The Ghost Bird Series

First Kiss

♥

Book Ten

♥

Written by C. L. Stone

Published by

Arcato Publishing

ISBN-13: 978-1532702334
ISBN-10: 1532702337

I pulled my bag onto my shoulders and stood, testing the weight of it. Did we have to hike to the campground? "Gabriel packed all my clothes. I need more?"

He shrugged. "Probably not. I just get used to hearing about girls packing half the house."

"Can we bring the house?" I asked. "At least the heater part?"

His smile faded. "Peanut, don't tell me you're an indoor girl."

I shook my head and leaned into him a little, putting a hand on his chest. "I like the idea of camping, but I was thinking of how cold it's been at night."

His blue eyes were intense and he pressed himself against my hand before he put down his bag on the bed and covered my hand with his. "If it's too much for you, you tell me. I'll make sure you stay warm."

Books by C. L. Stone
FROM THE ACADEMY

The Ghost Bird Series

Introductions
First Days
Friends vs. Family
Forgiveness and Permission
Drop of Doubt
Push and Shove
House of Korba
The Other Side of Envy
The Healing Power of Sugar
First Kiss
Black and Green (Coming late 2016)

The Scarab Beetle Series

Thief
Liar
Fake
Accessory
Hoax (Coming 2016)

Other Books By C. L. Stone

Smoking Gun
Spice God

♥

$\mathcal{T}$HE $\mathcal{R}$ECOVERY

$\mathcal{K}$ota Lee brushed strands of my dirty blond hair away from my forehead and then pressed the back of his palm against it. "You feel warm still." He sat next to me on his bed, wearing green and white plaid flannel pajama pants and a green T-shirt. He studied my face.

Dr. Green stood in front of us, eyeballing me and waiting for the thermometer in my mouth to finish reading my temperature. His arms were folded over his chest, making creases in the untucked, unbuttoned yellow shirt, and the white T-shirt underneath. He wore jeans, too, so I guessed he wasn't going to work at the hospital today. "Let's let the gadget thingie tell us if she has a fever."

"The thermometer?" Kota asked.

Dr. Green dropped his hands, stuffed them into his pockets and shrugged. "I get so many gadget thingies. That's what they all are."

I smiled with the thermometer in my mouth. Strands of my hair fell over my cheeks, and while I tried to brush it back, Kota knocked my hands away from my face and gave me the eye to tell me not to move so they could get an accurate reading. I breathed out through my nose and waited, the loose hair tickling my forehead and cheeks. My hair was a mess after sleeping over; I must have thrashed around a lot in my sleep.

After about a week of being sick, the other guys had slowly started to get back to normal, returning home. I'd stayed at Kota's house, at first because I was sick, and later because I was helping the others to recover. There were times when I'd run over to Nathan's house to take care of things while he was sick. I'd also or occasionally gone to the diner to help while Luke and North were recovering.

My home base had shifted to Kota's house because that was where everyone else usually ended up. Kota's mother checked on us on occasion, too.

Apparently everyone taking over Kota's upstairs bedroom while being sick was normal for them, and she didn't say a word about me joining the guys.

We had all just starting to feel right again when my temperature had jumped in an odd spike last night. I was feeling a little run-down but had assumed I was only tired. Kota checked my forehead, said I must have overworked myself into being sick again and sent me to bed early.

Dr. Green hovered over us with a soft smile and a few curls of his dirty blond hair hanging around his forehead as he waited. He and Kota had such worried, concerned shadows behind their happy demeanors.

I was going to say I was fine, but kept my mouth closed, hoping the thermometer would tell them for me.

When it beeped, he pulled it out and looked at the digital screen. "According to this, she's dead."

I giggled, sure he either was reading it upside down or just making a joke. "I'm fine," I said, probably for the hundredth time that week. "I feel normal."

Dr. Green held his smile but looked at the thermometer again. He pushed the button once, to turn it off, and then again to turn it on. "One more time, though. Seriously. I think you opened your mouth."

I hadn't but was willing to sit through it again just to prove I wasn't sick...or dead.

Dr. Green put the thing under my tongue and then looked at Kota. "It's not like we should be in a hurry. Right now, your schedules are all changed. You'll go to homeroom and then to Music Room B while we figure out our next steps."

"Sang, too?" Kota asked.

Dr. Green nodded. "She's already pinned as one of us by most of the staff and her schedule is out of whack. Despite our efforts, she has been missing a lot of school. She might be getting straight A grades, but we weren't able to totally mark her as in attendance as we thought we could. We might get away with it with a fake Academy record that she's been at the other school on days off. Might as well officially enroll her with us full time so we can have control of her schedule." His green eyes sparked with amusement. "Did you hear that? You're stuck with us now."

I grinned, although it was more like barring teeth to keep the thermometer in and then closed my mouth quickly.

"What about Mr. Hendricks?" Kota asked, seeming to read my mind. "What happens when he wants something from her and tries to call her parents?"

"We're going to face it sooner or later," Dr. Green said. "What happens if we find this missing money? Hendricks will point fingers, including at her. The people he keeps close are ones with a lot of skeletons they want to keep in the closet. She's not a threat to involve any police, but he could change that in a few seconds with a phone call. Based on who he is and his status, he could make things escalate very quickly and he's not above lying. If we kick his beehive enough, he might do it."

"We can stop it, though," Kota said.

"We may need to get her off the radar before that happens." He looked over to the window, to the street outside. "We're taking a lot of risks trying to keep things as they were. The best thing to do right now is to get her away from the potential for harm when it all falls down. We were kidding ourselves. Extracting her from the school was never going to be easy, and we've made it ten times harder involving her as much as we have."

Kota caught my attention with a stare and then winked at me. It wasn't the first time I suspected things might change after this year when I'd possibly join with the Academy, but Dr. Green made it sound like they'd been planning for a while to get me out of Ashley Waters High School.

Dr. Green continued going over how we'd handle the next few weeks. Since we'd gotten sick, Academy meetings had been held in person, usually at Kota's house. With Volto getting closer and more dangerous and clearly listening in on any phone calls, despite Victor's efforts to evade him, no one was taking any risks. Phone calls were only for every day normal things—no Academy business.

I hadn't turned on my new phone all week. Since mine had been compromised, Victor had provided a new one that had a unique heart sticker on the inside of the cover so I'd know if it'd been switched. Once we returned to school and the diner I'd have to carry it with me, but I planned only to use it for emergencies. I was paranoid now and waited until people were around to talk to them about anything, including simple, friendly things.

When Dr. Green took the thermometer from me again, he shook his head and pouted. "Yup. Dead. Is this one broken?"

"What does it say?" Kota asked.

"Ninety-five point eight," he said. "I thought you said she had a fever last night. This is the opposite of a fever, Kota. You should get her a heating blanket."

"Ninety-six is my normal," I said. Had this not come up before? Maybe not, since I hadn't really been sick around them before. "If my temperature is ninety-eight, I'm uncomfortable and if it's ninety-nine, I'm feeling really sick."

Dr. Green smirked and put the thermometer away. "You just break all the rules, don't you? I wouldn't mind taking a few blood tests to be sure it isn't anything serious. It could be your normal or it could be something else."

"Could it be serious?" Kota asked.

"Well, she doesn't have a whole lot of other symptoms," Dr. Green said. He raised a quizzical eyebrow and looked at me. "No internal pain?"

I shook my head.

"We don't have to hurry with it," Dr. Green said. "But I'll put you on my schedule."

Kota sighed and shook his head. He stood up and adjusted his shirt and pants from the mess they were in since we'd both just woken up. "Well, as long as she's not very sick...or actually dead."

He headed toward the closet, pulling out clothes for himself. His brown hair was sticking out in the back in a way I liked; I'd come to enjoy his fresh-out-of-bed look. He was a lot like Mr. Blackbourne during the day, with hair just right and glasses polished. In the mornings, though, he was almost human, casual, and occasionally without his glasses. I found his face handsome, and admired it.

Dr. Green waited until Kota was in the bathroom, and then reached for my forehead, pressing his palm to my skin. He held there and then eased back to brush some of my hair away from my eyes. "Almost ready to get back into the saddle, pumpkin?" he asked.

I tried to smile, but I was shaking my head at the same time. Could I ever be prepared to go back to school now? Every time I showed up, something strange or awful happened. I wasn't even worried about the other students anymore. The teachers and staff were unpredictable enough.

"Well, you don't have to go back right now," he said.

The door to the bathroom opened and Kota stepped out, dressed and ready for the day in jeans and a thin, green sweater. He had cleaned his glasses with a microfiber cloth and his brown hair was brushed neatly aside on his forehead. "So today's the day, huh?" he asked.

"I figured with the two of you, we can get through them all in one day," Dr. Green said. "Unless we're missing any items. Hard to keep track. There's a mountain."

"Today's the day we find out if we're missing anyone," Kota said. "A couple weeks out should be enough time to get more. And if that's the case, we'll just order things from the internet to be delivered. We've got time."

I looked from Kota to Dr. Green and back. "Huh?" I asked.

"Wrapping Day," Dr. Green said. "I've got all the gifts at my house for Christmas this year. Now that everyone else is busy, you and Kota are going to help me sort and wrap them all up. You just don't get to see your own, and you two have

5

to wrap mine so I can pretend I don't know what they are." He finished with a satisfied grin.

I started to get up but froze as I thought about gifts. I'd started my shopping with Luke and Gabriel. Gabriel had tucked those items away, promising to send them on to Dr. Green to wrap. I hadn't thought about it since.

I hadn't finished shopping for everyone. And Gabriel had the rest of the cash I'd brought to buy them with.

Dr. Green stepped away from the bed to talk to Kota. "We'll have to be careful, though. Volto doesn't seem to like me being around her. I don't want to kowtow to his demands, but we're in a dangerous position as it is."

"Luke was onto him," Kota said, putting his hands on his hips. He wore a determined look with a tight smile. "We were close enough that he took some drastic steps to stop us. Which means we need to know what Luke knows."

"We debriefed him," Dr. Green said. "And we've got a list we're working from." He eyeballed me. "Is that what you're wearing?" he asked as his smile lifted. "I think it's adorable. You should just come in your pajamas."

Heat burned through my face. It was tempting to simply hop into a car wearing what I had on, but going to Dr. Green's condo might mean running into Mr. Blackbourne, and then I'd feel foolish and wish I'd changed. I stood up and found my phone on the side table. "I'll get dressed," I said.

The guys went downstairs, leaving me to pick out a few things Kota had in his closet for me. There was a pair of nice slacks that Gabriel had bought on impulse last time he was out shopping. I put on a casual pink blouse, too, and a light windbreaker—it had gotten cold now that it was December.

I avoided the shower in the bathroom, and simply did a quick wash of my face in the sink. I'd take a bath that night before going to school.

I typed out a quick text to Gabriel, and even then I hesitated, knowing Volto was probably reading it. Still, it was a normal thing and not Academy related, so it probably didn't matter.

Sang: I never finished shopping for gifts for the other guys. Do we need to go again?

By the time I'd brushed my hair, the phone was vibrating on the counter, making a funny echo in the bathroom. Instead of returning my text, Gabriel was calling.

"We got a few extra things for you," Gabriel said when I answered. "I went back out two days ago and had to figure out all that shit by myself."

"Why didn't you tell me?" I asked.

"You were at the damn diner again. And Luke was cleaning up after Sprinkles the skunk snuck into North's room and made a doodie in his laundry basket."

I giggled at the news. I hadn't heard that story yet but hoped Luke wouldn't let Sprinkles get into too much trouble with North. It had been hard enough to get North to agree to let Luke keep the pet skunk.

"Don't worry," he said. "You'll see them if you're going over there today anyway. I got for everyone but Mr. Blackbourne. I never know what to get him. Just ask Dr. Green. He can usually come up with an idea."

"Thanks, Gabriel."

"Trouble, you owe me a week without your clip in your goddamn hair now. You've got money left over though from that night. I took care of the rest of it."

"You didn't need to do that."

"It's fine. I keep forgetting to bring the cash back, though. It's sitting on my dresser. I need to move it at least so what's-his-fuck, Pam's boyfriend, doesn't take it. Oh, and I bought another game for our 3DSs, too with the money I had left over. That's our gift to us."

"Thanks for taking care of it. Take some money since it was me getting gifts for you all, technically." I didn't know we were to buy gifts for ourselves, but I assumed he meant my gift to them was a game and he got me the game, too. The surprise was spoiled now but I didn't mind. I was getting excited to see what else 'I' got for the others.

It also had me excited to think of what else the guys got for me. Not in a greedy way, but all of the things Gabriel, Luke and I had picked out, we could all enjoy together. Nerf swords and toys and games: Fun things.

♥

$\mathscr{I}$NSIDE $\mathscr{T}$HE $\mathscr{H}$EART $\mathscr{O}$F $\mathscr{A}$ $\mathscr{D}$OCTOR

$\mathscr{O}$nce I got off the phone with Gabriel, Kota, Dr. Green and I got into Dr. Green's car.

I sat in the front passenger seat beside Dr. Green and Kota was in the back.

I'd had a coffee and a quick Pop Tart on my way out the door; Dr. Green had promised a proper lunch at his house later on.

"I want to make sure we get a good head start on it all," he said with a chuckle. He glanced at me using the rearview mirror. "This will be a lot of fun since we've got you this year." He turned the car onto the highway and headed into Charleston.

He and Kota talked about if they had enough wrapping paper. I was half listening, but mostly I stared out the window at the blue sky, feeling the slight chill of winter, wondering about how different living in the south was going to be; there wasn't going to be any snow.

Anything to take my mind off of returning to school soon.

I must have been dazed out because the ride seemed to happen in a split second. We were suddenly pulling into the drive that led to his condo. His was the last in a line of five and there were cars parked in the other drives. I wondered about his neighbors though I didn't see any at the moment.

Dr. Green's was the most lavishly landscaped; roses growing from most of the available garden space, compared to the simple green bushes everyone else kept.

Dr. Green parked in his drive and turned to me. "Ready?"

I blinked rapidly to focus and then nodded. I hoped there were simple boxes I could stick with. The few gifts I'd wrapped had been for Marie, at the request of our father for birthdays and Christmas. It was something I didn't exactly excel at. Marie was actually better.

I joined Dr. Green and Kota on the porch, waiting to go in, when Kota asked, "Did you put her gifts away?"

"Yeah, they're in my bedroom," Dr. Green said and pushed the door open.

"All of them?" Kota asked. "I dropped a few off yesterday morning."

I'd started inside, but Dr. Green reached out and gripped my elbow, holding me just inside the short foyer before I could go deeper into the condo. "Uh..." Dr. Green said. "Hang on there, pookie. Let Kota double check... and also, Kota, check the kitchen and the spare bedroom. Make sure I didn't leave anything out that's meant for her. We'll spread out in the living room to wrap. Toss anything of hers into my bedroom."

Exactly how many gifts were there, that Dr. Green had them spread out all over? I grinned as Kota walked around me to get into the living room just beyond the foyer. "Keep her there," he said. "Give me a minute."

It was tempting to misbehave a little and peek around the corner, but I forced myself to stay still with Dr. Green near the door. I didn't want to know. I would forever second-guess the gifts I'd gotten for them, and had to trust that Gabriel got things that would be appropriate. I couldn't even imagine what they could be. Most likely toy swords and gumball machines.

I also considered something else: Did I want to try to get small individual gifts just from me? It was nice that Gabriel had gotten gifts for them, but I wanted to get them each something special. Something none of them knew about.

Only I didn't have the money. Gabriel had used the last of what I'd had from the diner. The few hours I'd worked this week at the diner were mostly to cover the counter, and the counter had been really slow the times I'd been there.

The rustling sounds of Kota fumbling through boxes

drifted to us as we waited in the foyer. I was still thinking of gifts and what I could do to surprise them when Dr. Green put his palms on the wall on either side of my shoulders, trapping me. I looked up at him and saw his playful smile.

"Hi Pookie," he whispered.

Thoughts of gifts slipped away, replaced by excitement, and then panic. I braced against the wall, hoping Kota didn't come back around the corner to spot us like this.

Dr. Green dipped his head to land a gentle kiss on my forehead. "I'm glad you're feeling better."

"I... missed you, too," I said quietly.

The smile on his face lit up his green eyes in a way that made him much handsomer than before. In the casual clothes, he looked younger, leaning toward my age of sixteen instead of nineteen. A curl of sandy blond hair fell over his eye as he looked at me eagerly. "May I sneak a kiss?"

I nodded. I wanted to, but also was mindful of Kota.

His lips pressed to mine. I puckered my lips, not going too far, just a peck.

He held his lips against mine for longer than I expected, but then backed up and his smile seemed even brighter than before. "I can't wait until it's not a secret anymore," he whispered.

"I hadn't thought of what it might be like," I said. I'd been so focused, waiting for the others to tell Kota about the plan, not thinking about what would happen after. I worried about how he might feel, and how best to talk openly with the others about the idea without fighting. It was all so complicated.

"Won't it be wonderful?" he whispered and then moved to brace his shoulder against the wall, tucking me in front of him. He had his back to the hallway opening, so if Kota came around the corner, it would look like he was preventing me from viewing what was around the bend. "I could kiss you openly. I could hold your hand. We could go out on dates together and let them all know. Without worrying about what anyone thinks. It won't matter how many pictures Volto takes. Won't that be great?"

Would I ever get to the point where I wasn't worried about what someone else would think about anything? Lily and her team hid away from the world to avoid what other people thought of them. Besides that, there was our own group to worry about, too. North and Luke got jealous at times, even though they were both for the plan. Would there always be the threat of jealousy? Or could we actually get beyond that?

Still, Dr. Green seemed so eager. How strange that it was such a normal thing—to kiss a boy, or go out on a date—things he wanted to do, but was prevented because of what it looked like from the outside.

How our lives had shifted. I'd once been the lonely girl in my bedroom, dreaming of normal life. Now here I was, out in the world, and still there were limitations, for them as well. The plan they'd presented, that I secretly desired, and yet was still hesitant to admit to, all centered on me. If we followed through, even if they were all in on it, we would still not be normal.

Maybe if I hadn't met them, and had continued on how I was, had grown to eighteen in my house, maybe I would have been normal. Eventually. Or would I have ever been? Would I always feel like I was on the outside, like I had for most of my life?

Kota whistled and then called out, "Okay, I think I grabbed everything."

Dr. Green took my hand and led me around the corner. At least no one ever seemed to mind my holding hands with them. Kota didn't say anything about it as we turned the bend.

I'd seen Dr. Green's home once before. Back then it was impeccably clean, with his DVDs organized, everything in its place, and his glass-topped coffee table spotless.

This time, while the space was clean, it was cluttered with boxes and shopping bags along the couch, the floor, and the coffee table.

"There's a few more in the kitchen," Kota said. "And in the spare room. But the only things that are in the master bedroom are Sang's and ours."

"Why'd you hide mine?" Dr. Green asked. "We're going to wrap them."

"Just to get them out of the way," Kota said. "Sang can wrap mine, you can wrap Sang's, and I'll wrap yours when we get to them. That way we can tell the others we didn't wrap our own gifts."

"I might not have everything for everyone," I said. "Gabriel mentioned he couldn't think of anything to get Mr. Blackbourne. I don't have anything for him."

Kota and Dr. Green shared a look. "Did you get him anything?" Kota asked him.

"Not yet," Dr. Green said, scratching absently at his temple. "The man has everything, doesn't he?"

"And doesn't want much of anything," Kota said. "He's as minimalist as they get sometimes."

Dr. Green pressed his lips together and surveyed the mountain of boxes and bags scattered around his living room. "Well, let's get through this and then we'll figure out that part." He winked at Kota and then put a hand on top of my head, messing up my hair.

I smiled, but then my hair loosened and the clip fell out. Dr. Green swooped to pick it up for me, but when I went to put it back, my hair was tangled.

"We can start sorting," Kota said, going to the couch and opening up a white department store bag. He checked the contents and then pulled out folded sets of clothing. "I'm going to need boxes."

"Sang," Dr. Green said, going to the coffee table and sliding boxes around, adding some to a pile on the floor. "In the spare bedroom, there's a large green tote box. All the gift boxes are inside. Go grab it? And no sneaking a peek in my bedroom."

I nodded and went to the hallway. The furthest door to the right was the main bedroom, which I'd been in before. That door was closed. All the doors were closed except one.

The smells of the condo were filling my nose, Jasmine, citrus, ginger and cedar. There were other scents, too, like cleaners and carpet and other indescribable house smells. This was Dr. Green's home. No parents. No one to hide from. I liked being here. It was one of the few places where I simply felt safe. Some of the boys had nice homes, but it often felt like someone could walk in, like a parent, and not all of them were nice.

I went to the open door, assuming that had to be the spare room but found a bathroom instead. I stood inside it for a moment combing out my tangled hair with my fingers. I looked for a brush on the counter to borrow, couldn't find one, and settled for twisting my hair and clipping it as neatly as I could.

When I came back out of the bathroom into the hallway, the house was quiet.

I listened, hoping to hear Dr. Green and Kota. The place was so still. I couldn't even imagine they were still inside. Had they left? Or had they gone into the kitchen and I couldn't hear them?

There were two more doors down the hall, one near the bathroom, and one at the very end, opposite the main bedroom. I still wasn't sure which one was the spare bedroom, and what the other room would be. Then I remembered him, or someone, had said there was an office.

I padded my way down the hall until I came to the next door down the hallway. I pushed my ear to the wood, listening for any sign of Dr. Green or Kota, just in case they had slipped in while I was in the bathroom. When I didn't hear anything, I opened the door and peeked inside.

It was dark but light enough that I could see that it looked to be an office, with a desk and bookshelves. The room was on the small side, smaller than my bedroom back home, or even Gabriel's tiny bedroom in his trailer.

Out of the corner of my eye, I caught a winged shadow flutter overhead.

My heart leaped into my throat and I froze.

Another shadow to the left shifted, flying toward me.

I took a step back and started to shut the door in a hurry,

thinking there was a flying bug in the room and I was going to let it out. The door stopped against my shoe before shutting completely.

A flurry of activity within the room caused me to cringe, and then pause to listen. The sound was like the rustle of paper blowing in the wind, but it was coming from above my head. It wasn't just a bug. It had to be dozens of them inside. Was the window open?

I closed the door until there was a crack left so I could peek in. The sound died quickly, and I waited. I knew I should find out what was inside, and then go back and tell Dr. Green right away if there were bugs in his office. He'd want to know. However, I wouldn't want him to go charging in if the bugs were wasps and not beetles or something else.

I opened the door slowly, peering into the darkness. My heart flew into a frenzy when it looked like there were birds and butterflies flying overhead.

I jerked back in surprise until I realized they were motionless, only moving with the smallest bit of breeze that I had created by opening the door.

I breathed in slowly, smelling ginger and cedar, and…construction paper? There was a hint of glue as well, along with the unmistakable chemical tang from markers.

I found a light switch along the wall and flicked it on.

There were actual birds and butterflies floating above my head. They were so perfect, almost lifelike. My brain wanted to insist that they were real and hovering over me; I kept ducking, assuming one would finally flutter down toward me.

I eased in further, curious. There were more butterflies and birds hanging down the deeper I went in, but also fish and bugs. They were suspended by fishing wire, barely noticeable until I caught the light above reflecting across the string.

The animals all looked so real, swimming and flying above me. Vivid blues, reds, and greens: all sorts of colors mixed in together. The birds looked so soft and the fish appeared to wriggle with life at the most subtle of air movements.

I stepped closer, looking up at the display, until I bumped into the desk, forcing me to look down and check out the layout of the rest of the room.

I froze, finding myself in the middle of an entire display of delicate paper animals.

I'd found the door to Narnia.

Nearly every inch of space was covered in paper craftwork. Animals hung from above. Shelves held pedestals, and on top were homes and entire neighborhoods, both Japanese and American in style. Some looked familiar, and one looked so similar to Bob's Diner, and another like the hospital he worked at. Some of the buildings were so small, they were the size of a small cell phone. Some were so detailed that they had tiny blades of grass around the edges and numbers above doors and on mailboxes. There were flowers in vases on his desk, and picture boxes along the walls depicting scenes of the ocean, of people sitting to eat at a meal.

I tiptoed further in, drawn to every surface, my eyes wide as I tried to take in everything. My breath caught at the sheer number of tiny items around, the paper animals above my head, the wall full of paper-crafted flowers and trees. While there were some origami pieces, many were cut paper, pieced together.

A gentle cough came from the doorway.

I spun, my palm planted hard against my chest to stop my wild heart, amazed at what I'd just seen, and terrified at being caught snooping.

"I was wondering what was taking you so long," Dr. Green said.

"I … I was looking for...," I said.

"I figured you got lost," he said with a teasing grin spread across his face. His eyes went to the walls and ceiling. "Not bad for a bit of paper and glue, huh?"

My eyes widened in surprise. "Did you make it all?"

"Paper craft is pretty popular in Japan," he said. "Picked it up a while back. It's one of those things I can do that doesn't involve thinking too hard. Just creating."

"It's…it's…." I didn't have a word. What he created was nothing short of magic. The doctor who could heal also had a talent for practically giving life to paper.

He curled his fingers at me, urging me to stand in front of his desk. "Come on. I'll show you," he said quietly.

"Show me what?"

He wriggled his eyebrows. "How I'm going to win your little heart."

I couldn't hide my smile. Did he not know he was already winning it? He was very flirty, but I was still too in awe to say anything.

I stood, nearly holding my breath, as he pulled out a couple of sheets of paper in shades of green and red, a ruler, and a slim paper knife from a desk drawer. As he bent over the paper, I noticed his desk was padded, so he could cut at ease without hurting it.

Dr. Green focused on the paper, bending and folding. He worked so quickly, it was like when Victor's fingers swept across the piano, or when Nathan lunged with a kick. It was the same precision and artistry that had to come from practice. Bending here. Cutting there. First one piece of paper, and then another.

Before I could ask him what he was making, he covered the papers with his hands. I got that he wanted it to be a surprise so I then looked at some of the creations that had only been partially completed.

He reached into the desk again, drawing out a pen. He marked on his hidden creation, in what looked like dot marks. It wasn't writing, at least, it didn't look like it from his movements.

As I waited, I noticed a panda sitting on top of a pile of paper. It had what looked like delicate fur and two green gemstone eyes.

At last, he sat back, still masking the craft he'd put together with his hands. "Ready?" he asked.

I pushed my heart back into my rib cage, willing it to stay calm no matter what it was. "Yes."

Dr. Green stood, coming around the desk. When he was beside me, he shifted so the light fell in front of him.

In his hands was a delicate rose, curled up like a new bud on a stem, the petals just beginning to open. It was so realistic and so beautiful; if I hadn't seen him make it in front of me, I would have believed it to be a real flower.

"Wow," I said, unable to control my heart anymore. My fingers trembled and I reached to touch the delicate petals.

"Not yet," he said softly.

I didn't know if I could handle much more of this surprise but he shifted his hands to begin a twisting motion from the stem.

As he moved, the rose opened, slowly unfolding into a full bloom. It was like watching a time-lapse camera, with petals unfolding one layer at a time.

Across the petals, there were ink markings. Together, they spelled out a line of Japanese hiragana:

こいする

I didn't know the Japanese, but I was struck with the beauty of the rose and how he'd made it bloom. Dr. Green had a skill; his work could be displayed in museums.

"What does it mean?" I asked.

He offered me the rose. I was hesitant, afraid to break it, but took it, pinching the little stem he'd made for it.

"Let me know when you figure it out," he said with a soft smile. "I'll give you bonus points."

My heart fluttered like one of his paper birds above my head. I guessed they meant something sweet, but not knowing exactly left me excited and happy to find out.

It was amazing how he could do that. With just one little smile and joke, he made me feel so much lighter. He made it easy to feel comfortable with him.

"I guess this isn't the spare room," I said. "I didn't mean

to intrude."

"Darling, my house is yours. Go wherever you want. Just not into the bedroom right now because your presents are in there."

He moved to the door. "But we've got a gigantic pile of presents to wrap. Kota's measuring presents to figure out what sizes of boxes we'll need. Little does he know I just eyeball and if it's too big a box, I just throw in more tissue paper."

I held onto the flower, unsure where to place it while we'd be working. I looked for a spot to put it down in his office.

Dr. Green moved back to me and caught my wrist gently.

I froze, mostly affected at his holding my arm when I was already feeling excited. His touch was soothing.

He took the rose and lifted his arms. I felt him adjusting the hair clip at the back of my head. When his hands returned empty, I assumed he'd managed to put the rose in the clip. I was tempted to reach around to touch it but didn't want to damage the delicate paper.

"I don't want to lose it," I said.

"I'll keep an eye on you...it...No... I meant you." He winked at me and then urged me to the door. "Go back to Kota. I'll get the boxes."

♥

ℛEPARATION

he rest of the morning consisted of endless wrapping paper cutting, tape dispenser refilling, and bow selection. I learned a lot under Dr. Green's tutelage as he gave me some boxes to work on. Still, I wrapped simple, small boxes, while Dr. Green focused on the more complicated items. Each one of his carefully-wrapped gifts ended up as a beautiful paper creation like I'd only seen on television or in magazines.

Kota kept a list of who got what and who was left to shop for. He also put tags on gifts and marked which items were to go to which homes. Some were to go to a particular family's homes, like the Korba's or the Morgan's. Some were for people I didn't even know: Dr. Green's colleagues at work, Academy members they were friends with, and family of the boys' I hadn't met yet: cousins and aunts and uncles. Most of them got small gifts, candy or other food items unique to Charleston.

The rest were put aside to take to Kota's house.

"We'll have our family Christmas there," Kota said. "It's tradition."

Saying it was tradition made me feel special for being included, but also slightly alienated as well since it was my first, and I was unsure of what to expect. Wouldn't Kota's mother wonder why I was there with them for Christmas and not with my own family? The Thanksgiving traditions I'd experienced with them had been so surprising and exhausting, too.

Since they'd kept their Christmas plans a surprise, I was prepping myself for another unexpected and crazy day.

By the time we were close to finished wrapping gifts, I'd

probably only wrapped a few dozen boxes. Dr. Green had not only wrapped faster, he'd created fancier ribbons. He'd made store-bought bows look like sparkling flowers once he was done with them. Mine paled in comparison, and you could see the drastic differences once they were together.

No wonder everyone sent their gifts to Dr. Green's to be wrapped. I was embarrassed by the state of mine. I encouraged Dr. Green to make bows for me, to at least cover up the boxes I'd wrapped.

Before we were done, the front door opened and closed, drawing our attention to the still-unwrapped presents. We shifted in front of them, waiting for whoever it was to make an appearance from the foyer.

Mr. Blackbourne turned the bend, followed closely by Victor. Mr. Blackbourne was pristine in his usual crisp gray suit, white shirt, and maroon tie. His steel eyes were shining and vibrant.

Victor seemed a little more relaxed, more curious about what was going on. He wore his regular white Armani shirt and black slacks, the silver medallion—a heart and shield symbol—around his neck. His fire eyes were not quite a blaze, but a simmering fire. With his head high and his unyielding stance, he looked incredibly handsome.

Mr. Blackbourne, however, looked almost as intimidating as when I had first met him, his expression serious and ready to take the lead.

"I was hoping you would still be here," Mr. Blackbourne said, looking at Dr. Green. He then turned his gaze to Kota and me. "I hope you're finished."

"Finished enough," Dr. Green said. He sat on an empty space on the couch, pushing over a few empty store bags to make room. "I think the rest is mostly up to me."

Kota had been sitting cross-legged on the carpet in front of the coffee table, using a Sharpie to mark names on tags. He finished what he was writing as he spoke. "I didn't know you were going to come here. Should we go?"

"We all need to talk for a minute, but we'll need to decide

who should take Miss Sorenson back home," Mr. Blackbourne said.

"I'll do it," both Kota and Victor said at the same time. They looked at each other with sheepish grins.

I shifted to stand front of the television so I could see all of them at once.

"You might want to hear this," Victor said to Kota. He put his hands in his pockets, his lean arms pressing against his torso, outlining his chest and stomach. "You might even want to stay after."

"We need to be prepared," Mr. Blackbourne said as he turned to me. His voice was much like it was in the first week of school when he'd tried to teach me how to hold a violin: sharp and powerful. "Unless you have other plans, we need you to be free New Year's week. The entire week."

My heart thundered. "I..." I didn't mean to stumble, but so many questions came to mind all at once and I was trying to piece together what to ask first. My schedule hadn't been my own practically since I'd met them. I'd go wherever they wanted me. Why would it change over New Year's?

"Owen, she knows about the Academy introduction. Why don't you just tell her what it is?" Dr. Green asked.

"Don't tell her," Kota said. "It's still kind of a Christmas surprise, too."

"She should be able to prepare for it," Victor said. "It might be a little unfair otherwise. You don't even know if she'll like it."

"I think she will," Kota said and looked at me with a smile. "I don't mean to talk around you. It's just I don't want to ruin Christmas."

I blew out a breath between my lips, wanting to be supportive but unable to really begin when I didn't know what their surprise was. I started at the beginning. "So, the Academy wants some sort of official introduction the week of the first?" I had to say *official* because last time they sprung a surprise on me at Thanksgiving, I'd met a lot of Academy people, only I didn't realize they were Academy until right before I met them. I also didn't know they were showing me off until after the event.

They'd called it an *informal* introduction, but apparently I'd passed the test. I imagined next time I'd actually meet them and know their names and see their faces and get to know them as Academy. The idea was intimidating; there were a lot of them.

"Correct," Mr. Blackbourne said. He smoothed out the front of his gray jacket and then unbuttoned it, only to re-button it again. He stopped himself and then put his hands at his sides. "This isn't just an introduction, however. This is to identify your potential for getting into the Academy."

"Do we have to do that part?" Kota asked. "And so soon?"

"If she gets more involved with us, she'll have to," Mr. Blackbourne said. "Besides, she's expressed interest. I don't think we'd be able to mask her potential from them."

"But she doesn't know what she's getting herself into," Kota said. He turned to look at me. "I know we've talked about it before, and you said you wanted to, but there're more complications than you realize. Especially with you..."

"Which is what the Introduction is all about," Mr. Blackbourne said, turning to me. "You'll learn the details and can then make your own decision. However, we have something more important to worry about other than your future Academy career at this moment. We're facing a delicate issue." He turned back to Kota. "The Academy may...no. I don't want any illusion here. They will want to try her out with other teams. And not just for a week. Most likely, they'll insist on asking her to join another team soon after the week is over and continue with them."

"I don't want another team," I said, straightening my shoulders and standing taller. "Can't I just tell them I want to stay?"

The others smiled, even Mr. Blackbourne, for a second. He collected himself quickly and turned toward the dining room adjacent to the living room and then turned back. "The problem is, they'll request it very early on. Not accepting a trial with another team, not being willing to at least listen to their suggestions, might make them think you are unwilling to listen to their direction at all. As well, they'll want to know why you're so connected with us. They'll want solid reasons."

I shared a look with Victor. He frowned, and the fire in his eyes was low. He didn't like this. Neither did I.

I suspected this was part of why the plan was so important. It was why we were still trying to figure it out, even at this preliminary stage. The problem was, Kota wasn't ready. I wasn't sure the others were ready, either. Nathan hadn't spoken to me about it, even though the others said he knew about it. Silas was unsure, and waiting for direction from the others. Most of the time, North seemed steady in his belief that it would work, but on occasion, he seemed to second guess. Usually, that was because I was unsure about the idea. But that he could have doubts made me wonder if he was confident at all.

I was on the fence. As much as I wanted to believe it *could* work, I still felt guilty about it, even if I faked my courage for the others like Mr. Blackbourne had suggested.

"Because she likes us—that's a solid reason," Kota said. "But you're right, it may not be enough." He removed his glasses and with his other hand, pinched at the bridge of his nose as he closed his eyes. "See, this is one of the many reasons why I didn't want her getting this interested. She can still help us and be around us without being in the Academy."

Mr. Blackbourne shook his head. "You can't control another person's interest, Mr. Lee. If she is interested, which she says she is, then she should be allowed to explore her options. All of them. On the other hand, they could just as easily ask us to give her space—because of the dangerous assignments we pick up—to keep her safe."

"I'm not totally against that idea," Kota said. He put his glasses back on, his green eyes filled with a new determination. He looked at and spoke to me. "You wouldn't have to go. You just wouldn't have to be as involved as you are now. It's not just for you. It's for us, too. We're not ready."

"Ready or not, they are asking for her," Mr. Blackbourne said.

"Then maybe she should be busy that week," Dr. Green said quietly.

Mr. Blackbourne turned to me. "It might be tempting," he said. "You do have a choice, but I don't think keeping you from it is the best solution."

My heart was in my throat as I stood quietly, staring at all the gifts I'd helped to put together, suddenly disinterested in it all. With all the secrets and Academy rules, where I stood and would stand in the future was unclear. I wanted to listen to all of their concerns without interrupting. I was trying to do what they taught me: to hear them all out, and to get the full scope of what I'd be facing, before offering my own opinion. "Would it hurt anything?" I asked.

"It would give us more time," Dr. Green said. "Maybe we should wait another year."

"I can't believe you'd suggest that, Doc," Victor said. "You don't think she should join?"

"I don't like when there's a risk of us losing her to another team," Dr. Green said, his voice getting stronger. His eyes went wide and his shoulders pulled back. "The odds aren't good for us right now. Why can't we just pause for the time being? Keep her where she is? There's no harm in it."

Mr. Blackbourne frowned, a small dip of his lips that made my already nervous heart drop into my stomach. "We can't keep her in limbo." He turned to me, his steel eyes flashing. "Miss Sorenson, are you comfortable where you are?"

There was so much behind his question. "I can be if it's necessary," I said, wanting to be sensitive to Kota and Dr. Green. Clearly the rule about boys and girls not being allowed on the same team was what they were concerned about. It was already causing a rift between them. If we weren't ready, then that was fine. It didn't deter my desire to stay with them.

"Waiting until later won't hurt. But I do want to stay with

our team. I was told it was a choice. If that's true, then why would they force me into another team?"

"They don't force anything, sweetheart," Victor said. He came over, stood close and wrapped an arm around me, squeezing me in a side hug. "You always have a choice. Sometimes, though, to be honest, they have a way of making us see things in a different light that gets us to try out new things. Sometimes that's a new team." He turned to look at the others. "That's not always a bad thing, either. She's not going to disappear into a black hole, even if she does choose to join another team. If in the end, if she wants to, how can we stop her?"

That wasn't really what I wanted, I knew that. I'd grown too close to them to ever consider leaving them. I'd simply have to prove it to them and to the Academy somehow. That was much harder to do when I didn't know what was ahead of me. Couldn't I just say flat out from the start that I preferred to stay with them?

The guys were quiet.

"She doesn't know she has options," Kota finally said. "Or what they are. What we risk is their influence when she has no idea what she can negotiate."

"Which is why it's important that she does go," Mr. Blackbourne said. "Perhaps now more than ever. She'll learn what she can do, even if she says she's not ready yet to join completely. It will at least give her what she needs to make an informed decision."

Kota stood, frowning. "There's a greater chance they'll place her somewhere else, or they'll ask her to leave. Or they could ask us to leave her alone and send in another team. She's too nice to say no, even if she might be unhappy. That's what I'm trying to prevent."

"I'll just tell them I don't want to," I said, more quietly than I'd intended.

He looked at me. "I know you—a little at least—and you'd do anything to help other people, even if it means leaving us behind. It may not be the wrong decision when you're presented with it." He turned his eyes back to Mr. Blackbourne, standing tall, his shoulders back. "But is it wrong to hold off the question when we have so little to offer to Sang right now? They see us as a troubled team with a tough job--and she's in the middle of it. We offer more danger than actual protection and any opportunity for learning at the moment. I'm not sure how to convince them we need her, and that she should stay."

"They'll do anything to keep her, once they know her," Mr. Blackbourne said, his tone low.

Kota pressed his lips together, his eyes narrowing at Mr. Blackbourne. He said nothing, just continued frowning.

As the two of them looked at each other, I was grateful Victor was there. I breathed in his moss and berry scent for strength but found myself wanting to bury my head into his shoulder for comfort rather than say anything. I wanted to get Kota and the others to believe that, whatever happened, I wanted to stay with them.

This talk of changing teams frightened me most of all; what could the Academy offer me that would lure me away from them?

"I want to stay with you," I said into the quiet room. Victor reached for my hand, squeezing it encouragingly as I continued. "If that means I have to skip the introduction this time, I'll do so. But if we go through with it, I'll tell them from the start..."

Mr. Blackbourne cut me off. "You should listen to your options first," he said, but then bowed his head in a clear apology. "Believe me, I'm just as eager to get you on our team, Miss Sorenson. But you should wait until the end of the week. Let them introduce you to other people. Giving them a chance to show you some options may be just enough to demonstrate to them that you're at least willing to listen and consider alternatives. By the end of it, you'll have to make some sort of decision." He sighed. "The truth is, the offer might be very hard to ignore."

An offer. That's the result they were worried about. The

Academy provides so much for the guys, I knew that. What offer would the Academy provide for me that would convince me to leave the boys to stay on a girl team?

They didn't have to say it because suddenly I was aware of the real fear. It wasn't my decision to make right now. It was the offer they feared. At the end, when the Academy saw me and talked to me, they'd give me choices. I couldn't predict what it would be.

Mr. Blackbourne looked again at Kota intently. "But we also have to be ready with our position if she says she wishes to stay. So we all need to be ready to tell them we want her in, without hesitation."

Kota was still frowning. "I suppose I don't have much choice if they want to invite her into the Academy. It's the worst time for her to join with us."

I gritted my teeth and then released Victor's hand to step forward to look firmly at the others. "If all I have to do is wait until the end to say I want to stay with the team, then I'll keep quiet and do as they ask until the end."

"You'll be provided the opportunity during a final review," Mr. Blackbourne said. His face was calm, but his eyes betrayed a flicker of worry behind the gray.

That flicker added to the doubt in my heart. I didn't want to believe that I'd choose any other group. Their questioning my loyalty hurt in a way. If they didn't really believe in us as a group, then would the Academy see that and think I'd be better off somewhere else?

Victor took my elbow, holding me comfortingly. The fire in his eyes settled on Mr. Blackbourne. "As long as she's aware, she can at least prepare herself for that moment. If you're not going to tell her anything else in advance, then you shouldn't scare her with any more. The introduction into the Academy shouldn't be scary. You'll make her think they're all bad guys not willing to listen."

The rest of them nodded in tense agreement. I swallowed, unsure about all of this. Their concerns and doubts now slipped into my heart.

Maybe I didn't have to be afraid of the Academy, as they did good things for other people, but what I did fear was if they shined the light too brightly on us and discovered secrets we weren't ready to reveal. Maybe they'd call us out for being silly and unrealistic, planning an impossible outcome. Maybe they'd try to shut us down.

The answer was up to me. But because I was new and, as Kota said, too nice, they weren't sure I'd be able to convince the Academy I really wanted to stay with them. At the end, I would have to face the Academy and stand firm, telling them I didn't want to leave them, no matter the cost.

But the offer still remained a mystery. Maybe even they didn't know what they would offer to keep me within the Academy.

The boys couldn't help me with this. Maybe it was better to face the Academy now instead of waiting it out like Dr. Green had suggested. If the Academy learned my decision, then this whole worry would be behind us.

I simply had to make that final choice, which meant I had to work on my resolve and conviction. They doubted; I had to believe.

"I wish we could tell you more," Kota said to me. "Unfortunately…"

"It's okay," I said. "Please, don't worry. You said it should be fun and we should make it fun."

"She's right," Dr. Green said. "It's uncomfortable because we don't know what will happen. She wants to stay. We want her to stay. How could they tell us no?"

"We shouldn't worry," Mr. Blackbourne said. "Perhaps someone should take her home. We can finish up here."

"I'll take her back," Victor said. "Or can I take her to lunch?"

"Take her somewhere random and low-key," Mr. Blackbourne said, turning his attention to Dr. Green and Kota. "We have other things to talk about."

This was one of the reasons I needed to belong to the Academy. There were certain things I had to leave for because they had secrets and I couldn't be involved. As much as I was curious, I had to respect that boundary. For now.

The others talked about upcoming Christmas decorations and eventually Victor and I started saying goodbye as I prepared to go with him. Dr. Green and Mr. Blackbourne shifted boxes and gifts to other parts of the living room. Mr. Blackbourne took over my spot and said he'd help with the wrapping process to get it done.

Victor guided me toward the door.

♥

$\mathcal{S}$ECRET $\mathcal{G}$IFTS

$\mathcal{I}$ didn't really begin to breathe normally until we were out in the fresh air, realizing I'd desperately needed that break from the conversation.

At least I was aware of what I needed to do, even if I didn't know how to do it. For the next several weeks, I'd go over what I would say at the end of it all. I might not know what would happen between now and then, but I thought it would be like preparing for a speech in class. *I want to stay with my group. I want to join and be part of their group. I appreciate suggestions, but I prefer to stay with my group.*

The words repeated in my head as I followed Victor. Next to Dr. Green's car was Victor's BMW. Victor opened the passenger door for me. There was a chill in the air, although the sun was out and warmed the inside of the car.

I buckled in as Victor got behind the wheel.

"I hope you're not too nervous, now," Victor said as he pulled the car out of the drive and onto the road. "I know I was when I first went for an introduction."

"Did they not tell you about it, either?" I asked.

Victor tightened his hands on the steering wheel, his knuckles turning white. "Normally, you wouldn't even be aware it was happening. Us telling you about it is an exception, because of what we just talked about. I'm not sure how much I'm supposed to tell you about the process at all. But they're all nice. All of them. I don't want you to stress out about that."

I sighed, lowering my head, absently looking at my shoes against the gray of the carpet of the bottom of the car. I fiddled with the zipper of my jacket, watching the light from the window spark against the silver. "Tell me what you can? I don't want you to get into trouble, but the more I know, the better I'll be prepared."

He waited until he turned onto the highway, headed west toward Summerville. He leaned back in his seat as he turned on the cruise control.

"Sang," he said, glancing over at me for a moment. "Our setup was different. We had Mr. Blackbourne and Dr. Green, who had already graduated by the time they found us. So our entire introduction and entry into the Academy might be different than what you'll go through. We were in a lot of danger. Not myself as much, but the others were in a whole lot of trouble with their parents. Nathan especially, since he was so young and his dad was home more because his mom had just left. Then there was Gabriel. Kota..."

"Kota?" I asked quietly.

He pressed his lips together, looking out at the road with a low but steady fire in his eyes. "Nathan and Kota got along so well when they were little because they dealt with the same issues."

Nathan's father had been very abusive. Nathan had watched his father beat his mother, but then when his mother escaped, his father turned to Nathan, beating him instead.

Kota's father wasn't around now. I had a hard time picturing the scene with his mother and sister.

But could this be what had happened? Kota's story was still in shadow. Would it do any good to bring up his past now? I sensed Victor didn't feel comfortable talking about it, so I filed my questions away.

"Not that your parents treated you much better," he said. "Your situation is more complicated, though."

"It doesn't matter," I said, clutching the zipper in my fingers. "If mine ends up being different, that's okay. You all are my team. That's what matters."

Victor smiled at this and flicked his eyes to me for a moment before refocusing on the road. "Just keep thinking that, Princess. It won't be easy, but being determined to stand your ground is a good attitude going in. They'll ask you dozens of questions, but if you keep that in the center of your mind, and really believe in it, then they won't be able to dissuade you."

I hoped that was the case. I was tired of thinking about it. I needed to prepare, but not right now. "Where did you want to go for lunch?" I asked.

This brightened his face even more and he pressed down on the gas pedal to disengage the cruise control.

♥♥♥

Later, we were sitting facing each other in a red booth in a small salad buffet restaurant that Victor had said he wanted to try. It was after the lunch rush; only a handful of the dining tables were occupied, and some of the staff were looking a little sleepy.

There was a long silver buffet filled with not just lettuces and vegetables, but also potato, tuna, and broccoli salads with creamy sauces, as well as a baked potato bar, various fresh breads, soups, and chili.

We'd filled our plates with heaping salads before returning to the table. I also had a baked potato and a buttery biscuit, and he had chili and cornbread.

I hadn't realized how hungry I was until I could smell the butter and potato, as well as the sweet French dressing on my salad.

"North would be proud of us," I said to Victor after I'd had a few bites of lettuce.

"I might recommend this place to him," Victor said. He had a hand in his lap while he ate his chili gracefully with a spoon. "I wasn't sure if you'd like it. You seem to like pancakes."

"I like different things," I said.

"Apparently you like salad," he said, looking at my heaped plate. "That's something I didn't know."

"I used to join the salad line at my old school for lunch. It was usually the least crowded. They usually had more variety, and not the same chicken nugget or pizza options."

Victor's gaze held mine for a long moment. I often saw the fire in his eyes, but now that I was looking at him, I realized the color of his irises was brown, something I often overlooked.

Then I realized I was staring and dropped my eyes back down to my plate as I picked at my food. "I'll try most things," I said.

"There's a lot to try," he said softly. Out of the corner of my eye, I could see he was leaning in, trying to get my attention. I looked up and he caught my eye, holding my gaze. "How was it at Dr. Green's before we arrived? Did you get a lot done?"

I was still getting used to them wanting me to look them in the eyes while we talked, but this was a little harder to do. How was I supposed to eat if I was constantly looking up?

"There's a lot of gifts," I said. "I don't even remember what most of them are." Not to mention Gabriel helped with buying a lot of them. I was very grateful he did so I wouldn't run the risk of forgetting anything. I fiddled with my fork. "I still need to think of what to get Mr. Blackbourne for Christmas. I meant to work that out with Dr. Green, but then we got busy with wrapping."

"Mr. Blackbourne is the hardest to buy for," Victor said. He looked down briefly to take a bite of his salad and then looked back at me. "So you finished shopping? What did you get for me?"

I grinned. "I can't tell you." I honestly had a hard time remembering. There were lots of gifts, and a few were for him, and in the chaos of wrapping, I couldn't remember which one was from me—and technically Luke and Gabriel—and which were from the others. "I almost wish I could have gone shopping alone. That way everyone would be surprised. Kota and Dr. Green, Luke and Gabriel already know what they're getting from me."

Victor lifted an eyebrow. "You'd want to surprise them?"

I shrugged and then picked at my salad some more. "Just seems to ruin the fun when they know what they're getting."

He was quiet for a long moment, poking his fork at a slice of cucumber. "Do you...want to surprise them?" he asked.

"Gabriel has the cash I had leftover right now," I said. "Although I'm not very sure how much is left or if it's even enough. I mean I have a little more at home from this week, but it's not a lot."

Victor placed his fork down on his plate and then leaned toward me, the fire in his eyes igniting. "Don't worry about that," he said. "Wait here for a minute. Let me go grab something from the car."

As he slid off his seat, my heart froze in my chest, nervous to be left alone, but as I watched Victor leave, I could see the car from where I was. I turned back toward my plate, taking the opportunity to eat what I could while he was gone. As I chewed, I kept an eye on him as he opened the trunk of the BMW and pulled something out.

When he returned, he was carrying a small iPad. "There's no reason why I can't give you this," he said, and placed it in front of me, next to my plate. "Turn it on."

Is this an early gift? It wasn't wrapped, and the device looked to be used. It was still very nice, though. I took some napkins from the dispenser and wiped at a section of table in front of myself to make sure it was clean and dry so I could move the tablet closer. I looked at the darkened surface, found the power button and turned it on, curious as to what he wanted me to do.

The screen lit up, asking for a numerical code to unlock it.

I looked up at him, and he flashed four digits with his fingers. I entered the code and got beyond the splash screen to the front page. "Now what?" I asked.

"Use it to shop," he said.

I raised an eyebrow, angling the tablet his way. "Victor..."

"If you're going to start with Luke and Gabriel, then you might want art supplies for Gabriel, or get them all a game they can play with you."

"But I can't pay in cash," I said. It was a nice idea. My family had never bought items over the Internet, so it hadn't occurred to me. I realized online shopping was a normal thing and I suddenly felt silly I hadn't thought of it. "I don't have a credit card."

"Here," he said, pushing his plates of food away and reaching for the iPad. "Let me show you how to get it to work."

He placed the iPad between us, facing me, and used it upside down to show me different websites. Some were his favorites to shop at, and others were ones he often used to buy things for Gabriel, Luke, and the others.

Then he went to a bookmarked page: a retail department online.

"I'll show you how to use the credit card autofill app," he said.

"Victor," I said. I'd been leaning forward to look at him, and then reached out to stop his hand before he could touch the screen again. "I shouldn't use your card."

"Don't worry about it," Victor said. "They all use it when they need something."

I'd not seen anyone use a credit card that was like Victor's. Most of them had their own debit cards or carried cash. "I can...give you the money I've got so far from the diner this week," I said. "To help pay for it. And I can get more..."

"Sang," he said, his eyes brightening. "Just say thank you."

I sighed. It was normal for them to share what they could without asking for anything in return, like when they had taken me clothes shopping. I settled back into the seat. "Thank you, Victor," I said quietly.

"Don't feel awkward," he said. "I agree with you that they should get some surprises this Christmas. They've gone too long always knowing what they're going to get. It's hard to surprise them anymore. It'll be good for you to give them a surprise, especially if they think they've wrapped everything already."

"How can I get the gifts and make sure they're wrapped

and at the house?" I asked. "I can't just get them sent to Nathan's house. Any one of them might open a box that comes in. Or at the least, they'll know I've gotten more stuff. It'll ruin the surprise."

Victor drummed his fingers on the table, his fingers tapping like he was playing a tune at his piano. He did this quietly for a moment and then nodded. "You'll send it to my house," he said. "I'll make sure they are wrapped and will bring them on Christmas. I'll hide them under the tree when I'm sure everyone's asleep."

I got more excited about the idea, liking that the others would really be surprised. "You'll know what I got you."

"Maybe the shop you buy from will have a gift wrap option," he said. "But you'll just have to trust me this year if we're going to surprise the others. Maybe next year you can surprise me."

I smoothed my fingers over the surface of the now dimmed tablet, bringing it to life again. I might not be able to collect all the boxes without the others noticing, but maybe I could get one sent to Nathan's house. Nathan would understand, and wouldn't give away my secret. I'd pretend I only did it for Victor, and then Nathan would still be surprised at his own.

I asked Victor for ideas of what to get for Mr. Blackbourne as we lingered over dessert.

"What do you know he likes?" Victor asked as he spooned out some chocolate swirl ice cream.

I went over what I knew about Mr. Blackbourne. "He likes music," I said. "Both violin and piano. And I kind of know what types of songs he likes."

"He composes sometimes," Victor said. "You could buy him sheet music."

I made a face. It wasn't exactly the kind of gift I wanted to give.

He laughed at my expression. "What else?"

I thought some more. I tapped at the little iPad as if staring at it would give me some ideas.

When we were done, and after he paid and left a tip on the table, we walked out together, me still holding onto the tablet. Items filtered through my brain, but I dismissed them all. He had ties and that was a boring gift anyway. He already had a violin, and that would have been way too expensive, even if he didn't.

Once we were in the car, I was ready to give up. "Victor," I said, placing the tablet on my lap as I buckled in. "What would you get for Mr. Blackbourne?"

"I'm the one that usually gets him new music sheets," he said. He started the car and pulled out of the parking lot, heading back to Sunnyvale Court. "And I usually buy him new bowstrings for his birthday."

I sat up straight, staring out the windshield but not really focusing. "His birthday? When is it?"

"On the twenty-second," he said. "I try to get something sent to his house, so he gets it on the day. Sometimes I won't see him that week until Christmas, and I don't want the gift to blend in with the others."

"Shouldn't we do something?" I asked in a rush. I'd missed a few birthdays, and had barely been prepared for Gabriel's. This time, I had a chance to prepare and do things better. That was important to me, especially for Mr. Blackbourne, who had done so much for me since I'd met him.

"Maybe we should do a little dinner. Or..." I wasn't sure what else to do for him. Take him to a concert? Would he like that?

Victor pressed his lips together, remaining quiet for a few minutes as he drove. His eyes darted to the mirrors. "Princess, I've known him many years, and I have no idea what he does on his birthday. He usually disappears for the day and tells us all he's busy with Academy business or something else."

"Do you not believe him?"

"I don't think he really enjoys his birthday," he said. "I've never figured out why. Maybe it draws a lot of bad memories. It's the only time he ever really withdraws from the rest of us. I've asked Dr. Green about it, and he says that for now, we should just let him be. Just send him birthday wishes and gifts—from a distance."

I settled into the seat, staring off at the line of trees whizzing by. I was curious, wondering what happens to Mr. Blackbourne on his birthday.

If Dr. Green said to leave him alone except to send a gift, it made me determined to pick one that would be perfect.

♥♥♥

For the rest of the day, I curled up in a couch or in bed, looking at the iPad. I kept a novel ready on a reading app, so when Nathan or someone came close, I'd tap on it to bring it up, claiming to be caught up in a new book.

In secret, I carefully went over gift options from every store I could find. One by one, I picked out different gifts for all of them. I had them sent to Victor's house, and then I'd send him a text message or call him, letting him know which items were for who, so he could label them correctly.

He approved of my choices. "You should shop with me for gifts next year," he said. "We'll work with two iPads and drink coffee by a fire while we pick out what to give. We should do that for birthdays, too."

I adored his idea. I told him I wanted to do that next year.

I'd still go out with Gabriel and Luke if they wanted, but I'd save special gifts for shopping with Victor.

♥

$\mathcal{T}$HE $\mathcal{S}$OUND $\mathcal{O}$F $\mathcal{S}$NOWFALL

$\mathcal{S}$chool whirled by in the couple weeks that were left. No Volto. No Mr. Hendricks. I saw the inside of Music Room B and we cleaned the room and worked on homework as a group. We did homework that would last us several months through the next year, so when we returned, we could focus fully on the task at hand there. Everyone was busy with mid-terms and closing up school for the holidays anyway, so nothing eventful happened.

I was grateful for that.

♥♥♥

Early morning light woke me first. It was the gray glare of winter, with the sun starting to rise, and the surrounding trees and neighborhoods hiding its arrival. The day promised to be cold, and sections of my body was chill, even with the blanket around me.

Without opening my eyes, I sensed Kota in the bed next to me. I knew that Nathan slept on the roll-out cot next to us. North, Gabriel, Silas, Luke and Victor were nearby in sleeping bags spread out along Kota's bedroom floor. I smelled them in the air: Kota's spice, North's musk, Luke's vanilla, Silas's ocean, Victor's moss, Nathan's leather, and Gabriel's new blend, which I thought to be cranberry.

To me, that was what smelled the best. I didn't have to look to sense they were there, and they smelled wonderful. My heart fluttered, even while I was still partially asleep, warmed simply by the different scents blending together.

It was winter vacation. We had two weeks to ourselves. Two weeks without a crazy principal and vice-principal looking over me, or sneering students trying to look into my life. It would be the longest amount of time I'd spent with all of them for any length outside of school, without having to work at the diner, deal with school work, or do anything for the Academy.

"Everyone needs a break," Dr. Green had said. I could almost envision him trying to lecture me like he did in class at school, but failing to hide the grin on his lips. "That includes you. We work hard, but we take holiday breaks very seriously."

My skin tingled with chill, waking me further. I hadn't realized while sleeping that parts of me were almost numb. Despite the sheet and blanket, I was still freezing. It was usually moderately warm in Kota's room; why was it so cold now? Perhaps the weather had changed quickly, and the heater wasn't able to keep up.

It felt odd to be upstairs, with Erica, Kota's mother, and Jessica, his sister, sleeping downstairs and knowing I was up here with the boys. Maybe they didn't know that I shared the bed with Kota, but Erica trusted the boys to not do anything "unbecoming of a gentleman" as she called it, with a laugh and a teasing wink at Kota. Kota blushed when she said that.

I turned in the bed slightly, drawn to Kota's warmth and peeked at him, trying not to get caught looking.

His handsome face was still. His chest was bare, which surprised me because I thought I remembered him wearing a T-shirt the night before. The glasses were gone, although there was a spot on his nose, close to his eyes, where his glasses normally rested on his face. He didn't open his eyes, but he must have sensed I was awake anyway because he started to move. He threaded his arm around my shoulders, inviting me in.

I rolled into him and snuggled up against a firm chest and my legs folded near his, drawn to body heat. When I was pressed up against him, he tucked the blanket around my body. How the boys managed to keep their bodies warm when I ended up cold was beyond me.

He didn't say anything and I didn't either. I thought I should be shy about snuggling with Kota when the others could wake up and see us, but if Kota didn't have a problem with it, I wasn't going to object. I was too cold to move away. The boys were still sleeping, too. It was probably the quietest I'd ever heard them when they were together.

I settled and stilled. I thought maybe I'd fallen asleep again, but was listening to their breathing.

As I was listening, something caught my attention. My eyes opened a little, staring at Kota's chest, unsure of what I was hearing though I'd heard the sound before. My half-asleep state wasn't putting to words what it was. It was a very delicate sound, soft, crackling like a fire hissing...but softer.

There was also a familiar taste in the air.

I knew it. I knew it in my bones.

Excitement surged through me. I forced myself to still, grinning against Kota's chest. "Guys," I called, nearly cooing, the sound muffled against Kota.

Someone grumbled, though not Kota.

"Guys," I said louder, pulling my head away so I could be heard.

A grunt. A rustle of a sleeping bag as someone flipped over.

"Guys, wake up."

"Go back to sleep, Sang," North said, his voice gruff and deep, sleepy. "It's too early to get up."

That was a first. I was usually the last one in bed. The boys had a habit of waking me, urging me to get up and move quickly.

I quieted and listened again for the sound, not wanting to be wrong, but it was so distinct, unmistakable. "We should get up," I said.

North cleared his throat. When I peeked over Kota, I caught North dragging his blanket over the top of his dark head of hair. His broad shoulders caused the blanket material to tent around him. "Baby, sleep."

Kota reached a hand up, rubbing my back. "Sang," he said softly. "Let them sleep. It's vacation."

"No," I said, even as I closed my eyes. I would normally agree with them, but they wouldn't want to miss this. "Get up. Guys, we have to go outside."

Gabriel gave off a loud groan. "Trouble, I love you and everything, but shut the fuck up and go back to sleep."

I dismissed the love comment, knowing it didn't mean anything. It's what he said when he wanted any of us to shut up or do something he wanted. "Guys," I said. "It's snowing."

Kota's hand at my back stilled. "Sweetie, you're dreaming."

"No really. It's snowing."

Kota chuckled. "You can't even see the window."

"It's snowing. I swear. I can hear it."

There was a dead silence and I knew the boys were listening.

Someone snorted and then laughed. "You're so full of shit, Trouble."

"Meanie?" I sing-songed his name.

"Trouble," he mumbled, his voice slurred.

"Go look."

Gabriel groaned. "No. You're tricking me."

"I swear," I said. "It's snowing."

"No, it isn't."

I turned away from Kota, lying on my back. "I bet you a dollar."

"I'm not getting up for a dollar."

"I'll bet you...what do you want?"

"Gabe," Luke said. "Don't fall for it. She'll get you to get up and then while you're up, she'll get you to get something for her. Like a cup of water or something. It's an evil girl trick."

"Guys," I said in a more urgent tone. Why did they never believe me? "I swear. I'd bet my soul..."

43

"No betting your soul, Princess," Victor mumbled.

I grumbled, frustrated. "Gabriel," I called. "Go look."

"No."

"Please?"

"Fuck, no."

"God damn," Nathan said. "Someone get up and tell her it's not snowing so she'll go back to sleep."

I shoved my hands into my face, yawning and stretching. I could have told them I heard gunfire and they'd still sleep. I turned enough so I could peek out at the boys, over Nathan bundled up on the cot nearby. He was on his back, but his eyes were closed with an arm draped over his face to ward off light. I spotted Gabriel on the floor nearby, his hair sticking out from just under his blanket. The blonde mixed into the russet and the locks were wild, twisted about and sticking up in places. "Gabriel, I'll give you anything you want if I'm wrong. Cross my heart. It's snowing outside right now."

Gabriel grunted into his pillow, arched his back and slowly drew himself up until he was sitting back on his heels. His shirt was off, his bare chest a ripple of lean muscles. He eyeballed me through narrowed, sleepy eyes, focusing on my face. "I swear, Trouble, there is no possible way it is snowing. This is South Carolina. South. It hasn't snowed here in like a hundred years."

"And I'm telling you, I can hear it. It's snowing. I'm from Illinois. It snows there. I know what it sounds like."

Gabriel shoved his blanket aside, crawled over Luke, and started to knee-walk over to Kota's window. "Trouble, you asked for it. You can't hear snow. It's impossible. I'm going to want a massage. I'm going to want you to wash my hair for a month. I'm gonna get you to paint my nails a thousand times." He got to the window, wrapping a fist around the strings to tear open the blinds. His head tilted toward the window. "I'm going to make you wear skirts for the rest of winter. I'm gonna...holy Jesus motherfucking Christ; it's snowing."

"Now *you're* full of shit," North said.

Gabriel spun around, staring at me. "How the hell did you do that?"

"Do what?" I asked, my chest warming and happy I was right. While I had been arguing, part of me was worried I might have been wrong. Or maybe it would have stopped while Gabriel was delaying. I sat up, sucking in air and stretching again, suddenly wishing I'd worn more than a cami tank shirt and shorts to bed.

"You must have looked," he said. "You must have gotten up and saw it was snowing."

"She hasn't moved," Kota said, rolling onto his back. "Is it really snowing?"

"Told you guys," I said. I crawled off the bed, stepping, wobbly, over Nathan on the cot, and almost falling to land on Luke. Luke got up on his elbows, but I moved away quickly, weaving my way between Silas and North, and headed to the stairs.

"Where are you going?" Gabriel asked.

"Gonna go see the snow before it's gone," I said. Like I was going to wait for them when the first snow was outside. Sure, I'd seen it a million times, but there were palm trees here. I wanted to see a palm tree in the snow.

"What? Wait." It was Kota, who had sat up in bed, rubbing at his eyes. "You can't go out wearing that."

I was already past Victor, who was at the end, closest to the stairs. I thumped my way down to the bottom, opening Kota's bedroom door. I had been right. I could hear it snowing. I was going to go see it.

I was opening the door to the garage when I heard the others moving and their footsteps down the steps behind me. I hurried out into the garage, met with an even stronger wall of cold the moment I stepped into the space.

Max was in his crate wagging his tail and gave me one bark in greeting. I smacked the button to open the big garage door, urging it to hurry.

Gabriel and Kota were the first ones to arrive behind me as the garage door finished opening. I smelled them coming before I even turned to look at them. Kota had shoved on a T-shirt, the one he'd worn last night. He'd also put on his glasses. His green eyes were wide awake now, looking beyond me. Gabriel was bare-chested, his crystal eyes wide, his lips pressed together. I stood just inside the garage, gazing out into the morning.

A clean dusting of white covered the yard and the driveway. It was a wet snow, with big fat flakes that fell heavily against each other. It was just cold enough to keep it building for a while, but I knew once the sun came up over the trees, the snow was done for. My skin prickled with cold but I ignored the feeling. The twin palm trees in Kota's back yard looked strange with a layer of snow trying to collect at the base. There were a few trails from car tires already in the street, where the snow melted quickly. The neighborhood, for the moment, was still.

Kota and Gabriel fell in line next to me, staring out to the winter scene. I wondered if either of them had seen snow. They were from here, but I didn't know if they'd been out of the state before. Kota kept his arms tucked into his body. Gabriel shifted up his black sleep pants, the edge of his boxers poking out around his waist.

I didn't want them to waste a moment. I snagged Gabriel's hand, marching forward to drag him with me.

"Sang," Kota said. "Don't walk barefoot in the snow."

"It's not going to be snow much longer," I said. I marched out, leaving the dry cold of the garage floor, and meeting the wet, freezing bite of snow against my feet. The instant my foot touched the snow on the drive, it melted, leaving my footprints to mess up the pure sheet of white along the driveway. "Come on, Gabriel."

Gabriel hesitated for only a moment, before he stepped out, letting the snow melt around his feet. "Shit," he said. He clamped his arms over his bare chest. "It's cold."

I marched ahead of him, making a path and heading toward the end of the drive. The snow swirled around my face. I breathed in the icy air. I thought I wouldn't see snow this

46

year, or within the next few years living in the south. I didn't know where I was headed, after all. Since the boys came into my life, nothing was predictable anymore.

But knowing it was snowing outside without looking was apparently one thing I could do that they couldn't, and I was going to revel in this for as long as possible. I may not get another chance, if it truly didn't snow in the area except maybe once every hundred years, like Gabriel had thought.

I weaved my way across the driveway and back. It was cold, but knowing the house was right there and I could go warm up made it easier to enjoy being barefoot in the snow. I'd done it before up north, in Illinois, at my family's old home. A few minutes in the snow wouldn't cause frostbite. I'd return and warm my feet up inside quickly, maybe finding a pair of shoes before doing it again.

When I turned at the end of the drive, North emerged from the garage. His wore his black t-shirt and, his black pajama pants stuffed into boots he had shoved on. He held out a pair of Kota's green rain boots and a leather coat. When he was close, he dropped the boots at my feet. "Baby," he said, "don't walk around barefoot in the cold. You'll get sick again."

I mumbled a thank you in response and stuffed my feet into the rain boots. I let North slip the coat over my shoulders. He zipped up the front, then leaned down and planted a kiss on my cheek. His lips warmed my chilled skin.

"Told you it was snowing," I said, grinning.

"I still think you cheated," he said. "You saw it somehow."

I stuck my tongue out at him, marching away to go back toward the garage.

Kota and Gabriel both had boots on now. Gabriel had a jacket on, too. Kota had pulled on his coat. The others emerged in various stages of dress, with shoes stuffed on and jackets in place. They all stepped out, glancing around the yard and neighborhood.

Nathan was out front, making a trail with his boots on the

pavement. He went to Kota's car parked on the far side. He touched the snow there, picking some up and shifting it through his fingers. His red hair was starting to catch some of the flakes, making his hair look frosted.

Silas stretched his arms over his head, twisting his neck until it cracked. He scratched at the hair on the back of his head. "*Aggele*," he called to me. "Get the snow to come later in the day next time."

I rolled my eyes, bent over and scooped up a handful of snow. I had to gather a lot as it was starting to melt in my hand the moment I picked it up. I tossed it at Luke, who had turned, staring off at the back yard.

It hit him square in the neck and he cringed, his shoulders hunching. He looked back at me, making a face and moving stiffly, like moving made the snow colder.

Revenge lit up the brown eyes and I knew I was in trouble.

I turned and started hauling myself away across the yard. I'd only plotted my assault; I didn't have an escape plan. Dive in head first. That's how I worked.

The splat of wet snow hitting my thigh told me Luke was right behind me. I made a wide turn around the house, sailing toward the back yard. It was hard to run in Kota's boots, as they were too big. It was more like a quick, stomping march, and I was leaping more than running.

I ran smack into Gabriel coming around to catch me. He caught me by the waist, and we both went tumbling to the ground, sliding against the grass.

"Ow," I said, rubbing my hip that had crashed into his. I was still wearing the shorts, despite the coat, so I got my butt and lower back wet with snow, and my legs were freezing.

Gabriel had his hand pressed against his chest, laughing. "Oh my god, it's too cold for this."

"Sang," Luke said, standing above us. As I looked up at him, he dropped a handful of snow onto my face. Cold, soaking wetness smeared down my cheek, circling my body against my jaw and neck and dripping away.

I wiped furiously at it. I leaned over Gabriel, grabbing more snow and tossing it at Luke, but he dodged it and started running back around the house. He called out to me and then made a taunting, sing-song tone as he ran.

I jumped up, ready to run, when Gabriel caught me by the ankle. He did it so quickly, I nearly fell on top of him again. "No, wait," he said. He picked up a handful and got up. "You wait here. I'll chase him back around."

This led to each of us scooping up handfuls of snow, making slushy snowballs and flinging them at each other. Nathan joined the game. He caught me and held me up, allowing Luke to toss one at me. I struggled against him, but when Luke misfired and caught Nathan in the face, he released me and started running.

I circled around and managed to get up on the porch, where I discovered a fresh bundle of snow collecting in a drift in the corner. I gathered what I could, making a huge ball, and when Nathan was chasing Luke in loop number three around the house, I threw and then ducked.

"Ugh!" Nathan cried out. "Peanut! That was my eye. And my mouth."

I grinned, knowing if I stayed where I was, I'd be cornered. I flew over the other side of the porch and started to run, collecting a snowball as I went.

Luke and Gabriel continued to chase. I was just aiming a snowball at Nathan's head when I caught one in the ear.

I turned, finding Kota grinning guiltily, pointing a finger at Silas. Silas was smirking as he pointed a finger back at Kota.

I wasn't sure which one to believe in the moment and made a dash after them, a melty snowball in hand. Kota started off running and I gave chase. He was running carefully, though, trying not to slip on the snow, where I was already dirty and wet so I didn't care. I got close enough that I could aim my snowball. It hit him in the back. Not as satisfying when he had a coat on.

Kota laughed, turning around. He caught me by the waist and picked me up off the ground until the boots almost slid off my feet. I was breathless and hot around my chest and neck with the coat on, even though my legs were numb.

"You missed," he said, swinging me around.

"I got you in the back," I said.

He released me and reached for his shoulder, brushing at the clump of slush. He turned back around, catching my chin and smiling. "Are you all satisfied with yourself now?"

"Yes."

"Good," he said and looked over my shoulder, winking at someone behind us.

That someone hooked fingers into the neck of my coat and dropped a big handful of snow down my back.

I stiffened, turning. Silas wriggled his eyebrows at me.

I playfully shoved at him, scooped up some snow and prepared to throw it but stopped short. He was standing still as if he didn't care if I threw a snowball or not. Plus, he was wearing his coat. It made tossing at him less fun.

I changed my mind and was about to run off after Gabriel and Luke again when I did a second take at Silas. I thought of what I could get away with. Keeping my eyes on his, I hooked my fingers into the front of his pants and dropped the dripping snowball down the front.

"Shit," Silas said, smacking my hand away and pulling back from me. He opened up his pants, shoving a hand in and moving things around, scooping out the little bit that remained and hadn't already melted against his body. He shivered. "She even cheats at snowballs."

"That wasn't cheating," I said, laughing, although it probably was. I felt a little guilty about it but Silas was smiling and that seemed to make it okay.

"How did you know it was snowing?" Victor asked. He'd been standing quietly to the side, his hands in the pockets of his long trench coat. His hair was nicely mussed on the side where he'd slept. His fire eyes were lit to a simmer, subdued for the moment, but still curious. I wondered if he was bored or too cold to participate, but he looked curious now.

I shrugged. "I just heard it."

"What does it sound like?" he asked, stepping forward. His wavy brown hair fell across his cheek, a little longer these days. Even in pajama pants and a coat and just having woken up, he had an elegant look to him, and carried himself with his shoulders back, and his head high. "Can you show me?"

Heavy flakes were still falling around us. I'd been sure it wouldn't last but it was building on the ground. If it continued after the sun came up, it'd turn into a slushy rain, which would get rid of the snow quicker. I looked around the yard. With the other boys playing and scrambling for snowballs, I wasn't sure it was quiet enough to listen.

I held out my hand to Victor. "I'll show you," I said.

Victor perked up at this, as did Silas, Kota, and North. Victor took my hand. He lifted it and held it between his palms, at first warming my cold, wet fingers. I led him away from the snowball fight and toward the two palm trees in the back yard, and the opening they provided between them through the thick section of trees.

I crossed underneath the trees, heading into the flattened grass of the path in the woods behind Kota's house. Once my hand had warmed a bit, Victor's fingers intertwined with mine, his thumb sliding between my forefinger and thumb, smoothing out the skin on the back of my hand and warming me. I stepped until we were in the middle of the wide path, away from the hovering tree branches, and where we had a clear view of the clouds above us.

I stopped, stood still and listened. The snow fell around us. "Can you hear it?" I asked.

Victor lifted an eyebrow, shaking his head. "What am I listening to?"

I twisted my lips, finding it as difficult to describe as what music would sound like to someone who had never heard it before. Instead of answering him right away, I closed my eyes and listened harder. The wind blew softly, causing the snow to drift a little. The birds had stopped singing. Cars weren't driving by. This was how I'd heard it up north. When it snowed, especially the first snow of the season, the world stopped, watching and waiting. Animals stopped moving. Birds were quiet.

I slowly curled my fingers into his palm, trying to warm them. "It's like the world fell asleep, and all you can hear is it breathing," I said, my cheeks heating as I realized it was probably stupid. I tried to correct myself. "It's like fire crackle, very soft. The world's just quiet enough to be able to hear it."

Victor didn't laugh. He covered his fingers over mine. Together we fell into the silence, watching our world blanket with snow.

I turned slightly to see if Kota and Silas were still there.

All six of the others were standing behind us, eyes open, quiet and listening. Their heads were crested with white, as I'm sure mine was. Nathan, Luke, and Gabriel were muddied and wet. Silas had his arms wrapped around himself. North's breath drifted from his nose in visible puffs. Kota touched the corner of his glasses, the lenses fogged at the bottom.

My heart melted like the snowflakes that landed on my cheeks. I don't know how I knew it in just that moment, but I did.

Snowfalls were better with the boys.

As with many things in my life, they made everything better. Now that I'd experienced it with them, I wouldn't be able to imagine a snowfall without them. As much as they had things to show me, to teach me, I had my own little tricks to show them.

It was the first time I felt I was part of a family and wanted to go through many more experiences with them, sharing everything I knew, and exploring new places with them. I finally felt what it was like to have a family, where you cared what they thought, and wanted to share your world.

Our world. The boys and I. Dr. Green and Mr. Blackbourne, too. I wished they were here to share this. I knew someday, though, that they would be. I wasn't sure how I knew, I could simply feel it. They were home.

My heart melted like the snowflakes that touched my cheek. I don't know how I knew it in just that moment. I wasn't sure if I was supposed to. The moment I felt it inside me, I was sure it was wrong.

But I did.

I loved them.

All of them.

And that was the worst feeling I could have because the plan I knew about, the plan some of them wanted and the others struggled with... This new feeling inside of me troubled me terribly.

If I really cared about them, how could I ask them to do something so difficult?

♥
SECRETS TOO FRAGILE

I was one of the last people to return to the house at the finale of the snow fights. When Luke finally admitted defeat due to being too cold, we returned to the house. We left our boots by the back door, and Luke went to find out if the downstairs shower was open.

I went upstairs, finding Kota's bedroom empty, but the bathroom occupied.

Shivering in my soggy clothes, I contemplated whether I should go downstairs, or strip in the closet and put on warm clothes there.

The warm-looking bed called to me, and I kept my clothes on, crawling between the sheets. I suspected Kota or one of the others would yell at me, but I was too cold to wait for a bath, and stripping in the closet meant I'd get even colder once my skin was bare.

The sound of the shower spraying in the bathroom was starting to get to me, too. Lately, that had become very hard to ignore.

I pulled the pillow over my head, appreciating that it was helping to get my face warm, and using it as a sound barrier.

A hand grabbed my ankle and then tugged at the blanket, but I held on, keeping it where it was.

"Sang," Kota said, his voice muffled through the pillow. "Don't fall back asleep."

"I'm too cold to get up," I said.

"Let me walk you to Nathan's house," he said. "We'll shower over there. The hot water here will probably run out soon. It's probably gone already, even with the new bigger tank we installed. My mother is up, and so is Jessica and they've already had their showers."

The thought of trekking over the road through the cold and snow back to Nathan's house wasn't appealing. I had just started to warm up underneath the blankets. Still, I shivered after all the excitement had drained away. We'd gotten up too early, and now I just wanted to get warm and sleep.

"I'm fine," I said. "Just wake me up in a few hours." It was meant to be a joke because there was no way they would let me sleep after I'd woken them so early over snow.

"Hurry up," he said. He rubbed his hand over my calf, warming me a little over the blanket. "You're not going to want to miss pancakes."

With Erica at home, there would be chocolate chip pancakes. It was what Luke requested every time we were together. The thought of melted chocolate and maple syrup made my stomach rumble. I pushed the pillow and blanket away in a heap and was hit by a new wave of cold air against my wet clothes. A shiver started at the base my spine and moved upward through my body, finishing at my neck. I gritted my teeth. "Cold," I bit out.

Kota stood over me, wearing a clean pair of jeans and a new green sweatshirt. His brown hair was still a little damp, combed neatly to one side of his face. I suspected it was something Gabriel had suggested, slightly different for Kota, but stylish.

The thought of getting back into my boots in my bare feet caused another shiver. "The boots are going to be icy," I said.

He gave me a considering look before he said, "I was going to pick you up, but I don't want to drop you on the stairs," he said. "Just get to the garage. I'll carry you over so you won't have to put your boots back on."

I winced as I stood, feeling guilty for being such a baby. I was the one who'd walked outside in my bare feet. I was the one from Illinois who was supposed to be used to the cold. Cold was still cold, though, no matter where you're from. And I was freezing. "You don't have to do that," I said. "I can run over. Just go ahead of me and open the door."

Kota smirked and then turned toward the stairs, but

before we started to descend, his bathroom door opened. Victor stepped out wearing only his usual black slacks and a towel around his bare shoulders. His torso was trim with delicate lines around his abdomen and deep indents at his hips. His wavy hair was still wet from the shower and appeared much darker than normal, almost black and contrasted against his light skin. His fire eyes were dim; he looked tired. He noticed at us at the steps and raised a smooth brown eyebrow. "Is she showering downstairs?"

"I'm taking her over to Nathan's house," Kota said. "There's not enough hot water now."

Victor dragged his eyes from Kota to me. "She prefers baths," he said. "Your bathroom has a tub."

He was the only one that knew about my fear of showers. I shivered where I stood and not just from the cold. I didn't want to talk about showers right now. "I can take one in the other bathroom," I said.

Victor pressed his lips together as he looked at me for a long moment. Then he nodded slightly and turned toward the closet, picking through the hanging shirts.

Since he didn't say anything else, I assumed had kept his promise not to tell the others until I was ready. As I descended the stairs behind Kota, I hoped he understood why I hadn't said anything to Kota this time.

Being cold wasn't the only reason. I didn't know where to start. Every time I hesitated, I felt the guilt of holding back. At first, it seemed such a stupid little thing to worry about when we had *real* worries like Mr. Hendricks and his people following us, Mr. McCoy hunting for me, and all the other problems we had been facing. Maybe back then when it had first come up, it had been the wrong time to talk about something like that.

Now, after almost a month of quiet, of all of us going about our routines, and forcing Mr. Hendricks to stay put by not drawing attention to ourselves, I could have told them but I hadn't. At first, I didn't want to trouble anyone with a new problem. It's not like they could have solved it, anyway. All I had to say was that I wanted a bath; no one had questioned it.

Still, I knew it was probably best to tell them. I wanted to wait until I got a moment alone with Victor; maybe he could help me figure out how to tell one of the others.

I followed Kota to the back door, and the salty, greasy smell of bacon frying hit my nose as we passed near the kitchen, making my stomach rumble.

Kota encouraged me on. "Hurry and get a shower in," he said. "By the time you get back, it'll be ready."

I got out in the garage before he had a chance to close the door behind him and descend the few stairs. The big door was open, and I could see the snow had already started to get soggy and melty, only patches remaining now that it had warmed up. There was the start of a very soggy snowman at one corner of the house, the one we had given up on when the boys finally realized they wouldn't be able to collect enough snow before it all melted.

My clothes were sticking to me, and I sniffed as my nose started to run. I wiped at it with the sleeve of my jacket.

Kota came up behind me. "You sure you don't want me to carry you?"

I looked over at him. "No, it's okay."

He grinned at me and then blurted out, "Ready, set, go!" before he took off in a jog.

Finding a spurt of energy, I raced behind him, catching up only when we got to the road. Once he realized I was about to leap ahead, his run turned into a faster sprint, aiming right for Nathan's front door.

I was breathing in cold air and had to go around the wet grass so I wouldn't slip on it in my bare feet.

He was able to get the key in the door right before I crashed into him, breathing heavily. The short run wouldn't normally have winded me so badly, except I was already exhausted from playing earlier.

I leaned on him, tired and needing support.

Kota eased me back a bit. "Hang on," he said with a chuckle. "I can't open the door and hold you at the same time."

I pulled back, waiting. Kota opened the door and reached back around my waist to pull me against him, picking me up to carry me into the hallway.

I was met with a wave of heated air—Nathan's house was warmer than Kota's—and I breathed in deeply, catching the leather and wood scents of the house.

Kota locked the door behind us and urged me on. I shuffled forward, and then stopped and listened when I heard an unfamiliar sound.

Someone was in the bathroom in Nathan's dad's room. I was usually the only one who used it since everyone else liked Nathan's new shower.

Kota turned his head toward the sound. "Looks like someone beat you to it," he said, before turning me toward the hallway bathroom. "You'll have to settle for a warm shower instead of a bath."

A memory of being inside the shower at Victor's house sent waves of nausea to my empty stomach. I almost whimpered but coughed to cover it. "I could wait."

"You're freezing," Kota said with a chuckle, though his eyes were concerned. "Your lips are turning blue. You need to get warm."

As I stood still in the kitchen, hesitating, I touched my lips. The sprint here and fear were warding off the cold, but that wasn't the point. I pressed my lips together, secretly hoping whoever was in that bathroom would finish quickly. There wasn't an argument I could make that would make sense.

I could wash in the sink, but wouldn't he notice if I never turned the shower on?

Before I could say anything, Kota moved ahead of me to the hallway bathroom. He opened the door, turning on the light, looking at the fog on the mirror. "Someone's been in here already," he said. "Hopefully, there's some hot water left."

I stood in the doorway, holding myself together as Kota got a towel from the linen closet. "Go find some clothes so you can change," he said.

I escaped to the bedroom, finding some breathing space as I searched in Nathan's closet. Not a big deal. So I'd go into the bathroom, wait until Kota was distracted and wash up in the sink. I pressed a hand to my chest, over my heart beating rapidly against my ribs. I searched for clothes that would be appropriate to wear today since it was cold. I found a pair of black cotton slacks and a large sweater that would fall over my hips and grabbed underwear and a bra.

I dropped all of the clothes at the sound of the shower turning on in the bathroom.

"Sang!" Kota called out to me. "Hurry up. I'm getting the water ready."

I gasped in panic. I bent over, picking up the clothes with shaking hands and hugging them to my body so I wouldn't drop them again.

But I couldn't stand up. I remained frozen in fear, knees bent, head down, eyes closed. The patter of water spray hitting the shower tiles echoing in my head was all I could hear.

Telling myself to calm down, I tried to talk myself into moving. I could go into the bathroom. I had gone in before with Nathan when he thought he might be hurt. I didn't have to actually go into the shower stall. The water didn't have to touch me.

"Sang?" Kota called, his voice louder.

I forced myself to stand, to suck in some air and draw some courage. *Don't look at the shower. Just walk in and face the sink.*

I turned, carrying the clothes close to my chest.

I passed Kota in the hall, although I didn't say anything.

"It's ready," he said quietly. "You have everything?"

I nodded quickly, and before I could reconsider, I stepped into the bathroom and shut the door.

The shower was much louder now. I stood with my back pressed to the door, staring at the floor, and the clothes in my arms. The cold tile chilled my already cold feet. Steam drifted to me from the running shower, and I breathed in the warmth.

I was still standing. That's progress, right?

I put the clothes down on the counter and I started to strip out of the soggy things.

In order to not pay attention to the shower, I spent a lot of mental energy focusing on each task. Remove pants. Remove shirt. Strip off bra.

Once I was naked, I considered how to clean up. I sucked in a breath, found a washcloth in the bathroom closet and kicked the wet clothes away from the counter.

I turned the sink on, wetting the cloth. I focused on my legs, first checking for dirt, wiping away any and using the hand soap on the counter to wash properly.

It was a slow process since I forced myself into a daze, the sound of the shower echoing around me.

If I hurried, I could get out of here quickly enough.

Washing my hair was more difficult. Once I made my hair wet, I realized I couldn't get to the shampoo. That was in the shower.

I couldn't go in there.

I stood there, wet hair dripping into the sink and contemplating my next step. Thinking was made difficult as my brain could only function on a basic level as I tried to not focus on the shower running behind me.

At first, I considered opening a new shampoo bottle that might be in the closet, but then I remembered the boys kept kits below the sink.

I bent down, opening a kit and finding someone's shampoo which I used to wash my hair. From the ponytail holders inside, I suspected it was Luke's.

I did everything I could, even shaving, simply by using the supplies I'd found under the sink.

Then I realized my final problem. The shower was still running. There was no way I could reach in and turn off the water. I'd have to go into the stall to turn it off, and I was sure I wouldn't be able to. It was too close.

I wrapped myself in one of the big towels and made up an excuse. I opened the door an inch and called out for Kota.

He came quickly from the direction of the kitchen. He'd rolled up the sleeves of the sweatshirt. "Everything okay?" he asked and then stopped in his tracks when he saw me in the towel.

I was covered pretty well. Maybe I should have gotten dressed first. I was getting used to Gabriel being around whenever I was getting dressed, and I was already embarrassed by what I was about to ask him. I hadn't thought about him seeing me in the towel.

Heat radiated through my cheeks and I secured the towel with my arms over my chest. "I can't seem to turn the shower off," I said quietly. Technically true. I'd meant to add that perhaps the knob was slippery, but after a long pause, I couldn't get myself to continue.

Kota looked on toward the shower. "Is it stuck?"

I shrugged. "I'm sorry," I said. "I tried." More than he realized.

Kota entered, pushing the door back but leaving it open an inch. He stepped around the half wall, using the edge to hang on to as he leaned into the shower, avoiding the spray as much as possible. He twisted the knob and the water stopped.

"There," he said. "Maybe it was a little slippery. Did you turn it right or left? You have to turn it all the way to the right and down."

I blew out a breath of relief, mostly because the shower was off, and also because Kota had accepted that I'd had trouble with the faucet.

Emotion was weighing on me and I just wanted to get ready for the day. "Sorry," I said.

Faint footsteps echoed in the hallway like someone was trying to tiptoe around.

Kota tensed, turning toward the door and stepping out in the hallway. "Who's there?"

"Hey," came Silas's voice, deep and reverberating against the walls. "Kota, you should come out and see this."

"Hang on a second," Kota said, his shoulders relaxing. "Just helping Sang."

"She should come see this, too."

I shared an intense look with Kota, curious and wondering why Silas hadn't included me when he entered. Hadn't he seen us standing in the doorway?

Had he been trying to give us some privacy?

I let out another breath and then nodded to Kota. "Go out," I said. "I'll get dressed and catch up."

"We'll be right outside," he said. He reached for my head, kissed my brow, and then released me. I heard his footsteps getting quieter as he headed through the kitchen and toward the front door.

When I heard the door shut, I closed myself in the bathroom and proceeded to get dressed. I brushed my hair out as well as I could, but while it was still wet, I threw it all into a clip and secured it.

Once I was ready, I went to the kitchen and paused. Did I want to know? I did, of course. Something told me that if it was nothing, Silas wouldn't have bothered to come inside and ask us to look.

I pulled the front door open. Kota was right at the step, blocking me from exiting, holding his hands up. Silas was behind him, with a confused look on his face, dark eyes questioning me. He was dressed in a dark sweater and jeans and black boots, a look that almost mimicked North's. His expression was almost as grave as North's, too.

"What's wrong?" I asked.

"We don't know," Kota said. He reached out for my wrist and then tugged me outside. "We came back to get you."

I swallowed down my sudden trepidation and allowed Kota to pull me out to the walkway. Once we were in view of the street, he stopped and turned toward me, his eyes only focused on my face. "Look behind me, at your house."

I sucked in a breath and focused, looking around his shoulder toward the two-story gray house a couple lots down from Nathan's. I'd passed by the house so many times, not paying it any attention since it always looks the same, the only occasional difference being if the garbage had been taken to the street that day.

Otherwise, it looked empty it was too big a house for one person. Not that I saw Marie these days.

But now, the house had all the lights on and the windows were open. On a cold day like today, it seemed an odd thing to do.

I stared at the house, trying to figure out why when Marie appeared at the door inside the garage. She came down the steps with giant bags of trash. She wore a sweater and jeans and her long brown hair was tied back into a ponytail. From the distance, I couldn't tell her expression.

They wanted me to watch her taking out trash? And why did she have the windows open?

Then I noticed Derrick behind her, also carrying trash bags. He walked around her quickly and lifted the lid to the bin. It was already full to the top with bags. The trash collection wouldn't be on this block for another few days yet.

They shoved the bags down as far as they could. As Derrick closed the lid, it remained ajar, overflowing with bags peeking out. They didn't seem concerned and shuffled back into the house, closing the door behind them.

"They're...cleaning," I said, staring at the closed door and then at the windows.

"Yeah," Kota said. He still kept his eyes on me, even though I could tell he really wasn't looking. He was thinking. "It looked like they were *deep* cleaning. Doing a lot more than usual."

Silas had come over to stand next to me and while his head tilted toward Kota, his eyes were on the house. "Why?" he asked. "And why now?"

I shrugged. "Maybe she realized if she had the house to herself, she's the only one who can keep it clean."

"Maybe Derrick said he wouldn't come over again unless she cleaned," Silas said with a small smile. "He's never been messy. Maybe he'd had enough."

"Let's keep an eye on them," Kota said and turned toward his house. "When someone's out of a routine, there's usually a reason. Let's just make sure it is just a change of heart about a clean house, and not something else."

I couldn't imagine what other reason there might be, other than... "Kota," I said quietly. "My stepmother. Is she...would she be sent home for the Christmas holidays? Is she well enough to come back?"

"Not yet," he said. "Although we might have to face that soon. Dr. Green would have alerted us if there were going to be changes to her situation. Last time I checked in with him about it, he said she was recovering but her mental state was still off with all the medications she is on. The doctors are trying to work with her. Otherwise, she might come home with the same pills, and fall into overdosing herself again. She does need medication for her condition, possibly for the rest of her life. But if she can stabilize and not take more than what is needed, she can be somewhat normal."

"Whatever her normal is," I said quietly. I couldn't help it. My stepmother had been sick for so long, it was hard to remember what she was like before that time.

If she got better, would she regret what she'd done to me?

Would she even remember?

♥

A Visit
To The Past

reakfast was fluffy buttermilk pancakes and crisp bacon, with a few chocolate chips for Luke and me. We had to eat in turns at the small round table in the breakfast nook, making Erica comment that she should get a bigger table, along with a bigger dining room, to house us all.

I volunteered to wait for a seat while brushing out my wet hair and allowing it to dry. It was only during this moment that I remembered that it was Mr. Blackbourne's birthday.

We wouldn't see him today. He spent the day alone.

I wished we could do more for him, but since Dr. Green had said it was fine to send a gift and well wishes, I hoped a small text message would be acceptable for now until I could give him the gift I had picked out. I found my phone and sent a quick message.

Sang: Happy birthday. I hope you're well. Perhaps we can do another breakfast date soon. I do have a gift for you, so hopefully I'll get to see you soon to give it to you. Best wishes.

I read it once more and then sent it. As soon as it was gone, I questioned my choice of words for 'breakfast date.' I'd really meant to say something more vague, instead of flat out calling it a date, but I had been so focused on wondering if saying Happy Birthday was enough, or if it needed more.

He didn't send a reply within a few minutes, so I suspected he was either busy and couldn't answer, or he really did break off contact with everyone for the day. I tried not to dwell on it. He'd always told me to contact him whenever I felt the need, and this wasn't so important that it needed a response.

After breakfast, Jessica got picked up by a friend to spend the day with her. Luke, Gabriel and Nathan went to work at the diner, which they had said would be busy that week; we were all going to take shifts. Erica left for work.

Silas, North, and Kota were cleaning up in the kitchen. I tried to help, but North kept finishing whatever he was doing quickly and then would take over my task. I was feeling like he was silently criticizing me until I noticed him doing the same thing to Silas.

Silas looked to me after the third time North told him he'd put away the leftovers and to go do something else. Silas left him to it, and walked over, leaning against the counter near where I was standing and watching. I felt short next to him, so I hopped up to sit on the counter.

We shared a look and then smiled at each other. Something told me this was normal behavior for North. Silas understood.

Sitting on the counter had brought me closer to him. I leaned into him and whispered. "Should we go do something else? Maybe play a game or watch a movie?"

He backed up so he could put his mouth to my ear. His lips tickled my skin as he whispered. "One second." He looked at me with big brown eyes and then over at Kota, who was scrubbing the bacon pan in the sink. Silas returned his gaze to me and then Kota again. He was anticipating something, and I waited with him.

North found the right sized container to store the last of the bacon in and put it away. When he finished, he swept his eyes around the kitchen and then moved over to Kota, standing at his elbow. North shifted his weight in his black boots, a length of his dark hair dropping over one eye, making him look dangerously appealing to me. He nudged Kota's arm with his elbow. "Let me finish up."

"No," Kota said flatly and continued to scrub the pan.

North frowned. "Come on."

"You're not at the diner. You're off duty." Kota rinsed the pan and then put it onto a rack to dry. He picked up the pancake pan and dipped it into the soapy water. "What are you going to do after? Scrub the kitchen from head to toe? Sweep the cobwebs from the attic spaces?"

Silas grunt-chuckled. North threw him a look, but then refocused on Kota. "If I'm getting time off, I can do whatever I want." He looked at the countertops, clean and neat. There was nothing to scrub, so he turned away from them and looked at Kota. "I could take your car to the garage. Give it a tune up."

"I don't need a tune up," Kota said, beginning to scrub. "You did that two weeks ago. You've become a workaholic lately. Go watch a movie. And I don't mean straighten up the living room and then watch a movie. I mean sit down with Sang and Silas and watch something. Relax." Kota looked up from his scrubbing directly at me. He nudged his glasses up a little with the back of his wrist since his fingers were soapy. "And don't let him watch a documentary on cars. Try a Christmas movie."

North breathed heavily out of his nose, scrubbing his palm against his face. "Fine. Sang, go pick out something."

"Keep on him, Sang. Don't let him sneak off to mop the bathrooms. Sit on him if you have to."

I grimaced and slid off of the counter. He might have been joking, but the looks that being exchanged between Silas and North at the moment had me considering lap sitting and what that meant. Did Kota really mean it, or would Silas be jealous if I sat on North's lap during the movie? Would Erica walk in and then I'd have to explain it?

Just when I was thinking it was normal to hold hands with them or sit in laps and had gotten used to it, I now questioned such things from so many angles.

North did try to straighten the pillows on the couch, but Silas sabotaged him by tossing the extra pillows onto the floor and telling him to sit without them.

I pulled up Netflix with the remote and picked one of the first movies that I could find about Christmas. I started the movie and then sat between Silas and North, with my hands in my lap. Feeling small between them, I focused on the movie.

North started out with his arms folded across his chest. He barely moved except to loosen his arms a little so that his bicep touched mine.

Silas sat with his legs apart, and the questions crawled back through my brain unbidden.

What would happen if they noticed what the other was doing? Had they meant to sit so close? Were they just sitting casually or were they making a point to touch me?

Twenty minutes into the movie, with a live action Grinch going into a tirade, I was trying to focus on the plot instead of Silas and North, when the doorbell rang. At first, I thought it was coming from the movie and was trying to figure out why that sound was happening in the scene. Silas and North must have thought the same because they didn't look up.

Kota came into the living room and looked at the three of us on the couch. I looked up and noticed he was drying his hands with a towel. "Did the doorbell go off? Or was that the movie?"

We exchanged looks and before any of us said anything, Kota crossed the room to check the front door.

I presumed it had to be the mailman with a package. I thought about some purchases I'd made for gifts for the others, and if any of them might accidentally come to Kota's house. There was no reason for me to believe that might happen, but I had had one delivered to Nathan's house, which was hidden in Nathan's closet until Christmas.

With my thoughts focused on gifts, Kota's surprised tone of voice jarred me. "Oh, good morning. Did you see the snow? Wasn't that unusual? I didn't expect to see you today."

A powerful, steady male voice that I recognized as Mr. Blackbourne's replied. "That *was* unusual. I don't mean to interrupt. Did you need Miss Sorenson for anything today?"

My heart and lungs stopped working at the same time. I

checked my clothes, the black cotton pants and light, oversized sweater I'd picked to wear. Was this too casual for him? Had he come because of my text?

Had I upset him? Maybe I should have waited until the next time I saw him to wish him well and to give him a gift. Had I misunderstood Dr. Green? He'd said to leave him alone on his birthday, but I didn't think a text would be bad. I wondered if Mr. Blackbourne was here to lecture me to leave him alone when people told me to.

"Sang?" Kota asked. "No, I don't think so." He coughed and then called out my name.

I got up. I was so nervous that I'd done something wrong, I didn't even look at North and Silas until North reached for my hand, squeezing it.

I caught his eye, and we shared a long look. "Don't look so scared, Baby," he said.

I tried to smile at him and then at Silas, who sat forward, elbows on his knees, a wary expression on his face.

I started toward the foyer. The couch creaked behind me, and I looked back. Silas and North were leaning out as far as they could, peering toward the front door.

Mr. Blackbourne stood tall at the door, shoulders back, his head high, but his steel eyes were shadowed. He wore his usual gray suit, but with a black tie—a striking difference from his normal maroon one. What had he been doing? Had I interrupted something? I regretted bothering him.

Once I was in view, he focused on me. "Would you join me, please?" he asked in an odd voice.

The request didn't feel like his usual commanding tone. It was a plea. I panicked. Maybe this was something else. Like he didn't want to be here and yet something was forcing him to do so. Mr. Hendricks? Volto? "I...need shoes," I said, looking briefly at the floor as if there were a pair there. I wanted to follow him instantly. "And a jacket."

"I'll wait by the car," he said, turning quickly toward the door. "Join me when you're ready."

Not good. On a day he was supposed to be unavailable,

I'd kicked the hive and now he was here. Or worse, something bad was happening and he was forced to come find me on a day he didn't want to be bothered. The more I went over what it could be, the more I was sure there was trouble.

Kota closed the door after Mr. Blackbourne left. He came after me in a hurry, shooing me toward his room. "Do you have boots you can wear? Do you need me to fetch anything from Nathan's?"

I expected more questions from him, and North and Silas. But those two stayed on the couch, watching but not talking.

"I...have something upstairs. They're fuzzy on the inside. More like slippers. It's been snowing, so it might rain. Should I wear those in this weather?"

"The Uggs?" Kota said. He turned toward the front door. "You can wear those. They'll go with your outfit. I'll grab a proper jacket from Nathan's house for you."

"And I had a gift for him." I slumped my shoulders and looked down again. "Do you think I should give it to him now?"

Kota paused, turning toward me. He approached me and put his hands on my shoulders. He slowly and steadily massaged my muscles. "Sang, for whatever reason, he wants you to join him today. He's never turned away any gift we've given him. If you give him one, he'll open it when he's ready. You don't have to push him."

I breathed in slowly, finding my courage in his touch, soothing the shaking that had started in my heart. "I want to hurry," I said. "I don't want to make him wait."

"I know," Kota said, and he kissed my forehead before he gently urged me on. "If you need anything, call me right away."

I nodded, although I sent a long look to North and Silas, knowing they'd seen the kiss.

North frowned, adjusting his weight on the couch to lean more on the armrest. He shared another look, something I couldn't understand, but I wondered if he was uncomfortable witnessing this.

Silas was still, looking toward me, but with unfocused eyes. His broad nose dipped down slowly until his gaze dropped to the floor. I noticed his hands clenched, one on the arm rest, one at his leg.

I retreated to the bedroom upstairs, finding the boots. I didn't dare linger, not wanting to make Mr. Blackbourne wait.

If he came for me on this day, the day he never went out on, I didn't want him to change his mind.

♥♥♥

Moments later, I was in boots and a light gray jacket, holding the gift that was wrapped in gray paper and a maroon bow.

I couldn't hide it as I approached Mr. Blackbourne's BMW. He stood beside the car, holding open the door for me, but his eyes dropped to the gift.

I offered it to him, unsure of what else to do. "I didn't want to forget," I said, and then quickly added, "You don't have to open it now. I just wasn't sure..."

"Thank you," he said. He reached for it, grasping the bottom of the box, and waited for me to get in.

I slipped in, reaching for the seatbelt as he closed the door for me. He opened the back door and placed the gift onto the rear seat snugly, using a floor mat as a brace so it wouldn't shift around. He left the gift there as he circled the car to get in.

Good enough. I second guessed getting him a gift for his birthday. Maybe I should have just gotten him a card. Maybe he didn't want a gift. Maybe I should have held off until tomorrow.

Mr. Blackbourne backed up the car from the drive in silence. I kept an eye on the house, suspecting Kota and perhaps North and Silas might have been peeking out from behind curtains, wondering as much as I was right then as to where we were headed.

As Mr. Blackbourne drove, I kept my eyes on the brown

grass on the lawns we passed by. The sky was gray and overcast, but I wasn't thinking about the scenery.

With his somberness and black tie, a thousand concerns flew through my head. Maybe something important had happened, and he was about to tell me terrible news that couldn't wait. The police were about to arrest me for not going to school. My stepmother was demanding to see me or she had threatened them. The Academy had rejected me the moment they talked about me and I wasn't going to be invited to the important introduction the following week. Something drastic had clearly forced Mr. Blackbourne to come out today despite his usual desire to be alone.

It was something they'd all respected, an unspoken rule, but I was breaking that somehow.

I wanted to talk to him, but my tongue was glued to the top of my mouth. I was afraid to say the wrong thing. He never spoke, his eyes focused through the windshield as I got more and more nervous.

Since his gaze never left the road, I stole long glances at him, trying to gauge his mood. His light brown hair, trimmed perfectly, was as neat as ever. The scent of his spring soap was strong today. His fingernails were manicured. I wondered if he did that himself, or if he went to a spa like Victor often did.

I was unsure of where we were going until he took a turn into a park when the lane and surroundings started to look familiar.

I wasn't positive until we got to the end, where there was a playground, a picnic area, and a dock stretching out to a lake. There was no one at the park today, probably because of the cold. There were remnants of people having been there recently, though, with a child's forgotten shoe on top of a picnic table, and footprints in the sand near the playground.

Mr. Blackbourne had brought me here before, the time I'd been angry with North and he had given me guidance. He had told me about how his mother had brought him here when he was young. Perhaps his mother brought him here on his birthday, and while those had been happy times, now that she was dead and gone, he continued the tradition even though it made him sad.

Would he have brought me here if that were the case? Maybe I'd angered someone else without realizing it and he was had brought me here to talk about it.

Afraid to make a move before I knew why he'd brought me, I waited quietly as he parked and got out. He walked around the car to open the door for me, holding it expectantly.

I kept a soft smile on my face, trying to not appear as anxious as I felt. I got out and stepped away so he could close the door. I kept my hands behind my back to hide the shaking. The air was chilly, but with the jacket, it was just my nose and face that were exposed to the wind.

He moved to the trunk, opening it.

I stepped closer as he lifted out a picnic basket. It was something I hadn't ever seen in person, only in movies. It even had the red checkered cloth sticking out of it.

He closed the trunk, holding the basket in his left arm, and then turned to me, his steel eyes softer now, turning silver.

Surprise surged through me, replacing my anxiousness. I stepped up beside him, allowing him to lead the way. I was still unsure what he had in mind but understood I'd been wrong in my previous assumptions.

This wasn't about me at all.

He headed toward the dock. I checked for other people that might have been behind the picnic area, or further down the beach, but I didn't see anyone else. We were alone today.

We walked the dock, our shoes the only sound, creaking against the wood beams as we walked over them. At the very end of the dock, he stopped and gestured for me to stand aside. He put the basket on top of a post at chest height, and then opened it, taking out a heavy blanket that had been on top. He put the blanket down on the wooden planks. I stepped toward him with a hand out to help but then paused, unsure if I should get involved, afraid to do something wrong.

He looked at me with a lifted eyebrow, and then held out a corner of the blanket to me.

I took it from him, and together we lay the blanket over the dock.

Once it was smoothed out, he nodded down toward it. "Please, sit. Get comfortable."

I was grateful in that moment that I hadn't switched the pants for a skirt. Still, I sunk down to my knees, choosing to sit on my heels. The blanket was only a thin cushion against the rough boards of the dock. I wanted to be ready to stand if he needed any more help.

He brought the basket over, sitting it on one corner of the blanket, and then knelt down. He removed his shoes that looked a little too stiff for sitting on, and kept those at another corner of the blanket. I considered if I should remove my boots but they were comfortable and flexible enough. Also, it was chilly, and I wanted to keep the warmth.

Mr. Blackbourne reached his hand into the open basket, bringing out three boxes. The boxes reminded me of Chinese food containers, made of some kind of paper, but flat like a bento box—something I'd seen in Dr. Green's Japanese textbook. He handed me one of the boxes along with a fork, also made of a strange material, like a thick stock cardboard. Next, he put a second box in front of himself, and then the third, he placed nearby, as if he were expecting someone to join us.

I looked up and around, looking for someone else who might be approaching.

Mr. Blackbourne took out a bottle of water, offering it to me. I took it and opened it to take a sip since he hadn't opened the boxes yet. I smelled food, something greasy like fried chicken, but the boxes were cold.

He took a Thermos from the basket and then a small paper cup. "Do you like tea?" he asked. "It's black tea. I've got sugar packets if you'd like."

"I've never had regular black tea," I said quietly.

There was a slight lift to one of his perfect eyebrows but he said nothing. He poured out some tea into the cup and passed it to me. I was more interested in holding a warm cup in my hands than actually drinking it. Still, I tried a sip, and the flavor was bitter to me. I did my best to press my lips together in an attempt to mask my soured expression.

He poured himself a cup and then another one, placing it near the third bento box.

I looked around us again, back toward the shore and toward where he had parked, expecting someone else to arrive.

He passed over a couple of thick cloth napkins. I suspected they were to replace paper napkins that could blow away in the breeze.

When everything was laid out, he settled back and opened his box.

I opened mine, finding small pieces of fried chicken, bite-sized to eat with a fork, along with potato salad and diced peaches in the other compartments.

He held his box close to his chest, and picked out a piece of chicken, looking at me and waiting.

I sensed he wanted me to eat first, so I chose a piece of chicken and began to eat it. It was white breast meat and was tasty, despite being cold.

Once I'd taken a bite, he began to eat too. I couldn't think of what to say, so I focused on the food, enjoying the comforting tastes in an otherwise very curious situation.

The entire time, I waited for someone else to arrive, but no one ever did. He never looked for a third person behind him to arrive, but also seemed to ignore the place setting for the third person. He hadn't set out a water for the person, just the tea.

I finally realized no one ever was ever going to arrive for the food and a haunted feeling washed over me, wondering who it was for, but not daring to ask. As we ate, I occasionally glanced at the third set. I shifted as I sat, uncomfortable and feeling out of place.

When there was nothing left to eat, I sipped at my water until Mr. Blackbourne was finished.

When he did finish, he put his empty box down and sipped at his tea, looking out over the lake. I did as well, getting lost in watching the water lapping against the shore. In the distance, bare trees stuck out over the water. Without a strong wind, all was still. The gentlest of sparkling light reflected against the water, despite the light covering of clouds overhead.

After a while, the silence between us became less awkward and I felt myself relax. Feeling like we were almost meditating, the quiet trance-like, I was aware of my full stomach, the cool, crisp air, the nice park surrounding us, and his close, silent company.

It was an hour before he finally sat up, having shifted to sitting cross-legged after lunch. He collected the empty boxes and forks and emptied my unfinished tea into the water.

The lunch for his third person, our invisible guest, he simply slid aside to sit on the dock, while he collected the other items. I stood and helped him collect the blanket which he refolded and put it back in the basket.

We walked away from the dock, leaving behind the paper items and the food. I imagined animals and bugs would be by to eat what was left over, and the paper items he used wouldn't hurt the environment, being biodegradable. Isn't it still bad to leave it behind?

With my tongue glued inside my mouth, I followed him back to the car. I recalled something from Japanese class, where Dr. Green once talked about how the Japanese often left food for those who have passed away on different event days just for their ancestors. Leaving behind purchased or homemade bento, fruit, or other items.

But wasn't the food left at grave sites?

Mr. Blackbourne was doing something similar but had added his own twist to the tradition. For whatever reason, on his birthday, this is what he wanted to do.

I waited while he placed the basket back into the trunk and shut it.

He walked around to the passenger side, and I followed, presuming he was going to open the door for me.

Instead, he stopped at the back door, and opened it,

pulling out the gift. He held it in his hand, looking at it, tracing the gray paper and maroon-colored bow with a finger.

I was compelled to break the silence, even though it felt like I was somehow breaking a spell. "You don't have to open it now," I whispered. It felt silly to have even brought it up at such a time. I should have held onto it and given it to him when all the others had had a chance to.

He moved forward, and I backed up, allowing him space. He placed the box on top of the car's trunk, and delicately removed the paper and bow, to get to the white gift box underneath.

He opened the flap and pulled out the protective paper to uncover a crystal flower vase.

I panicked, feeling silly. I'd remembered the roses, and some comments he'd made about other flowers, making me think he had a fondness for flowers. I thought something as perfect as crystal, a nice vase, might be a unique enough a gift.

Though as I stood there, it occurred to me that if he did like flowers, wouldn't he have plenty of vases? It was too late to change my mind now.

He held the vase in his hands, smoothing his fingers over the curves. The store had described it as a bud vase, slim, meant to only hold one flower at a time. It narrowed in the middle, giving it a slight design, but otherwise, it was clear and simple.

"Thank you," he said, his voice a gentler version than his usual strong tone. He looked over the vase once more and then gently put it back in the box. "You have a unique way of understanding, Miss Sorenson. I couldn't have imagined how perfectly..." He quieted again.

Saying, "You're welcome," was on the tip of my tongue, but I waited to see if he was going to say more.

He pressed his lips together, sighed gently, and picked up the box. "I should get you home," he said.

I understood. It must have been very emotional for him, to think of his dead mother on a day like today. I didn't know why he brought me along. He hadn't done it for any of the other boys. What about Dr. Green? Did even he know what Mr. Blackbourne did on his birthday?

Why, of all days, did he pick his own birthday to be so somber, making it like a memorial? It was more like visiting a grave than a celebration.

I held on to those questions and more while he placed the box and the paper gently back into the rear seat. He opened the door for me, and soon we were off for him to drop me back at Kota's house.

I never told the other boys what happened, and they never asked, although questions filled their eyes when I returned. I couldn't offer any explanation. It wasn't my story to tell them.

They respected my silence, and never prodded me with a single question. I sensed their respect for Mr. Blackbourne.

Mr. Blackbourne had shared something big with me, inviting me along. Would I ever learn the mystery behind it? But I didn't need to really know. I sensed it that day, felt it. Through it, Mr. Blackbourne reached out to me and again, like many times before, something profound had happened between us.

Mr. Blackbourne had let me in.

I would never forget.

♥

CHRISTMAS MORNING

or the first part of the holiday break, it was a whirlwind of decorating. I found myself in awe of how much care the boys took to decorate every one of their homes.

Most of the time was spent on Kota's and Nathan's, and then Victor's estate and Silas's apartment. We didn't do the whole house, just Victor's and Silas's rooms, and then certain other areas. I wondered if Charlie, or if Victor's parents would notice. They didn't seem worried about it. To me, it seemed they simply kept themselves busy to pass the days.

Dr. Green had no problem adorning his condo with fancy crafted snowflakes made out of paper.

Pam decorated the Coleman trailer, despite Gabriel pleading with her to let him handle it.

North said not to bother decorating their house; no one would see it except for him, Luke and Uncle. But despite his protests, Luke and I spent an afternoon putting up a tree and hanging simple holiday wreaths at every window. North only disapproved of the ones on the second story windows, telling us not to walk on the roofs.

Compared to my past Christmases, this one was full of activity. In what I'd started to think of as my old life, my stepmother had my sister and I put up and decorate the tree from when we were very young. At first, decorating was different, and different in the house that was always the same was exciting. My father was always working so it was usually up to us.

As we'd gotten older, when my stepmother was sick in bed and had directed us to put up the tree a week before Christmas, it had started to become a chore, and one that I often did alone.

There was little appreciation for it; no one wanted to help or even looked at it until Christmas. I did it more out of something to do because it was something I'd always done. There was little joy in the holiday.

Still, I knew Christmas this year would be different.

Leading up to the holiday, I had dreams of Academy people behind walls, whispering to me that something was coming. I kept those dreams to myself, not wanting to admit to the guys that I was stressed about the upcoming introduction. Being busy kept me just distracted enough during the day, but at night, with the long stretch of time between lying down and actually falling asleep, I worried about what was to come. Every evening, I practiced in my head what I would say when I was finally asked which group I'd like to join.

The next thing I knew, it was Christmas Eve. The boys all collected at Kota's house, save Dr. Green and Mr. Blackbourne, who would join us the next morning. We watched a marathon of Christmas movies until midnight when Kota proclaimed Santa couldn't deliver gifts unless everyone was asleep.

Kota's mother allowed us all to sleep upstairs, under the condition that Jessica was allowed to as well. Jessica took the roll away bed and I took Kota's while The others spread out on the floor. It was a surprise to me that any of them were here at all and not at their own homes. What about Charlie? Or Pam? Wouldn't they want their families at home on Christmas Eve?

I did worry about Marie. I'd sent her a small gift, which Nathan walked over to give to her as I wasn't sure if she wanted to see me. Nathan said she said thank you but there was nothing from her, which I wasn't surprised by and didn't expect.

I also sent along something small for my step mother, that I'd told Nathan to tell Marie to say it was from her. Kota made arrangements for Marie to go visit with her on Christmas alone. I hoped she wouldn't feel left out, but then we didn't do much for Christmas before. Some guilt weighed on me still. I was leaving her behind and it didn't really feel right.

I fell deep asleep. I'd suspected I would have been awakened to help put Christmas presents under the tree in the middle of the night, but no one woke me.

♥♥♥

The moment I opened my eyes Christmas morning, I panicked, sure I had made a terrible mistake.

I was positive that all the Christmas presents for the guys under the tree were all wrong. I wanted to take them back and get them all something different.

Maybe it was because I'd never given Christmas presents to anyone before, and I second guessed every item, and in some instances, couldn't even remember exactly what I'd selected. Gabriel had picked out some of my gifts. Victor had assured me that the extra ones I'd picked out would be under the tree. The problem was, I had never seen them myself in the flesh. Were they what I'd thought they were? What if I'd gotten a wrong order? Victor had told me what he received and I told him what was for who.

Silent whispers of breathing and light snoring came from around the room. I stared at the ceiling for a long while, gazing at the gray light coming in from the window, pondering if I could slip downstairs and possibly find the items before anyone woke up. Could I take them away and hide them? Where would I even put them?

"Sang," grumbled Gabriel before he yawned. "Trouble..."

I turned in the bed, looking down at sleeping Jessica, her brown hair a frizzy mess, coming out of her braid. Her glasses were on the table that had been scooted over, her frames next to her brother's—pink next to the black.

Looking past her, Gabriel and the others had their heads pointed toward the bed, their feet toward the far wall. Silas's lump was the biggest in the middle, moving as he breathed steadily, North and Kota on either side of him.

Gabriel was at the far end, closest to the bathroom. A stripe of blond hair stuck out from under the blanket.

Had I dreamed him talking?

"Sang," Gabriel said. "Is it snowing?"

I listened and heard nothing. "Not today."

"That would have been fucking cool," he said, his voice huskier than usual. He coughed and it returned to his usual baritone. "Sang, go get me a coffee, please?"

I was bundled warmly in Kota's bed. I imagined that was the same reason he didn't want to get up. "Gabriel, I tried. I failed. I'm sorry." I giggled, unable to stop it from spilling from my lips.

Kota and Victor snickered from underneath their blankets.

Silas shifted to his back, letting out a rumbling groan as he stretched long, lifting his hands so he wouldn't hit Jessica's bed. "I'm going to need a good Greek frappe if I'm going to survive."

"We've got Sang's baby coffee," Kota said, still lying down. "I think the only other coffee we have right now is instant unless you want to go over to Nathan's house."

"Sang's coffee is baby frappe," Silas said. When he spoke the word *frappe*, there was more Greek accent. "Frappe is a Greek invention made from instant coffee." He rolled onto his side before sitting up, holding himself up with strong bare and bulging arms as his blanket slid off of his chest. He stared at the wall, blinking.

"Frappe?" I asked. It was on my tongue to say Frappuccino but his accent made it sound different. I'd once tried a sip of Kota's normal black coffee and it had tasted so bitter that I didn't think I'd ever get to the point that I'd want to drink it. Would a frappe be the same?

Silas breathed in deeply through his nose and then let it out from between his lips. He turned a little to look at me once and then twisted back around to sit up. "Frappuccino is a

Frappe cappuccino, *aggele*."

Would it really be the same? I supposed if Silas wanted to make one, I'd try it.

"Learn something new every day," Nathan said. He slowly flipped around onto his stomach, did a pushup and then was up to sit on his heels. His red T-shirt was halfway up on his stomach like he'd tried to push it off while he was sleeping. His boxers were slung low on his hips. "Are we awake now?"

"Yes," a few of them said at once. North and Gabriel started to get up. Victor remained stationary with the blanket over his head. He was the one closest to the window sea, and the stairs. I wondered if he picked that spot so he could sneak downstairs silently during the night when everyone was finally asleep.

How late had he stayed up?

Kota nudged Victor in the shoulder. "Are you going to get up?"

"I don't see the point," Victor said and then flapped open his blanket in a huff. His hair was a mess and he quickly combed it with his fingers, only having moderate success at controlling it. His eyes were barely open. "We have to wait for Mr. Blackbourne and Dr. Green. Who knows when they'll show up?"

Nathan picked up a pair of black pajama pants and turned around to put them on. "Remember when Dr. Green was sick all night on Christmas? And then he slept in until one in the afternoon? We had to wait until two when they arrived."

"Worst Christmas ever," Luke said with a groan. He had been next to Gabriel and was already rolling up the sleeping bag. "He got here and fell asleep on the couch, so we had to wait *another* two hours. It was nearly sunset before anyone opened anything; too late to play with some of it."

The boys continued to talk about the different Christmases they had. Jessica eventually woke up and even joined in.

Not having anything to add, I curled up with the blanket around me, listening to every detail. I was sorry when a few talked at once and I couldn't pay attention to everything; I wanted to know everything.

I wished I had been there myself. The guys'd had years and years to be together, and I felt so left behind. Would I ever feel completely included? There would always be a past that I hadn't been a part of.

I got up, found my clip, and used my fingers to comb through my hair, twisting it before clipping it back.

The pajamas I wore were a black and pink plaid, with Victoria Secret's VS logo embroidered on the pocket. They were made of a light flannel, not too hot, and very comfortable.

The other boys didn't seem to be in a hurry to find other clothes but Mr. Blackbourne would be here at some point. "Should we get dressed?" I asked.

Nathan shrugged, picking up his pillow and sleeping bag and adding them to a pile of stuff tossed to the side of the room for now. "Nope," he said. "I mean, you can if you want. But the rest of us usually just stay in pajamas."

"That's the part my mom likes," Kota said. "She loves days where she can wear pajamas all day. If we change, she'll want to change." He had his glasses on now but strands of hair stuck out on the back of his head. He smoothed his hands over the green T-shirt and then down to his matching flannel pajama pants. He picked up his neatly folded blanket and his pillow, adding them to the collection of bed things. "I guess someone should heat up breakfast."

Gabriel was the first into the bathroom and Victor waited for him to finish to go next while the others went downstairs. Watching them leave, I stayed in the bed, waiting my turn behind Victor.

Victor smiled, though with dark shadows under his eyes—a tired ember glowing inside them. "Morning."

"How'd it go?" I whispered to him, worried Gabriel could hear us.

"Fine. Everything's ready to go. I hid yours pretty well, so they might not even notice them until we start passing gifts out."

I smiled and pressed my palms against my thighs, itching to ask a million questions about my choices. Too late now, I supposed. Maybe they would forgive me if I'd picked things they didn't like.

"You go ahead of me," he said.

"You were in line."

"I can wait."

"So can I."

The toilet flushed and the door opened. Gabriel appeared in his black pajama pants and a bright orange tank shirt. His blond locks were brushed back neatly, blending with the russet. His crystal eyes landed on us and he jerked his head back, cheeks reddening. "Give a man some room. Geez. Listening in..."

"We didn't hear anything," Victor said. He waved me on. "You go ahead."

Gabriel's face reddened some more until his ears were pink. He put an arm around my waist and then urged me on toward the stairs. There was an odd collection of smells, but the thickest was a fresh spray of Kota's spice scent. Had Gabriel sprayed it on himself just now? "You go, Vic. She should go downstairs."

I shared a curious look with Victor and then walked away with Gabriel.

"I'm not in a hurry," Victor said but moved in toward the bathroom.

"It's fine," I said. "I can wait..."

"Trust me," Gabriel said with a stronger tug I couldn't resist and let him guide me down the stairs. "Remember, Sang. Boys are smelly. You can't judge."

It was clicking in what he was referring to when Victor cried out, "Gabriel! Oh my God. You drank too much milk again, didn't you?"

Gabriel rolled his eyes and grimaced. He spoke through his clenched teeth. "Motherfucker needs to shut up right now."

"You can't drink milk?" I asked. We'd reached the bottom of the stairs and I pushed the door open, stepping onto the wood floor in my bare feet, feeling the chill compared to the carpeted stairs.

"Not quite as much as I did last night," he said, landing behind me with a thunk and shutting the door back behind us. "But Luke was trying to eat all the cookies by himself, so I had to hurry to get into the contest. I couldn't swallow as much cookie without milk."

"What contest?"

"Who could eat the most cookies," he said. "We do it every year."

"When did this happen?" I asked, blinking at him. "Where was I?"

He stopped in the hall, his orange shirt clinging to his body, the flannel pants sagging a little around his hips. He lifted the hem of the pants to adjust them on his narrow waist and looked over my shoulder at Nathan setting the table before returning his gaze to me. "After you went to sleep. When we put out the presents. We ate the cookies that were set out for Santa."

I remembered they had done that, a whole plate of sugar cookies had been set out on the coffee table. "Aw," I said and pouted. I had missed things simply by going to sleep.

"Hey, hey," he said in a stronger tone, and shoved a finger into my lips, pushing them back against my teeth. "Don't you start."

"That just sounds fun," I said. "A cookie-eating contest."

"Breakfast," North said in his deep voice, coming out of the kitchen with some paper plates. His face had a night's growth of beard, and it made him appear a little older and dangerous. He positioned the plates around the table—settings for nine. "No cookies until after breakfast. Or maybe not even until after dinner. I don't think there's any left."

"Fuck, how do you hear us?" Gabriel asked. "Every time..."

"You're all noisy," North said. When he was finished setting the plates, he went back into the kitchen.

Gabriel and I padded along behind him into the kitchen,

where Nathan was toasting bread, and Kota had the microwave running; I could smell bacon cooking.

"What did she want?" Silas asked from the other side of the kitchen where he was leaning against the doorframe.

"Cookies," North said. "And the answer is no."

"Cookie contest," I said. "Luke and Gabriel had one last night."

Silas laughed in a boom that echoed through the kitchen. He folded his arms across his broad chest, appearing bigger than usual in his blue tank shirt. His arms bulged as he leaned against the wall. "You couldn't survive a cookie contest with any of us."

"I could, too," I said, even as I doubted it. But I did have an idea how I might be able to although it did require cheating. "It's whoever eats the most, right?"

"Usually within a minute or two," Kota said. The microwave beeped and then he pulled out the cooked bacon. "Otherwise, Luke would make himself sick. North, you might as well let her. It won't be long until they have their Christmas candy anyway."

"Moot point," Gabriel said. "I don't think there's any cookies left. Luke and I finished them."

"Give me a minute and I'll find some," Kota said.

I used the time to go to the bathroom down the hallway. By the time I returned, Gabriel, Luke, and Victor were sitting in the living room around the Christmas tree. Max was with them, lying on his side in front of them as they examined the gifts piled under and around the tree.

I'd never seen a room so full of gifts before. I could have stacked them into a mountain shape and it would have been taller than the house. Some of the packages even appeared bigger than me. Shiny wrapping paper glittered under the dozens of lights on the tree.

The tree itself was dazzling. I'd seen it the night before with the multicolored lights glittering against all the different decorations. While there were a few red and silver balls, a lot of the other ornaments were handmade, or were filled with photos of past Christmases.

There were stockings hung over the small fireplace and more were scattered around—at the base and some on top of the mantel. All were stuffed full.

I'd been surprised people in South Carolina even had fireplaces in their homes. I'd heard a rumor while I was still living in Illinois that people in the south didn't have them.

I couldn't see the names on all the stockings, but I counted that there was enough for everyone, including Max.

Gabriel, Luke, and Victor sat quietly together, gazing at all the items. They said nothing, and I watched quietly from behind them, unsure if they even knew I was behind them. Luke, bare-chested and wearing baby blue pajama pants, was gazing sleepily at the tree. Gabriel petted Max absently. Victor was sitting cross-legged near a heap of presents, simply looking over the pile of packages.

Not wanting to disturb them, I snuck away quietly. When I got back to the kitchen, there was a paper plate on the stove, heaped with sugar cookies.

"My mom keeps a stash in a tin in her bedroom," Kota said. He stood beside the stove, grinning. "It's so Luke and Gabriel won't try to eat them all on Christmas Eve."

"Kota!" Erica's voice traveled from the kitchen table. "Grab the strawberry jam, will you?"

Kota winked at me and then went to the fridge, getting out a jar and taking it to the table.

Silas remained with me in the kitchen. He was leaning against the counter with his arms crossed over his chest. "You couldn't beat me at eating cookies," he said.

He was one of the few I was pretty sure I could beat. I smiled slyly and then picked up one of the cookies from the counter. They were glittering with red and white sugar crystals on top. "I only have to eat more than you do in a minute," I said.

"My mouth is bigger," he said with a grin. "If you're going to try, you're welcome to. You'll just owe me after."

I'd almost forgotten that they wanted things when you

lost their games. I hadn't considered that would be part of it though it didn't deter me from the challenge.

I held the cookie in front of my face, inhaling the sugar. "Who's got a timer?" I asked, not answering Silas directly.

North appeared in the doorway, found us hovering over the cookies, and then narrowed his dark eyes at Silas. "Don't encourage her."

"She started it," he said.

North shifted his dark eyes to me. With the shadow of a beard on his face and the deepening frown on his lips, he was terrifying. "Sang," he said. "If you make yourself sick on cookies, you'll have to go back to bed and then we'll all have to wait to open our gifts."

"I'm not going to get sick," I said. I put the cookie down so I could hop up and sit on the counter. My plan required being able to brace myself, and I could do it better if I was at least almost level with Silas. I brought the plate over to my lap to hold for easy access--the important part of my idea was having control over the plate. "Will you time us?"

North groaned and then shrugged in defeat. "Hang on. Let me get some milk out before you two choke to death."

Voices from Erica, Jessica, and Nathan drifted from the table as they ate and talked. Kota returned for napkins but then lingered in the doorway to watch.

North placed two cups of milk next to us on the counter and then got his cell phone out. He pushed at the timer to set it up. "One minute only, you two. And that's it." He held it up and showed it set to count sixty seconds. Then pushed the button as he said, "Go."

I let Silas grab a cookie. I held onto the plate with one hand and used the other to take a cookie and took a bite. It was a lot of sugar and more than I would have liked, especially first thing in the morning. I had a fleeting thought that it probably would have been better to do this after breakfast.

Silas was teasing me by eating slowly, slower than I knew him to normally eat. Still, in three bites, the cookie was gone.

I stuffed the rest of the cookie into my mouth, the red and

white sugar crystals falling from my lips back onto the plate. Before I'd finished, I grabbed another one.

Silas reached for one more, but I moved the plate away by tucking it almost behind me on the counter, keeping a wide grin on my face as I chewed.

Silas smirked and then stepped closer. "Hey," he said.

I lifted my foot until it was in the middle of his chest and pressed it against him, holding him and the plate away while trying to finish...and not laugh, choke and die.

Laughter erupted from the two doorways to the kitchen. Nathan had was standing next to Kota in the dining room entryway, his face reddening as he snorted with laughter. Victor stood at the opposite end on the living room side. He chuckled and his fire eyes sparked to life.

North rolled his eyes but still smirked.

Kota crossed his arms over his chest and leaned against the counter. "Come on, Silas. You can get more if you want."

I quickly braced my foot and leg against Silas's chest and then tucked the plate more behind me, out of his reach. Then I lifted another cookie and shoved it into my mouth.

Silas leaned against my foot, smirking, but then started pressing against my leg a little at a time using his strength and weight. He was testing me, but I put every ounce of energy I had into holding him off.

I laughed and then choked a little on the cookie in my throat. I coughed but didn't give up the fight.

Silas froze immediately and then eased off of my leg. "Give me some."

I passed him a cookie and then picked up another two. Again I grinned, and coughed, a bit of sugar stuck in my throat.

Victor moved around so he could pick up the milk and hand it to me. "Drink," he said.

I put the cookies onto the plate and then took up the milk, drinking, eyeballing Silas with a wary gaze over the glass. He finished his second cookie but then held his hand out, but I was busy drinking. I gave him a piece of a broken one before I picked up more for myself.

Kota rolled his eyes. "You're going to let her cheat like that?"

"She almost choked," Silas said, holding his ground. My foot was still on his chest, but he wasn't fighting anymore. He looked at me with pleading eyes. "Come on, Sang. Let me have a few."

"No-o-o," I said with a chuckle, but then stuffed another cookie in my mouth.

North looked at the timer. "Fifteen seconds left."

With that, I ate one and a half more cookies. I offered Silas another half.

He rolled his eyes, but then leaned down and let me feed him the cookie from my hand.

North said stop when the time was up. I'd eaten four and a half cookies and Silas had eaten three.

North shook his head. "Well, at least you didn't puke."

"I didn't have to get sick if Silas didn't actually eat them all while trying to win," I said and slid off the counter. "Besides, there's still some cookies left over for everyone else."

North smirked and poked me in the shoulder. "Smart ass."

Kota groaned and shook his head. "Silas," he said. "You let her cheat and get away with it."

Silas lifted his shoulders in a heavy sigh. "Look at her face," he said. "She wanted to win."

I grinned, offering around the plate of cookies freely now that the contest was over.

Silas turned to Kota. "Are you telling me you can resist her?"

The way he said it, made me still because I wanted to hear Kota's answer.

"You can't baby her," Kota said, although he said it with a smile. He gave me a different look than I was used to. It reminded me of Mr. Blackbourne: challenging, making me want to sit up straighter. "Make her play fair," Kota said, keeping his eyes on me.

"It was just cookies," Silas said. "Besides, now she has to ask me a favor."

I reached for the glass of milk to give myself a moment to think because I hadn't thought far enough ahead to what sort of favor I'd ask of Silas.

"Do you want to give them to her, or have her earn them?" Kota asked.

He was smiling, but the way he straightened his stance and sent a challenging look my way told me he was talking about more than a cookie-eating contest. "Play time is fine; I'll give that to you. You might not always be around us, though. You might need to play by the rules. Not everyone will understand or be accepting of your cheating."

His suggestion hinted at my future within the Academy and possibly a future that put me on another team. I put the glass down, looking for someone else—anyone—to provide a little reassurance.

However, the others kept their heads down, looking at their feet, or the counter, or something else—anything that wasn't me. Clearly the possibility of me being on another team was something they all knew about and considered to be a possibility. Were they worried about the outcome at the end?

The playful mood was broken. Somberly, I put the plate down on the counter. How could I believe if they didn't?

"Sang!" Gabriel cried out from the other room. "Did you eat yet? Come see."

♥

𝒦OTA'S 𝓕EARS

*N*orth begged me to eat some bacon and drink more milk. He suggested I avoid toast since that was just more carbs on top of the sugar I'd already had. He sat next to me at the table, eating his own bacon and sliced peaches. "You're going to crash hard in an hour and sleep through the whole thing."

Erica paused while clearing her plate and cup from the table, waving a hand toward his face. "Don't fuss at her so much," she said. She had on her large gray T-shirt with yellow USMC lettering across the front and gray sweatpants. "It's Christmas, you big grump. Let her relax."

North bowed his head. "Yes, ma'am."

Erica winked at me and then went to the kitchen. She left her dishes in the sink, grabbed one of the sugar cookies and headed toward the living room.

Already mostly full on the cookies, I could only get in so much bacon before my stomach was weighing me down. I drank some milk and then a cup of water.

I had to skip the coffee by the end of it; I was too full. Silas seemed to have forgotten his promise to make frappes.

I was the last to finish eating, so when I got to the living room, the others were already gathered around, admiring the gifts and the stockings arranged in front of the fireplace. The coffee table had been pushed into the hallway, leaving us room to sit on the floor. The television in the entertainment center was on, showing a Charlie Brown's Christmas movie, but the volume was muted. Some presents along the wall reached the edge of the entertainment center, blocking part of the view, but no one seemed to be paying attention.

Still in bare feet, I stepped into the room, dazzled by the

scene in front of me: the gifts wrapped in countless colors, the glittering tree, the overflowing stockings, and the boys at the center of it all. My brain couldn't focus on one thing, possibly from the cookie-induced sugar rush.

Or maybe I was just excited. I'd never had a real Christmas before, where I was actually looking forward to not only receiving gifts but seeing what everyone else got.

Erica was on the couch at one end, with Jessica at her feet. Erica combed and redid the braid in her daughter's hair while Jessica sleepily stared off at the presents. Kota was on the other end, leaving a space in between. He was watching the movie, his eyes occasionally darting at the others.

Luke, Gabriel, Nathan, and Silas were on the floor in front of the presents, making guesses as to what might be inside the boxes. It was funny to see Silas in the middle, not really talking, but taking in what Luke, Gabriel and Nathan argued over.

While North remained in the kitchen, finishing up the last of the dishes, Victor came in, looked around, and then eased himself to the floor where the coffee table had been. He sat quietly watching and listening to the others as they speculated.

I moved into the room to sit next to Victor. He looked up at me and at first started to scoot over, but then stopped, looking over his shoulder. He nodded slightly toward Kota, silently trying to tell me something.

I didn't understand until I looked at Erica. Even though we'd all been hanging around the house, I seemed to end up sitting next to Kota a lot. I suspected it was because Erica assumed Kota and I were dating. I supposed we sort of were. Maybe Victor was suggesting I should sit with Kota now just so there wasn't any confusion.

I tiptoed hesitantly over to Kota. He had seemed a little irritated with how I'd handled the game earlier. Now, with him spacing out like he was at the television, I wondered if something else was bothering him.

As I got close to the couch, Erica looked up from her braiding. She'd undone the braid and was doing it again. She paused and patted the space between her and Kota. "Come on, Sang," she said. "The other two should be here at any minute." She looked over at Kota. "They're on the way, right?"

Pulled out of his daze, Kota blinked and focused on his mom first and then blinked again and looked at me, seeming surprised to see me there. He stretched out his arm, patting the spot next to him. "Did you want to sit?"

"How late did you stay up, Kota?" his mother asked while I took the spot between them. I sat back so his mother could see him as they spoke, but she returned to her braiding. "You're usually up at all hours but today you're sleepwalking. You're not getting the flu again, are you?"

"No," Kota said. He moved his arm along the back of the couch, his fingers resting on my shoulder. "I'm fine."

"One of these years, you won't be able to bounce back as quickly," Erica said. She smoothed out the tail of Jessica's braid and then folded in a hair tie to finish it off. "There, darling daughter of mine. You've got the braid of an archeress."

Jessica scooted forward. "Thanks," she said, looking at Max, who had come into the room. He sniffed at various gifts and at the boys, who shooed him away from the present pyramid they were starting to build. "Can I give Max something out of his stocking?"

"I don't see why not," Erica said. She pointed out the stocking with Max's name on it, lying on its side at the foot of the fireplace.

Jessica adjusted her pink glasses on her nose and padded over to the stocking, her braid swaying behind her. She pulled out a chew bone, drawing Max's attention immediately. She had him sit down next to her near the presents to let him chew on it.

Erica sighed, looking over all the gifts and then looked at me, catching my eye. "Did you want a braid?" she asked.

I was surprised to be asked. She'd want to brush my hair? I glanced at Gabriel, who was distracted by the present pyramid, directing Luke to find some smaller presents for the top.

"It would look cute," she said.

I nodded.

She smiled. "I'll need more hair bands. Do you want to go fetch them?" she asked. She waved her hand toward the hallway. "They're in... one of the drawers. I'm drawing a blank as to which one. I just reorganized it this week."

My heart was beating fast though I wasn't sure why. Besides Gabriel, no one brushed my hair out or did anything with it.

I stood up quickly, trying to figure out why I was shivering at the idea of her braiding my hair.

I went down the hallway to the bathroom. I was looking at the drawers, trying to figure out which one of the three had hair stuff in it, when footsteps sounded in the hallway. I waited, watching the doorway.

Kota appeared with mussed hair and a tight-lipped expression. He leaned against the frame of the door, arms folded at his chest, and nodded at the cabinet. "It's the top one," he said.

"Oh," I said. I waited, only because he seemed a little irritated. Was it still about the cookies? Nervous, I turned and opened the drawer, finding a packet of hair bands. "Should I bring the whole thing or just one or..."

"Probably two," he said. He yawned, and then covered his face with his palms, rubbing his cheeks. I might need a nap later."

"Are you okay?" I asked. I'd never seen him so sleepy. Maybe Erica was onto something when she'd asked if he was getting sick again.

His eyes shifted down and his head tilted forward as he looked at the sink. "I haven't been sleeping much at all lately."

"Why not?" I asked, now very worried. I put the hair bands down on the side of the sink and then started to reach for him, but then retracted my hand. I wasn't sure what to do. Check his temperature?

He stared at the sink and then bent his head to the side,

resting it wearily against the door frame. A lock of hair fell across his forehead, shadowing his face more. "I can't think of a solution."

His tone was wary and his expression was somber. I reached out, touching his arm. "Kota..."

He lifted his head to look at me, and then down at my palm still on his arm. He sighed. "I'll be okay. I don't want to spoil Christmas. I didn't mean to fuss earlier. I know you were just having fun."

"I'd be more worried if you don't say anything and look as down as you do," I said. "I'd be wondering what's wrong."

"You know what's wrong," he said in a quieter tone, his green eyes locked on my face, his expression one of desperation, fear.

I frowned, suddenly afraid of the Academy. Could my future be so uncertain that he'd be this stressed out about it? "Why won't you believe I'll stay with you?" I asked. "I thought you said I could stay?"

"I'm not even sure if you staying here with us is the right solution," he said. He looked over his shoulder down the hallway, seeming to listen for a moment before he shooed me further into the bathroom and shut the door behind himself. He leaned against it, the cloth of his T-shirt tightening across his chest.

"Sang, you're in constant danger around us. It was bad enough with your parents or Hendricks, but now with Volto... And we have other problems—there's still so many unknowns. It could be the end of the school year before we're free to leave the school, and if you're with us, you'll be involved."

"Wouldn't I be involved even if I wasn't technically in your group?" I asked. "I'd still have to go to school. Hendricks would want to know why I wasn't with you all anymore. What if..."

He raised a hand to quiet me. "I imagine once the Academy talks to you, even if it's decided you shouldn't join for whatever reason, they'll take steps to make sure you're removed from your house. Maybe you'll be placed with any family that exists—any relatives that will take you in. Or possibly with a foster Academy family.

"If you do join a group, you'd probably be put in a starter group with other girls joining up at the same time you are."

"But I want to stay with you," I said, suddenly afraid of the options he was laying out. How could those be the only solutions? "Mr. Blackbourne said it was possible. You're in danger, too. Why do you get to stay and I have to go?"

"Because there's more to your story than mine," he said. He reached out, putting his hands on my shoulders to hold to me, looking intently into my eyes. "Things will only get worse for us at Ashley Waters, not better, until there's a resolution. On top of that, your parents could come back at any second, complicating things. While we have strategies to deal with contingencies, we're never going to be free of the complications until you turn eighteen. There's always the chance of the police or social services getting involved if we're not careful. Volto's involvement has made it clear that anyone can get to us if they really wanted to. Hendricks could easily make things so much worse. He doesn't know that one phone call would mean disaster for you. The goal right now is to pull you out of harm's way before he even thinks to try."

I pressed my lips together, searching for an answer. Despite not wanting to believe him, what he was saying was true. "Mr. Blackbourne believes it'll work."

He sighed and then looked down while he held my shoulders. "I'm sure it would, but I'm not sure it's the right solution."

"What are you saying?" I asked. "That I should go?"

His shoulders dropped and his head bent forward more. His usually steady and concerned green eyes closed behind the glasses. "I can't see a scenario where staying with us is better for you and safer than staying with anyone else. Not for a long time."

I swallowed back the sudden thickness in my throat. Staying with them was the only solution for me. Despite Volto, Hendricks and McCoy, the school, my parents and everything else, I believed being with them had to be right. What about the plan?

But did the boys really even believe in that? We weren't ready for the Academy yet because Kota didn't even know, and I wasn't supposed to be the one to tell him. Outside of that, some of the others weren't coming around to the idea.

Kota sighed again and then pulled me into a hug. I buried my head into his shoulder, desperately trying to come up with solutions to ease his fears.

"Maybe I've just been selfish," he said. "Being around us meant I could see you more. You being with another group doesn't mean we won't ever see each other. I'd still come find you. We could go on normal dates. You can always come over."

Free time was limited with all of them. If I was with another group, there would be long stretches of time between seeing any of them, especially the more involved they got with the school.

Besides that, it just felt wrong. My heart sank at the thought of being away from them. If it was the right thing to do, why did it feel so wrong?

"It wouldn't be right to keep putting you in danger when you could be with another group that didn't have a Volto or Mr. Hendricks to worry about in addition to your parents," he said. He held onto me tightly and then pulled back to look down at my face. "Family first. Your safety is more important."

I couldn't speak. Could he be right?

When I met his eyes again, his were shiny with tears. "I'd hoped there was another way. I don't really see one, though."

"Kota," I whispered. No wonder he hadn't slept at all, staying up all night to come up with solutions that would mean I could stay. Maybe the reason why he couldn't think of an answer was because he was so tired. If I could just give him some hope, maybe he'd sleep and a solution will come to him. "We don't know what will happen but I prefer to stay. I want to."

"I wish we could put it off until we figured out another way," he said. He pressed his warm palm to my cheek. "Sang, you've never been a burden, but we have to be prepared to let things change if that's the right answer. Maybe we're making too much out of it, making it harder on ourselves. One of these days, we'll look back on how silly we were worrying about staying together when it would have been easier to get you into a safe place. Just because you start off with another team, doesn't have to mean you'll never come back."

I hadn't known I could switch teams like that. Or perhaps he meant when we were older, we'd be able to move around easier, not having to worry about parents and what they thought.

He bent down, kissing my forehead, staying close, breathing against my skin. I inhaled the spice scent that warmed me through, usually such a comfort to me when I was afraid.

"We can't worry about the future," I said to him quietly, something Mr. Blackbourne said often. We both needed some hope, or we'd be defeated before we got started. "We can't play a what-if game and make guesses. We'll have to deal with it as we face it. It's still my decision to make ultimately. I don't see how being with another team would be easier when I'd be bringing my own problems to them. I'd still have to leave Ashley Waters to get away from Hendricks and the others. That's not going to be easy for anyone. I bet there's answers weren't not seeing. We're too close to the situation to look at the big picture. Maybe the Academy will help us go over all our options, and it won't mean me leaving at all."

I could almost hear him thinking in the silence around us. He swallowed heavily and nodded against my forehead. "You're probably right. Even you leaving might not be so easy. I know it's your choice. Maybe I am stressing myself out too much." He kissed my forehead again and then backed away, opening the door before he paused. "I'm going to make a coffee. Would you like one of yours? You haven't had one yet."

"Sure," I said, although I didn't really want coffee, or anything else.

Kota left me alone in the bathroom, giving me a few minutes to think and calm down.

While before I'd been going over and over what to say to the Academy about what I wanted, I hadn't stopped to consider the other side. Kota was right to contemplate what options the Academy might give me. What would they think of a girl who was desperate to stay with a group that was in the middle of danger? Would they think I was crazy and unable to make good decisions? I hadn't considered other options because I was so sure staying with them was the solution.

As I finally left the bathroom, I took the hair bands with me. I needed to actually believe what I'd said to Kota. I had to believe there was a solution that would mean I could stay with them.

Though if that was true, why did I feel weighed down with doubts?

GIFT MOUNTAIN

When I got back to the living room, I sat down at Erica's feet, facing the television as the muted Christmas movie played. Erica brushed my hair and then braided it just like Jessica's as the others were still distracted with the gifts and their guessing.

I tried desperately to drown out the thoughts in my head. I drank the coffee Kota had fetched for me and held onto the bottle as Erica twisted and braided my hair.

"Okay," Erica said, patting the top of my head. "You're an archeress, too."

I suddenly shivered, coming out of my thoughts and feeling awkward at resting at her legs.

What was wrong with me? Why was I so uncomfortable?

"Are you cold?" Erica asked.

"Hey, Sang?" Luke called before I could answer her. They'd finished their pyramid and now they were making forts out of the rest of the gifts. He and Victor were behind one by the fireplace. He stacked a smaller box on top of their wall, making it slightly higher. "Come get behind my fort. Quick."

"No, come over here," Gabriel said. He and Nathan were crouched behind a wall of boxes closer to the tree. Nathan was trying to balance boxes on top of each other though they were swaying dangerously.

"You're going to break all those presents," North said as he came out from the kitchen. He was about to sit on the couch when the doorbell rang. "About time." He straightened and headed to the door.

I stayed on the floor, trying to get the feeling inside of me to ease; I wasn't in the mood to play fort.

Erica got up to meet Mr. Blackbourne and Dr. Green at

the door so, in an effort to get my feelings under control, I crawled up to where Erica had been sitting on the couch. I wanted my back against something solid and to be sitting properly when the others came into the room. I pulled my knees up to my chest, waiting nervously.

Dr. Green arrived first, wearing jeans and a dark yellow T-shirt, with a faded design of white-capped mountains on the front. He shrugged off a gray jacket and dropped it on the arm of the couch. He winked at me quickly and then surveyed the forts. "Hey," he said. "Where's my fort?"

"Fuck the forts," Gabriel said, accidentally dropping one he was trying to balance on the pile. He picked it up carefully and examined it for damage. "We didn't have ammo yet, anyway."

"They're all in the boxes," Nathan said. "Can we open these yet or what?"

"Gotta wait for the stragglers," Dr. Green said. He sat down cross-legged near the outside of Luke's fort. He picked up one of the top boxes. "You all play a dangerous game with these. How do you know I didn't get you all delicate glass figurines for Christmas?"

"I hope mine's a candy jar if it's glass," Luke said.

Gabriel started up the guessing game again and even Dr. Green joined in, although his guesses were always random, things like "dinosaur" or "San Diego".

Sitting nearly shoulder to shoulder with the others as they took down their fort walls, it was like a group of brothers sitting together. I wished Dr. Green got more time off from the hospital to be around. He was a lot of fun.

Erica came in with a potted dark green holly plant. "Isn't this lovely?" she said. "I'm going to put it on the table."

Mr. Blackbourne followed behind her. He wore the dark gray slacks and the white shirt, but today he had on a gray sweater over the shirt. No tie. The collar was unbuttoned, giving him a more casual look.

It was one of the rare moments when I saw the nineteen-year-old that he was. Young, with a strong energy that came

103

from within. He was perfect, as always, with the black-rimmed glasses over the steel eyes, moving into the room smoothly, always with his shoulders back and his head high.

I didn't want to tattle on Kota and his feelings, but I was rattled after our conversation and wished I could talk to Mr. Blackbourne right then. I wanted to ask him again about this plan, looking for some validation that what we were considering was the right thing.

I also wanted him to sit next to me. I wasn't sure I could last through opening gifts without betraying my dark thoughts unless I felt him beside me. I needed to steal some of his confidence that we'd stay together.

Erica paused on her way to the dining room to turn around and plant a delicate kiss on his cheek. "You're such a sweetheart," she said. "So thoughtful."

"You're welcome," he said as his cheeks turned a shade of pink.

He seemed happy, relaxed. It wasn't right to worry anyone else today. Kota was already stressed, but maybe he was wrong. But I had to believe what Mr. Blackbourne and the others said, that there was an answer out there somewhere, even if we couldn't see it yet.

Don't let the doubt overshadow today, I repeated to myself, and refocused on the boys who seemed so happy, capturing the Christmas spirit. They began to settle down around the tree.

Mr. Blackbourne sat next to me on the couch as though he'd heard my silent wish that he sit with me. I kept my eyes on the boys as they started reading tags and sorted the gifts into piles.

He watched quietly with me, but after a few minutes, he leaned ever so slightly, his arm against mine, drawing my attention.

"Merry Christmas, Miss Sorenson," he whispered, his eyes still on the gifts.

Heat filled my cheeks. "Merry Christmas, Mr. Blackbourne."

♥♥♥

It took several more minutes before everyone finally settled down. North sat on the other side of Mr. Blackbourne, arms crossed but aware and watching.

Silas, Kota, and Erica sat in beanbag chairs they'd brought in while Jessica sat in her pink and purple one she'd dragged from her bedroom. The others spread out on the floor, making a circle around the tree, leaving some space between them and the tree.

Luke and Dr. Green passed around the gifts one by one. It took a good ten minutes and the pile at my feet grew.

And grew.

Everyone had plenty, but mine either came in really large packages or very small ones I could hold in my lap. Most had pink rose bows on top, thanks to Dr. Green's handiwork.

As Luke and Dr. Green were finishing up, Erica waved her hand and said loudly over the boys' chatter in the room, "Okay you guys. Remember the procedure. Open quickly and toss all your wrapping paper in the middle. Don't wait on the others. It takes too long to go around the circle. We tried that before and we don't have all day. We can admire it all at the end."

I'd never realized how many gifts they all had until they were all passed out and stacked in individual piles in front of each person. The ones who sat on the floor could have made their own mini-forts.

Once Luke and Dr. Green finally sat on the floor with their own collections, Erica signaled for us all to begin.

I was eager to see what everyone else got, but I listened to Erica, and soon there was too much noise and distraction to do anything other than to read the tag, open the box, see the item and toss everything that wasn't the gift to the floor in the middle of the room. I didn't want to be the last one opening gifts, so I did my best to hurry along.

I started with the smaller gifts in my lap so I could clear

out those before getting to the bigger ones. The first was a 3DS Nintendo game from Luke and Gabriel: A dress-up game called Style Savvy. There were also arrows for the toy bow we all got. Jessica got a bow, too, which she seemed to really like. There were also the matching foam swords that Luke and Gabriel and I had bought, technically for Nathan, but we each got a set, so we could all play.

Then there were gifts I hadn't known about in advance: a pair of pink gloves and a warm jacket—mostly black with some hot pink throughout. There were thermal pants, too. The clothes had me looking at Gabriel, wondering if he thought the weather would stay cold and we'd be outside more. But when I checked the tags, I was surprised that they were from Nathan. Had he and Gabriel gone Christmas shopping for me?

There were many items from Victor: a pink sleeping bag, a folding cot, a small stereo, a pink heater, and a travel pillow with a waterproof case.

I liked them all but wondered about why he'd buy me these things. Were they planning more sleep-overs? I really appreciated the gifts but wasn't sure where I'd store them.

The item from North confused me. It was a small tool kit in a pink case, a multi-tool knife, a lantern and a travel kit that had a poncho and an umbrella and a small case.

I supposed I could use the tools and the lantern might come in handy if the lights ever went out.

I was looking over the items and sorting them at my feet when I almost dropped the knife between the couch cushions. I shifted my leg to grab it, inadvertently pressing it against Mr. Blackbourne's thigh.

He'd just unwrapped Victor's gift: a stack of sheet music. He set it aside and picked up the knife for me. He examined it and then passed it over. "That's an interesting choice," he said. "Don't you think?"

"It's very...practical," I said. "I've never had one. I'm not sure when I'll use it."

"I think you'll figure it out soon enough," he said. "Why don't you open some of the bigger boxes?"

There was something to figure out?

I checked on what everyone else was opening. Luke and Gabriel got plastic blow-up punching bags, which they said would be used as targets for the weapons they got. Dr. Green had received craft paper and some DVDs from Japan and a simple cookbook for children learning how to cook. The others got gifts that fit their personalities.

I put what I'd opened so far on the floor and then started working on the biggest box. I ripped away the paper and had to scoot the box around in front of me to actually see what was inside.

It was a three-person tent.

A tent, a sleeping bag, a lamp.... "I'm going camping?" I asked quietly, not wanting to sound unappreciative, but confused.

"We go every year," Mr. Blackbourne said. He'd paused in his own unwrapping to watch me open this gift, and helped me tear away the rest of the paper from the box and toss it toward the growing mountain of wrapping paper in the center. "On the week of the first."

My mouth hung open as the realization settled in. They'd been looking forward to it and they'd all gotten me camping equipment for Christmas. It was why they hadn't wanted to spoil the surprise. "Wow," I said, examining the tent. It wasn't big enough to fit all of us. "Do you all have tents?"

"It's for you to use if you'd like," Mr. Blackbourne said. "You can sleep in the bigger tent they have although we might bring it along just in case you want to try it out. Better to have an extra anyway."

I smoothed my hand over the side of the tent box, trying to picture when else I'd use the thing. Maybe Nathan would want to go camping sometime; he liked being outside. "I've never been camping," I said.

"We thought as much," Mr. Blackbourne said quietly. "Which is why we got you the supplies you'd need."

The more I opened the gifts, the more excited I got. They'd all given me camping gear as if I'd be going for weeks and weeks. Luke gave me a small digital camera in a waterproof bag. Silas's present was a fishing kit, complete with a pole and a cooler for keeping fish fresh and small portable chair. Gabriel gave me lots and lots of outdoor clothes, boots, and even a hat. It was enough to last through a month of camping. Dr. Green's gift was an extra blanket, waterproof card games, some folded towels inside a pink panda carry bag, and a bath kit with organic soaps.

Mr. Blackbourne gave me some music CDs for the stereo, a set of flashlights, a journal with some fancy pens, and an emergency whistle, which he said I'd need if got into trouble since my voice hadn't worked properly in a while.

Kota's gifts were all kits: a fire-starting set with waterproof matches, compass and a waterproof map of South Carolina, a first-aid kit, an emergency food stash and water cleaning supply kit, and bug spray and sunscreen.

Amid all the camping gifts, there were other items, too. A small plush bear, a tennis bracelet, books, my own iPad, gift certificates to spas, tickets to a play sometime in the spring, and many more things that made me start to get overwhelmed.

I opened up a necklace from Mr. Blackbourne—it was a crystal rose pendant. As I was looking at it—watching how it captured the light, Kota spoke from across the room.

"I thought we all agreed just to get her camping equipment," he said with a smile.

"I just got her one other thing," Luke said.

"Me, too," Victor said. "Or maybe two. I thought she could actually use the spa after a week of camping so that technically counts as a camping gift."

"Well, then her own iPad should count as a camping gift," Nathan said. "She was borrowing Victor's all last week. I figured she wanted one—and she can use it to pull up maps and survival books."

Kota chuckled. "I guess the books count as camping gifts, too."

"It's okay," Victor said, opening up a jacket he'd gotten from Gabriel. He folded the collar of it neatly. "She got everyone else something extra, too."

I didn't mind him spilling the beans; if they knew, then they might not feel awkward for getting me extra. But as I looked around, I couldn't tell if any of the boxes were from me. Victor had wrapped them, so I wasn't sure what colored paper he used.

The boys looked at each other at the same time, blinking in confusion.

Gabriel moved first, diving into the few remaining gifts in front of him. "Where? I don't see anything." He held up a box and examined the label. "I love the fuck out of you Doc, but I want to see Sang's gift." He glanced up at Erica and then at Jessica, each watching with amused smiles. "I mean fudge. I love you like fudge...Don't listen to me." He put the box down and sorted through the gifts he hadn't opened yet.

"Did I miss it?" Silas asked. "I got the Wiffle ball set."

"They're in the tree," Victor said with a grin, leaning back on his hands. "You've been looking at them all day and you never saw them."

He'd hidden them in the tree? Even I hadn't noticed. I looked at the tree from where I was, but was dazzled by the lights and their reflections on ornaments, and couldn't see anything.

Gabriel and Luke scrambled to get up and check it out.

"Get mine for me, Luke," Silas said, pushing his pile of paper toward the middle of the room. "I'm going to step on someone's things if I try to climb over everything."

"Yeah," Nathan said, kneeling amid a pile of wrap. "I can't get around this stuff. We got too much this year."

Luke reached in among the branches and then pulled out one gift: a small box wrapped in silver paper with a delicate pink bow on top. He checked the label. "For North," he said.

"What the fu...*fudge*, Vic?" Gabriel said, reaching in and pulling out a longer box. "Why didn't you just put them with the rest?"

"I didn't want them to get lost in the shuffle," he said. "It's her first Christmas with us. She should get to see us open them."

I pressed my lips together to hold back the swell of emotion. I could have kissed him in front of everyone. He was so clever.

"I should get yours, too, then," I said. "Although I left it at Nathan's house." I hadn't had a chance to escape the night before to go get it, and there had been so much going on this morning that I'd thought I'd wait until later to hand it to him personally.

I started looking for a way to get out from the maze of paper but Mr. Blackbourne placed a palm on my knee, stilling me instantly.

"Don't you dare," Gabriel said, pointing at me and snapping his fingers. "Sit the fuck down." He cringed, glancing once at Erica. "Fudge. Sit down fudge." He smacked his hand over his mouth and then spoke through his fingers. "Whatever. Goddamn it."

Mr. Blackbourne's millimeter smile appeared. "What he said...or rather, what he meant. Please, stay."

"I know where it is," Nathan said and before I realized what he was doing, he used Kota's head to do an almost flip over the beanbag chair and raced to the door. "No one open anything until I get back."

Gabriel and Luke continued to hunt down gifts that had been tucked in the tree. Everyone other than Victor got a silver-wrapped present, including Erica and Jessica. I wanted to get them something nice as a thank you, for letting me join in on their Christmas.

Gabriel and Luke were just sitting down when Nathan returned. He passed Victor a gold-wrapped gift; I'd used the only wrapping paper Nathan had at his house.

As they began unwrapping, my heart was in my throat the entire time, as I second-guessed all the gifts I'd gotten for them, sure that I'd made mistakes.

Gabriel was the first to open his tiny box. He tossed the silver paper to the floor and flipped open the lid.

Inside was a pink crystal dangling from a small hoop

earring—also pink. I'd agonized over the color, but Victor said it was perfect when I'd shown him the picture and asked his opinion.

I held my breath, nearly bursting as Gabriel examined the gift for a good minute.

"Fuck me," he finally said, and then put the box down. He pulled one of the red earrings out of his right ear and replaced it with the pink one. As he was putting it in, he turned to Luke. "Go get the piercing gun."

Luke was opening his gift, a flat square box. "I'm not getting it right now," he said. He opened the lid and froze, looking at the gift. Inside was a one of a kind, handmade pancake pillow, complete with a butter patch on the top. "Where in the world did you find this?" he said, his brown eyes widening and his grin broadening. He brought it to his face and then breathed in. "Oh...it even smells like pancakes."

"Yeah, pancakes," Gabriel said, and then shoved his arm. "Now come on. Piercing gun. One, two, three, go." They both started to get up.

North snapped his fingers at them. "Enough," he said. "Sit down. You can pierce your ear after you finish. Do it now, and you'll pierce your eyeball or something."

"Aw," Gabriel said and then brightened. "You mean I get to pierce my eyebrow this time?"

"I don't think that'd be an appropriate look at the moment," Mr. Blackbourne said with the small smile still on his lips. "Stick with the ears for now."

Gabriel shrugged and then got a pancake pillow in the face.

"Smell it," Luke said, holding it to Gabriel's nose. "Pancakes..."

I darted my eyes at Victor and smiled. In a way, I was sharing these small victories with him. I couldn't believe how much fun it was simply watching them open the gifts. He'd been right about making it a surprise. He almost always was right.

Silas opened his next: tickets. "What's this?" he asked,

curious. "An exhibit?"

"There's a boat and RV exhibition coming to Charleston this spring," I said. "Apparently they'll have all the boats out on display and we can go in and look inside them all. I thought you might like to go."

He grinned and nodded. "I haven't been to one of those." He looked down at the box and pulled out a silver anchor on a black cord. "Hey, I got two gifts."

It hadn't seemed fair to get him tickets to something so far in the future and not have anything he could use now.

I waited for his reaction, worried he'd find the necklace a little girly.

He immediately put it on, grinning wide, the white of his teeth a contrast against his olive complexion.

North opened his next: a cover for the Jeep's spare tire that was mounted on the rear door. It had a compass emblem on the back, with an N for North at the top. He smoothed his hands over the surface. In a way, the compass was like a star.

Erica and Jessica opened their gifts at the same time.

Jessica held up a set of leather charm bracelets, the main elements being a bow and arrow. "I like these," she said as she put them on. "They'll go with my bow set."

Erica held up her gift in a victory fist pump. "Yes!" she exclaimed, waving a package of fuzzy socks. It was a large stack, in varying vibrant pinks, purples, yellows and oranges, and more. "Best gift ever."

"Mom, you're insane," Jessica said with a blush on her cheeks. "You got socks."

Erica broke open the package, picked out two in mismatching colors—one red and one green—and put them on her feet. "You'll understand when you're older the pure joy of fuzzy socks," she said. She wiggled her toes then she stood up and shuffled across the carpet around the back of the couch.

"Mom," Kota said, blushing, too. "It's *socks*."

Erica reached around my shoulders, giving me a hug and then kissed me on the forehead. "Only girls get these things. You guys will never understand."

I was happy she liked the gift, but her sudden touch made me want to shrink away from her. I gritted my teeth, resisting the sudden urge to pull away, knowing she hadn't done anything to cause it.

The hug was over quickly and then as she walked away, I shook off the feeling, wondering why it felt so weird to me. When the guys had first started to hug me, or hold my hand, it was new, but also, I had liked it. I appreciated Erica and did care for her and wanted to please her, but for some reason, her touch made me uncomfortable.

In my soul, I knew she was a normal woman. She hugged her daughter and son regularly and they hugged her back. She did this with all the other guys on occasion—like how she'd kissed Mr. Blackbourne on the cheek earlier.

I was so used to the guys touching me, shouldn't I be okay with Erica doing it?

I was still working out my feelings when Mr. Blackbourne caught my eye, a concerned on his face. "Are you okay?"

I nodded, although I wasn't sure.

I felt his eyes lingering on me as Kota opened his gift.

Kota held up the dog tag on a chain. He flipped over the tag and read what was engraved on it. "It's a formula?" Kota asked, looking at me.

I nodded though I was still rattled, my feelings tripping me up. I looked to Victor for help.

He was holding his still-wrapped gift in his lap. "Put it in your scientific calculator. In the graphing part."

"I found it during homework those last couple of weeks in school," I said. "For geometry."

Kota pulled out his phone, entering the numbers in his scientific calculator app. When he was finished, he stared at the screen, blushing.

Mr. Blackbourne nudged me slightly with his arm. "What is it?" he whispered.

I swallowed, keeping an eye on Kota as his eyes brightened. He put his phone in his lap and lifted the chain over his head, putting on the dog tag around his neck. "It's a heart curve formula," I said quietly. "When you put it in..."

"It makes a heart on the graph," he said, and then smiled. "It's brilliant."

I felt my entire body flush with warmth; I wasn't sure I could take any more of this emotion.

Dr. Green opened his special paper construction kit that had come all the way from Japan. It was for a replica of a temple from a popular tourist destination.

It also had two paper people to make: a couple, as though on a date in the garden of the temple.

He touched the box, studying the picture on the outside.

Nathan opened his box, pulling out an underwater MP3 player with headphones. I'd checked his phone when he was in the shower and Victor helped me figure out what music he listened to when he went for a jog or worked out. The player was preloaded with some rock and country songs that we knew he liked.

He put the headphones on, despite being out of the water, wrapping the band snugly around his head. He turned it on and moved his head along with the music.

Mr. Blackbourne opened his gift: A silver and maroon fountain pen. The silver part of the clip was shaped like a musical note and there were music symbols engraved along the band in the middle. He plucked it out of the case, carefully looking it over. "I've heard of these," he said. "The tips are shaped specifically for making music notations?" He looked over the pen at me.

I nodded. It had been the hardest gift to find, but I'd dug around in a forum on the internet where musicians spoke about gifts and this pen had come up a lot as a favorite among composers.

Mr. Blackbourne carefully put the pen back in the black case. "Thank you," he said.

I whispered, "You're welcome," but so softly that I wasn't sure he'd heard me.

Once everyone was done, they looked at Victor and

waited.

He sighed, realizing it was his turn to go. He bit his lower lip as he plucked the tape off the bottom of the box, and then eased it from the wrapping paper.

Inside were tickets for two to a foreign film that would be playing in the next month. I'd remembered once when he'd talked about buying out a theater for a date. I hadn't gone that far but thought he might want to go.

Along with the tickets was a pocket watch. I'd gotten it engraved on the inside with simply: *For Victor. Love, Sang.*

The watch itself had taken me a week to take apart and manipulate, and a required lot of patience from Nathan for putting up with my taking up nearly his entire table with all the parts I'd had to move. But now it ran backward, like the clock I'd made for his desk.

For a guy who could get anything he wanted, I wanted to give him something he couldn't buy. The front had the same symbol from the necklace he wore: the heart shield.

He held the watch in his hands for a long moment, looking at the inside and then flipping it over in his hands.

"Best Christmas ever," he said.

♥

On The Way

With the camping trip coming up, I began to pay attention to the weather. It wasn't going to snow again, but the temperature regularly dropped down to the high thirties during the night. While I'd never slept in a tent, I'd spent lots of time in the snow in Illinois and I wondered how it would be spending the night outside. Would a tent keep us safe? I worried about us freezing to death. I would have to rely on the others and the gear they'd purchased, trusting that since they'd done it before, they knew what they were doing.

I kept myself busy with other things, too, because the meeting with the Academy was still on my mind. Whenever the boys were around me, though, I did my best to fake some courage and got into the habit of being silly and distracting them when they were feeling down, especially Kota.

There was also the issue of there being other people around while on this trip. This wasn't just a vacation and meant to be fun, but also an official meeting of the Academy. The boys couldn't tell me much about what would happen. They tried to tell me to relax and have fun.

The looming question about what the Academy would ask of me, to join another team, hovered over us. Meeting new people, even Academy people, was daunting enough. Nervous and antsy, I was quiet and

Still, when I fell asleep at Nathan's house the night before we were leaving for the camp, I was up past midnight thinking of what would happen, worrying about my future, the Academy, and freezing to death in a tent.

Nathan poked me in the shoulder at the crack of dawn. I waved him off, flipping over and curling back into the bed.

Waking up meant facing all of it, and I wasn't ready. The bed was warm and cozy. Nathan had slept with an arm around my waist the entire night, staying close, as if sensing I was awake with worry.

But he'd been up this morning already—I'd heard him crawl out of bed to throw in some last minute items in the bag.

He poked at me again, but I ignored it. He plopped down next to me and began to rub my shoulder and arm in slow circles. "Sang," he called, cooing softly. "It's snowing."

"No, it isn't," I said. "I would have heard it."

He shook my shoulder a little. "There's zombies."

"Not in this neighborhood."

He laughed and released my shoulder. "Chocolate chip cappuccino muffins?"

I sat up, rubbing my eyes. "I swear, if you're fibbing..."

"Morning to you, too, Peanut," he said. He leaned over, planting a kiss on my cheek. He was still in his boxers, his reddish-brown hair pressed against his head in spots, and sticking out wildly in others, giving him an almost punk look. The tan was fading around his broad shoulders, revealing freckles.

"Kota wants us over at his house early to pack up. Victor should be here soon. Want to shower before we leave?"

I bit my lip and turned away to hide my panic at the mention of a shower. I put my feet on the floor, facing the window, staring at the blinds. "I'll go find clothes," I said, not answering his question.

I took a bath and washed up. If the camping trip was going to have us outside all day, I thought a hot soak was the best way to warm up my body in preparation.

Gabriel came by the night before, hanging up thermal pants and a jacket to wear. I put a T-shirt on for underneath the jacket. I felt the thermal pants, and wondered if it might get too warm, but put them on. He'd even put out matching pink finger gloves and a woven cotton hat. I stuffed the hat and gloves into my pockets for now as I zipped up my overnight bag that contained general stuff, complete with iPad, a book,

CDs, the journal and other items. The tent and camping gear were sitting with the others' stuff at Kota's. Gabriel had made suggestions and helped me pack my clothes and had a bag somewhere ready to go for me. All I had to decide on was what fun items I wanted to bring along. I tapped at the phone in my bra. Should I even bring it? Would it work out there?

"Ready?" Nathan said. He stood near the bed, putting on his socks and then a set of old Nike running shoes. He had pulled them from the back of the closet.

I crinkled my nose at the old-shoe smell and forced a smile. "I guess," I said, going to my bag, shuffling through the items again to make sure I had everything. I looked in the closet once more, wondering if I would need more underwear.

He tapped at the sides of his shoes once he was done lacing them up. "Got to wear your old shoes camping. They get so gross."

I looked at my shoes. They were brand new, what Gabriel had put out for me.

He didn't notice, and stood up, wiping his hands at the jeans he wore, and then put on a red jacket. He picked up his own bulging red Nike duffle bag. It took up his entire back and I'd watched him stuff it with pants, shirts and underwear and other supplies. He glanced at my pack that was only backpack size and was still only half full. "That's it?"

I pulled my bag onto my shoulders and stood, testing the weight of it. Did we have to hike to the campground? "Gabriel packed all my clothes. I need more?"

He shrugged. "Probably not. I just get used to hearing about girls packing half the house."

"Can we bring the house?" I asked. "At least the heater part?"

His smile faded. "Peanut, don't tell me you're an indoor girl."

I shook my head and leaned into him a little, putting a hand on his chest. "I like the idea of camping, but I was thinking of how cold it's been at night."

His blue eyes were intense and he pressed himself against

my hand before he put down his bag on the bed and covered my hand with his. "If it's too much for you, you tell me. I'll make sure you stay warm." He bent his head to look at my face. "We'll have fun."

I nodded, but a shiver swept up my spine, thinking about how tired I would be today since I had been up all night worrying. Despite his words, I was still worried.

He cupped my face between his palms, forcing me to look up at him. "We'll have a good time," he said in a more determined tone. He leaned in and kissed my lips.

At first, I thought it would just be a peck, but then I realized he was lingering. I wanted more, too. I opened my mouth slightly, responding. I let the pack slide off my shoulders to the bed.

My heart raced as he kissed me. Couldn't we just stay here? Maybe Dr. Green was right; maybe I could fake sick and just not go.

His kiss deepened and I quickly forgot about the Academy. He moved his hands to my waist, holding me at first, and then lifting me. He started back toward the bed, and then changed direction to the dresser, where he sat me on the surface. I was now slightly taller than him, tilting my head down to kiss him.

After a moment, he broke the kiss and then looked up at me with a steady, serious gaze. "I think I know what we need to do," he said.

"You do?"

He nodded once as his hands smoothed along the outsides of my thighs. He tilted his head up to kiss me again and then broke off to look at me. "I just don't want to tell you."

"Shouldn't I know?" I was trying to figure out what he was referencing to. Was it about camping or something else?

"You should, but I don't like the idea," he said. "I've been struggling with it." He frowned then, darkness surrounding his blue eyes. "I think I can be okay, though, if you'll help me."

"What do you mean?"

"I think you need to stick with Kota," he said. "I think

you need to...to convince him that you care too much about him to just walk off with another team. Know what I mean?"

My heart raced against my ribcage. My hands were on his shoulders and I felt my fingers tightening, steadying. "Nathan..."

"I talk to him about you sometimes," he said. "I try to gauge how he feels; he gets really quiet when I go too far." He looked down at my lap, brushing his palms along my thighs. "I know he's not convinced you'll be around later. I know him; he's trying to distance himself from you to prepare himself for if that happens."

"So I shouldn't push him?"

"I think if you just hung out with him more, tried to get him to know you're really into him. It'd change how he feels and he won't be such a grump ass about all of this."

I bit my lip, unsure of what to say. Kota must not have been keeping his feelings to himself.

"I know I have a hard time with seeing you with the others," he said. He looked at me, the intensity unmistakable in his eyes. "I like things better when I've got you to myself. I couldn't stand it if you left. I'd probably go, too."

"You can't," I said, although without conviction. But I realized in that moment, if I left, they'd follow. They'd all said it in one way or another.

This meant that now—more than ever—we'd have to make this work, or it would all fall apart. "Nathan...I know about the plan. I know what Mr. Blackbourne wants us to do."

"Crazy, isn't it?" he said with a frown but searched my face for my reaction.

I looked away, at the wall, the window. It was hard to talk about because I knew how he felt. "I don't see another way for it to work. Not if everyone wants to stay together. Maybe Mr. Blackbourne is right to do this now. If the Academy doesn't make us split up, then we have to make it work. It might break everyone otherwise."

His fingers pressed into my thighs as he breathed out slowly. "Sang, look at me, sweetheart."

I slowly shifted my gaze to him.

His eyes shone as he looked at me, his eyes steady on mine. "I don't know what's going to happen," he said. "All I know is it would kill me if you left. It'd kill me if Kota left, or any of the others."

I nodded, unwilling to say what that meant. I didn't want to push. It was the plan, and I'd heard he was having a hard time with it. I couldn't get myself to be the one to start talking about it.

He continued. "I...just..." He bent his head down, bending over low and cuddling it in my lap. "This is fucking hard."

I brushed my fingers through his hair as he rested and sighed against my leg. I was afraid to express how I felt, but despite how hard it was, he needed to hear it. "I care about you, Nathan. I don't want to see you unhappy." I took a breath and forced myself to continue. "I don't know what will happen, either. I don't know what this will look like a week from now or even a year from now. I don't want to let go, though."

He brushed his cheek against my thigh and then straightened himself up, looking back at me. I dropped my hand from his head to his shoulder. "You can't go anywhere," he said, his tone a notch higher and huskier than before.

I nodded, biting my lip again.

He seized me around the waist, pulling me toward him until my knees were against his sides. "Tell me you're not going anywhere."

"I don't *want* to go anywhere. I mean, I want to stay with you all."

"Then that's what we're going to do," he said. "We've got to get our game plan together."

Give them confidence, and they'll never fail you. That's what Mr. Blackbourne had said. Maybe he was right. "You said to convince Kota."

"Yeah," he said, nodding. "I know he cares about you, but he's trying to cut himself off. He's being really distant whenever I try to talk about you. I think we just need to push him. You...*you* need to push him."

"What do you mean?"

"Mr. Blackbourne is right; focus on Kota. We need to convince him. Convince him you're staying and you're with him, that you won't go anywhere." He pressed his lips together for a moment, tightly enough that they started to turn white. He released and then leaned into me, his nose almost touching mine. "If that means I have to watch you sitting in his lap all week, kissing him...just don't think anything of me walking away if I need to."

"I don't want to make anyone uncomfortable."

"We're going to be uncomfortable for a good while," he said. "I don't know if we'll ever be comfortable, but I'd rather be uncomfortable and keep you around than see you on some other team that won't understand you. Or...just...Kota's wrong. He's not thinking right. He worries too much, and not just about himself, but about all of us. If you can get him to stop worrying for five minutes, he might calm down."

I nodded. I pushed him back so I could slide off the dresser. "I guess I can stand a few cold nights to convince him."

He pressed his lips together again and nodded before he leaned down and picked up his bag. "I get you here with me nearly every night. It'll be hard to go a week with you sleeping in another cot. Possibly on the other side of the tent, depending on how this goes."

I put my pack back on and smiled. I needed to make them all happy and if I kept being positive, maybe it'd make things easier. I was glad he'd told me how he felt. Maybe he wasn't okay with the plan, but he, too, was starting to realize it might be the only way to keep us all together. "It's just one big sleepover week. You like those, don't you?"

"The warmer, the better," I said with a smile.

He grinned, wrapped an arm around my shoulders and nudged me toward the bedroom door. "I'll keep you warm. Let's go, Peanut."

The morning was chilly, but with the thermal pants, I was comfortable. Only my face and fingers felt any of the cold.

The street was still. I checked on my old house, but it was quiet today. I left a note at the house that I'd be on a camping trip for the week and the number to call if there was an emergency, but I wasn't sure I could be reached if the signal wasn't good out there, so I gave her Kota's mom's number as well.

I looked ahead as we walked over to Kota's house, breathing in the cold air. I worried about leaving Marie behind for the week. Kota had said he'd asked Erica to keep an eye on her as well as Nathan's house since we'd be away.

Sometimes I suspected Erica knew more about my situation than she let on, but I never talked to her about it.

Kota was outside in the drive, standing beside a mountain of supplies near the open garage door. Luke, North, and Silas were nearby. Luke had on thermal pants like mine. North, Silas, and Kota were in jeans, and all were wearing jackets in their favorite colors: baby blue, black, dark blue and green.

Kota was holding a clipboard and started listing off supplies. Luke dug out each item from the mountain, handing it off to North or Silas. They took turns bringing each item to the back of North's black Jeep and loading it in. Tents and coolers and other larger items were tied up on the Jeep's top.

I stepped over to stand beside Kota. He looked up briefly, gave me a small smile, and went back to his clipboard.

I looked to Nathan, wondering what to do.

Nathan nodded toward Kota.

I stepped closer to Kota, touching his elbow.

Kota looked at me, lifting an eyebrow. "Need anything?"

"No," I said. "Unless you want me to help with something?"

He shook his head. "I can't think of anything. We've got a system."

"How are we going to fit everyone in the Jeep?" Nathan asked. "Why aren't we taking the SUV?"

"Two cars," Kota said, refocusing on his clipboard. "Just in case anyone has to leave." He seemed to want to work and I wasn't sure if I should let him; I hoped I wasn't pushing him.

"Like if Sang gets scared and wants to come home," Luke said, pausing to brush some of his blond hair away from his face. He undid the twist in his hair, re-twisting and clipping it back into a messy bun. "Because she'll freak out the first night."

"I'm not going to get scared," I said.

"She's tougher than she looks," Nathan said.

"She is tough," Luke said with a grin and a wink. "She'll kick nature in the face if it messes with her. I was just teasing."

I wasn't so sure. I'd been on hikes but always went home after a few hours. I smiled and was about to respond when a dark silver BMW came around the bend of the road and then parked at the end of Kota's driveway. Gabriel jumped out of the front passenger seat before Victor could fully stop, and started running toward me. He was wearing jeans, Converse sneakers, and a thick purple sweater. He also had on a neon orange beanie, covering all the russet in his hair, leaving out the blond streaks.

His ears had three black rings on one side, the pink ring on the other, and a pink and orange crystal stud in each of his lobes. He'd worn the earrings the same every day since Christmas.

I thought he was going to tackle me and braced myself for it, but instead, he caught me up in a hug, picking me up off the ground. He held me like that as he staggered forward.

"Sang's *my* camping buddy," he said to Kota.

"This isn't the cub scouts," Kota said. "We don't need to assign buddies. There's eight of us. As long as you're near someone, you're fine."

"Hi Meanie," I said, hugging him back, smelling the mix of the new car smell from the BMW, a bit of Victor's berries and moss, and Gabriel's own mix of flowers and sweet scents.

"Hi camping buddy," Gabriel said. He dropped me, finding my hand with his. His palm was warm and I held on while he addressed Kota, "Let's go."

"We just need to load up Victor's car," Kota said. "And figure out who is riding with who."

"Sang's my car buddy," Gabriel said, picking up our hands over our heads as if we were tied together, even though we were just holding hands.

I grinned, glad that Gabriel was being a little silly and lightening the mood a bit. Maybe Kota needed that.

Kota rolled his eyes. "Let's load up the cars and we can figure it out."

Taking his direction, I carried my bag and a couple others over to Victor's trunk. Kota knew exactly what would fit where, and helped us jigsaw piece it together the way he wanted.

When the cars were loaded, we all gathered around Kota, waiting for instructions.

Kota passed North some papers. "Here's a copy of our reservation for the campgrounds, the address, and a map I printed off from the website."

North glanced at the map. "Hunting Island? Not sure if I like this place."

"There's no hunting going on where we'll be. There's a campground near the beach that I hear is quite nice."

I perked up. "Beach?"

"It's winter, Sang," North said. "No swimming.'"

I huffed.

"Who's riding with who?" Kota asked.

"I'll take Sang," North said. "Easier to keep an eye on her."

I glanced at Nathan, but he said nothing. Maybe the ride over wouldn't be a big deal. It was just a car ride—I had all week to get closer to him.

Dr. Green and Mr. Blackbourne were coming along on their own so we didn't need to wait for them. In the end, Gabriel, Luke, Silas, and I ended up with North. Kota, Victor, and Nathan were going to take Victor's car.

"Neener neener," Gabriel said to Nathan. "We get Sang."

"It's two hours," Nathan said. "All three of you will be cramped in the back of the Jeep."

"We'll be fine," Luke said.

I giggled, excited about being on a vacation with them for a whole week. No school. No Volto. Just us in the middle of nowhere. I was having fun already, distracted by what was going to happen this trip. It lifted some of the doubt in my heart. *Remember what Mr. Blackbourne said,* I repeated to myself. *Just tell them, at the end of it all, I want to stay with them.*

Silas rode shotgun while North drove and I sat between Luke and Gabriel in the back of the Jeep. It was tight in the back, with our thighs touching and our butts squeezed together. It got warm quickly, and we stripped off jackets and sweaters down to the T-shirts we wore underneath.

It made me wish I'd worn jeans instead of thermal pants.

Soon, we were off. I saw little of the trees as the Jeep flew down the roads. No one said much at first. Luke and Gabriel were gazing out their windows. Silas had his head against the headrest and appeared to be snoozing. North was focused on the road. Since it was early morning, the roads were pretty clear as we followed behind the BMW.

I was worried that the stuff on top would slide around, but North took turns with caution and braked early around stop signs.

The moment we were out of Summerville and on an interstate headed south, Luke yanked out his phone. "Hook me up, North."

"I don't want to hear that techno shit this early," he said.

"I loaded up a bunch of songs that Sang likes."

North huffed, tensing his hands on the steering wheel as if he wasn't going to say anything.

Silas sat up and opened up the center console, finding a cord that was hooked up to the stereo system. He passed it back to Luke.

"You guys spoil her," North said. He slid a glance at Silas. "You know that, don't you?"

Silas shrugged. "It's her vacation. Let her have fun." His phone started to ring. He answered it, listened, and hung up. "We're stopping for coffee."

"Fuck yeah," Gabriel said.

Victor took the next exit, pulling into a Starbucks. North followed.

We weren't there long, but in that time, I downed a mocha Frappuccino, a half of a slice of pumpkin bread that I split with Luke, half a coffee cake that I pinched from Kota and a bite of North's egg muffin when he begged me to eat something with protein in it.

By the time we were on the road again, I was bouncing.

Luke flicked through different songs to find one I'd recognize. I hung over his shoulder, watching as he flipped through lots of music. "Got us covered for the whole trip," he said. "Won't have to use Internet once."

"No Internet on the island," North said.

"I said that," Luke said, and turned the volume up on his phone.

Soon, Gabriel, Luke and I were bouncing around in the back seat to Korean pop music.

North made a face, and then stuck his finger in his ear, wriggling. "What is this?" he bellowed back at us.

"K-Pop," I said loudly over the music.

North gave me an eyeball in the rearview mirror. "You like this?"

"I like a lot of things," I said. I started shaking shoulders. It was really the only move I could do in the limited space. Luke and Gabriel echoed my moves.

"I don't know if I can take this the whole way," North said, reaching for the volume control.

Silas's hand shot out, blocking North before he could touch the volume. "No. Please," he said. "Don't make her stop."

North frowned. Silas nodded toward the rearview mirror. North gave Silas a questioning look, then glanced back at us in the mirror before returning his gaze to Silas. "You fucking pervert."

Silas raised a dark eyebrow. "What? Pervert? Do you see her face? She's so happy."

"Oh," North said and sat back. "Never mind." He moved to adjust the mirror.

Silas put a hand over North's to stop him and grinned. "If you don't mind, leave it. It's my vacation, too."

North rolled his eyes, but he didn't touch the mirror again.

My cheeks were already warm but they were on fire after listening to this. I stopped bouncing around so hard in the back seat, but it was hard to completely stop when Gabriel and Luke were still having fun.

"Sing," Gabriel told me, mouthing the words.

"I don't remember the lyrics," I said. "Maybe the next one."

The next one I did know. I blushed, unsure if I should start singing when North was already annoyed with the music. When Gabriel and Luke started singing next to me, I started low. It was another Korean pop song with fast lyrics. I'm sure I got most of the words wrong though no one could hear me because Gabriel and Luke seemed to be making up their own lyrics. Eventually, I was laughing so much, I had to stop.

Between the laughing and all the coffee and sugar, my heart was racing.

Maybe this wouldn't be so bad. We were having fun and no one seemed worried.

We were going on vacation.

I'd never been on vacation and was suddenly determined to make the best of it.

♥

ℋUNTING ℐSLAND

After another thirty minutes, North couldn't handle the noise anymore and switched the music to rock, but turned the volume down.

We were already sweaty in the back and had stopped bouncing around. Luke had his shirt off. Gabriel had stripped down to a tank shirt. I wished I could take my T-shirt off like one of the guys. North did his best by rolling down the windows to give us fresh air.

"Maybe I should wear jeans," I said. "I'm all sweaty."

"You'll want the thermal pants tonight," he said. "Maybe even over the jeans."

It was taking longer than I expected to get there. At the beginning, I didn't think it would feel like such a long car ride and started to wonder if I should have joined the other car and be around Kota. I wanted to have fun, but I still had something I needed to do.

Victor's car was ahead of us and we were following. North poked his finger at his phone, but the GPS kept losing us, despite us staying on the same stretch of the state road for several miles. He focused on a map Kota had given him instead.

I leaned forward a little, propping my elbows up on the middle console, studying the map and trying to figure out our location. "Why did we get a map if we're following Victor?" I asked.

"Just in case we have to stop for gas. Although I don't know why we bother. Kota likes to keep the caravan together. I'm just using the GPS to count down the miles."

There was a long stretch of nothing in front of us. There were trees along the side of the roads and the occasional cutoff.

C. L. Stone

We passed by farms and over some bridges as we traveled further south. "Are we going to Georgia?" I asked.

"We're getting close," North said. "But we aren't leaving the state."

"I've never been this far south," I said.

"You've never been anywhere," Silas said. "One day, we'll go to an Atlanta game."

"Maybe this summer," North said. "After we get out of this school in the spring. We won't have time before then."

I smiled to myself, liking how they were thinking of the future with me around. I kept an eye on the map, trying to pinpoint Hunting Island without moving it from where North could see it. "Do we need to follow Victor? Do you know where to go?"

"We're headed to the same place," North said. "I've got directions. Just sit back and relax. We'll get there soon."

"But they'll get there first," I said. I leaned over the console more to check his speed. He was going just under the limit. "And they're taking forever."

"Kota really likes the speed limit," North said. "He'd fuss at Victor if he went any faster."

Silas grinned. "I think she's in a hurry to get to the beach."

"I just want to get there before Kota," I said for no reason. I thought it would be a silly way to have fun with Kota. Maybe it'd help him relax if we were having fun before we got there.

North grunted. "I can fix that. Sit back and make sure your seatbelt is on."

I sat back and made a show of snapping my seatbelt at my waist.

North checked his rearview mirrors and then stomped on the gas. The Jeep raced ahead, nearly meeting Victor's bumper. He cut around Victor when it was safe and zoomed off ahead, weaving in front of him, and then continuing at a higher speed down the lane. The Jeep's engine roared, making my heart race along with it.

North's phone rang. Silas picked it up and answered it.

"Sorry," he said. "Sang wanted to beat Kota."

I turned and looked back at Victor's car. There wasn't anyone along this stretch of road so no one was behind him now. It followed behind us for a moment, but suddenly the car slowed a lot.

My heart stopped. "What's wrong?" I asked in a panic. "Did something happen to the car?"

Silas laughed, poking at North's phone to hang up. "Victor heard you wanted to beat Kota there. So he's helping."

I laughed and turned to face forward. I leaned against Gabriel. "Victor's cheating for me."

Gabriel had his eyes closed and nudged me with an elbow. "You're Trouble for him, too. Kota's going to give us all a lecture later."

I avoided looking at North's dashboard, though when I did look, the speed remained at ten over the speed limit, keeping us way ahead of Kota and the others.

I was leaning back, staring off and daydreaming when Luke finally elbowed me. He pointed to a sign outside, a brown one with white lettering: Hunting Island.

"Is there really hunting?" I asked quietly. They'd said not at the camp, but I was wondering where the hunting would be happening and if we'd hear gunshots at all.

"Only for Sangs," Luke said with a grin. "Good thing I brought a few Nerf guns." He reached for my hand and held it, his fingers weaving between mine, squeezing as we shared our excitement.

Once we crossed a river onto the island, we were surrounded by trees. Eager to see a beach and what a campground would be like during the winter, I kept looking out the side windows, leaning against both Luke and Gabriel as I did. I had pictured a field that just ended at a beach, not woods like what I was seeing.

I struggled back into my jacket, sure that we'd be hopping out of the car into the cold at any moment. I scanned between the trees; all I could see was more trees and the road in front and behind us.

"I don't see a beach," I said.

"It's somewhere around here," North said.

He followed the signs that led the way to the campgrounds. Soon we approached a gray building, nestled in a cluster of trees. There was a barrier in the way, cutting off access down the road.

North pulled up, talked with the attendant in the booth and showed him our reservation, telling him there was another car following. The attendant passed him a map of the campgrounds with our camping spot circled in red.

"Your group has the campgrounds to yourselves this week," the attendant said. "It's low season, so we let the canteen and other attendants have the week off for the holidays, although someone should always be here at the security office, and one of our rangers lives on the property. Some visitors come for the open parks, but probably not this week." He tipped his brown hat our way. "Enjoy. Come see me if you need anything. And don't feed the bears. There's information on the back of the map if you need it."

"Bears?" I whispered as North eased the Jeep forward and made a left as the map directed.

"He's kidding," North said. "There's no bears."

"There's bears," Gabriel said, picking up his head, rolling it on the headrest and partially opening his eyes. "And coyotes."

"There's no coyotes," North said.

"It's fucking *Hunting* Island. What do you think they hunt around here? Look it up on Google."

North squinted at the road he was following, and then at the map of the campgrounds. "Don't look it up on Google, Baby."

I was sure he was just saying that so I wouldn't be afraid to camp. Secretly, I wondered if we could safely see bears this week without getting hurt.

He passed the map to Silas as he continued down the road. We took a few turns we assumed we needed to take, but he hesitated at a five-way intersection. There were signs, but the paint had faded and were hard to read.

North scratched his head and glared at the faded signs. "The map doesn't show this kind of intersection. We were supposed to hit a three-way split. Did they add a couple roads since the map was made? Which way?"

Silas looked at the map and said, "He wrote instructions. We're going the right way. This says head north for two more signposts and then east."

"Great," North said and leaned forward, checking the sky. "And it's overcast. So which way is North?"

I pointed a finger straight ahead, between North and Silas, to the road in front of us.

Silas and North turned and stared at me, blinking.

I stared back, my eyebrows arching up. Wasn't it obvious?

As a joke, I aimed my pointer finger at North's face, then grinned and pointed back at the road.

"She's fucking with us," North said.

"No, I'm not," I said. I jabbed my finger toward the road ahead of us. "That's north."

North grumbled. "We've been twisting around on roads surrounded by trees. There's no sign of the ocean, and there's no sun in the sky because of it being overcast. How the hell would you know?"

"The ocean is that way," I said, pointing east, down the crossroad. I return my finger to aim ahead of us. "That's North."

"I'd listen to her," Luke said. "It's crazy. She's got this wicked sense of direction. She can point it out in the dark. I've seen her do it."

"Someone find a compass," North said, twisting in his seat. "I want to see this."

Gabriel pulled out his phone and punched at something on the screen. "I'm not getting a signal, so I can't download the app. My compass is in the pack in the back."

"I've got the app," Silas said. "I might have just enough signal." He held up his phone, showing a compass. The needle spun at first but came to point in the direction I had picked out. "She's right."

"Son of a bitch," North said. He smacked at the steering wheel before driving forward. He glanced at me in the rearview mirror. "How'd you know?"

"I just feel it. I always know where North is," I said, meaning it literally but blushed, realizing what I'd said could have a double-meaning.

North glanced back at me, smirked and shook his head.

As we drove on, I noticed sites were marked off with spikes in the ground, each one numbered. North soon found our camping space. He parked in front of the flat patch of grass designated for parking.

I pushed at Luke to let me out. We'd been riding for forever and I was anxious to get out into the fresh air and stretch. I wanted to get all my stuff out and set up everything so I would be ready to have fun with Kota and the others. And then I wanted to find a beach. Maybe I could get Kota alone by asking to walk around and explore.

When everything was out of the Jeep, North planted his hands on his hips. "Should we wait for Kota? He'll want to organize everything."

"Sang," Gabriel said, picking up the pink bag that held the tent components. "Do you want to set up your own tent? You should probably try it out. Give you some practice living in the wild."

"I can?" I asked.

"Yeah," he said. "It's your first camping trip with us. You know what that means?"

I shook my head, my hand drifting up until my finger was hovering over my lower lip, pinching it to my teeth.

He reached over to me, gently patting my hand away from my mouth. "Means you've got to go rustic," he said. "You're with us now. This is initiation. Our first time out, we spent the night in the tents by ourselves. It's like a tradition."

I glanced at Luke. Luke perked up and nodded. "Yeah, Sang. Rite of passage. We all did it. One night all by yourself."

My heart fell. I had to sleep by myself? That was horrible. I had hoped to spend the nights with them all. This camping trip wasn't going to be fun after all.

But then I thought of what they'd said: Rite of passage. They all did it. If that's what it took to be part of the group, I had to do it.

I swallowed back my protest. I held out my hands for the tent bag. "Okay," I said, trying to sound confident. Maybe I would only have to sleep in the tent? Hopefully, I got to spend the rest of the time with them.

Gabriel smiled, handing off my tent. "It's light enough. You can carry it. Part of the fun is doing this yourself."

The tent wasn't heavy—not much heavier than my book bag filled with textbooks. "Where do I set up?" I asked.

Gabriel glanced around and then pointed toward the west wall of trees surrounding the campsite. "Follow me."

Luke and I followed Gabriel until we crossed through a thin line of trees.

We ended up at another space where there was a small fire pit, a flat section for a tent, and a picnic table within a small area. I noticed another spike with a different number on it by the road. "Is this another site? Are we supposed to use it?"

"We've got this one and the one on the other side," Gabriel said. "They give us plenty of room to stretch out, but we all usually just pile onto the one site." Gabriel stopped at a leveled section of ground. "You can set up here. It's close enough to your fire pit. You might not freeze tonight."

I dropped my tent on the ground. "Can I light a fire?"

"If you can light one, you can light one," Gabriel said. "I'll give you two sticks to rub together. Technically I'm not supposed to help."

"Aw," Luke said, grinning. He sat down on the picnic table bench, putting his elbows behind him to lean back on the table as he watched. "You're going to find sticks for her? I had to find my own."

"It's these modern times," Gabriel said with a wink.

"Have to do everything for these kids."

"I think I can find sticks," I said. At least they could hang out while I was trying to figure it out. "Can you at least tell me what to do? Or do I have to get my iPad and read the survival stuff."

"We'll help you with stuff you don't know," Luke said.

I started opening the tent bag—the fabric was pink.

As I pulled it out of the bag, Luke and Gabriel found a couple of rocks to sit on near the fire pit so they could be closer and make comments while I figured out how to put it up.

I supposed the first thing was to set up the tent properly. If I could do that, I thought I could figure a fire later.

I read the directions and counted pieces in the kit. It wasn't difficult to figure out, but with the way it was designed, it required two people at the end to lift it into place. I did as much as I could alone, but when it came to having to lift it up, I glanced at the guys. "Can someone help me lift it?"

Luke and Gabriel shook their heads simultaneously. Luke was staring into the woods, chewing on a piece of grass. Gabriel was flicking some dirt from his shoes. "Sorry, Trouble," Gabriel said. "No helping. You've got to do it yourself. Think of the boy scouts...I mean girl scouts. I bet they do this alone."

"But there's scouts," I said. "That's plural. There's more than one. And don't they have leaders?"

"Right," Gabriel said. "Think of us as camp leaders and you're earning a badge. This is basically survival training. This is Academy camp after all."

"He means we were never in the scouts," Luke said. "We don't know."

"I've read the manual," Gabriel said. "It's all about learning how to do this shit yourself so if you ever needed to do it alone, you could. We had to do all this. What if I was unconscious?"

"If you're unconscious, you don't need a tent," Luke said. "You need a doctor."

"You never fucking know."

I sighed. I got the concept of trying to do this myself, but the instructions said to lift while putting in a tent stake. Was I supposed to do that at the same time? If so, I needed two people. The instructions weren't clear and the pictures showed two people. I was tempted to call on Silas to help out, but I had a feeling Gabriel and Luke would have thrown a fuss.

I stepped over the fabric, pulling where I could. The tent lifted, but as I was setting up one end, the other started sagging over, jerking the pole out of the ground until the whole thing collapsed.

Gabriel stood up, dusting off his hands. "Sang, if I have to help you, this doesn't count," he said.

"Hang on," I said. "I'm not done yet."

Gabriel smirked and waved his hand dismissively. "Come on. It's your first time. I get it. Don't worry about it."

I glared at him. I found the edge of the poles. It took some maneuvering, but I managed to single-handedly stab the pole in the ground far enough that it wasn't going to move though I was worried it was going to break, so I moved quickly. I bent the pole over the tent, picking the whole of the frame off the ground.

I had to run around the tent to get it set up right but eventually I had it up.

The boys came over and we stood together near the entrance after I opened the flap, looking into the space and admiring my work. It wouldn't withstand a bear attack, but it might stand up all night. If it didn't get too windy. Was it waterproof? What would happen if it rains?

Luke nudged Gabriel in the arm. "She set up her tent on her own. She's going to sleep out here alone now."

"Naw," Gabriel said. "Just wait until dark. She'll be begging to sleep in the tent with us." He grinned at me. "It gets a little scary out here, you know. By yourself. Alone. In the dark."

I poked him in the stomach, and he leaned forward. He was just trying to scare me, but I didn't want to think about it. I didn't want to be afraid.

If the boys had done it, I had to, too. "Nu-uh," I said. "Where's my stuff? I want to put it inside."

"Most of yours is in Victor's car," Luke said.

"Maybe they're here," Gabriel said. He put his arm around my neck and walked with me back toward the other camp area.

We followed the path back to the main camp area where I noticed their site had two picnic tables, a large fire pit, and space to put up three or four large tents. Had that second picnic table been there before?

Victor's BMW was backed up next to the Jeep with the trunk open.

Nathan and North were unrolling a large tent in the very center of the tent area while Silas unloaded the BMW. Kota and Victor were separating packs into different piles.

Kota and Victor turned when we approached. Victor waved at me.

Kota smirked. "You really wanted to get here before me?" he asked.

I shrugged and glanced at the others, but then went to him, standing next to him. I didn't want to reach for him with the others around. Maybe I should tell them what Nathan had suggested I do with Kota so they'd understand why I was focusing on him. "When else do I ever get to beat you at anything?"

He smiled more. "Are you going to play fair this week?"

"I will. I promise. It was just this once."

He looked around and then toward the site we'd come from. "What have you been doing? Having fun?" He picked up a pack and opened it, looking at the contents.

"I set up my tent," I said. I unzipped my jacket for some air, warm after moving around so much to get my tent set up. "Can I bring my other things over there?"

Kota's eyebrows hunched together and then he looked at Gabriel and Luke and then surveyed the area around us. "Where's your tent?"

"Over in the other campsite,' I said. "The spot next door."

"Why all the way over there?" Kota asked. "Why not next to us?"

"So I can spend the night by myself like you guys did."

Kota's eyes narrowed at Luke and Gabriel. He put down the pack he was holding to place his hands on his hips. "I can't believe you two."

"Oy," Gabriel said, shrugging. "We did it. We can't treat her differently."

"I don't like the idea of her being out there alone like that," Kota said and then turned to me. "I know we're camping but…"

"Come on Kota," Luke said. "We did it. She'll have one night to herself and then she can join us."

Kota frowned. "I don't like this."

Gabriel's face shifted from joking to serious. "You know what? She set up her tent. She doesn't have to actually sleep in there, right? Maybe we can just get her to light our campfire and do a few things."

Luke walked up to me, nudging my arm. "I guess you don't get to spend the night alone."

"I am, too," I said, suddenly feeling like they were going easy on me. I turned to Victor, hoping maybe he would help. "How else am I going to fit in with you all? If each of you spent the night in a tent alone, then I have to, too, don't I? Where's my pile?"

Victor glanced at Kota. "I don't think we should..."

Kota didn't say anything for a moment but then waved a hand in the air. "No, it's okay. If she wants to spend the night alone in her tent, let her. It's her tent. We got her everything she'll need and she'll just be on the other side of the trees."

"No," Gabriel said. "Make her stay with us. You were right before."

"She wants to," Kota said. "We should let her."

I considered it a victory, though a bittersweet one. I did want to sleep in their tent with them, but I wanted to fit in, too. It was just sleeping. I grinned, gathering my supplies up in my arms. Before I passed Kota, I stopped, rocking up on my feet to kiss his cheek. I needed to not let the others make me too nervous to do what I needed to do. "Thank you, Kota."

Kota looked at me, an eyebrow raised and a surprised smile on his face. "You're welcome, Sang. Need any help?"

"No. The guys said I had to do it alone." I hefted my book bag on my shoulder, heading back to the trail between the campgrounds.

This time, when I went, Victor followed. It was the first time I noticed he was wearing black jeans instead of slacks, and a light gray jacket over a white V-neck T-shirt of some sort. It was so casual for him.

He knelt outside my tent, checking out the inside while I crawled inside and unrolled the sleeping bag. "Do you want your cot instead of sleeping on the ground?" he asked.

"Will it fit in here?" I asked, checking the space. It was a good idea, but it was barely big enough for the sleeping bag to spread out fully. While the tent said it could fit three people, it didn't seem to be realistic to fit two. Silas wouldn't be able to sleep in it without curling up.

"They didn't have a pink one in a larger size," he said. "Although I wasn't really sure you'd use it. I thought you'd want to spend the night with us."

"Luke and Gabriel said it was a rite of passage."

Victor smirked. He combed his wavy brown hair back off his forehead. "They did, huh?"

I nodded, then knee-walked to the entrance. Victor held out his hand, and I took it, letting him help me up and out of the tent.

"You know you don't have to," Victor said. "I think I'd prefer if you slept with us in the big tent."

I wanted that, too, but I also wanted to be part of the group. "I have to. They said everyone else did. It's fine," I said, smiling. "It's just sleeping, right? I can hang out with you all the rest of the time?"

Victor smiled but didn't say anything. He held my hand as we walked back to the other campsite.

By then, North and Nathan had the big tent spread out. It

was so wide that it took up nearly all of the plots meant for tents.

North stood back. Nathan was in the middle, fiddling with a handle. I looked for poles and rope like I'd had to use to put mine together.

"What's this?" I asked, looking at the setup. "Where are your poles?"

North turned back to me. A dark eyebrow arched over a brown eye. "Huh?"

"Mine had poles. Where's yours?"

North smirked. "Just watch."

I stood next to North as Nathan hooked his fingers around a handle and yanked it. He jumped off the top of the mass of plastic sheeting on the ground until he got safely to the grass on the other side.

The tent unfolded, widening even bigger than before, automatically setting itself up. Nathan ran around the tent, pushing already-attached spikes into the ground. Within a minute, he had the whole thing set up.

My mouth hung open. Academy boys had automatic pop-up tents.

North tapped at my chin, reminding me to close my mouth. "You might know a few tricks, Baby, but we've got a few, too."

"It's totally cheating," I said.

North's dark eyes lit up and he put an arm around my shoulder, hugging me sideways. "So you approve?"

I poked him in the side so he'd release me and then I marched off toward the supply piles, pretending to walk away in a huff. I was impressed, though. It had been so easy. Gabriel and Luke had made such a big deal about making me put mine up by hand!

Kota read from the clipboard, designating different piles for coolers, general equipment, beds, clothes and personal items. He put the clipboard down on the picnic table and pulled off the green jacket, laying it neatly next to a green book bag. It was getting to be mid-day, and while there was still a chill in the shade under the trees, the sun was starting to warm the air.

Kota picked up his clipboard, flipped a page, and then spoke to Silas, pointing to a stack of cots. "Let's start filling in those first, putting more toward the back and the sides, to give us room in the middle and front areas for our stuff. We should store the coolers in the cars to keep the bears out."

"Stop talking about bears," North said from the other side of the tent where he was adjusting the pegs.

The others shared a look and a smile. I was starting to wonder if North was afraid of bears.

I wasn't sure what to do, so I stepped beside Silas and awaited instructions.

Kota finished with Silas and then turned to me. He touched the corner of his glasses with a forefinger. "Are you missing anything? Did you get all your things?"

"Tell me what to do," I said. I pointed to the pile of supplies. "My stuff is done. What's my job?"

"We've got it," Kota said. "Once you've got the tent up and your stuff is inside, there's not much left to do. Go have fun."

I pursed my lips, sliding my eyes to Victor, who was standing by. Victor rubbed my back, but he addressed Kota. "She wants to help," he said.

Kota smiled and then reached to my forehead, wiping away a strand of hair blowing in my face, tucking it behind my ear. I beamed at him. I liked it when he did that. "If you want to help, go scout out the area. Go find the latrine."

"Latrine?" I asked. I knew what it meant, but it was surprising to hear him say that and not just calling the bathrooms. Was there something different about bathrooms at campgrounds?

"He wants you to go find the bathrooms," Victor said.

I smiled at his effort to be helpful. "I could help organize stuff here."

Kota touched me gently on my forehead to get my attention. "We need to know where the closest ones are. This map seems to be old and might not be accurate. Use the map, check the layout. We should all get familiar." He pointed to some empty jugs. "Fill up some drinking water, too. And a water bucket for the fire for when we need to put it out. You might want to fill one for your own camp area, too."

That made sense. "Okay. I'll find the bath—*latrine* first and then will come back and fill up the bucket."

"I'll go with her," Gabriel said, walking up beside me, finding my hand and grabbing it.

"It doesn't take two to scout," Kota said.

"We're camping buddies," he said. "We're supposed to stick together. Besides, I have to pee." He tugged at my hand. "Come on, Trouble. You're lucky I'm not making you dig a hole in the ground. That's in the scout manual. I think you earn a badge for that."

I shared a look with Kota. He released a small sigh and shrugged before he picked up his clipboard again and turned toward Victor.

I was glad Gabriel was coming with me so I could tell him about the plan with Kota.

"Meanie," I said to him when we were out of earshot of the others. "You know how Kota's kind of stressed out?"

"Because Kota has a system," Gabriel said, squeezing my hand. "He's not trying to be fussy and dismissive. And because it's your first camping trip and he wants you to have a good time. He doesn't want to weigh you down with a bunch of work."

Not what I was talking about, but I appreciated he was defending Kota. "I don't mind the work..."

"I wish he'd let me take a break like that. He's usually on my ass to do more." He pointed to a wooden sign at a crossroad. "Are these signs faded, or what? That says latrine, right?"

We had to get closer to figure out it was a latrine sign. We headed in that direction.

"I just meant to say, I'm trying to get on Kota's good side."

Gabriel looked at me. "Are you kidding? You're already on Kota's good side."

"I mean about...the plan, sort of. Nathan said I needed to work on him a little. He said Kota's been distancing himself from me and..."

Gabriel stopped in the middle of the road and turned to me. "Are you fucking kidding me? Kota's the one that hasn't stopped talking about you since you've been around."

I pressed my free hand to my heart, my mouth hanging open. "Oh..."

He dropped my hand and made a face like Kota, imitating his voice. "Don't be so rough on Sang. Why are you always in the bathroom with Sang? Do you think she'd want this pink shit? Fucking ape hamster shit fuck, Sang, Sang, Sang." He stopped and then smiled, picked up my hand and kissed my knuckles. "I'm not complaining, but that guy bugs me more about making sure you've got enough clothes and things than anyone else. I tell him I've got it covered. I'm not going to let you walk around naked."

I turned my head to hide the blush heating up my face. "Nathan said he talks to Kota about me but Kota wants to talk about other stuff."

"Not as far as I know," he said. He scratched his chin absently. I suddenly noticed he hadn't shaved and there was a shadow of stubble across his jaw. I liked how it made him look.

"But we do need to get him in on the plan," he said, not seeming to notice me admiring his face. "Mr. Blackbourne keeps putting it off. Honestly, I think he's waiting on Nathan and Silas to come around on the idea more. Maybe he's worried Nathan could talk Kota out of it."

"But we need Kota in on it to convince *Nathan*," I said. "Maybe I can do something this week, spend more time with Kota. If I can get him to where he seems like he might be comfortable with it, Mr. Blackbourne can finally tell him about the plan. We can all get on the same page."

"That might be a good thing." He tugged my hand to get us walking again. "I can't wait to be able to talk to them all about it openly. All this secret keeping is driving me batshit."

"Can you let the others know, though? It might be hard for me to pull them all aside right now without Kota noticing now that we're all here."

Gabriel lifted an eyebrow, reached up and touched the pink earring. "No trouble, Trouble."

We found the latrine and it wasn't too far from our campsite. The gray stone building had two sides, with girl and boy sections, thick dark wood support beams, and overhangs on all sides. There were water fountains out front, with spots to plug in hoses, too.

Gabriel and I stood on the concrete porch just outside the girls' side. The door was propped open with a rock. We glanced inside, our heads close. It was dark. The tile looked dingy, covered with sand in spots. The stalls had rusty patches flaking from the old green paint. There were initials and words scratched into the walls, some faded, some inappropriate for children.

And all I could think was that there must be a hundred creepy, crawly things in there.

"Gabriel?" I asked in a quiet voice, a finger pinching my lower lip. "Will you go in there?"

"I don't want to go in there," he said. "*You* go in there."

"There might be a spider," I said. "You should go see."

"I don't want to see a spider."

I stepped closer, but still held his hand, taking him with me.

We leaned in the doorway. There were several stalls on one side, sinks on the other. Beyond it was an even darker area, like a back room. I didn't know what it was for. I kind of didn't want to know. The area was shadowed, smelling strongly of old soap, rusty water, and dampness.

I glanced up. Gabriel's eyes followed mine. The beams of the building were exposed and the windows were wide open above the stalls. There were screens in the windows, but they had holes in them. I couldn't see the corners of the ceiling because of how dim the building was, but I imagined hundreds of spiders above us, waiting to fall in our hair the moment we stepped inside.

"What the hell?" Gabriel asked. "Why not just plant a toilet in the ground outside?"

"There's spiders in there," I said. "Go get rid of them."

"I'm not going in for a spider," he said. "I don't like spiders."

"I have to pee," I said. Now that we were here, I wanted to get that part over with so I wouldn't have to go for the rest of the day. I couldn't imagine going in at night. I'd have to make sure not to drink too much. What was I going to do for the rest of the week?

"I have to pee, too," Gabriel said. "I'm a second away from using a tree. At least out here in the sunlight I can see if anything is crawling on me."

"I can't pee on a tree. I don't have a...the...plumbing."

"Ha," Gabriel said with a chuckle. "You almost said penis. That's so cute."

"Who are we going to get to go in and kill the spiders?"

We stared at each other for a minute. We needed someone who would actually kill spiders and wouldn't laugh at us. At the same moment, we both turned our heads back toward the campsite and shouted. "Silas!"

Silas materialized a few moments later, coming up the hill to the latrine. "What?" he asked as he marched toward us. He'd removed his jacket, wearing just a blue baseball shirt. The shirt made him look bulkier around the shoulders. He towered over me as he got close.

"Will you go in and kill the spiders?" I asked.

He peered into the girls' bathroom, squinting into the dark. "You saw spiders?"

"No," I said. "Can you go see if there are any?"

He laughed, and the white of his teeth contrasted against his olive skin. His voice was rich with amusement. "You made me run down here to see if there were spiders?"

I blushed. Maybe he was laughing, but he hadn't said no. "Please?"

Silas glanced at Gabriel. "You wouldn't go in?"

"I'm not going in that shit," he said. "They've got those big ones around here. The ones with the furry knees."

My mouth fell open. "Furry knees?"

"Don't tell her that," Silas said. "She won't be able to sleep tonight." Silas nudged us out of the way, stepping into the bathroom. He tilted his head around and then slapped the wall.

The bare bulbs overhead flickered to life, but there was little improvement.

Silas sighed. He marched to the first stall, opened the door, and disappeared into it for a second before he came back out, announcing, "There's no spiders in here."

"Did you look under the toilet?" I asked.

He grunted and shuffled back into the stall, stepping out a second later. "*Aggele*," Silas said. "Will you get in here, please? There's no bugs. It's clean. It's not bad. It's just a little dark because you're out in the brighter light outside."

I wasn't sure if he was right or if he was just trying to make me happy. I edged forward. Once inside, I wrapped my arms around my stomach, trying to become as small as possible so I wouldn't risk touching a wall or a sink. I gazed at the painted brick walls, and the concrete floor with an ominous drain on the floor. Why was this so creepy? Maybe I wasn't a camping sort of person.

"Good luck, Trouble," Gabriel said from the door. "I'm going to go find a tree to make friends with." He dashed off towards the trees where I couldn't see him.

"Argh," I said, making a fist and shaking it, although I didn't really blame him at all. I wasn't so sure a tree wouldn't be better. "So much for having a camping buddy."

Silas chuckled and then leaned against the stall wall, folding his arms over his chest. He seemed taller than ever— definitely older than sixteen. "Gabriel thought you'd be the one to squash the spiders. Usually, we make him do it."

"He doesn't like spiders."

"We're probably why he doesn't. We get him to take care

of all the spiders; he complains every time." He took a step back, took hold of the stall door, and held it open for me. "Go ahead."

I peeked in at the toilet. It looked clean, but my skin crawled thinking about touching it. "Silas?"

"Yes, *Aggele Mou*?"

My next thought was that if he went back to camp, some ax murderer would come in and get me while I was in the bathroom. Or a bear. Or spiders. "Will... will you stay? I mean not in here but in this bathroom?"

He smiled and rolled his eyes. "I'll be your temporary camping buddy." He bent down, planting a kiss on my forehead. "Just whistle or something if you see a bug."

"I can't whistle," I said. I snapped my fingers. "I forgot the whistle they gave me."

"You need to take the emergency things out of your kit. This is where you use your whistle."

I entered the stall, locking the door behind me. I stared down the toilet. Now that I was here, I had another problem.

"See a bug?" Silas asked after a few minutes.

"Can you run the water?"

"Huh?"

"I can't go when I think you're listening."

"I'm not listening."

"Please?"

He let out a small, amused groan and then one of the sinks started up. Then a second one. It was enough noise that I felt I could pee without him hearing. I might have let Gabriel in the bathroom with me, but none of them had been around when I was using the toilet, and it was too strange to do so with him so close.

When I was finished, I flushed and walked out of the stall. The sinks were flowing at full speed across the room but Silas wasn't there.

I tiptoed out, suddenly fearful the ax murderer got him instead. "Silas?" I called. He wouldn't have left me alone: he'd promised.

Silas appeared at the far end of the room, at the shadowed area in the back. "Yeah?"

"What's back there?" I asked.

"Showers," he said and disappeared behind the wall again. "I was checking for spiders back there, too, just in case you wanted to take a shower tonight."

I turned from him, washing my hands, but mostly to hide my panic. I smothered a shiver. Worse than a shower was a creepy shower with rusted pipes and spiders. It made for a ready excuse to do hobo baths all week.

At least the girls had separate showers, so it wouldn't be a problem to do hobo baths out of the sink all week. I wouldn't get super clean that way, but I'd have to do my best. It was camping, right? I'd have to deal with being a little dirty.

Silas returned from his shower expedition. He rubbed his face. "This place isn't that bad," he said.

I looked at the rust on the sink. "Really?"

"Last place we were at, the showers were outside."

I spoke through gritted teeth. "You're kidding."

"Bare ass to the world. The Academy girls had to take showers on the far end of the camp. Not that we'd bug them, but just because it was exposed and we weren't sure if there weren't other people around. First day, they rigged a setup to hang a shower curtain."

I smiled. "And you guys didn't?"

He shrugged. "Barely took a shower that week, from what I remember. Too cold. I think we just dealt with being dirty."

So that's normal, I thought, relieved. I reached for his hand. "Come on," I said. "Let's go camp."

On the way back, I told Silas about the plan for getting Kota on the same page.

He was quiet and before we got back, I stopped in the road, looking up at him. "Do you not think it's a good idea?"

"I don't know what to think," he said. "When you're around, I'm fine. When you're not here, I'm...I don't know. I second-guess things."

I smiled, squeezing his fingers. "I do the same thing."

He lifted his head, a thick eyebrow going up on his olive skin. "Really?"

"I worry," I said. "I don't want to make anyone mad or jealous."

His thick lips pursed. He released my hand then put his hands on my shoulders before he bent and gently kissed my lips once. "I feel guilty for asking you to stay with me if you're interested in someone else. It's stressing you out."

My lips parted and I stared at his dark eyes, at his dark hair dancing in the breeze. "I'm more worried about you."

He nodded once and reached for my hand, holding it firmly between his palms. "Sang, you've got a lot to think about besides us and this plan."

"Kota was worried about that," I said, suddenly not wanting to talk about it now, worried it would stress him out more. "Mr. Blackbourne has a plan. He's sure it'll work."

"I've never seen Mr. Blackbourne fail," he said. "But there's always the possibility it won't work out the way he thinks it will."

I breathed in deeply and then put a hand on top of his still holding my other one. "I'm staying," I said, trying to look him steadily in the eyes steady, faking some confidence. "Silas, I'm staying with you and the others. Right now, I need to convince Kota, but this is what I want. I may need your help, though."

He pressed his lips together, swallowing. "You know I'd do anything for you, *Aggele*."

I nodded, sensing there was more to what he needed to say.

He looked toward the woods. "I'll do anything for you...as long as it doesn't hurt you. If in the end, we're hurting you more by keeping you with us, then I have to..." He turned his head away, his dark eyes storming.

His words were familiar. "You were talking to Kota," I said. "That sounds like what he's been saying."

"He's not wrong," he said. "You wouldn't want any of us

to suffer just by staying together if it was the wrong thing?"

I gritted my teeth and loosened my hand from his. Hurting them was the one thing I truly feared. "Would...am I making you suffer?"

He lifted his head quickly, eyebrows up. "I just meant...I was giving you an example."

"I don't want you to suffer at all," I said. I pointed to my chest. "And I know I make things more complicated just by being around. You all have to work harder because of me. And you all wouldn't have to even consider this...plan if I wasn't here. It makes everything more difficult."

Silas reached for me and then dropped his shoulders. "I said the wrong thing. I'm not suffering."

I closed my lips, trying to swallow back my emotions. I breathed as steadily as I could. It was everything that haunted me at night, fueled my nightmares. The last thing I wanted was for them to be hurt.

Silas stood by as all this went through my head, staring at his feet.

I looked at him, at his tall, broad figure. I remembered the day I first met him. He'd been so scary at first, and yet just a couple hours after that, I'd been in trouble, and he'd come to my defense, protecting me. From that moment, I'd yearned to be his friend. Later, when he'd saved me from my stepmother by pulling me out of the shower, he was there for me. He was *always* there for me.

Here he was, unhappy, but willing to give everything up if it meant protecting me again. Could I be selfish and ask to stay?

I shivered and swallowed back a wave of tears. "Silas?" I said, my voice quivering.

He reached for me again. "Don't," he said. "I'm sorry."

I swallowed again, wanting to get the words out without crying. "If it's the right thing to do, why does it feel wrong?"

He rested his hands on my arms, but stood still, looking at me. "What do you mean?"

I bowed my head, unable to look at him. "I've been trying

to consider how it would work with you. But I was ignoring that maybe you all would have it so much harder. But...when I think of leaving, everything hurts."

He rubbed my arms, warming them with his big palms. "If it hurts," he said softly, "then that is the wrong answer."

I breathed in slowly, tilting my head to meet his gaze.

His eyes glistened but held mine steadily. "Mr. Blackbourne is right."

"What do you mean?"

"He told me once that if it hurts really bad, it was the wrong decision to make, and your body knows it." He circled me with his arms, slowly picking me up off the ground.

I let him pick me up and buried my face into his shoulder, letting his body warm me as I breathed in his ocean scent. It felt good, comfortable. "I like this," I said.

"I do, too." His deep voice rumbled through to my bones. "Kota's wrong. You shouldn't have to leave if you want to stay. Not as long as everyone wants you with us, there's no reason for you to go."

"What about all the trouble if I stay?"

"We've already faced death and hell, *Aggele*." He squeezed me tighter. "That might never change for us. Do we face it separated and miserable? Or together and stronger?"

I sniffed, keeping my cheek against his shoulder. "Silas..."

"It hurts too much to even think about letting you go off alone or with another team. Before, I thought perhaps I was being selfish, but how can it be wrong if you really want to be here, too? It's not just you who needs us. We need you here."

Did they? I sighed.

"I'm sorry," he said. "Don't give up. Work with Kota. Bring him back to believing it will work with you here." He slowly put me back down on my feet and looked at my face. "Don't hurt."

I pushed a breath out through my lips slowly, trying to steady my feelings. "I'll try."

Silas nodded grimly. He traced a couple of his big fingers

across my cheek. "Let's have fun. Do you want me to catch a spider and show it to Gabriel?"

I smiled but shook my head.

He put his hands on his hips. "What do you get when you cross an elephant with a kangaroo?"

I cringed. "What?"

"Great big holes all over Australia."

The answer was so surprising that I snorted before I could laugh.

He smiled again and reached for my hand. "You were right; we'll think of something. You'll convince Kota. You just watch. If Kota can be on the same team as Mr. Blackbourne, we'll all be fine."

I hoped so. "Where is Mr. Blackbourne?"

"He'll be here tomorrow morning. He was finishing up some things. The rest of the Academy wouldn't be here until tomorrow. We're early."

I breathed out slowly. I'd been trying to ignore the thought of other people being around the camp site. Academy people.

I nodded and followed him on the path back to camp. I wished Mr. Blackbourne were here now. It would make it much easier just to get confirmation about what I should do. I could really use some confidence.

Could I call him? I pulled out my phone while we were walking back. No signal. Maybe I could try to get a message to him later somehow. Even a text message from him might be enough.

Maybe I didn't have to convince Kota tonight. I just had to get him to open up a little to believing.

I didn't want to even think of what might happen if I failed.

♥

𝒰NEXPECTED 𝒢UESTS

𝒲hen we returned, the guys were gone except for Nathan, who was pulling a few sleeping bags into the tent.

Silas went in and I followed. Their big tent was one huge room, with a little extra tunnel-like space in the front for the entryway. At the opposite end of the door, along the largest length of tent wall, was a series of cots, foot to head parallel to the wall. More cots had the head facing the wall, the feet to the door, taking up space in the middle.

"I thought Kota said to put them all along the sides?" I asked.

Nathan rolled out a sleeping bag on one of the cots. "We had them all around the edges, but adding an extra cot made it more complicated."

"An extra cot?"

"The one for you," he said.

I was going to say I was sleeping in my tent tonight, but then I realized later this week, I might need a cot in the big tent. They would have had to rearrange everything. I counted the cots. "There's only eight."

"Mr. Blackbourne and Dr. Green have their own tent away from us," he said. "Where family leads sleep."

"Shouldn't Kota be with them?" Silas asked.

"Kota wanted to stay here," Nathan said. "He'll join the family leads when it's time."

"Kota's a..." I broke off, not sure what it was okay to ask.

Silas and Nathan looked at each other. Nathan shrugged and responded. "There's two leads in a group," he said. "Mr. Blackbourne's our main contact for the Academy, he tracks the jobs we go on and lets us know what jobs are available."

"Then there's a family lead and that's Kota," Silas said.

"It used to be the doc," Nathan said. "But when Dr. Green got into his final year of medical school and had to be away so much and then had to do his internship thing, someone else needed to take over. That was Kota."

"What's a family lead?" I asked.

"We might need to wait," Silas said. "She'll learn it all this week."

"It doesn't matter if she learns some in advance, does it?" Nathan asked. When Silas shrugged, Nathan turned back to me. "A family lead is the person who keeps tabs on all of us. So like Kota checks in with Gabriel at home and makes sure things are running smoothly. He'd get groceries delivered to you if you were too busy with stuff that week. He makes sure everyone's bills are paid on time and everyone that needs a job has one."

"It's a lot of work," Silas said. "If we're too tired to do an Academy job, he'll veto it, even if we say it's okay."

"He rarely ever does that," Nathan said. "He usually keeps us pretty together. And if we need help somewhere, he'll go along rather than have us cancel."

There were more responsibilities on Kota than I had realized. No wonder he was so stressed. "He has to do that alone?"

"He's pretty good at it." Nathan smoothed out the sleeping bag and then found a pillow. "Sang, North's over by the beach. You wanted to go, didn't you?"

I nodded, trying to summon up some good feelings after the earlier intense discussion with Silas, and now learning about Kota having so much on his shoulders.

"Go run on ahead. I'm almost done."

"Which way?" I asked.

Silas moved to the small pile of items inside the tent, ready to be put into place. "Let me take care of this," he said to Nathan. "You go and show her."

Nathan nodded. "Thanks, man."

We left the tent and Nathan walked with me from the

155

campsite to the road, holding my hand along the way.

We were quiet for the first part of the walk.

"Did you get a chance to talk to Kota much?" Nathan asked.

"Not yet."

"You'll get more of a chance tonight," he said. "I tried when you were at the bathroom, but he kept saying his was busy and would talk later."

"Gabriel said he doesn't stop talking about me around him."

Nathan looked ahead, his blue gaze intense on the woods around us. "He used to be the same way when he spoke about you with me. But now, he's not."

Maybe Gabriel wasn't talking with Kota about the same things.

He squeezed my hand and focused on me. "You've got all week to change his mind. Hang in there."

We had to walk a while before we got to a clearing in the woods where the gravel path turned into sand, stretching out between sand dunes.

The beach.

I jolted forward in excitement. I released Nathan and broke into a stumbling run, climbing the dune.

The ocean met with a river to the north and the rest of the island to the south had really wide stretches of beach. This beach was much bigger than Folly Beach where I'd been before. The ocean rolled over on itself over and over in gentle waves. The breeze picked up, chilling my nose and face, so I zipped up my jacket again. I breathed in the salt and the moisture; it was so much better than the woods. Why couldn't we have our tents out here?

There was a picnic table on a dry patch of sand. Nearby, North stood next to a barbecue grill. He was bent over, opening up a bag of charcoal.

I ran toward him. He saw me coming and tensed, shoulders rounding out, but he held still. I jumped onto his back, circling his neck with my arms, holding to him for dear life.

"North Star," I said, my legs dangling off of his back.

"Sang Baby," he said, and he lifted the bag of charcoal, carrying me along with it as if I were just a scarf around his neck and not a person.

"Can I go touch the water?"

"Hell no."

I pouted, but since I was behind him, he couldn't see it. "Please?"

"The last time I took you to the ocean, you fell in." He shook charcoal from the bag into the grill. "I don't want to save your ass today. The water's freezing."

"I won't fall in," I said. "There's no undercurrents here, right? Please?"

"I don't know that and no."

I released his neck, dropping to the ground. I heard other people coming and turned to find Nathan jogging toward us. Gabriel was a few dozen feet behind him.

"Can I go if Nathan goes with me?" I asked North. If he was worried about my safety, maybe someone willing to go along might make it safer.

North chuffed. "Only if he stays right next to you."

I grinned, running back down the path. Nathan saw me coming and broke out into a sprint toward me, arms open. When I was close, I bounced up, catching him around the shoulders. He caught me around the waist, swung me around in a circle once before wrapping his arms around me. He held me by my thighs as he carried me back to the beach.

"Hi, Honey," I said, feeling silly because we were just talking a minute ago.

"Hi Peanut," he said, grinning. "Miss me?"

"Yes. Will you go with me to touch the water? North won't let me."

"North said no or North said no unless I go?"

"I can if you will."

Nathan smirked and glanced around. Gabriel was still struggling to get over the dune behind him and North was busy

157

with the grill. He whispered to me. "I'll do it for a kiss."

I leaned in, kissing his cheek close to his mouth. Then I gave him another on the opposite cheek.

"Ah," Nathan said. "A bonus. I guess you really want to swim."

"No swimming," North said. He was opening the package of lighter fluid. "And don't let her fall in."

He could hear even with the waves and wind blowing? His hearing was amazing.

"I won't," Nathan said. He patted me on the thigh with his palm. "Drop down for a second, Peanut."

I did. Nathan sat on the picnic table, where he removed his shoes and socks and rolled up his jeans until they were about to his knees. He stepped back down again, his bare feet in the sand. He gritted his teeth. "Fuck. Even the sand is cold."

I took my jacket off. "I don't want to get that wet."

Nathan put it next to his shoes and then focused on me. He bent over, hooked an arm around my back and then caught me around the knees with the other. He cradled me in his arms as he lifted me against his chest. "Let's go."

I snuggled into him, holding onto his broad shoulders. The wind from the ocean was biting into my exposed arms and neck. I loved the thermal pants just then, as they did keep my legs warm. I knew the water would be freezing, but I couldn't help it. I just wanted to touch it.

Nathan marched forward until he got to the soggy part of the sand and stopped. I felt him shiver. "Shit. It's really cold."

"Do it quick," I said. "I just want to touch it."

"Hang on," he said. He turned me over until I was dangling upside down, facing out toward the ocean. He hooked his arms around my waist, my legs over his shoulder. "You okay like that?" he asked.

It was perfect. I was upside down, but I could reach to feel the waves with my hands. He marched forward and I spread my hand out over the surface and touched the most chilling water I'd ever felt before. If it would keep still, I was sure the water would turn to ice.

"Got it!" I said and burst out laughing. "Holy crow, it's cold."

Nathan laughed and hoisted me a little higher on his shoulder, though leaving me upside down, as he bolted for the dry sand. I dangled in his arms, jostled by his movements.

When we were away from the water, he hauled me up even further until my stomach was over his shoulder. I giggled and patted this butt as he marched back to the picnic table.

"Are you done playing with the ocean?" North asked as we got back.

"Yeah," I said. "It's too cold to swim."

"No swimming."

Gabriel was putting a stereo on the table and then he adjusted an orange wool hat over his head. "Oy, Trouble, where's your hat?"

I stuffed my hand into the pockets of the jacket, pulling out my pink gloves and hat.

Gabriel walked over, taking the hat and adjusting it, pulling it over my head. "No sense in buying you shit if you don't wear it." He reached his fingers into the hat, stuffing my hair in, and then tugged out two locks of hair to frame my face. "You can leave those out," he said.

It was like how he wore his hat, with his two blond locks sticking out. It was a funny look for him because it made it appear like he had only blond hair and blue eyes with his contrasting dark eyebrows.

I put on the gloves, too. My nose was chilly, but it wasn't that bad.

North hovered over the grill, looking at the ocean and then down at the coals. "I don't know if I should light this."

"Just do it," Nathan said, brushing his feet clean of sand while sitting on the table. He groaned and wiped and wiped at his feet. "This is going to be my life this week. Sand in every little cranny."

"You like dirt," North said and then eyeballed me as I inched closer to the grill. He waved a hand at me. "Don't," he said. "Wind is blowing. I'm pretty sure I want to keep your face flame-free."

"Pretty sure?" I said, although I was joking and took a step back.

He said nothing. He took out a stick from a kit, and lit one end of it with a lighter, shielding the flame with his body. He stuck the still-burning stick into the coals.

The coals flamed up instantly. The breeze wasn't horrible, but there was no protection from it off the ocean, so it was constant, bending the tall flames away from the water.

North backed away from the grill. "Maybe we should eat sandwiches. This might be too dangerous."

"I can eat cold hot dogs," Gabriel said.

"The coals will simmer down after a bit," Nathan said.

"I don't have a lid to this thing," North said. It was a standard park grill, sticking out of the sand on a pole without a cover. "I should have brought one."

"There's a grill back at the camp," Nathan said. "And I bet it's better because the trees block the wind more."

Gabriel and I stood behind North, watching the flames. Nathan put his shoes back on and took turns poking at the charcoal. Eventually, the charcoal started glowing more and the flames simmered down, so North could place hot dogs on the grill to heat up.

North turned his head, looking toward the dunes. When I turned to see what he was looking at, I spotted Silas, Victor, Luke and Kota materializing over the hump of sand.

Luke broke into a run toward me, hurrying down the path while scooting the others out of his way.

He was carrying a soccer ball under his arm. "Hey," he called to us. "Let's play something."

The others carried ice chests and extra folding chairs and started to set them up around the table.

Gabriel took one of the ice chests, dragging it down the beach to where the sand had flattened out and was relatively dry.

Nathan tagged along and he and Luke set up a few lines in the sand.

"Sang's on my team," Nathan said.

"Are we playing soccer?" I asked.

"I guess," Nathan said.

No one said anything about rules, so I assumed we were going to play was basic soccer. The only rules I knew were to use your feet, or any body part except your hands, and kick for a goal.

I started out trying to just chase the ball, but they were all really fast. I ended up just aiming to block Gabriel and Luke while Nathan took over trying to kick the ball over the goal lines.

Nathan and Gabriel were struggling for the ball near the middle, and I zagged in front of Luke. Luke held his hands out as if he was going to catch me. I sprinted and when I thought he was going to zag out of the way, he held out his arms instead, catching me around the waist. I lost my balance, folding over in his arm toward the sand, but he shifted quickly, bringing me down on top of him as he sat down hard on the sand.

I luckily caught my knees in the sand and not in his stomach or groin.

"Ow," he said, laughing. He wrapped his arms around my shoulders, drawing me in to kiss my cheek. "It's too cold for tackling."

"You started it," I said.

"Oh yeah?" Luke slipped his hands under my jacket and shirt, his chilled fingertips finding the bare skin of my stomach.

Icy waves seared through to my center and I yelped, slapping at his biceps as I tried to crawl off of him. "No," I whined. "Let go."

He laughed but didn't release me. "Warm up my hands." He sat up, sitting cross-legged on the sand and kept his arms around me.

"Argh," I said, but I found both his hands, pulled the off me and stuffed them into my jacket pockets instead, securing them with my own arms. I bit my tongue as if that would stop the shivers—remnants of his cold hands on me.

"Oy," Gabriel called to us as Nathan made another goal. "Get your hands out of her shirt."

"Warming them up," Luke said.

"Wear your gloves."

"You've got gloves?" I snapped at Luke. I should have known, but had gotten caught up in the moment, not thinking of them. I wasn't really annoyed, but he had ice fingers.

"Maybe," he said. "But you're a better heater."

I pushed to try to knock him back over into the sand, but he was too strong and remained upright. He yanked his hands out of my pockets, capturing my hands and grinning.

He had such a wicked, yet warming smile. I had to scramble out of his lap; my heart was melting too much around him.

When I made it back to the center of our soccer field, Kota called for Nathan. They were going to move the table out a little and wanted an extra hand taking all the stuff off and carrying it over.

Gabriel turned up the radio. It was a little hard to hear around the waves, so he faced it our way and turned it up loud. "Oh my god, this song is awesome," he said. He twisted around again, kicking the ball away where it rolled into a hill of sand and stopped. He dashed toward me, snagging my hands and pulling me toward the stereo and then to a section of smooth sand in front of it. "Come on, Trouble. You've got to learn this one."

I didn't recognize the song at first until I heard the guitar intro as we got closer. "*Beat It*?" I asked.

"Michael Jackson." He positioned me in front of himself and then backed off a couple steps. He started snapping his fingers. "Learn this. Next time we go to a club, we'll do it."

I hesitated, looking at the other guys, but they were busy moving around supplies for the picnic. I'd danced once in front of them before. I focused on Gabriel moving around and I tried doing the same thing next to him.

Gabriel stopped instantly, snapped his fingers again at me

and then pointed to the spot beside him. "No, no, just watch first. I don't want you to learn it backwards."

How do you learn a dance backwards? I grunted, stopping. I learned better by diving in. Luke sat on the ice chest next to the stereo, turning up the sound more.

Gabriel started swinging his arm out, snapping his fingers. He did some hip swivels and spins. The more he did, the more I vaguely remembered a music video with this song and the dance he was doing.

Gabriel did the moves again and started explaining how he was swinging his body. He clapped his palms together, gesturing to me. "Come on, you do it now. Luke, start the song over."

Luke pushed a button and the song stopped suddenly and then started fresh from the intro. I stood quietly at Gabriel's left. He started snapping his fingers. I snapped mine. His arms went up and slid down. I did it. He pumped his arms out. I followed.

I repeated every move. We replayed the song from the start again and I was about a half step behind him for each movement.

By the second chorus, I had at least that chorus part and was keeping in time with him.

"Oh my god, you're beautiful," Gabriel said. He ran at me after we'd done the chorus and caught me around the waist, swinging me off the ground and then brought me back down into a hug. He kissed my eyebrow. "You and I, Trouble. You're the only girl who can keep the fuck up."

He'd kissed me so openly that I glanced at the others, but no one said anything about it, even though I had to think at least some of them had seen it. They were letting things slip a little. Kota was going to start asking about things.

Luke hit the repeat button on the stereo and jumped up. "Let's do it."

Gabriel positioned himself a step in front. Luke and I took up positions just behind him. When the chorus started, I let the guys start first and I joined them a half bar later. I followed

Luke, trying to be his match. Occasionally Gabriel would spin out and do his own thing, but for the most part, we synced up.

Nathan strolled over, followed by Kota and the others. Silas hit the repeat button again when the song ended.

I was blushing now that the others were watching, but I wasn't about to stop or mess up. Nathan surprised me by jumping in after the first chorus. He fell in step next to me and followed me closely. I thought I'd trip over him but he managed to stay out from underfoot. When it looked like he was staying, I moved over a bit, still behind Gabriel, and Luke stepped aside to give me more room.

Gabriel might have taken the lead, but Luke danced more smoothly than any of them. He swung his hips with a dip and tucked his knee in at certain spots that made it look cooler. I tried to mimic his moves, but he was much faster than me. Gabriel could sing, though, and did. Nathan mouthed the words and did okay with the dancing.

I was going into another turn when I spotted Kota holding up his cell phone. I thought he was taking a picture but he kept holding it up.

When the song finally ended, I was breathless after dancing for so long. Luke fell on his butt on the sand. Gabriel practiced a few moves and Nathan picked the sand off of his shoes. I went over to Kota as he lowered his phone and hit a button.

"Taking pictures?" I asked.

"Video," he said. He hit the replay button to show me. The other guys were visible, but mostly the camera was on me. My cheeks heated as I watched myself on the small screen. I had my head turned a lot, watching Luke and the others and the video captured every time I slowed down or misstepped.

Gabriel came to stand behind me, looking at the screen. "I want a copy," he said. "Sang and I could do YouTube."

"No YouTube," Kota said.

"Aw," Gabriel said.

"I'm not allowed?" I asked.

Kota shot a look at Gabriel, as if blaming him for my

question. He sighed and turned to me. "We want to try to keep you as low profile as possible."

"Why? What does low profile mean?"

"Sorry, Sang," he said. "No getting famous for you."

"I don't want to be famous," I said and meant it. Famous meant a lot of attention, and I barely tolerated what I got at school now. I couldn't imagine being someone really famous and having all those eyeballs on me like Victor had to deal with on occasion.

Kota smiled and swept a fingertip across my cheek. "Good."

"Do I have to be low profile for the Academy? Is it so I'd be able to get in?"

Kota said nothing, but winked at me and turned away back toward the table. He must not be able to tell me that much, I thought. Victor caught my eye and he winked at me, too. He picked up my hand where Kota left off.

"Hey!" a voice shouted.

Victor released my hand quickly, stepping around in front of me as a shield.

Nathan pointed down the beach. "From there," he said. Everyone turned, eyes darting toward where the voice was coming from.

There was a group of people coming from the southern part of the beach, walking our way. One ran ahead of the others, waving his hand to get our attention.

"I thought we had the place to ourselves," Victor said in a low voice.

"The Academy has this whole place," North said coming up from behind us. He stared ahead out at the approaching group, squinting his dark eyes, a hand lifted to his brow to shield the sun. "Unless it's park rangers, they've got to be Academy. They aren't dressed like rangers."

"How do we find out if they are without asking directly?" I asked.

Victor turned his head back toward the people approaching. He remained in front of me, standing close.

"Random," he said.

I knew it meant something, but in my panic, I couldn't remember what. Kota told us to stay put, breaking away from our group with North and Silas following. We inched forward to stay within earshot but held back.

The group consisted of three guys out front with three girls trailing behind them at a slower pace.

When the three guys got close enough that Kota could talk to them, the lead one spoke. "Caught you all dancing. Are we missing the party already?"

My cheeks burned in embarrassment. They had seen us? I ducked a half step behind Victor, putting my cheek to his shoulder to peek around. That they had watched us dancing made me super self-conscious.

Kota held out his hand toward the guy who had spoken. "Taco," he said.

Taco?

The guy smiled and looked Kota in the eye as he shook his hand and said, "Copernicium."

Kota's head bobbed in an approving nod. Silas and North relaxed behind him.

I remembered suddenly that if Kota said something random, and the other guy said something random as well, that was a sign that they were Academy. Anyone else would have asked why he said taco.

"That's number one-twelve, right?" Kota asked.

"Of course. Much better than the old name," the guy said. "Did you hear Japan might get to name a periodic element soon?" I couldn't see much of his actual face, but he was wearing jeans, a blue sweatshirt, and had on a New York Yankees baseball cap. He was the same height as North. The guys behind him were a little shorter, but broader.

All of them were casually dressed. One guy was just wearing a long-sleeved T-shirt but had his hands in his pockets like he was cold. The guys looked to be eighteen, maybe a little older. The girls looked older than that, like twenty-five.

Looking at their group, I suddenly felt so young and

small. Would I be the youngest here this week?

"I'm Ian," New York guy said.

"Kota," Kota replied.

"This camp is better than the one from a few years ago," Ian said. He adjusted the cap higher on his head. "The one with the outdoor showers."

"We didn't know another team was coming in today," Kota said.

"We weren't going to, but then we didn't have anything to do today. At least my team didn't. Thought we'd at least come check out the place." He turned to the girls.

The three girls stood close together, and I got the feeling they had followed the guy team over but they weren't really familiar with them. "Us, too," said one of them. She had long brown hair, wore a brown sweater, and had brown glasses. "We wanted to set our tent up. We like getting to places early."

"We did a sweep of the camp," Ian said. "There's a couple of girl rangers that live in a trailer on the grounds, and the guy is in the booth right now. He'll leave for the night. I hope no one else decides to come in after he takes off later."

"There's another campground, though," the girl in brown said. "It's a few miles out, but other campers might stop here, thinking this is it. It's a camp for hunters."

As they started talking about the campgrounds, what was close, and where their tents were, Nathan, Luke, and Gabriel moved in, joining Kota.

I lingered behind, standing next to Victor. He started to move forward but stopped when I grabbed his shirt and didn't move.

He paused and looked over his shoulder at me with his eyebrows up, a spark of curiosity simmering the fire in his eyes. "Sang? You okay?"

Was I ready for this? After this morning, I'd assumed I had a whole night with the guys to myself before I needed to prepare myself for meeting other people. My heart was beating a mile a minute. What was I supposed to do? I looked at the boys and the girls but wasn't sure what would happen now.

C. L. Stone

Suddenly, one of the guys looked right at me and nodded. "What about her team?" he said. "We didn't see another girl team around." He spoke directly to me then. "Where's your campsite?"

Kota started to do a side shuffle to block me from view but then stopped, shoulders relaxing. "She's with us," he said.

Curiosity filled all of their eyes. Ian spoke, "She's new, huh? That's cool." He smiled at me. "Sorry, I don't mean to talk around you. There's plenty of new recruits showing up this week. You won't be the only one."

Kota coughed. "Yeah, for now, she's staying at our camp," he said in a final tone.

"Are you hungry?" North asked, motioning to the picnic area. "We probably have enough hot dogs for everyone."

Grateful when North changed the subject, I eased closer to Victor, but he didn't grab my hand. I sensed it might not have been appropriate to do so.

Nathan joined me on my other side. I shared long looks with both him and Victor: *Don't leave me.*

Maybe they were Academy, but I didn't want to be separated from either of them. I was suddenly realizing there were going to be other people around, and they'd ask so many questions about me. I wasn't sure what to tell them—I wasn't prepared.

I suddenly had a million questions to ask the guys about what I should say. The only thing I'd prepared for was the end when I'd declare that I wanted to stay with the guys.

Nathan and Victor seemed to understand and when we returned to the table, they sat down on the bench, leaving just enough room for me between them.

Ian, Kota, and Silas talked about dragging over another table from a nearby camp and then left to go find the closest one, taking a guy from the other team. The third guy talked to North at the grill, watching as North turned them over with tongs.

The girls sat down on the picnic table bench across from us.

"Do you all want anything to drink?" Luke asked, standing at the far end of the table. He slapped his hand to his face, rolling his eyes. "Why do I feel like I want to say 'Welcome to Bob's' suddenly?"

"I dream about waiting tables at Bob's sometimes," Gabriel said. He stood next to Luke and then turned toward one of the coolers that were parked in a sand dune nearby. "We've got sodas and water."

"I could use a coffee," one of the girls said. She had an oval face and while she had brown hair like the other girls, hers was up in a sloppy bun in the back of her head. She sat to the left of the girl who wore brown, who was in the middle. "But I guess it's wishful thinking at this point. I only brought instant, but even that won't taste right without some hot water. I brought an electric stove, but I didn't see a place to plug it in except for the bathrooms."

"There's a picnic area," Nathan said. "It's on the map. It's got a couple of shelter areas, but I didn't see any outlets. There might be some, though. I think I remember seeing bare lights inside."

Gabriel opened another cooler and fished out two flavors of Frappuccinos: mocha and vanilla. "I don't suppose you like these."

The girl's eyebrows lifted and she started to smile, reaching out for the vanilla bottle. "It's coffee and it's in front of me. I'll take one. Thanks."

"You really need to work on your addiction," the girl in brown said. She tilted her sharp face as she peered over the table to the open ice chest. "I'll take a Sprite if you have one."

Gabriel passed me the mocha coffee in his hand and then fished out other drinks for the others.

Coffee girl's face was neatly made up, her skin looking smooth and contrasted with dark red lipstick. She pulled off the plastic safety wrapper and then snapped open the lid with a pop. "Ah," she said and then grinned at me. "Isn't that the best sound in the world?"

I wasn't so sure, but I shook mine and opened it, giving

169

her a small smile when mine popped the same way hers had.

Luke chugged half of a bottle of Coke and then wiped at his lips. "I'm starving."

"The smell is making me hungry," the girl in brown said. "What's your name again? Sorry."

"Luke," he said. "Wait, what's your name?"

"April," she said. She pointed to coffee girl. "And this is Taylor and..."

"Ha!" Luke said, cutting her off. He pointed to North and then back at himself. "Our last name is Taylor."

April laughed, smoothing the sleeve of her brown shirt. "They let brothers on the same team?"

"Stepbrothers," North said. "But we're still family."

"That's rare," Ian said. "And you've got such a big team."

"There's actually two more," Kota said. "They'll be here tomorrow."

"I barely recognize some of you," he said. "But then we couldn't make it to the camp last year. You all must have grown some."

"I remember you," Taylor said, nodding toward Gabriel. "You had the same hair and earrings last year, but you were shorter."

"There's always so many people to meet at once, you easily forget faces," April said, absently twisting her coffee lid.

"I think that's why it's so many of us in one place at one time," Kota said. "It's not always good to remember all of our faces. There's some security in that."

The others introduced themselves. I was half paying attention, more aware of the girls across from me. I was studying them, imagining they knew so much about the Academy. They were a team. What did they do?

April took a long sip and then wiped her lips on the sleeve of her gray sweater. "This is good. I was about to get the headache."

The third girl, Emma, who had already downed half a bottle of water finally spoke. "We've been walking forever," she said. She was chubbier than the other girls, with round cheeks that made her square face appear softer when she turned her head. She had bright blue eyes, a striking contrast to her brown hair. "This camp is huge and the map isn't great. It's outdated and wrong about some things."

Nathan perked up. "Maybe that's what we should do this afternoon. We could make a new map."

That started a discussion about how one starts a map and how we could scour the campgrounds, and then who would track everything.

I leaned into Victor. I was interested in making a map, but my voice was gone right now.

Victor was quiet, too, not joining in the conversation. He leaned into me but did nothing else. His eyes flickered to life with a low flame of curiosity.

When Kota returned with Silas and the other guys, towing another table, Nathan jumped up to give them a hand. They settled the table at the end of the first, making one long table together.

"Good," North said, piling hot dogs on a plate. "These almost burned."

There were black grill marks on the hot dogs but they looked fine. There was a flurry of movement as Luke got out more drinks for everyone. Each one of us got a hot dog and bun, and bags of chips got passed around. There were basic ketchup and mustard passed around.

I sat quietly through the bustle. Victor made my hot dog. Nathan made sure I had enough corn chips on my plate. It was easier to be out of the way rather than bumping into everyone trying to reach for anything. I told them thank you.

"Aw," April said. She'd finished her coffee and had gotten a second one. She looked over at Nathan with a smile. "You guys are so sweet to her. That's so nice to see."

Nathan, Victor, and I shared glances, and then I happened to look to Kota.

Kota's attention had shifted to us. He stood at the head of the table, a plate in his hand. He smiled weakly. "I hope it's not inappropriate," he said.

Taylor put up her hand to stop him and put down her Sprite to speak. "No, guys, you don't understand. So many girls these days complain about guys doing nice things, that some have stopped doing them because they don't know what to do. Opening doors, or fetching a soda. Those are things you can ask your friends or family to do, but if a guy offers to do it for his girlfriend, suddenly it's an issue."

"Oh my god, I hate that," said Emma. Her bright blue eyes opened wider as she spoke. "There was a girl—not Academy—but she got a compliment about her hair that she just had done. Some guy complimented it... and she yelled at him about how sexist he was." She sighed and shook her head. "I feel like the level of girls trying to fight for equality goes a little overboard in some areas. Compliments and niceties should be extended on either side. We shouldn't be complaining. We should be offering niceties back."

April picked up her hot dog. "I'll admit, I like the change of thinking in some areas, but attacking nice deeds is getting out of hand. I've opened doors for other people, including guys. And I rather like the door being opened for me. The way some girls talk, I'm supposed to yell at you about being sexist."

Gabriel spoke up. "What the hell?" he said. He looked right at me. "So you're supposed to snap at me when I open a door for you now?"

"No!" All three of the girls said together. They looked at each other and laughed.

April continued, pointing at me but looking at Gabriel. "Listen, don't start this. Open her door. It's a nice thing. She might open your door, too. But some girls, if a girl opens a door for another girl, they're okay with it, they say it's nice. If it's a guy, though, they say it's sexist, like they assume she can't open her own door."

"It's just wrong, though," April said. "I mean, okay, sometimes you have to be a little careful, but you should always be respectful and realize if someone is doing a nice thing for you."

"Doesn't look like you guys have that issue," Emma said to me. "Sometimes you work out in the field and you have to pretend to get friendly with people." She looked right at me. "You'll see. You have to be aware of social trends, be prepared to talk to anyone."

Me? Talk to anyone? I looked at the others. Did I need to learn social trends, like yelling at guys who opened doors for me?

"Hey," Nathan said, looking at Kota to get his attention. "We're talking about making a new map of the camp since this one is outdated."

Kota liked the idea and the dynamic changed as it turned into a plan. It was Ian, April, and Kota who started organizing who should do what.

I thought of things to say, but the others talked so fast and freely, that I never got a chance to say anything at all. I finished my hot dog and chips before anyone else because they were talking so much, seeming to forget about food.

The only other one who was quiet was Victor. He finished his plate, too, and then I felt his hand on my leg. He squeezed encouragingly.

I held onto his leg, too. I craved that stability the support of having him close.

I was about to face a week of activity with other Academy people. The two groups were friendly and helpful, what I'd witnessed in the guys, especially when I was first getting to know them. They were so eager to help and to jump in and get things done. These new faces seemed to ignite energy into them, and the plan to map the campground sent a wave of excitement through them all.

I shared glimpses with Victor, though, and while I was curious about the other teams, nothing changed in my heart. I wanted to stay with them. In a small way, I didn't want to know other teams at all. Being around them meant I couldn't hold hands or do other things with the guys. It meant watching what I said. I didn't know if they'd ask me personal questions and what I should say if they asked simple things like about my parents or school.

When Kota talked about mixing up the groups to help scout, my hand tightened on Victor's leg. The new teams seemed okay, but I wasn't really ready to get mixed together with other teams yet. What would I talk about with them?

His grip on my thigh held firm, his thumb slowly rubbing back and forth.

I leaned into him. "Stay with me?" I asked, hoping that no one could hear it but him. I didn't want to appear rude, but I felt a little awkward at the notion of teaming up with the others when I didn't know them that well.

He leaned in and whispered, his lips against my ear. "I will. Don't worry. You won't be out of our sight while we're at camp. Ever."

I knew he'd never break his promise. I swallowed back a little wave of emotion and tried to calm my nerves.

Luke spoke up loudly, drawing our attention. "Sang should be on my team since I'll be doing the drawing," he said. "She's got the best sense of direction."

"I can help," Ian said. He took off his baseball cap, scratched at his short brown hair and then put his cap back on. "I can draw a decent map."

"She can come with the girls if she wants to," April said.

Victor almost spoke up Taylor beat him to it. "I don't think we should split up like that," she said. "I know it's fun, but we should really focus on our skills. You'd be better with..." She looked at Luke and then Kota. "Well, let's figure out a plan."

Emma had brought her tablet and turned it on, and someone pulled up a Google map of the island, showing a bird's eye view. We compare it to someone else's phone showing a Google Earth overview, but it was hard to see any roads through the trees. We looked at the map given to us by the camp, and then another paper road map someone had picked up at a nearby gas station. It showed the roads and the entrance to the camp, but none of the details of the campground itself.

Kota pointed to the campground map. "This is our site, on the north side of the island. There's a few trails on the south side of camp, but I don't know how far they go before you hit wild section of woods. Somewhere beyond that set of woods is the other camp, the hunting camp, but it's a good few miles."

"We could go south along the beach," Ian said. "And mark on a map where there are paths going in and where they lead."

"And then follow the last path in again and make sure they connect with the camp properly," Kota said. "Start in the corner and work our way in. We could go," He pointed to Ian, himself and Nathan in turn, and then looked at the girls. "Are any of you wearing boots?"

Emma raised her hand. "And thick jeans—the brush is pretty thick."

Kota nodded. "You can join us if you'd like. We'll be in deep woods, though. We might need to go get some bug spray and water. I've got radios we can use back at camp, but I've only got nine."

"We should only carry maybe two per team, making sure to leave one for Luke and whoever stays with him to draw the map," Ian said.

"I'll stay with him," one of the guys said. I couldn't see who it was from where I was sitting, but Luke waved and gave a thumbs-up.

Kota pointed back to the map. "And then the rest of you can split up, following the main roads. There should be cabins and an RV section as well. Let's make sure we know where everything."

"Do we need put echo trackers for the campground managers or the rangers?" one of the guys of the other team asked. "Do we need to worry about that?"

Kota touched at the corner of his glasses, looking at the map but clearly thinking. He looked up at me and then at the camp's map. "I don't think we really need to. Unless they start getting too nosey about us. Do we have supplies just in case?"

"I've got trackers," the guy said.

"I've got some, too," Victor said. "They're in my car."

"We could put them on their cars now without much harm," the guys said. "So when they drive out, we'll know."

"Better to put them on their shoes," Victor said. "They might not take a car with them everywhere."

Mouths fell open across the table.

"You put them in shoes?" several people asked together.

The question surprised me. I hadn't been surprised to hear their suggestion to track the rangers, as I'd heard them track with phones. But why were the other teams' members shocked? What kind of things did other Academy groups do?

"They don't last very long," Victor said. "Because when you walk, it puts pressure on the devices and they can break."

"And no big battery support," Luke said.

Victor continued. "But they'll go for a while with a fresh battery on them, and by mid-week, we should know their patterns well enough. I'd say tap their cell phones, but it's a little extreme and there's hardly any signal out here."

"They probably have radios, too, though," April said. She leaned on the table with her hands pressed to the wood. "We could keep the signal going with the battery attached to it."

Victor shook his head and made gestures with his hands like holding a radio. "Radios are trickier because they pick up on signals and will create feedback noises. It might be more noticeable, probably not worth it." He smirked. "Speculation of course. We don't need to do all this but always good to think it out just in case."

Ian blew a breath out from between his lips. "What kind of jobs do they have you all on that you're doing this type of stuff?"

"PE classes," Nathan said with a small smirk.

"And lunch," Luke said and chuckled.

"This is nothing," Gabriel said.

"It's a long story," Kota said. "But let's focus on this map making."

Everyone split up as evenly as we could. Gabriel would

come with my group to fix the faded signs along the way using paint one of the girls had on hand.

Luke and Victor decided it was better if they teamed up to introduce themselves to the rangers, and also scope out their place and determine if we needed to worry about them.

Gabriel, Silas and I were joined by Taylor and April. Before we left, April grabbed one more coffee for the road.

"I'm going to have to grab some more for you for the rest of the week," Gabriel whispered to me as we fell behind the two girls. "She does have a coffee addiction."

Taylor—who seemed to be her team's leader—led the way, giving us directions. April stayed up front with her while I walked with Gabriel and Silas trailed behind us.

After a stop for the girls to get the paint, we tracked back to the road that came in from the main gate. Starting there, we took every right until we hit the end of the paved road areas. April wrote on the map where things were. Gabriel painted signs along the way.

I walked beside Silas, saying nothing and following along.

It took up a good portion of the rest of the afternoon to get through even half of the campground, and there were roads that continued beyond where we were focusing on, turning from paved to gravel. It was suspected the gravel roads led to campsite areas, although one sign marked a path as a hiking trail.

We stopped to let Gabriel paint the marker.

"They gravel their hiking trails?" April asked, holding the map and a pen. "That's kind of distracting on a hike."

"It might just be the start of the trial," Taylor said. She blew a breath out and shifted some of her long brown hair away from her sharp-featured face. "This might be a two-day job. We're not covering nearly enough ground, and it'll get dark soon."

"We could split up," April said. "Cover more ground and get more done."

"I don't know if that's a good idea," Gabriel said,

painting white letters on the wood post. "We've only got the one radio."

"Those with the radio should be the ones going out in the gravel sections," Taylor said.

"I don't like the idea of splitting up, though," Gabriel said. He looked up toward the cloud-covered sky, through the tops of trees. "You could end up on the other side of the camp in the dark."

"Girls aren't afraid of the dark," Taylor said. She looked at me and winked. "Are we?"

I shrugged in reply. I really didn't want to be far away from our camp in the dark, especially when the temperature was starting to drop. My tongue hadn't moved the entire time we were out. I wasn't needed as a directional navigator since we were following the roads.

Taylor lifted a brown eyebrow. "Do you talk at all? I don't think I've heard your voice yet."

I smothered a frown. I didn't like getting pressured into talking. I didn't really have anything to say.

"She talks when she wants to," Silas said, his voice spooking even me. The others jumped slightly, except for Gabriel, who remained focused on the sign.

"She's fine," Gabriel said. "All I'm saying is that it's getting late. It's going to get really fucking cold soon. This isn't an emergency map-making project. We should focus on the paved roads as much as we can and then head back. We can get up early in the morning, and finish out the paved road maps before the others get here."

"We should have taken a car," April said. "It would have been faster getting from place to place."

"Someone can do that tomorrow," Gabriel said. He stopped his painting, stood up straight, and wiped his forehead with the back of his hand. "Take the gravel roads and see how far they stretch out. If we took a car on these main roads, we would have been getting in and out to see what was where."

April continued walking up the paved road. Taylor hadn't stopped looking at me since Gabriel had changed the subject.

I looked down at the road and started following April, walking next to Silas.

Taylor lingered back behind us and then came next to me, making me drift even closer to Silas.

When we got to the next sign, April worked with Gabriel to interpret what the sign was trying to say. Then Gabriel painted while April marked the spot on her map.

"So you guys go to high school?" Taylor asked Silas and I as we waited, but she was mostly looking at me.

I turned to Silas. I knew she was just trying to get me to talk, and I didn't like it if she at all understood I didn't want to. It felt like almost a challenge.

"Yeah," he said, and that was all.

Taylor's eyes shifted slowly from me to Silas and then back to me again. "You, too?"

"Yeah, she does," Silas said before I even opened my mouth.

I pressed my lips together after that, willing to let Silas answer for me and let him be my voice right now. It wasn't to be mean or rude, but Taylor made it awkward with her obvious desire to hear from me.

Taylor lifted a brown eyebrow and it disappeared behind her bangs. "What's it like?"

Had she not gone to high school? Then again, I remembered the boys didn't go to a normal high school before, either. They'd gone to a regular elementary school, but I didn't think they'd returned to a normal school until this year. Were all Academy students taken out of public schools?

"It's shit," Gabriel said. "We're in a fucking dump of a school so we can—."

April smirked and rapped him on the head with the map. "Your momma let you curse like that?"

Gabriel covered his head with an arm, ducking away. "God. So-o-orry. Let me shut my mouth."

"There's homework," Silas said. "You study enough to get the answers right and then forget it again to study another test. Really hard to learn anything when it's short term

179

memorization."

April's smile dissolved. "You really don't learn anything?"

Gabriel straightened after finishing painting on the post and put the cap on the paint. "It's stupid. The teachers don't really care if you learn anything, just as long as you fill in bubbles on tests. If you get something wrong, they don't go over it and help you. There might be a lecture, but half of the time we're reading out of those boring textbooks in class. Half of the stuff doesn't even matter. Will I ever be held at gunpoint and asked the specific date Eisenhower came into office? Probably not. Better they teach me how to look it up on Google."

"You don't use a computer?" April asked.

"Fu-nope," Gabriel said, catching his curse after getting an evil eye from April. "We just read textbooks. But then you've got these tests where you have to come up with all the dates and stupid details. Can't even use your phone; you have to memorize lots of useless material. I'm not saying it isn't interesting stuff, or it couldn't be if presented in a good way, but there's so much important stuff they don't even bother with. Practical things like how to manage money, do taxes."

"Balance a checkbook," Silas said.

"How to change a tire," Gabriel said. "None of those kids know how. They don't even train them to how to look it up, or even who you call."

Taylor slowly shook her head, her eyes wide. "That's crazy. That's like basic entry-level Academy stuff."

I was trying to appear casual, but my heart was beating a mile a minute. *I* didn't know how to balance a checkbook. I didn't know the details of how to change a tire, although I thought I could figure it out...but was I really sure? I rubbed my nose with my gloved hand, as if warming the chill on my skin, but more to hide the blush.

I had a thousand questions—ones I didn't dare ask—mostly about what Academy classes were like. I wanted to ask Silas or the others after we got away from the girls.

But would we get away from the girls later? Or the other guys, for that matter? Taylor made me nervous. I didn't get a sense that she was a bad person, but she was overly curious about me, and it made me uncomfortable to have her staring and asking questions.

It suddenly got a lot darker.

Gabriel lifted his head, concentrating on the clouds. "Sun's down over the trees. We should head back."

Taylor groaned. "You know what the worst feeling is? A job half done."

"We'll do more in the morning," Gabriel said. "We got a late start today. When's the initial group meet up?"

"Nine, maybe," Taylor said. "Maybe earlier."

"Then we'll have a few hours if we're up at dawn," he said.

Taylor made a pouty face but then reached for the map April held. "If we head this way..." She looked up, glancing up the road we were on, then swiveled her head. "Hang on, I got turned around. Which way is the beach?"

April reached to pull out her phone, as did Silas, but then I pointed east, toward the beach beyond the trees.

Taylor focused on me, her eyebrows raised. "That's the beach?"

I nodded. I would have said yes, but my tongue felt stuck after not talking for so long. I didn't mind talking as long as it didn't feel like a silly challenge.

"Okay," she said. "I trust you." She looked at the map again and then pointed to a side road winding eastward. "If we follow that, there's one more turn and then we should be back at that spot on the beach. And it's a road we haven't been down yet, so we should be able to map it on the way."

"Good job, Trouble," Gabriel said. He came over and wrapped an arm around my shoulders as we walked on. "All this painting and walking makes me want another hot dog. Even cold ones. Something about camping makes me hungry."

I said nothing but smiled over at Gabriel. As I did, I caught Taylor leaning toward April, talking quietly to her.

April's eyes drifted to me.

I was sure they had as many questions about me as I had about the Academy. This was just one team, too. Soon—tomorrow—I'd face who knew how many more, and many of them would have questions. My spine prickled with the thought of so many questions to answer, the whispers, the eyes on me.

I was an oddball. They'd said it wasn't normal for a girl to be on a guy team.

If I joined with the guys, I might never escape the whispers and questions for as long as I stayed within the Academy.

I'd once longed to be normal, but now maybe I wouldn't ever be.

Would I be able to last the week? At the end of it, would I be strong enough to say I wanted to stay with them?

♥

A **C**AMP *A*T *N*IGHT

*T*he other teams returned to the beach as they finished. The rangers didn't seem interested in us, according to Victor and Luke. They even told them about updating their map, which they appreciated. No one had done it in years.

Luke collected maps. He and Ian drew a more up-to-date version with what everyone had managed to piece together.

Eventually, Ian and Taylor decided to take their teams back to their own campsites. It was getting dark and cold and they wanted to get to sleep early so they could be up at dawn to help with the final parts of the map.

I had been quiet the entire time and remained so as I followed the guys back to our own camp. I tried not to think about other teams being around. In a way, I'd hoped it would be more like school when everyone finally showed up. I could blend in a little more, and become a forgettable face in the crowd.

No one held my hand or did much more than the odd friendly pat or offer a nice comment. It normally wasn't a big deal, but now I was questioning my every move. No one had said anything about how we should act around each other, but were we supposed to not give the impression we were more than just friends?

I wanted to ask, but as soon as full night hit, it was getting very cold out. The boys tried to teach me how to light the campfire near their tent, but I was shivering pretty hard to strike flint. I made a few sparks but it was hurting my fingers. Kota ended up getting it going, saying I was on the right track.

Kota had us take out lanterns that were now scattered about the site. We huddled together on the rocks around the fire pit in front of the boys' tent, watching the flames and listening to the crackles and pops of the burning logs.

The latrine lights were on, but from where we were, it sent up a spooky gray glow above the trees nearby.

As a group, we visited the bathrooms, with Silas and Nathan checking my side for spiders before I went in. I used the restroom and washed my face and hands in the sink. If I kept on top of keeping clean, maybe I wouldn't get so grungy down the road. I felt sand in my shoes, but I figured we'd all be stuck with that for the week.

Back at camp, I sat between Silas—the human furnace— and Nathan, who cuddled close. I was hoping Kota would come back and sit down, but he was constantly up checking things, running back and forth from the tent and looking at stuff on the map we'd created. He never seemed to stop long enough to relax.

We ate sandwiches because no one wanted to cook other than heating marshmallows over the fire. No one wanted to move away from the heat.

"It'll be different tomorrow," North said. "We'll be more used to the cold."

"It's going to drop down close to thirty-four tonight," Kota said. "Almost cold enough to snow."

I bit my lip, thinking of my tent far away from the others. That was really cold. I'd freeze to death.

I was stuck, though. One night. There was no guarantee other nights would be any warmer and I wanted to get my one night in my own tent over with.

While I wanted to talk to the others, the fire was mesmerizing and I could only stare while thoughts whirled around in my head. I kept my glove-covered hands tucked into my arms, my knees and face warmed by the heat. My hat was doing okay but I was thinking of a blanket and bed so that I could get the first night over with.

Yet, I didn't want to sleep yet, because that meant I'd be up for tomorrow, and I wasn't sure I was ready for tomorrow.

I hadn't been prepared for people to show up so soon, and

I was working through what had happened. Embarrassment rattled through me as I thought of the others finding us dancing. I knew it wasn't a big deal, but that normally wasn't something I would do in front of anyone else. Not talking at first made it harder to talk at all as the day drew on, and eventually, it seemed like it was best if I didn't.

What could I have to say to anyone?

The guys talked about the map and the other teams.

"She said I've grown up," Gabriel said. He sat closest to the fire, and from where I was sitting, it looked like his knees were practically in the flames. He huddled on the log he was sitting on, his hat low on his head, his jacket tight as he hugged himself. "Did I really get taller? It doesn't feel like it."

"You keep buying new pants," Kota said. "You haven't noticed?"

"And she hit me for cursing."

"You've been slipping a lot more lately. I told you once you make it a habit, you might not be able to control it. Not everyone sees them as just words."

"Yeah, well, not everyone likes violence either."

"She hit you with paper," Silas said, his deep voice rumbling through me.

"And the corner of it got me in the scalp," Gabriel said, pointing at his hat. He rubbed at the ribs of the material near the top of his ear. "I could have gotten a papercut."

"If you're that offended, you should have said something," North said.

"Will you all let me gripe? Can't I talk shit about another team a little without the therapy session? Geeze. I'm just talking."

Kota stood on the other side of the fire, opposite to me. The glow lit up his face in an almost spooky way, reflecting off his glasses, the flickering shadows making him look fierce. He put his hands on his hips to address us. "Well, it's not getting any warmer out here. Do we want to call it an early night? I know it's just after eight but might as well try. We should get up before dawn to take advantage of the light when it comes up to finish the maps. It'll be a long day tomorrow."

There were a lot of grunts but North stood up, and then Victor. That seemed to be enough to motivate the rest of them to get moving.

I didn't want to get up because it meant going to my tent by myself. I'd already promised I would, and while I didn't want to, I had to endure it for one night.

I stared off to the fire as others started moving around me, putting things away and getting ready for bed. Nathan and Silas had stood up, picking up lanterns and helping to put out the fire. Luke and Victor wandered off to the latrine once more.

I was thinking about how I was supposed to be getting some time with Kota but was running out of opportunities if the rest of the Academy would be arriving tomorrow.

"You look sleepy," Kota said from behind me.

I nodded, but really, I was sure I'd be awake most of the night, again, going over what I would talk to him and other campers about tomorrow. I'd been distracted all day and lost my focus on whatever I was supposed to tell him about. Could I do it now?

Not to mention it was freezing. I'd probably be up all night shivering. Do tents really keep you that warm?

I breathed in some courage and started to rise, but when I turned toward him, he was gone, lifting a cooler to put it in the back of the Jeep.

Maybe now wasn't a good time anyway. I was tired and nervous, unsure what to say. He was probably tired, too.

Maybe spending the night in the tent by myself, proving that I was part of the group, would be a good thing to talk to him about in the morning. I could ask him to take a walk with me, or perhaps escort me to the latrine and talk to him there.

With a plan in place, going back to the tent to try to get some sleep seemed like a good idea. I'd need more energy for everything tomorrow.

I didn't want to freeze once the fire was put out before getting a head start to my tent. "I'll just take one of the lamps with me, I guess."

"Oy," Gabriel called from just outside the big tent. He stood with his arms wrapped tightly around his chest, his teeth clenched. He shifted from foot to foot. "Where do you think you're going?"

"I'm gonna go find my tent," I said. "And get some sleep."

"Aw no," Gabriel said. "You've got to stay here with us. It's too cold out there. And it's dark. There's bears."

"Nope," I said. "I'm going to my tent. You said I had to."

Kota had returned from the Jeep, coming toward the tent now that most everything else was put away. He took off his glasses and used a cloth from his pocket to clear the dust from the lenses. "You did say that," he said with a squinty glare at Gabriel.

"Your tent doesn't have a heater," Gabriel said. "You can't stay in there. Didn't I just say bears? I'm sure there's a bear over there right now."

"You can't lie to get her to do what you want her to do," Kota said.

Was he lying about the heat or the bear?

"Kota, make her stay," Gabriel said. "She can't be out there alone."

"You started this," Kota said.

"Goodnight," I said and marched off toward the trees. The more Gabriel pushed, the more I wanted to do this. Being part of their team meant so much to me that I would do everything they said they'd done. Kota would think I was brave and capable.

I headed toward the line of trees, to the small trail that stretched between the sites. I listened for someone following but didn't hear anything except Gabriel still arguing with Kota about why I should come back.

As I strolled away from them, I realized I hadn't taken a lamp with me. Clouds had cleared once the sun had set, giving us some view of the stars and a glowing half-moon. I could follow the path on the other side easily, and the tent stood out among the dark landscape. I marched, lifting my feet so I wouldn't trip over anything, and headed straight for the tent.

I climbed inside, but then nearly fell over a pile of stuff. Had some of my things shifted? I had placed a lot of it along the back and sides so I'd have room to get in. I zipped up my tent and then secured a lock on the zipper. The lock came with the zipper so I assumed it was to keep animals...or people out.

I used the phone I had in my bra for a light and looked around. There was a cot set up along the back side of the tent, along with a stereo in a different spot, and a small electric heater hooked up to a battery unit. There were also carefully placed items like the iPad and a light hanging off the side of the tent. I turned it on, checking out the set up so I could turn my phone off and put it down on the little cot.

Kota and the others must have set things up for me, knowing I was determined to sleep out here. I didn't think a cot would have fit, but there it was with my sleeping bag unrolled on top of it.

If I was going to be out here alone, they'd made sure I would be comfortable. It was sweet. I hoped they knew I wouldn't continue to stay out here, though, if I had the chance to stay in their tent tomorrow.

Still, maybe while I was on my own tonight, I could work out how I'd handle tomorrow with all those other people. If I tossed and turned all night thinking, I wouldn't keep anyone else awake.

I tucked the thought away, sitting on the cot and clicking the heater on. I wanted to get into bed quickly and let my body warm up the sleeping bag to keep me warm along with the heater. I turned on the stereo, finding some familiar music, similar to what Luke had on his phone. He must have made a CD for me.

I thought of sleeping in my clothes, but there was a bit of sand in my shoes, and I wanted to keep the sleeping bag as sand-free as possible. I rushed to get out of my clothes, leaving them in a pile on the ground before brushing off my feet and then slipping into a T-shirt and pink flannel pants. While it was freezing, the heater was starting to warm the space up. I adjusted it to point at the cot. I jumped into the sleeping bag on the cot, finding a pillow and settled in.

The coolness of the sleeping bag faded as my body warmed it. I ended up getting up only once to scoot the heater closer, warming the underside of my cot a little. I hoped the power wouldn't run out before morning. I'd have to leave it on all night. I wondered where I would have to charge it for tomorrow.

About an hour later, while I had dozed a little, I wasn't really sleeping. I counted and listened to the music to avoid thinking but it didn't work. I felt tired, but between the new place, a lack of someone else around, and the expectations for tomorrow my brain was working in overdrive to try to piece together some solutions.

The problem was, there wasn't a solution. I didn't know what to expect, so speculating was pointless and just made me more tired.

Over the sound of music playing on the stereo, there was a rustle outside my tent.

I turned over in the bag to listen. I'd had a feeling one of them might come to check on me, but I was also aware it might be one of the other Academy people checking the place out, so I stayed still and quiet. Hopefully, if it was Taylor or the other girls coming to check on me, they'd think I was asleep.

Or it might be animals.

I suddenly wondered about the bears. And the coyotes.

It was Hunting Island, after all.

A faint shadow came close to the door of my tent.

I watched it, waiting. Would a bear make that shape?

It bent down like it was looking for the zipper of the tent.

"Oy," Gabriel called softly. "Trouble."

I sighed in relief. Not a bear. "Meanie?" I wanted to stay in bed, fearing the cold; if I had to spend the night here, I didn't want to get up and freeze.

He fiddled with the door, tugging on the lock. "Open up."

I lifted an eyebrow, staring at his shadow. "Why?"

"Let me in."

"Nu-uh," I said, not moving. "I'm fine. Did you need something?"

He yanked at the outside of the tent door, causing the material to flutter. "Yeah. You. Open up and let me in. It's cold."

I sat up but kept the sleeping bag tucked around me. "Go back to your tent."

"You're not staying out here by yourself," he said. "It's too cold. There's wild animals. It's not safe. You're too far away. Open up."

"No," I said. "*You* said I had to spend the night by myself."

"You're not doing that shit tonight. There's bears and it's freezing. You really shouldn't go camping by yourself anyway. Open up." He yanked at the door again as if he were going to rip it. "Come unlock this thing."

"No," I said. "Go away. I'm trying to sleep."

"Sang, you either let me in, or you come back with me to the big tent. Let me in and we'll just count it to say you slept all night in here."

I fell back onto the bed. Was he that worried about bears? "That doesn't count. You're the one who said I had to spend the night out here by myself." I'd curl up and sleep, even if he was standing out there all night.

"You're not sleeping out here alone," he said.

"Why not?" I asked. "You're not going to let me do the rite of passage?"

"I told you. It's not safe," he said. "Unlock the zipper thing."

"Nu-uh," I said.

"It's too cold for this. Trouble, I'm going to count to three. If you don't open..."

I didn't totally disagree with him, but it felt like I couldn't give in so easily. That and I didn't really want to get up when I was already warm. It wasn't the best but I thought I could sleep through it. If he just left me alone tonight, it'd be over and I could say I did it.

I hit the buttons on the stereo and turned the music up loud to drown him out. I wasn't going to the big tent. He was trying to mess with me and I didn't want to be the one who chickened out of sleeping in the tent alone.

Beat It started playing.

Gabriel quieted for a moment. "Are you... are you telling me to fuck off with that song?"

"Go away," I called to him, turning the music up even louder. I hadn't noticed what the song was, I just wanted to tune him out. The song choice was a coincidence, but it made a nice point.

"Oh my fucking god, Sang. That's it. That's not even Michael Jackson. That's Fall Out Boy."

There was shuffling outside. I tensed, ready for him to pick the lock or break it so he could get in. I wondered if I should yell for Kota. He seemed to think it was fine.

Suddenly the top of the tent started to cave in on one side. I sat up in a shot. He was pulling up the stakes!

There was a snap, and the tent billowed as it fell. The material covered me over the sleeping bag, and I reached up, giving myself some breathing room. The heater knocked over and automatically shut off. It got cold quickly.

"Gabriel!" I cried out, my voice squeaking by the end. Words twisted on my lips and I couldn't get out what I wanted to say though it would have been mostly a lot of name-calling.

Gabriel climbed over until he was sitting on me on top of the tent. His weight sank into my thighs as he trapped me. "I will fucking sit here all night until you get out. You can't sleep out here by yourself with bears walking around."

He'd been talking about bears so much, I wondered if he didn't psych himself scared for my life thinking about them. I struggled and punched him, mostly mad that I was being sat on, but he wasn't moving. I yanked the phone out, but in the dark, I couldn't figure out where the button was. Gabriel rolled his butt against my body, and I dropped the phone somewhere beyond the cot. I couldn't reach it after that.

"I'll get up when you promise to come back to the big tent," he said. "I'm not going to let you freeze to death tonight."

"Silas!" I tried to cry out, but my voice broke and the word was no more than a squeak. I punched at Gabriel. "Gabriel," I cried out. "Get off of me."

"Are you coming back with me?"

"No!" I cried. "I'm going to fix my tent, kick your butt and then I'm going to sleep in my tent all night. You told me I had to sleep alone. I'm going to do it. I was fine until you came by. There's no bears. The heater was on. Now fix my tent and let me go to sleep."

Gabriel bounced and settled on top of me harder. "Joke's on you. I broke your tent. You're too far away and you can't scream if something came in after you. You're not going to sleep with a whistle in your mouth to choke on. I've thought it all out and you can't sleep out here alone."

He did have a point, but I kept punching at him through the tarp anyway. I was so worked up, I didn't care if he was right. I was just so mad he broke my tent to get me to come out.

"Sang," Nathan called out.

"Nathan!" I called back, relieved. "Get Gabriel."

There was some shuffling, and suddenly Gabriel was gone from on top of me. I tugged the tent up on my head, giving myself space to find my way to the door. My body quaked, shivering as the collapsed tent seemed to stick to my skin, prickling me with cold until my bones were rattling together.

"*Aggele*," Silas called. "You okay?"

"Kick Gabriel," I said, trying to find the zipper. "He broke my tent."

"Aw," Nathan said. "Peanut, you okay? Can you get out?"

I shifted through the tent material, trying to find the lock. "I don't know. I don't know if I can find a key now." I wasn't sure where it was, either. There was no way I'd find it in the dark.

A massive body shifted on the tent nearby. "Hang on, *Aggele*," he said. "Don't move. I'm going to cut it open."

My heart sank. Victor's gift! Silas was going to break it more. Still, it couldn't be helped. I was freezing. I couldn't stay out here looking for a little key in the dark.

Before I could protest, I heard the slash of the knife breaking through the material. The air grew intensely colder through the sudden opening. Hands reached in for me, wrapping around my body and tugging me through the hole.

Silas picked me up though I couldn't really see him or Nathan in the darkness.

"You okay?" Silas asked, holding me close, his body warming me up.

"Yeah," I said, hanging onto him, wrapping my legs around his waist to let him carry me. I finger-combed my tangled hair away from my face. "Gabriel broke my tent."

"I didn't really break it," Gabriel said. "Actually, I might have. I just pulled the stake out, but there was a snap to one…"

"Sorry," Silas said. "We'll get you another one."

Nathan fished into the tent, pulling out the heater and making sure the power was unplugged, and then shut off the stereo. He stepped back, looking things over. "Was that all you had turned on? What should we do with it?"

"Leave it for now," Silas said. "Let's come back in the morning for her stuff when we can see."

Nathan picked up the lantern and started on the path back to the other campsite. Gabriel followed behind Silas, his lips twisted into a smug smirk.

I pushed at Silas, urging him to put me down. "You mean.... Meanie," I called after Gabriel. "You ruined my tent."

He shoved his hands deep into his pockets and shrugged. "Got you out of there, didn't I? Now the bears aren't going to eat you."

"I was fine!" I lunged toward him, but Silas held me back. I couldn't believe that after all that effort I'd put into putting up the tent and the guys' putting together the nice set up for me, he had come by and ruined it. "You broke everything. How am I supposed to do the rite of passage thing now?"

I nearly slid off of Silas when he redoubled his arms around me. "Easy, *Aggele Mou*," he said. He pulled me up until I was dangling over his shoulder. "It's cold. You can fight him tomorrow. Maybe he was right. You can't fight a bear."

"I want him to sleep out in my tent," I said. I didn't care if Gabriel was right, I just wanted to argue. It felt like a defeat. "Gabriel, go sleep in my tent since you busted it."

"No," Gabriel said. "I'm going to the big tent."

"I thought you were my camping buddy."

"You can't be my camping buddy if you're sleeping in another tent. I tried to get you to let me in."

He was so frustrating! "How am I supposed to be part of the group now? You said I had to sleep by myself!"

Silas marched between the trees toward the other site. Dangling over his shoulder, it was hard to yell at him, so I let my anger smolder inside me.

When we got close to the other tent, I heard North calling after us. "What happened to her?"

"Gabriel broke my tent," I said through clenched teeth, so angry that it felt good to tattle on Gabriel. Silas set me down until I was standing. I threw my arms over my chest quickly to block out the cold.

North was in the opening of the big tent, looking out at us. He wore all black, and in the darkness, it was like his head hovered in midair. "He did, huh?" North said, his head tilting to gaze over my shoulder at Gabriel. He threw Gabriel a wicked eye, his lips tight. He side-stepped, taking part of the folded door with him, to allow the rest of us in.

"Yeah," I said, pausing outside, not caring about the grass at my feet or how cold it was. Tattling just felt too good. "He broke it so I had to come back. And then he sat on me. And then Silas had to cut it open to get me out. But it's Gabriel's fault."

"Oh," he said. "Sorry, baby." He turned to Gabriel. "You ass. You broke her tent."

"Sorry," Gabriel said though I didn't believe he meant it.

North shot out a hand, giving his head a chop. "Well don't break her shit." I started walking past North to duck into the tent when out of the corner of my eye, I caught North leaning into Gabriel. He patted him on the back and stage whispered. "Good job."

Gabriel smiled quietly to himself.

I huffed. They sent Gabriel out to bring me back. I bit my tongue, too angry and cold to argue. I'd beat them all up in the morning. Maybe I'd sleep in my own tent the rest of the week.

Not that I really wanted to sleep out there anyway. The more I thought about it, the more I was pretty sure if Gabriel had concerns and told North, North would have made the call to bring me back, due to cold and threat of bears.

If it had been Gabriel, I might have broken his tent, too, to make sure he was safe.

I was still mad, though. I couldn't help it.

The lanterns were on the floor in the tent, casting long shadows against the nylon walls, but it was enough to light up faces. The air was warmed by a similar battery powered heater.

"Sang?" Victor said, sitting up on one of the cots in the middle, sliding his sock-covered feet to the floor.

I shot a glare, ready to throw accusations, assuming they'd all been in on it.

He raised an eyebrow, lifting himself out of the cot quickly. "What happened?"

I realized he might not have known anything about what had happened. Underneath the anger, I was disheartened and sad that they had broken something Victor had paid for and had been set up so nicely for me. "They broke the tent."

"Aw," he said as he stood, holding his hands out. He came forward, enveloping me in his arms. It was a cozy hug, full of sympathy and warmth. He kissed my cheek. "I'll get you a new one."

"She doesn't need a new one," Gabriel said. I threw him an angry glare and he skirted around cots, looking at the floor with a frown, avoiding my eyes.

195

I didn't want to say more while I was still angry.

Nathan was sitting on a big, king-sized blow-up bed pressed against one wall. Luke was sitting up on one of the cots. Gabriel headed toward an empty one.

Luke patted his cot. "Come sleep back here, Sang. I can make room."

Nathan scooted until he could tug my arm while I stood next to Victor. "No way," Nathan said. "She's sleeping on the air mattress with us. There's room even with Silas on it."

Luke grunted. "Naw, let her come back here with us."

Silas entered the tent with my pink sleeping bag slung over his shoulder.

"I'll sleep next to Nathan and Silas," I said.

Luke pouted. "Aw. Why?"

"They're the ones that came to save me," I said. "And I don't want to go back there with Gabriel."

Gabriel had already climbed back into his cot, clothes still on. His hat was still on, too. He curled up, facing the wall of the tent. It almost made me feel sorry for him. He was the one willing to face the cold and bears to make sure I was okay and now he seemed so dejected.

Luke stretched out and kicked Gabriel in the head with a toe. "See what you did."

"Shut up," Gabriel said, his voice muffled. "You would have done it if I hadn't."

Silas chuckled. He dropped my sleeping bag on the air mattress between Nathan's and his own. "Finder's keepers," he said.

"I thought we were going to sleep," Kota's voice came from outside the tent. A moment later, he stepped in, dressed in pajama pants, a jacket, and a long sleeve shirt underneath. "It's cold, and it's late. Let's sleep." He blinked in surprise at me standing at the foot of the air mattress. "You came back?"

"Gabriel broke her tent," Victor said.

"Oh," Kota said, and then sat down on the cot farthest from the air mattress and took off his jacket.

He said nothing else about it. Had he been in on it, too?

Or was he not surprised by it? I smothered a sigh. Maybe none of them really wanted me to sleep out there alone, either. Gabriel was just sent to be the bad guy.

I missed them, too.

North came in, zipping up the tent behind him. "Are we all here now?"

"Yup," Gabriel said from underneath his blanket. "No thanks to any of you."

I took my spot in between Nathan and Silas, sliding into my sleeping bag and settling in.

"Let's just try to get some sleep," Kota said, smoothing out his sleeping bag and putting his glasses carefully on a little cooler near his bed. "We've got an early day tomorrow. Lights out."

Kota's request was followed by a few grumbles, but no one argued. Kota was on the very end closest to the tent door. Next to him was Victor, then North. Silas, me, and Nathan were on the mattress, and sleeping lengthwise at our heads were Luke and Gabriel.

Silas pressed close, providing some heat but not enough for me since he was wrapped up in his own sleeping bag. Nathan leaned against me on the other side. His fingers found their way to my face, and he slipped one between my lips.

I wanted to give him one of my fingers, but I was too cold to take my arm out of my sleeping bag. I chewed on his finger a little but then dozed off.

♥

$\mathcal{N}$IGHT $\mathcal{I}$N $\mathcal{A}$ $\mathcal{T}$ENT

$\mathcal{I}$ wasn't sure how much time had passed, but at I woke up freezing. Despite Silas being close to my left, and Nathan on my other side, my back and stomach were cold, even though the sleeping bag. My forehead was sticking out and cold. My feet were ice. The air from the mattress wasn't warm at all, and the tent itself had cold air throughout.

I exhaled a long puff of air, and could swear I was seeing my own breath hanging above my face.

I tried moving to my side, but my shoulders ended up freezing, and then Nathan and Silas weren't close enough. I either had to cuddle with one or the other. I tried Silas. As I got closer, he did turn into me, but I wasn't getting much heat along my stomach, and my butt and back were cold.

I moaned. My mostly-asleep brain was trying to work out a problem, and I couldn't do it if I was cold, so I was trying to figure out how not to be cold.

If I was cold, they had to be cold, too. We shouldn't sleep in the cold. I knew that. Extreme cold makes you sleepy, but if you fell asleep in it, you could die. I knew that from living up north and everything I had been taught in elementary school about staying safe during the winter. Have they ever been this cold while camping? Maybe they were so cold they were sleeping through it, and that was dangerous. "We need to get up," I said, hoping someone was awake.

I caught someone mumbling back but it faded. Either he wasn't concerned or didn't hear me. Was everyone able to sleep through this cold? What had happened to the heater?

"Silas," I said.

"What?" he asked, his deep voice vibrating the bed.

"We need to wake up."

"It's not snowing," he said.

"No. We can't sleep here."

Someone else groaned, there was a creak and thumping around, as if someone flipped over on a cot.

"North," I called. No one was listening! I was sure this was wrong. We couldn't sleep in these frigid temperatures— maybe they were groggy from the cold shutting down their brains. Freezing to death wasn't good. "North," I called again.

"Baby," North mumbled back. "Go to sleep."

"We *can't* sleep in the cold," I said, turning a little, allowing some cold air into my sleeping bag, enough that my body started to shake and rattle against the cold. "Did the heater break?"

"You can sleep," North said. "We're here. You're fine. Go to sleep."

"It's too cold," I said. "I can see my breath."

North groaned. "You've got a sleeping bag. It's not that bad."

"We can't sleep," I said. He was missing the point.

"Why can't we sleep here?"

"Because... if we sleep in the cold we may never wake up!"

There was a rustling, and I glanced over to see North sitting up. "Sang. Get your pretty ass over here before I come over there and thump you."

"Thump her," said a slurred voice of Gabriel.

I didn't want to get thumped, but it was really cold and I didn't want to get out of my sleeping bag.

"Come on," North said.

I only hesitated another moment. I pulled myself out of my sleeping bag. Silas and Nathan turned over as I tiptoed my way toward North's cot.

The air was so cold, I thought my feet would freeze to the bottom of the tent. Why did the Academy pick winter as the time to camp? Why was this a thing? I'd have to talk to North. He was reasonable. He approved of Gabriel getting me out of my tent because of the cold. He'd hear me out and he'd make everyone get up and go sleep somewhere else. Maybe he'd go get the heater from my tent. Maybe we'd sleep in the cars with the heat on. Anything had to be better than the ice cold tent.

Instead, North surprised me by opening up his sleeping bag. He found my hand in the dark and tugged me down. "Get in," he said.

I wedged myself into the bag, snuggled close against him while on my back. He reached over me, zipping us up.

North tugged the sleeping bag up around our heads. It was surprisingly warm and got warmer quickly when the material covered my head. He mumbled to me inside the darkness. "Now what the hell are you talking about?"

"It's too cold to sleep here," I said. "If you fall asleep in the cold, you don't wake up."

"Baby, we're not dying of hypothermia." He dropped his head against my hair and wrapped his arms even tighter around my body, drawing me in closer. "Now close those pretty lips and go to sleep."

North's sleeping bag warmed even more. Was his thicker than mine? I didn't understand, but chilled shivers took over my spine again. . North tucked his arms closer around my body. He pulled me around until my back was pressed up against his chest, my butt into his waist. He crossed his arms over my chest, and bent his head, until and pressed his lips to the back of my neck.

Our legs pressed together and I slid my fingers along his arm, silently thanking him. Maybe he hadn't realized how cold I was in my sleeping bag. Maybe the others had better sleeping bags. I'd have to inspect them in the morning and see what made the difference.

I dozed for a while. I woke when I felt North's lips against the back of my neck, trailing to my ear. The air was still, and it was dark. I strained to listen, even though I was sure the others were sleeping and no one was paying attention.

Maybe North knew that, too.

I stretched slightly, but the move made my body press

closer into his. His arms tightened around me. His lips parted until he was sucking at my skin.

His teeth grazed at the soft spot behind my ear and sent a wave of warm sparks through my body. My hands covered his forearms that were wrapped around me. It was the only spot I could reach. I rubbed my fingers against his arm as if to let him know I loved what he was doing. It was the first tender moment I'd had with any of them since we'd arrived, and I hadn't even realized how much I missed a touch like that.

Maybe this wouldn't be so bad.

Part of me wanted to stop him. His kisses, his touch reminded me of when we were at the hotel on the beach. Could I remain so quiet if he continued? Each gentle brush of his lips against the soft skin along my neck made my heart throb.

My body responded in ways to his kisses that felt good, but I was confused as to what I should do.

His mouth trailed down my neck to my shoulder. The coarse hairs on his face electrified me.

His lips parted. When his teeth grazed against my skin, I shivered into him again. I smothered a moan against his arm.

He was going to do it. I felt it inside me. Part of me panicked, sure the others would hear.

The other part of me didn't care and wanted it badly.

His arm tugged me tighter around the waist and the other was a cushion at my head, supporting me up and giving himself support to nuzzle against my shoulder.

He bit down slowly, his teeth sinking into my skin. It was only a half bite, less pressure than what I knew he could do.

At the same time, his arm holding up my head came down, sliding around my chest and holding strong. The other pulled me in tighter. A leg wrapped around mine, locking me in.

The jolt took over my body, diminished only by his strong hold. Electricity coursed through every nerve. There was nothing else except the bite and the feeling it brought.

My shoulder pressed back against his teeth with an instinctual reaction. I craved more. He was holding out and I couldn't bare this.

He held onto me with his teeth on my neck for a moment, before slowly easing up. He sucked at the spot, sending another wave of shivers through my body.

A minute passed before I could breathe again, sinking back against him. I swallowed a moan, forcing myself to stay silent.

His mouth lifted until he was nuzzling behind my ear again. "Baby," he whispered, his voice gruff.

My heart pounded, out of control. He'd stirred something inside of me. My brain whispered that I should be quiet and go back to sleep, but my heart was drawn to him, craving, needing.

North released the strong hold on my body, and I gently pushed for room to turn and face him. He pulled me in, his arm encircling my head to hold me close again, and his palm at the small of my back, urging me close, even as I was snug against his body.

He kissed my nose once, lingering there. I breathed in his musk, and it was all I could smell at that moment.

I listened for any sign of the others, but they were still.

I may have whispered his name, but it was so soft on my lips, I wasn't sure if he could hear it at all.

His head tilted, and his broad lips met mine.

The kiss was strong, like him. Cautious, careful North, for the moment, kissed recklessly, feeling every corner of my mouth with his lips. His tongue followed, circling, diving in.

I responded, and I only pulled back when I needed to catch my breath.

North ducked his head lower and kissed my cheek close to my ear. His leg covered mine again, locking himself against me. With my shorter legs, my toes curled into the material of the sweatpants he wore to bed.

I lowered my head, wanting to bite him back. The way we were positioned, it was too awkward to reach for his neck. Instead, I pressed my cheek against his chest, my hands smoothing out his T-shirt.

"Baby," he whispered, his body stiffening against mine. There was a slight edge to his voice. A warning? I couldn't tell. I stilled for only a second, listening, but only hearing light snores and breathing.

I tilted my head until my lips were pressed against his chest, kissing at the muscles of his chest.

North shivered. His mouth pressed at the top of my head, tense.

My teeth grazed along the shirt but I wanted to touch his skin. I tucked two fingers into the neckline of his shirt, drawing it down.

His hand flew up, catching mine, but he didn't draw my hand away. I hesitated for a moment, unsure what he wanted from me, what I should do next.

Maybe he was worried about the noise.

I exhaled slow and then took in as much air as possible. I held on to him, determined to remain quiet. I dropped my mouth to his bare skin and kissed it.

He sucked in a breath, and his chest pressed to my mouth and he let out the quietest moan. It was enough to make me kiss the spot again, wondering if his reaction had been from the kiss or if he'd been expecting a bite.

His other hand found the back of my head, rubbing the base of my neck and then finding the spot where he had bitten.

The pressure of his thumb over the bite sent a new wave of bravery through me. I opened my mouth, putting my teeth to his skin, and bit his chest, slowly. My teeth sank into his chest and my tongue darted against him.

North smothered a grunt in his throat, and I felt the rumbling through my bones. He pitched against me. A sharp metallic creak sounded as the cot jerked at his reaction. His hand at the back of my head held me to his chest, afraid to move, afraid to let go.

Suddenly his fingers twined in my hair, pulling my head away from him. He pushed me until I was almost teetering off the edge of the cot, held up only by the sleeping bag.

North quickly found the zipper, ripping open the sleeping

bag. He crawled over me, starting to stand up. He lifted me in his arms as he stood, and then stilled when he was fully up.

My eyes fluttered, trying to figure out what he was doing with me.

North released me until I was standing. I think he only meant to put me down so he could get around me, but he was walking away, and caught my ankle and I dropped in a heap on top of someone else. I managed to scramble to sit up, worried I'd hurt whoever was sleeping.

"Ug," a voice said underneath me and a body shifted in the cot. I scrambled as best as I could while trying to get out of North's way. Where was he going?

He lumbered toward the tent opening, unzipped it and stumbled out into the night. I heard the zipper again and then his footsteps as he stormed off, the crunch of grass getting fainter under his boots.

The body beside me shifted, the sleeping bag opened and a head appeared. I moved until I was sitting up on the edge of the cot.

"Sang?" Victor whispered.

"Hmmm," I whispered. My heart thundered in my chest.

North storming out worried me. He'd done it before. I felt like he had liked what he'd been doing, and yet when I tried to bite back, he'd pushed me away. If he didn't like it, he could have stopped me before that point, so why hadn't he?

Should I crawl back into his cot?

Would either of us sleep if he returned?

You can only push a guy so far. It's what he'd told me before. Why didn't he tell me before I got too far? If it hurt or he didn't like it, then I didn't want to do it anymore.

Victor unzipped his sleeping bag. "Hurry up and get in. It's cold."

How was I supposed to explain to Victor what had just happened? I couldn't even explain it to myself

But he didn't ask. Victor simply urged me into the sleeping bag until I was lying next to him. He reached around me to zip it back up.

"Princess," he cooed, as his arms remained around me, drawing me close until I was facing him. His hand moved against my shirt around to my back. He stilled at first, but then his fingers shifted, finding the spaces between my ribs and following them. He started at my spine and traced around, following the bone. It was a short, smooth movement like I'd witnessed him do to piano keys when he was thinking or considering a song to play. "What's wrong with your sleeping bag?"

"It was cold," I whispered, still thinking of North, worried that he'd gone off by himself in the middle of the night. "I was freezing."

"Aw, was it not working?" he asked. His lips met with my forehead. "I'm sorry."

"Working?"

He kissed my brow. It was just a sweet kiss, like one would do to a child who broke a toy. "What? You didn't turn it on?"

Even though it was pitch dark, I blinked, trying to figure out what he was talking about. I pushed back a little, looking at him, his face having a bluish glow from moonlight shining through the thin tent wall. "What do you mean it turns on?"

There were a couple of snickering giggles from Luke and Gabriel's direction.

Victor reached up and touched my arm. "Our sleeping bags heat up. There's a little button and then a dial where you can direct how much heat..."

I groaned. "No one told me about the button. I didn't see one."

"Luke didn't tell you?"

I blinked. Luke was supposed to tell? "Luke!" I said in a harsh whisper.

More snickering, louder this time. "I swear, I thought I said something," Luke said. "I thought you knew."

Maybe he thought he had, but no one else had bothered to mention it to me. I suddenly felt silly for not looking at the sleeping bag closer. I didn't know they could do that. No wonder North's was so warm. Were they battery powered? I fell back into the cot. Did none of them hear me saying I was cold? Or did they just assume mine wasn't working right?

"I hate you all," I said, grumbling.

I thought I heard Silas and Nathan giggling with the others.

"Sorry," Victor said, sounding sincerely apologetic. "I thought you knew. Seriously, I would have said something before."

"I hate everyone except Victor," I declared. I snuggled into him. He wouldn't kiss me and dump me on someone else. He wouldn't destroy my tent. He wouldn't refuse to tell me my sleeping bag heated up, and then giggle about it.

I hated to admit it, but a lot of it was at least partially my fault. I could have checked out the sleeping bag and noticed something was different. I should have known I couldn't bite North like that without things getting too loud and he felt he had to leave. If I'd at least let Gabriel into the tent and heard him out, I would have agreed with him about it being too cold and too dangerous to sleep there alone. My pride was more hurt than anything.

"Oh my god, Trouble," Gabriel said, shuffling as he turned over. "I love you, but please shut the fuck up and go to sleep."

My heart wanted to flip out at him saying he loved me, but I knew from his tone he was just trying to butter me up so I wouldn't yell at him. He didn't really mean it. "Gabriel…" I was too tired to fight him.

"Everyone go to sleep," Kota said in a groggy voice. He flipped over in his cot, facing the wall. "You're all ridiculous."

I bit back my retort to Gabriel, not wanting to anger Kota. Victor moved a hand around the back of my head, coiling a lock of my hair around his finger and drawing me into his chest. His lips brushed against the top of my forehead.

"Shh, Princess," he whispered into my ear. "Stay with me. I won't let them pick on you anymore."

I snuggled into his chest, my lips pressing against his

collarbone. I would stay with him. I'd be his camping buddy. I was still mad at Gabriel knocking down my tent, and I wanted to get back at him later for doing that. And maybe for Luke as well for not telling me about my sleeping bag.

In fun, of course.

Minutes passed and Victor soothed me with his fingers tracing against my ribs, and his head ducked down slowly against my brow.

Silence fell around us.

His lips quietly puckered against my skin. I closed my eyes. I tried to settle my excited heart, wanting to sleep and yet now awake.

I was gripping slightly at his chest as I was relaxing, and then uncurled my hands so my palms were against his chest.

Victor's head ducked. He slid his lips over until they were by my cheek. "Sang," he whispered.

"Victor," I breathed, surprised. Were my movements keeping him awake? I blinked repeatedly, my eyelashes traced against his collarbone.

His palm brushed back my hair that had fallen against my face. He shifted and tilted his head until his lips met my cheek, close to my jaw. "When we get home, I'll take you to the spa again. Want to do that?"

In his arms, I would have agreed to anything. He understood me.

I remembered the time we'd gone to the spa. "If we go, let's do something we can do together. Last time we went, Adam did my hair and everything. It was nice but I hardly ever saw you."

"Sang," he whispered, breathing against my face. His lips moved again, but he didn't say anything I could understand. His fingers traced my face, sliding until they caught the edge of my mouth. His thumb slid over my lower lip.

Out of instinct, I kissed the tip of it.

I could barely see anything other than the outline of his face in the dimness, but watched as he brought his thumb to his own lips, kissing where I had just a second before. I stared at him, confused though I sensed it meant something to him.

He reached down inside the sleeping bag for my hand, finding a forefinger. He brought it to his mouth. I was tempted to draw it back, thinking of Nathan and how he wouldn't like anyone to bite my fingers like he did.

Instead, Victor simply kissed the tip of it. He kissed it again before pulling it away, guiding it and pressing it to my own lips.

He leaned in and then whispered. "I won't be able to kiss you this week with other people around, not directly, but maybe we could get away with this."

My heart raced thinking of this week and the Academy and wondering if us kissing fingers would be sneaky enough to get away with. Maybe, if we were careful.

He'd been thinking about how to kiss me. The thought of it thrilled me through to my heart.

I feared we were already being too loud and I wanted a quick kiss before settling in to sleep. I wanted to thank him for being good to me when the others had teased. I drifted a hand up to the back of his neck, catching the gentle waves of his hair in my fingers as I held him and drew him closer.

He leaned closer at my bidding, lowering his face. His lips missed my mouth, kissing my cheek, his mouth warm on my skin. He cupped a hand under my chin, drawing my face up.

The cot creaked.

"Victor," Kota called.

Victor remained dead silent, his face an inch from mine. His breath fell against my face.

"Victor," Kota said. "Go find North."

"He's not lost," Victor said. His lips were so close. I held my breath, waiting, wanting the kiss a moment ago and now frozen.

My heart thundered. Had he just told Kota no? What was worse was that if Kota was looking at us, he might be able to tell Victor was hovering so close over me.

Did he know? Could he see?

"Please go get North," Kota said. Even though he'd said please, there was the tone of command behind it.

Victor lifted his head, looking over mine. I was sure he was looking at Kota. As if in protest, Victor landed a kiss on my forehead, letting his lips linger.

My heart exploded, sure Kota would have seen if he was looking this way at all. We were supposed to be getting Kota on our side. Why was Victor acting so defiantly?

"Victor," Kota said.

Victor grunted, released me, and sighed. I had to shuffle to the side so he could yank the zipper open. I pulled myself out of the way, but still got a waft of cold against my skin.

Victor started to zip me in, but I touched his hand, urging him on and not worry. He stumbled over me, stuffed his feet into shoes, and walked out into the night after North.

"Sang," Kota said after Victor's footsteps faded away. "Come here."

I blushed in the darkness, so hotly I was sure my cheeks would glow. He'd told Victor to go away. If Kota was really worried about North, he would have gone himself, or he could have sent anyone else. He had sent Victor for a reason. I could only assume he knew what Victor had been doing, and had seen that last kiss.

Guilt sent a gentle shudder through my body. Could Kota understand? Maybe I was too late.

I took forever to go to him.

The silence in the tent was thick and too quiet. I had a feeling they were all awake and knew. They were all waiting to hear what Kota would say.

When I finally reached Kota, he held open his bag. When my legs were inside next to his, he zipped us up and settled in next to me.

I started to turn toward him to look at him, ready to face the consequences, when he stopped me by grabbing my arms. "Nope. You've done enough tonight. You turn that way," he said.

My heart was going a thousand miles a minute, but I

obeyed him, afraid to do anything else. He nudged me until my back was against him. When I was settled, he turned himself, so his back was against mine. It was obvious he wasn't going to talk to me about anything.

I stared off at the wall of the tent, doubly embarrassed. I was angry again with Gabriel for breaking my tent and drawing me into theirs. I blamed Silas and Nathan and Luke for not telling me my bag was heated, and North for running out.

I couldn't blame Victor at all. He was the one who had understood and tried to make things better but had made a mistake with Kota.

Embarrassment blazed through me, heating me from the inside. Was Kota was angry with me?

I wanted to fix it and yet I didn't have the guts to say anything now. And if I did, what would I say?

He'd brought me into his sleeping bag, so he wanted me near him, but since he was turned away, I had no idea what to do. Maybe he was only angry that I had made so much noise he couldn't sleep. He was the one who'd said we all needed sleep if we were going to make it through tomorrow.

And if that's all he was concerned over, then did he not care that Victor had kissed my forehead in front of him like that?

I told myself over and over again that I was too stressed out to understand anything. I tried my best to sleep, staring until my eyes closed. I didn't hear North and Victor return, but I must have dozed for a few minutes because, at one point, I turned onto my back to get comfortable and saw their forms on their cots.

Through my tired frustration, I ended up facing Kota's back, cuddling close for warmth but trying not to make it obvious. My body was still, but inside, I was agonizing over everything that had happened today, at my own silly pride and then Victor's kiss and how Kota probably thought I was ridiculous like he said.

I could have insisted I stay near him. I could have asked

him for a minute and talked to him. Was it too late now?

When he turned over some time later and faced me with closed eyes, I remembered what I was supposed to be facing away from him.

"Sorry," I whispered, starting to flip over.

His hand found my arm, holding me and preventing me from moving. "Relax," he said.

I settled on my back stiffly, afraid to do anything. He wrapped an arm around my stomach, his hand holding my side. He drew his other arm around, tucking his bicep was under my head. He snuggled in close until his nose was nuzzled against my cheek.

His breath tickled the side of my face. I stayed still for as long as I could but wanted to turn toward him. I did it slowly, unsure because before he wanted me the other way and now it felt like he wanted me close. If I turned my head just right, we would have been nose to nose.

But he didn't move. He was letting me choose where I wanted to be now. Why had it been a problem earlier?

When I was finally facing him, I could see his eyes were half open. He gazed down at me, his lips curled up in the corner. Without his glasses, his face was softer, losing his commanding expression. This was just Kota now: human, my friend...or something closer.

I wanted to ask if I'd upset him, but he didn't seem upset now. I looked at his nose, his lips, his cheek. I wasn't looking for anything particular; I was avoiding his searching glances, him silently asking me questions I didn't know the answers to. I couldn't stand how he looked into my eyes for so long, seeing right into every corner of me.

"Are you ever going to sleep?" he whispered.

Now that he'd asked, I realized I'd been hopping from bed to bed, disrupting everyone and unable to rest. While I was tired, I was too wound up to sleep.

I sighed softly, shaking my head. Maybe camping wasn't for me but the least I could do was lie still for him so he could sleep.

Kota's lips shifted, almost a smile. He leaned in, nuzzling my nose. "You silly, beautiful girl," he said.

My heart lifted at his words. Wasn't he angry? What had happened?

He nudged me again until he could move his arms. He unzipped the sleeping bag, then dropped his head until his lips were near my ear. "Find some boots and a coat. Follow me."

I wondered where he was taking me.

I climbed out of the cot. Somehow I found a pair of boots, too big for my feet but ones I could easily stuff my feet into. I picked up a coat by the door, smelling North's musk. I peeked over at him, back in his cot and still. Was he paying attention now? Victor was still, as well, in his own cot and sleeping bag.

I wrapped it around my body to stave off the chill and to try to keep the warmth I had for as long as possible.

Kota put on a pair of boots and his own green coat. He opened the zipper to the tent and nudged me out.

♥

THE STARS, THE BEACH, THE WAVES, THE SHORE

There was a dark gray haze overhead. It wasn't sunrise, but the moon was masked by a thin layer of cloud. The cold threatened to steal the warmth from me, but North's coat was long on my body and covered my upper thighs. My legs got a little cold, but my feet were protected. As long as we weren't out here too long, I'd be fine.

After Kota zipped up the tent, he found my hand held them in his and held up a flashlight with the other. His glasses were on, though his hair was a little messy. In a green coat and boots, he led the way toward the paved road and then headed east along it.

We walked quietly together, his fingers intertwined with mine. He kept his eyes forward, scanning the darkness. For the others? For bears?

I took the opportunity to study him, trying to gauge if he was upset, but he didn't appear to be. He was holding my hand. That was a good sign, right?

With the moonlight casting a blue-gray glow down, his face had a pleasant expression. The angles of his jaw and cheeks stood out, and I thought he looked incredible.

He walked quietly and turned off the road onto a sandy path.

I breathed in the fresh salt air, hearing the waves before I ever saw them. They were softer now, rolling smoothly across the shore closer to the dunes, covering the areas we had used for dancing and soccer.

I thought he'd want to get closer to the water, and was going to head toward the benches, but instead, he stopped well back from the beach. He turned off the flashlight and tucked it into his pocket.

He sat down on top of the dune and tugged me down next to him where we sat, still holding hands.

We looked out at the dark water that occasionally sparkled when the moon shone out from the clouds.

We cuddled close and my free hand found sand to shift between my fingers. While he didn't speak, my heart continued beating intently as I was scared and wanted to please him, too. I wanted to say I was sorry and find out what he was upset about, or if he was upset at all.

Kota remained focused, eyes intent out on the water.

Maybe he didn't want to say anything. Maybe he just thought I couldn't sleep and listening to the waves might help make me get sleepy.

With the chill starting to seep into my bones again, I shivered. He wrapped an arm around my shoulders, inviting me to lean against him.

He pressed his cold nose against my forehead. "Enjoying the time off yet?"

"I was enjoying it last week," I said, with a small smile, even though he couldn't see. "Not sure if I've gotten the hang of camping yet."

He grazed the tip of his nose across my hair, pressing his mouth to the top of my head, not kissing, just resting his face against me. "You're doing fine. You should come tell me if the others a being a little rough. But maybe you should listen a little more, too? You can bet most of the time, they're only trying to help."

I said nothing, but I did agree with him. I needed to also ask more instead of assuming.

"Nervous about tomorrow?" he asked.

"Yes," I said. Wasn't it obvious?

"You didn't do too badly today with the other team members," he said. "Although I heard you didn't talk to any of them."

I shrugged. "I didn't know what to say."

"I know you're shy, but they're all family. You can trust them."

That wasn't the problem, or I didn't think that it was. "It just takes time..." I knew I was shy. I was learning more about myself thanks to them. I just needed to get to know someone more before openly talking.

"I know," he said and rubbed my arm, warming me through the coat. "Although...although I'm second-guessing you staying in the big tent with us."

I sat up sharply, suddenly ready with the million excuses I'd made up in the tent about Victor and North and how I hadn't known about my sleeping bag. "I was trying to sleep in my own tent, but Gabriel and..."

He tightened his hold around my shoulder. "No, sweetheart, I don't mean that. I was just thinking how it would look when we brought you here, and you're in the big tent with our team. A team of all boys. And what if someone had walked in while you were in my sleeping bag? It'd be hard to explain, for teenagers...I guess."

I'd gotten so used to being around the others that I'd stopped questioning it. "I hadn't thought of that."

"I didn't until today," he said and then pulled away from me gently, wrapping his arms around his own body, leaning forward into his thighs, and looking out toward the water. "Maybe if you don't want to sleep in a tent alone, one of us should stay with you. We can go get another two-man tent."

That would be good enough. "You think other people, the Academy, would accept one of you staying with me?"

"Yes," he said. "They trust us, but since we're trying to put you on a team with all guys, we should work on looking more...normal than we seem to be sometimes."

Normal. He felt we weren't normal. Adults in the

Academy, like Dr. Roberts, might question the group if we all slept in the same tent. I should have been more aware of that as well. There's a lot of things I hadn't thought through lately.

However, Kota didn't know about the plan yet. Would Mr. Blackbourne want us to pretend and be different than how we normally were or was Kota right by being careful? "If you' think it's best."

"At least until we get other things squared away," he said. He paused. "So I guess you should pick someone to stay in the tent with you."

Pick one? "We could switch out," I said, not wanting to hurt anyone's feelings.

"I mean for the whole week," he said. "Just in case."

Wasn't I supposed to be showing I got along with our whole team very well? I wondered what Mr. Blackbourne would say about this later.

Still, maybe this could be my chance to talk to Kota this week. We'd be really busy in the next few days with the rest of the Academy, so at night, when it would just be him and me, I could talk to him about the plan. "It can be you, right?" I asked. "Do you have to stay with the others because you're family lead?"

"I don't have to sleep in the same tent," he said. He looked at me over the bulk of coat on his arm. "But are you sure you want me?"

My eyebrows rose. The question stilled my heart, and I knew he was asking something much more meaningful than who would sleep in the tent. I ducked my head, partially covering my face with the collar of the coat. "I mean, if you want to..."

"I thought you might want to pick someone else. Like maybe Victor."

He had seen. How much did he know? "I think..."

"Or Nathan," he said at the same time. He looked out at the ocean again. "Or North? Gabriel?"

My heart began to thump harder at each name.

Did he not want to stay in the tent with me? Why was he

asking about the others? I didn't want to force him. "I...don't know..."

He turned slightly, looking at me. "I think any of them would if you asked."

I bit my lip. Maybe he saw me interacting with them and was confused. Maybe he thought that I was playing with their feelings, or worse, doing things behind backs and being selfish.

I couldn't risk choosing one of the others. If the plan was going to work at all, I had to choose Kota, and hopefully get him to understand. "Do you mind sleeping in the pink tent? I bet we could fix it, even with the hole in it. We could fit in the tent, right?" I asked quickly, trying not to reveal anything I felt about the others at this point. I needed to focus on him and then find a way to talk to Mr. Blackbourne about the situation. "It seemed kind of small with the cot inside."

He didn't answer my question for the longest time but just looked at me, searching, calculating. "We could fit in an air mattress. The double should fit in and still give us some room."

"We could give the cot back to the others," I said, trying to sound enthusiastic. I had to prove to him how important he was to me. "When the heater was running, it warmed pretty well, too. And now that I know the sleeping bag heats up, we should be fine."

He nodded and then looked out at the ocean again. "If you're sure."

"Of course," I said, at first thinking he meant the heater, but then realizing he was talking about himself. I dipped my head again until my nose brushed against North's jacket. "If you want to."

"I do want to," he said, although his voice was soft, distant.

He continued staring out at the water, not saying anything else.

Unsure, I leaned into him, worried, waiting.

He opened up then, moving his arm back around my

shoulders, leaning against me while he stared out into the darkness. "If you think you might sleep, we can try going back. Just for tonight, we'll sleep in the big tent."

I wanted him to be able to sleep, and I thought I'd have an easier time of it since we had been able to talk. I still needed to let one of the others know and to pass the word along, what was happening and why. But that could wait for morning.

He stood up and reached for me. I put my hand in his.

I thought we'd start toward the tent, but Kota continued to stand still and looked at me. It had been an intense conversation, and I sensed there was more that he wanted to say. I was terrified of doing something wrong at this point, so didn't want to ask. So much had happened and deep down I knew we weren't really being open about what we were thinking.

Was he going to say something now? I waited, holding my breath.

"Ready?" was all he asked.

I shrugged and nodded, unsure of what else to do or say.

Afraid to break this truce we'd found where both of us swallowed back our unspoken feelings.

$\mathscr{T}$HE $\mathscr{A}$CADEMY, $\mathscr{I}$NSIDE

$\mathscr{I}$ didn't wake up the next morning until Kota was shaking me hard.

"Sang," he called from above me. "I can't let you sleep in anymore. We'll be late."

Late? For school? Once I'd finally fallen asleep, I'd slept deeply and couldn't remember anything. I sat up quickly, trying to figure out where my clothes were and what we were late for.

The shock of cold as he unzipped my sleeping bag woke me quickly. The sun streaming through the mesh windows reminded me where I was. But as I looked around, I noticed the tent was empty, except for Kota and me. Cots were made up, things were put away. I didn't hear any shuffling outside.

"Am I late?" I rubbed my eyes.

"No," he said. He sat down on the cot we'd shared the night before. He reached for my leg and rubbed my knee. He wore another green sweater and jeans and without a coat. "I wanted you to get a few more hours' sleep. The others have been up finishing the map and making copies for everyone else. Some other teams have already started to arrive."

Other teams. Would I appear lazy after having slept in so much? "Sorry," I said as I stood, wavering on an uneven patch of ground.

Kota grabbed my elbows, steadying me. Grateful, I looked up at him. That was when I noticed the dog tag he wore around his neck, the one engraved with the heart curve formula that I'd given him. I'd never seen him wear it until now.

"Calm down," he said with a smile. His eyes were clear, the green bright. When I was steady, he slowly shifted his palms up my arms to my neck and massaged. "What do you need, sweetie?"

My eyebrows lifted as I thought of where to start. "Clothes...I guess."

"I'll get them," he said, still holding me for a moment. "Just stand here. Do you want your bathroom kit?"

I nodded.

He released me slowly and then turned to a small collection of items in the corner of the tent. I recognized the pink camping gear, the stereo and other items from my broken tent.

He found clothes and then the kit, and pulled them from the collection, along with a towel. Then he plucked out my coat and a pair of boots. "You might wear these just over to the latrine," he said. "It's getting a little warmer today."

I listened, but I wasn't completely paying attention to what he was saying. I was much more interested in his movements, at the way he smiled and how his features were all lit up. "Did something happen?" I asked.

"Happen?" One of his brown eyebrows cocked as he turned to me. He put down most of the things on the cot so he could hold the coat open for me. "No, nothing in particular. I saved you some breakfast. I hope you like oatmeal."

I shrugged. "I've never had oatmeal," I said, sliding my arms into the coat.

"Really?" he said, and his smile lifted more. He picked up one of my boots to help me get into them. "You'll have to let me know if you like it."

"Okay."

When I turned to pick up the items to go to the latrine, he scooped them up quickly. "It's okay. I've got these. I'll walk you over."

I bit my lower lip. I was glad he was so happy, but also curious. He had been so gloomy this last week, worried about me. Even yesterday, when we were walking back to the tent, he seemed a little on edge. What had changed?

Did he figure out a solution to keeping me on the team with the Academy? Maybe he had an answer now.

I tried not to think too much on it, but I couldn't help but let his happy nature affect me. As we stepped out of the tent and walked to the latrine, I held his elbow as he carried my things. I didn't say anything, but studied the clear blue sky, and checked the surroundings for signs of other teams.

I didn't see anyone at all until we got close to the latrines.

Then I heard the very distinct sound of showers running.

I stopped dead just as Kota passed me my things to go inside the girl's restroom.

He paused in his movements, stopped, turned his head to the latrine and then looked again at me. "It's probably just Taylor and the others in there. Or another team. Don't worry. It's just Academy people right now. No one else is here. No need to be afraid."

I hadn't even thought about who might be in the bathroom. The shower was loud, echoey, unavoidable.

I don't have to go into the shower, I repeated to myself. I didn't have to go anywhere near the shower this week and Kota and the others wouldn't even notice. I'd wash my hair in the sink at some point.

I held my things against my body, leaving Kota outside as I entered.

I couldn't see who was in the shower, but April, the girl who had worn brown yesterday, was at one of the sinks, brushing her teeth. She wore brown again today: a long skirt with boots and a sweater. She gave me a quick wave and turned back to her sink to spit. "Morning," she mumbled. She stood up straight and wiped her face with her towel. "Up late?"

I nodded and then swallowed. I had to make an effort to get along. "Yeah," I said, although then I didn't know what else to say.

I headed to one of the stalls and hung up my things on the hook before using the toilet and then changing. I wanted to finish up quickly and get back out to Kota. I smelled fruity shampoo, and the overpowering the dank damp of the latrine.

The shower turned off and then I heard Taylor's voice. "If I were concerned about the boys being perverts, I'd be worried about this bare window in here," she said. "This is an awesome camp shower, though."

"For now," April said, and I heard the scratch and swish of a hairbrush. "Wait until there's a hundred girls in here this weekend. There's only two latrines, and the other one is over near where the campers are, and that's a good long walk." Pause. "Uh...what's your name...sorry? Sang, right?"

"Yeah?" I called, surprised she was talking to me.

"Did you want a shower?"

No. But did I want to sound like I was gross and wouldn't shower? How was I going to get through a week of not using a shower? "I..."

"I wouldn't take one right now. I'm pretty sure I used up all that hot water," Taylor said.

"Darn it, Taylor. You can't do that this week."

That might be my answer. If I made sure to come in later in the morning, I could say there was no hot water left and had to wash up in the sink. I finished up, dressing quickly.

When I left the stall, wearing the clothes Kota had picked out for me—jeans, a pink sweater, and boots that were fuzzy on the inside—April was leaning against one of the sinks, cleaning her brown glasses with a wipe. Taylor had come out and was wearing tight jeans and a long gray sweater that was bulky and covered her butt, and a fuzzy pair of boots. She focused on the mirror, leaning over the sink, brushing her teeth. Even without makeup, she was still very pretty. She had supplies surrounding her, taking up her sink and the sink next to her.

One of the two girls was wearing some sort of flowery, potpourri-like scent that was a little overpowering. I suspected April since Taylor had just washed. I went one sink away from Taylor's.

I thought of Gabriel, and missed his expertise and wished he was there to brush my hair and even make his little demands about my clip.

I started washing my hands and face, thinking if I took long enough, Taylor would finish and then the girls would leave.

However, when Taylor finished tying her brown hair back into a ponytail and swiping on lip gloss, she just stopped and looked at me. She seemed to be waiting for something. "Going to walk with us?" she said.

"Uh, I think Kota's waiting for me," I said, giving her what I hoped was a nice smile. "If you'd like to go ahead..."

"Is he outside?" Taylor asked and then grinned, putting her tube of gloss away before she headed to the door. "Let me tell him to go away. We'll take you."

I gritted my teeth. I didn't really want to go with them, but I was also supposed to be getting along with them. I hoped Kota insisted on staying with me.

April and Taylor went to the bathroom door. I couldn't see out beyond them to Kota. When Taylor started talking, hers and Kota's voices were drowned out by my running tap. I shut it off quickly.

"...don't need to worry," Taylor was saying. "We'll make sure she gets there."

"It's not that," Kota said. "She...hasn't had breakfast yet. And then..."

"We've got leftovers," April said. "Our camp's on the way to yours."

"And her coffee," he said.

"We went and got more of those yesterday," Taylor said. "To replace the ones I took from you all, and for myself. I forgot how much I liked those. They're super easy compared to trying to make coffee out here, anyway."

"It's okay," April said. "We'll take care of her. We're going to the same place anyway."

Say no, I tried to yell at Kota without saying anything.

Maybe I wasn't being as flexible as I should be around other Academy people. Last night, I'd never really gave the girls a chance. I couldn't continue to do that if I was here to prove, in some way, that I wanted to be in the Academy. Mr. Blackbourne had said to get along with them. Reluctantly, I bit my tongue and waited.

Maybe Kota realized this as well, because slowly, he sounded like he was beginning to relent. "Well...she...if...tell her..."

"We'll tell her you'll be there," April said. "We know. Don't worry. She'll be safe with us."

April turned back toward me, but Taylor lingered in the door, whispering something to Kota.

Don't leave, I said in my head as I turned from April and looked into the mirror, a hair brush in my hand, hair half detangled. Despite knowing what I should do, it was very hard to do it. There was nothing wrong with April or with Taylor, or the others. I just wanted...my team.

I sucked in some air, seeking out the calmness that Kota had tried to instill in me earlier. I needed to be braver than ever this week.

Tonight, I'd be in a tent with just him. I could look forward to that. As long as I had time in the evening to relax with people I was familiar with, this might not be any different than a normal school week.

Or so I hoped.

♥♥♥

I finished getting ready, clipping my hair back away from my face.

"We almost match," Taylor said, and then showed me her boots: black with gray fuzz at the top. "April won't let me get her more fashionable clothes like this."

Gabriel usually picked out my clothes and what to wear. I wanted to tell the girls this, to let them know how great he was, but I didn't know how to say it. I missed him, despite our fight the night before. Now that it was morning, I still wanted to talk to him about breaking my tent, but I also wanted to say I was sorry for not listening when he was trying to keep me safe.

Taylor shuffled her boots against the concrete floor as she walked. "I just hope they won't get full of sand."

"I just assume all of our stuff will need to be replaced after this week," April said and then sighed. "It's why I said to bring old clothes along. I wish you'd let me shop for you at the Goodwill."

"They never have anything fashionable or in my size, otherwise I would."

When we left the latrine, as I'd feared, Kota was gone.

I pressed my lips together. I'd hoped he'd linger. I wrapped my arms around my stomach, squeezing my clothes and kit to my chest as I fell in behind the girls.

Just walk to wherever we are going, I told myself. *I'll be fine.*

As we walked to their camp, I paused. "Oh," I said, looking down at the things in my arms. "I should...take this back to our tent." It was a good reason to go back to camp, and maybe I'd see one of the guys there.

"*Our* tent?" April asked and then paused in the road. "Didn't you have your own tent?"

I grimaced. "Well, it sort of broke last night and I..."

"Oh, well then you can stay with us if you want," she said. "We've got room."

"No, it's okay. Kota was going to get another one."

"He doesn't need to do that," April said. "We've got more than enough room."

Taylor smirked. "You know he likes you, right? I asked him and he told me he does."

My cheeks had already been burning but now felt like they'd lit up in flames. I looked down at the road. "I..." What could I say to that?

What would they say of me if they ever learned about the others? That I'd kissed two of them last night before climbing into Kota's sleeping bag? They wouldn't be able to understand.

The fact that I couldn't say anything about it made me question what we were doing. Were we wrong to try the plan?

"Don't worry," April said, waving her hand through the air. "And never mind the crush right now. We've got things to do. You're new and most likely they'll stick you in a tent with other new girls. But you can stay with us if you prefer."

My mouth opened. "I don't...need to."

"No, it's okay," April said. She turned to walk toward their camp again. "You won't be the only one who shows up without a team. Sometimes you just know your group from the start and that's all you know. If you come into the Academy without a prior group, you get put with other people who don't have one already. It all works out in the end."

She assumed Kota and the others weren't my team, but that I was a straggler looking to join. "...Oh," I said. The guys never told me new people were put into random teams until they found one for them, but then, had they formed their group before they joined the Academy? It was Dr. Green and Mr. Blackbourne who had sought out Kota, Nathan, and the others, bringing them into an already formed team.

And then I remembered that Dr. Green and Mr. Blackbourne had been put into a team together. They'd said so. That's how they'd started. I wondered what other teams they might have been a part of prior to finding each other.

April headed into a campsite where there was a large tent, similar to the one North had set up, but this one was a shade of brown.

April walked over to it and opened the flap, showing me the inside. There were three cots lined up around the walls. Since it was only the three, their tent had more room in the center, but it was filled with small chairs and on top of the chairs, were three suitcases, identical brown.

The potpourri scent was strong here, as was the smell of other perfumes: sharp fruits and flowers, fighting the natural scents of pine trees and the ocean outside.

I couldn't sleep here. I'd suffocate.

"Just put your stuff on the cot," she said.

I entered and placed my sleeping clothes and the bathroom kit on the nearby cot. I was reluctant to leave my things; I didn't want them to pick up the strong perfume scent. "I can come back..."

"I'll make sure your stuff gets put in whichever tent you end up in." April poked at her temple through her long brown hair. "I think of these things."

"Thank you," I said. What else could I say? I had to be polite.

We emerged from the tent and I watched Taylor, who had wandered off toward a brown, old Jeep Cherokee. She opened the back to reveal a cooler inside. She opened it and pulled out two bottles: Coffee Frappuccinos. I followed April over and Taylor handed a coffee to me.

They were different from the ones the boys normally bought for me. I looked at the light brown label. "I haven't seen these," I said. "Coffee flavored coffee?"

"It's just coffee without all the flavor," she said. She reached further into the back of the Cherokee, and pulled out an aluminum foil packet, handing it to me. "April makes us easy to-go food."

I tucked the coffee under my arm and took the packet from her hand, feeling the contents. "A burrito?"

"It is," she said. "Don't worry. It's vegan."

I tilted my head toward April in a silent thank you and then forced a tight smile. Vegan what?

"Eat on the way," she said. She and Taylor headed toward the road.

On the way to what? And where was their other teammate? My only hope that wherever we were going, Kota and the others would be there.

I did my best to balance the coffee while I walked and tried to open up the burrito. For some reason, I was thinking potatoes, maybe eggs... No, she'd said it was vegan; do vegans eat fake eggs? What's even in fake eggs?

The outside of the wrap revealed nothing to me. All I could smell was tortilla bread smell.

I took a bite and got a mouthful of spinach, black beans, and mashed avocado.

I rolled the food around my mouth as I walked, working to get the full flavor and textures. Different. I had to give it a chance.

But the more I chewed, slowly, tasting the flavors together, the more I didn't like it.

There was something spicy inside that I hadn't noticed right away but grew hotter as I chewed. My eyes watered. I worked to swallow it quickly.

I rewrapped the burrito and tucked it under my arms so I could go for the coffee, taking a sip. It was cold, and slid down easy, but had a bitter aftertaste, or maybe was mixing with the burrito in a way that was overpowering. I wanted to go back and brush my teeth just to get the flavors out.

How could they eat this? Suddenly, I was craving oatmeal, even though I'd never had it. I'd eat anything that wasn't so spicy. I missed my mocha coffee.

The other two powered on, glancing back at me on occasion but mostly talked about the weather, how cold it had been last night.

I either had to find a trash quickly or somehow manage to swallow the food.

I tried another bite but then had to wash it down with the coffee. By then, I was down to half a coffee.

I considered starving instead.

I was so focused on looking for a trash can that I hadn't registered when I followed them down a path I was unfamiliar with. Suddenly I was hearing voices, more than just the boys, even if I couldn't see anyone at the moment.

We came to a gathering area, where there were rows of wooden benches, tiered on a slope, all facing the lowest area. At the bottom—the stage, I assumed—was a fire pit that contained a small campfire. Trees surrounded the area, so the place felt sheltered and secluded.

But what hit me wasn't the setup of the area, but that there were hundreds of people, talking, and moving around, finding places to sit. They had been masked by the hill before, and now their voices were overwhelming. Most were already seated while a handful was working their way down to empty seats available.

"Good, it didn't start yet," Taylor said. She scanned the area.

I looked around, too, and found a trash can at the edge of the seats. I slipped away from Taylor, crunching the burrito in my hands in the foil, pretending I was done with it and hoping they wouldn't notice there was more than half left. I tossed it and then downed the last of the coffee, eager to be finished with it.

After I threw out the bottle, I turned and realized I had lost sight of April and Taylor.

I scanned the open-aired theater for any signs that I was supposed to sit somewhere specific. People were sitting down and a small group had started toward the stage, engaged in conversation. They were older, and then I recognized Dr. Roberts among them, wearing brown pants, a white shirt, and a tie. Formal for camping, but still different since I'd only ever seen him in a doctor's coat.

I stopped focusing on him and was looking for the boys when there was a touch on my shoulder.

I turned to face not one of the boys or even Taylor or April, but someone very familiar to me, though I didn't recognize who he was until he spoke.

He had different-colored eyes and brown hair that was longer in the front. "Hey, it's the little doctor," he said, a grin on his face. "I remember you."

In my panic, I couldn't remember his name. He had to know I wasn't a real doctor. Would he be upset to know a real doctor didn't pull the nail out of his leg?

Behind him stretched a group of guys, all bulky and including two that were really tall, maybe even taller than Silas. They all stood together looking uncomfortable.

One of them stepped forward, a man wearing glasses with long dark hair hanging around his face. I remembered him: Mr. Toma. He'd talked to me before when I'd been with Mr. Blackbourne in the music room when Mr. Toma had been looking for someone. He scanned the area and then pointed.

"There's space for us down there," Mr. Toma said.

I'd been watching him and hadn't noticed the guy in front of me holding out his hand. "I'm Marc, remember?"

I nodded, shaking his hand. "Sorry," I said. "I was just...looking..."

"You're with the doc, aren't you?"

Dr. Green! "Have you seen him?"

"Not yet," he said. He looked over his shoulder at his own group already starting down the path.

I realized then that there was a girl among them. She was wearing a very bulky T-shirt and a loose pair of jeans and at first, I'd thought her to be a guy with long brown hair. As I looked closer, I saw she wore an angry expression, frowning deeply. She stomped in her boots as she followed her guys down the steps, to an area toward the front, close to the fire and the center staging area.

"Come sit with us," Marc said, moving back a half step to allow me to go in front of him. "It's okay. Don't we all split up after this part anyway?"

He was speaking like I'd been here before. Maybe he really did assume I was Academy.

I followed one of his team members—a bulky guy with a grizzly expression and a lip ring—down the steps. As I walked, I kept looking around, hoping to find the guys along the way.

I spotted Taylor sitting near the center in the middle of a row, but a distance from us. I turned my head away so she wouldn't see me. If I had to get put in another team for the week, I didn't want it to be their group. They were nice, but I'd starve to death and suffocate in their tent.

I sat at the end of the row, next to Marc. Their girl sat between Mr. Toma and the bulky grizzly guy. The two tall guys sitting on the other side looked alike, perhaps brothers, and somehow seemed familiar but I couldn't remember how.

They had a girl on their team?

Four guys, one girl? Or five? As I looked down the row, I noticed another guy on the far side. He was black with dark brown hair but I couldn't tell if he belonged to this team or the one on the other side of him. He had his arms crossed and appeared very displeased to be there and sat distanced from Marc's team. Beyond him, the other team was made up of older, middle-aged men, so it made me think he was on Marc's team, but didn't like it. Maybe he was new.

Marc's team appeared to be all in their twenties as far as I could tell.

Five guys, one girl. All on a team.

Hadn't Lily and the others said they spoke to other teams like ours, but none of them had seen it through? Was this one of them? Is that why they all had dour expressions?

A sudden loud air horn sounded from the stage area, and Dr. Roberts waved his hands, getting everyone's attention.

An elderly, thin woman stood beside him, and I recognized her, although it took me a minute to place her. Mrs. Rose? She'd been in the hospital and had spoken in sign language to Dr. Green. She was the one who had tried to hack down a palm tree with a chainsaw and had fallen off a ladder.

She seemed to have recovered fully. She was now holding the air horn and let out another short blast, grinning.

People still standing shuffled to find seats quickly, settling down. It took a fraction of the time that it took students at any school assembly I'd ever been to. Everyone here became dead silent, respectful and ready to listen.

Once everyone was seated, I could search the crowd easier. The majority of people were young—early twenties down to ten-year-olds at the youngest that I could see. There were plenty of adults, but most were young or middle-aged.

Had they grown exponentially in recent years as they recruited new, young members? Or did older members fall out of the Academy and no longer participate? Maybe there was a retirement age?

Dr. Roberts and Mrs. Rose took several steps back, allowing an older, dark-haired man, with white patches at his temples, take center stage.

He waved hello. "Welcome, everyone!" he said into a microphone, a huge speaker on the stage blaring out his voice.

A few in the crowd waved back but everyone remained silent. "I am Mr. Duncan. My associates and I would like to welcome you to camp. Thanks for coming. I know we're all anxious to get on with camp activities. I'm excited to let you all know we do have an arts and crafts section set up in a picnic area. Archery, hiking, fishing and some of the other usual activities: first-aid training, et cetera. are all available. You know the drill: do a circle around the camp, find a flag, it'll take you to a station to learn something new."

A murmur rippled through the crowd and then everyone settled down.

"There's no need for appointments, or to even stay with your teams. This is your vacation, a chance to learn new things and even meet a few new people. You don't need to try to get to everything, but I encourage you all to try something you're not familiar with. You never know; you might find something new you enjoy.

"We've got several new people, whom I want to welcome..."

A thunderous applause erupted just then.

The man with the microphone waved once and the crowd settled. "You can meet them all through the week," he said. "I just wanted to say hello."

I was still scanning the crowd but didn't see the guys. The Academy seemed bigger than Ashley Waters. How many people were here today? And how many hadn't made it in?

"New people, this is your chance to get to know us. You were invited to our Academy for a reason. You're smart. You're capable. You have a desire to help others. It's that simple, folks. I know it looks complicated from the outside, but this is your chance to learn it from the inside. We'll help you find your place and then we'll all work together to help others."

"I don't want to take up any more time unless we have any announcements?" He turned, looking at Dr. Roberts, who shook his head, but Mrs. Rose started signing at him. Her hands moved so fast and from this distance, I couldn't make it out.

"Oh, right," the man said and turned once again to the audience. "Most of your team and family leads will be in the cabins as we need to go over new protocols and train new leads for the year. If you need them, find the cabins. Maps will be handed out to you as you leave here. Grab two. Remember the rule of two."

Rule of two? I didn't know what that meant.

Also, what he'd said meant Kota and Mr. Blackbourne might be gone for most of the day, perhaps the whole week unless Dr. Green took over for Kota...

"Before everyone leaves," he continued, "I need all the new people down here with us. We'd just like to say hello and get to know you." He clapped his hands over his head and then spread them out. "I think that's it. Emergency information is on the map. We're all family here. Have fun."

Everyone stood, including me. My heart went into a panic as people started to move. Marc went to talk to their girl, who was angrily shaking her head and pointing to Mr. Toma.

I knew I was expected down at the front, but I felt like I needed to locate someone familiar, like Kota. Looking around and not seeing him or any of the boys, I felt misplaced. Did I have to go down there by myself?

"Miss Sorenson?" came a loud voice and then as I turned my head toward it, I recognized Dr. Roberts waving to me from the stage area to get my attention. He curled his finger at me. "Come on up here."

While he wasn't one of the guys, I was grateful for the familiar face and scooted out of the seats.

Then he pointed to the angry girl with Mr. Toma. "Miss Winchester. Would you please join us?"

The girl frowned, said something to Mr. Toma, but then followed. But instead of going around, she walked along the benches, using them as steps to go down into the center. When she got to the end, she jumped off the first row and shuffled her way toward Dr. Roberts.

I used the designated path and ended up beside her,

watching at Dr. Roberts, while he looked behind us.

I turned looked at the rest of the group assembling around me. Some of the girls were my age, and only two were older, one being the angry girl. The guys were varying ages, and there were many more of them than there were girls.

There were at least fifty of us, standing together and waiting.

I kept looking behind me, hoping for Kota or one of the others to find me.

Then I recognized one of the people handing out maps at the very top of the hill, near the garbage cans: Silas. He had on a ball cap, but I was sure it was him. Maybe they hadn't been sitting at all. Maybe they'd been stationed up there to pass out maps.

I should have insisted I'd stay with Kota. I would have been with them and could have asked them so many things.

Mr. Toma, Marc, and the rest of their team hadn't moved, and sat on the benches together, all eyes on the angry girl—Miss Winchester. Waiting.

Miss Winchester stood with her arms across her breasts, the T-shirt and bulky jacket she wore making her look frumpy. She was beautiful, with green eyes like mine, but hers were sharp and calculating like she could knife your soul or save it with just a look.

I didn't recognize any of the others.

I still felt out of water, but I waited, trying to calm my panicked heart, knowing this might be my future with the Academy.

♥♥♥

Mr. Duncan clapped his hands and we all turned and focused on him.

He smiled. He had a broad body, wide shoulders, and a protruding stomach, but he was friendly-looking. The rest of his body looked strong and didn't match his stomach. "Welcome," he said. "I know you all must be really confused."

"Tell me about it," one of the guys said. He appeared about my age and wore a dour expression. "I've got questions."

"Me, too," one of the young girls said. She stood tall and put her hands on her hips. "Why are we here? And what are all these rules they can't tell me about?"

Mr. Duncan spread out his hands and smiled. "That's what you're all here to learn about, although it's a lot to go over. You will be free to ask any questions you like." When the dour guy started to open his mouth, Mr. Duncan cut him off with a hand wave. "Hang onto your questions for now until after we're done here. We want to get to know you individually and have a discussion."

"If you all would get in a line," Dr. Roberts said, stepping forward. "We want to know your name, where you are from. You might have met one of us before, but we'd like to introduce you all formally now."

Introductions. Formal ones. Like Mr. Blackbourne had said. I scanned the stadium again, seeing the others at the top, still handing out maps. Did I have to do this part alone? I thought they would be here. My hand fluttered up, and I touched my lower lip once, but then paused and hid my hands behind my back. I didn't want to appear as nervous as I felt.

I wished I'd had some warning. Perhaps Kota had stayed behind to tell me but wasn't able to.

I glanced over my shoulder and saw Miss Winchester's team sitting away from her as well. A few other guy and girl teams were still in the stands, lingering and looking toward us. Maybe they were waiting to see what happened.

I started getting into line when Dr. Roberts walked by and pulled me casually out by the elbow, giving me a handshake. "Hello there, familiar face."

As the line was assembling, I worried I was going to be late for something.

Dr. Roberts ducked his head to catch my eye and kept a firm hold of my hand. "I have some more of those candies if you'd like one."

I almost said no thank you but then registered what he said. I nodded enthusiastically. He had no idea how much I needed something to get the taste of spicy avocado coffee out of my mouth.

Dr. Roberts handed me a foil-wrapped strawberry cream candy he'd pulled from his pocket. I opened it quickly and popped it into my mouth, suckling at the flavor. It was a funny taste at first, but soon it washed away the old flavors, leaving only creamy strawberry. It was such a relief.

Dr. Roberts glanced at the line again and then winked at me. "Sorry," he said. "Looks like you're last to get in line but don't fret; last is not least here."

He walked toward the line, seeming to size up the others. He guided Miss Winchester from her spot in the middle to the back of the line, putting her at the very end before he walked away quickly.

She gave him a glare before she pulled a strawberry candy out from her pocket, opened it and put it in her mouth. I hadn't even seen Dr. Roberts give her one. Had he dropped it in her pocket, or given it to her earlier? She seemed surprised to see it.

Why did he put her last in line?

Actually, I realized he had held me up so that *I* was last in line. He'd been distracting me on purpose. He had placed Miss Winchester in front of me, though. I wondered about his reasoning as I followed the line down and got into place.

The younger kids were at the front of the line, and since I was in the back, I didn't hear much of what the group of adults were saying to them. They invited the first one in and the adults closed in around him—a young boy--speaking to him privately, but still within view of anyone who was paying attention.

"This is so stupid," Miss Winchester in a low voice. Her hands were in her jacket pockets, but even then, I could tell they were clenched, shoved far in. "Why not just tell us? Why separate us out?"

Maybe it was procedure? Weren't we supposed to trust

that they were on our side? Maybe because she and I appeared to be older, we were being held back to wait. But that didn't make sense either because there were another couple of girls and a few boys who could have easily been our age, and they were scattered among the other younger kids.

I shifted from foot to foot, staring eagerly toward the front of the line. I smoothed down my hair, redoing it in the clip and straightened my sweater on my shoulders.

Nothing eased my nerves and it was worse being at the back. I couldn't hear what might be asked giving me time to prepare what to say.

It wasn't until we'd gotten through half the line that I figured out that once a kid had spoken to the circle of Academy adults, most of them would join people waiting for them in the bench seats. A team would then leave the area, new kid in tow, getting their maps and walking away.

Some didn't go to a team and instead were directed to sit on the bench closest to the stage area, waiting. They didn't sit close together, although some of them talked. I didn't think they knew each other.

There were ten adults with Dr. Roberts making up his circle. They were all middle-aged and older.

They would have the person at the front of the line step forward, then they'd surround the person to talk to him or her privately. It took only a few minutes, but then they'd be directed either to join a team or to the bench in front, what I started to realize was a spare team.

A spare team.

I might get put on a spare team.

When Miss Winchester was called up, I stood alone, but I eased a few steps closer, trying to hear so I could go in more prepared.

Dr. Roberts stood beside her in the circle. "I believe I've told a few of you about Miss Kayli Winchester. She's a very special recruit."

"I'm not a recruit, yet," she said. "I want answers. That's all. No promises." I could only see the back of her, but she stood tall, her hands clenched at her sides.

I almost envied her directness. Could I be so bold?

"We never hold anyone against their will," Dr. Roberts said. He then turned toward the group, introducing Mrs. Rose and the others, although, by the end of the list of names, I lost track of most of them.

"And you're a local, like me, aren't you?" Mr. Duncan asked, standing with his hands tucked behind his back. "Born and raised in Charleston?"

"I'm sure that's what my file says about me," she said. She eyeballed one of the women. "I know you've read it."

Mr. Duncan bowed his head and pressed his lips together. The middle-aged woman with fine wrinkles around her eyes looked her dead on. "I have," she said. "You're welcome to peruse mine if you'd like."

Kayli's head jerked back. "I...yes," she said. "I'd like to read it."

"I'll bring it over sometime," the woman said, a satisfied smile on her lips.

When no one said anything else, Kayli looked suspiciously around the group. "Well? Was that it?"

"Sure," Dr. Roberts said. "Unless you had questions for us."

"Tons," she said. "But most importantly, I want to stay with my current group. I understand that's possible."

There was a pause as some of the members of the circle looked at each other. I had a feeling they knew each other very well, like my own team. They could understand what they were thinking without saying it.

My heart beat wildly. Kayli was like me. She wanted to stay with her group of guys. I glanced back at them as they watched on intently, except for the one that sat apart, who looked fierce now. I cringed and looked at my feet, suddenly worried for her. Did he not like her? Did he not want her to stay with them?

Would Kota look like that if he knew about the plan?

Dr. Roberts broke the long silence. "Sometimes it's better

to get to know other teams. You can learn more by simply getting to know..."

"No, thank you," Kayli said quickly. She motioned back to her team. "I'll ask other people, but if I'm free to get straight answers from my team now, they've got a lot of explaining to do."

"As you wish," Mr. Duncan said, looking at her steadily. "We hope you find what you're looking for."

Kayli turned, but as she left, Dr. Roberts followed her, leaning in to say something. I couldn't help hearing as they passed right by me.

"I hope you'll remember, nothing you see or hear while with us here should pass your lips once you leave. Not even to Blake Coaltar."

"He can be trusted," she said.

"That's yet to be determined," he said. "But I'm not asking for myself. I'm begging you, for the safety of these kids here. You cannot comprehend the potential for tragedy if the wrong people get wind of this."

"Then maybe my team should explain it to me. From the outside, it looks like a cult that just happens to blend in with the rest of society, so no one notices."

A cult? She thought the Academy was a cult?

I couldn't hear anything else, but kept my eyes on them until I heard Mr. Duncan asking for the next person in line.

I turned toward the circle, to Mrs. Rose and then the others, waiting with their expectant eyes on me.

Dr. Roberts was still walking away with Kayli, leaving me to walk into the crowd of strangers.

♥

$\mathcal{N}$EW $\mathcal{R}$ECRUIT

I clasped my hands behind my back, the only way to hide their shaking, as I stood as tall as I could, keeping my spine straight. Even the kids waiting on the benches had quieted and it felt like everyone was watching me.

I entered the circle and waited, my eyes glancing from one face to the next but not meeting anyone's gaze. I wanted to appear friendly, but I couldn't push myself to look at them straight on. It was the best I could do while feeling so anxious.

Mrs. Rose started to move her hands, and that attracted my attention. "Would you like to tell us your name?" she signed.

"She's asking..." Mr. Duncan began.

"Sang Sorenson," I said quickly. I'd been practicing a lot more while we were sick and since we weren't going to regular classes. Luke had helped a lot.

"Oh," Mr. Duncan said. "Oh, I'm sorry. I didn't know you could read sign language."

"An impressive skill to have," someone else said, but I didn't see who as he was behind me.

There was a murmur of agreement and a few nods around the circle.

Mrs. Rose continued, smiling brighter now. "And where are you from?" she signed.

Did they mean the street I lived on? "I was born in Illinois," I said and then stopped. I wasn't sure what I was supposed to say beyond that. Kayli's demand to stay with her own team invaded my brain. Could I tell them I wanted the same? It didn't seem like they would stop me if I tried.

However, I remembered Mr. Blackbourne's words and

how he had wanted me to be willing to participate. He said to save stating my desire to stay with my team for the end. I wished I'd talked to him last night or this morning for one more check-in to make sure it was the right thing to do.

Dr. Roberts returned to the group and said, "Miss Sorenson has a very impressive skill list in her file. She volunteered to be of assistance for the camp, even though it's her first year. She's already started since the team who invited her came early."

Heat burned through my cheeks. Was I supposed to say something about this? I hadn't realized there would be a file about me, but it did make sense if Kayli had one. I wondered what mine said. Who put it together?

"Interesting," Mr. Duncan said, looking behind me toward Dr. Roberts and then focused his curious eyes on me. He shifted his tie as he spoke. "How were you able to help?"

My heart thundered in my ears. I couldn't focus on their faces at all now. I opened my mouth to answer, but no sound came out at first. I swallowed.

What had I done? "I...helped make the map," I said in a small voice. "And..." I couldn't think of what else to say, what I'd done that they'd want to hear about. My brain froze and seized my tongue.

"Miss Sorenson," Dr. Roberts said after a long moment.

I turned, looking at him for direction.

His smile lit up his clever eyes. "Show them where north is."

I assumed he meant North and picking him from the crowd. I started to look among my team handing out maps.

"Or east," he said. "Whichever."

Oh. I pointed immediately toward north. "That's north," I said. And then redirected my pointer finger toward the ocean. "That's east."

How was this interesting? They had a vast pool of talented Academy people. I'd seen what Kota and the others could do so I imagined they all could do extraordinary things, even if those things were different among them.

Heads shifted as I pointed, and then one of them, a woman, pulled a compass from her pocket. "She's right."

"How did you do that?" Mr. Duncan asked. "We're surrounded by trees. The sun isn't visible to tell direction."

"She helped make the map," one of them said before I could answer. "She's been here before, so she probably knows. She has a great memory, right? That's what you're saying."

Dr. Roberts stepped forward, shaking his head. His hands were clasped behind his back like mine were, as he addressed the group. "This girl can find her way north in the middle of a pitch black night. A testimonial from Mr. Lucian Taylor, validated by several members of her adoptive family."

"She can identify direction by feel?" one of them asked. "Like a sense?"

"Correct," Dr. Roberts confirmed. "As you know, research shows we have more than five senses, like our sense of balance for example. Miss Sorenson here seems to have a highly developed sense of direction."

"And knows sign language," Mr. Duncan said. "That's an asset. She's already got a head start."

"And she can do a lot more," Dr. Roberts said. "I've been following her progress for some time. We've barely scratched the surface with this one."

I bit my lower lip, unsure of what else to say. Dr. Roberts was interested in my abilities? I didn't know he'd been paying attention, or even that I was interested in the Academy. I'd only guessed him to be Academy after the others had mentioned the hospital he worked at was Academy.

"Then perhaps you'll grant us a favor," Mr. Duncan said to me. "You see, we've been assigned to be managers for the new recruits. We're about to split them into starter teams."

"I want to lead a team," Mrs. Rose signed. "But my translator is busy; your doctor volunteered for the first aid tent this year."

My doctor. She had to mean Dr. Green. Luke could read sign language, too, better than I could. I wondered why they hadn't asked him.

"I'll help if you need me to translate," I said. Was that good? I'd be helping out and showing I could support the Academy in whatever way they needed. If I had an assignment and participated in the different activities, the week would be over in a flash. Then, at the end, they'd ask if there was any team I'd like to join, and I'd just say what Kayli had said...only nicer.

Perhaps I wasn't the best interpreter, and I was nervous, but maybe it wouldn't be so hard. Why had the guys made such a big deal about it? I wished I knew sign language as well as Luke, though. I was getting better, but he occasionally had to spell things out for me.

Mrs. Rose smiled brightly and then nodded at Mr. Duncan. She signed to him, "I believe I have my volunteer."

"Take good care of her," Dr. Roberts said, giving her a small salute with a single finger. "And I trust, she'll take good care of you, too."

I pressed my lips together, forcing a smile. I hoped I appeared sincere, even if I was incredibly nervous.

Mr. Duncan clapped his hands together. "Okay, then let's pick out our temporary teams. Miss Sorenson, stick by Mrs. Rose this week. Don't let her talk her team into going into caves or doing anything crazy."

I glanced at Mrs. Rose, who was grinning, a wild look of excitement in her eyes. She had soft white hair tied into a bun in the back of her head. She wore a bulky sweater that had pastel flowers woven into the design, gray cotton pants, and brown hiking boots. She might look like a frail lady, but I sensed that Mr. Duncan was absolutely not kidding.

Hadn't she just gotten out of the hospital after breaking her hip? *Maybe I should keep my phone on speed dial for Dr. Green.*

Where *was* my phone? I tapped around my bra and pockets as the older Academy leaders shuffled toward the collection of boys and girls waiting for them. I suddenly remembered mine had fallen in my tent and I had no idea where it might be now. Hopefully, Kota or the others had fished it out.

I hoped it wasn't broken again. But even if it wasn't, I was without any means of communication now.

The girls and boys sat up straight in their seats as the adults approached. I stood a little behind Mrs. Rose at first but then realized if she needed me to translate, I wouldn't be able to see her hands, so I stepped forward. I couldn't remember if she was deaf but she seemed to react to sounds around her. Maybe she was just mute?

"Thank you all for waiting," Mr. Duncan said in a booming voice. I checked the stands. There weren't any teams left, save mine, waiting at the crest of the hill for the last of us to get maps. "You'll have a chance to find your friends and talk with them this week, but I want you all to get familiar with each other in this group. We're going to stick together."

"Is this our team now?" one of the guys asked. "What about—"

Mr. Duncan shook his head and spoke over him. "Hang on, and no. This doesn't have to be your permanent team. You may pick anyone you like. We're just keeping you together as something of an orientation so you can all learn together."

"Just for the sake of simplicity," Dr. Roberts said, stepping up beside Mr. Duncan. "If you are thirteen or younger, come with me to this bench to the right here." He pointed to the far right. "And split off into two groups. Boys and girls."

"Why are we splitting?" One of the girls asked. "I'm as good as a boy."

"Because, among other reasons, some of us have to have a birds and bees talk later and I don't want you embarrassed by having the boys giggling. Don't worry. You'll have a chance to show boys up plenty this week."

They got a sex talk here? Then I realized this was a group of teenagers meant to sleep in tents and with lots of woods and places to hide. I thought of Ashley Waters, where there were rumors of people having sex in the bathrooms. I supposed getting a talk of camp rules in that regard needed to be done first thing.

There was a lot of muttering as the new recruits split apart.

Dr. Roberts, one of the women, and four more men went to go talk with the younger kids. Each one of the men split the boys even further, and the girls remained with the woman. They moved into their own sections of the stands and talked quietly among themselves.

"You older kids," Mr. Duncan said, drawing our attention back to him. "You've all had basic sex education classes in school, right? That's the lecture they're getting. I'm just going to remind you about the legal mumbo jumbo. By South Carolina law, anyone fourteen and older *may* engage in sexual activity legally, but only with someone eighteen or younger, unless you're sixteen and then it's legal in general. But," he said, scanning his eyes around to look pointedly at each of us in turn. "Even saying this, you should know your parents or legal guardian can press charges against another teenager or someone over eighteen if they believe it wasn't consensual."

"Why are you telling us?" someone asked from the group.

"We give the same speech every year simply because we can't keep our eyes on you at every second while at camp. Also, because you should know about *all* the consequences of any sexual activity—including legal ones, not just the medical ones," he said.

"You're free to make the right choice for you and we encourage you to give a lot of thought to your choices, but any Academy boy will back off the moment you tell them no. It's drilled into them. Same with the girls. They'll never pressure you. Consent is of the utmost importance."

"But we have to talk about boundaries," another one of the men said, stepping up next to Mr. Duncan. He was tall and pale, with black hair sculpted to perfection around his head. He wore all black, and while the material appeared rugged, he didn't seem to be the outdoor type. He reminded me of Mr. Blackbourne: someone who would wear a suit and tie to the park. He gave a serious eye toward the boys mostly, but also to the girls. "We do not tolerate peeping toms in the latrine, or spying on other teams in their tents. Trust me, you don't want to find out what other teams will do to you if you're caught."

I glanced at the others, particularly the boys. Many had wide eyes and stern faces. They were taking this seriously.

"And you will get caught, so don't even think about it," Mr. Duncan said. "You know as well as I do what they're capable of. Always be respectful. You wouldn't be here unless we thought we could trust you, but that doesn't mean there won't be consequences if you break that trust."

"Also, hands off unless there's consent," the tall, pale man said. "Consult with any of our doctors if you are in need of supplies or have questions." He paused, giving everyone a long, solid stare. "I don't want to have to repeat myself this week on that topic. Anyone reporting that you've crossed a line and put pressure on anyone for sexual activity will immediately be sent home and will not be invited into the Academy. That decision is permanent."

"Are we clear?" Mr. Duncan asked.

I supposed it made sense to get this out the first day. It was strange to me to see they accepted sex among teenagers could happen and were so frank about it. But I appreciated that they were serious about unwanted sexual attention.

It hadn't been on my mind at all until now that it might be an issue with so many teens in one place. It made me feel safer that it was spoken out loud, and that they seemed to be taking it very seriously.

As people nodded in agreement, the tall man spoke. "However, you will be very busy every moment of the next few days, so I highly doubt you'll want to do anything but sleep at night. This brings us to rule number two. In your tents at ten, not a moment later. Anyone caught outside a tent at that time better be on fire, or have a solid reason. Tent walls are thin; respect your neighbors and give them a chance to sleep."

I wondered who was on his team. He had a power and directness in his eyes that I suspected only Mr. Blackbourne could match.

"Rule three," Mr. Duncan continued, smiling. It was like good cop, bad cop with the camp rules. "We are going to split you up into teams now. I want you to remember your team manager. That would be myself, or Mr. Buble." He clapped a hand on the tall, serious man's back. "Mrs. Rose or Mr. Olson here." He motioned to Mrs. Rose and the final man in turn.

I'd thought at first Mr. Duncan had called the tall man Mr. Bubble, but then stop shorter than expected. It made me secretly giggle to myself that such a serious man would have a funny name.

Mr. Duncan continued. "Every morning, your team manager will be at a designated spot where you will join them at the appointed time. They'll interview you to see how you're doing, and will be available if you have any questions. You can join them for the day's activity planned with new recruits, or you may go to one of our groups. No matter what, remember your team manager, his or her name.

"He or she will guide you throughout the week. Listen to them. They'll answer your questions in full. We've got scheduled hikes and other times where you'll be able to get our full attention and ask all the questions you'd like as we explain to you the true Academy way."

"If the girls will go with Mrs. Rose," Mr. Buble said.

"Why are we getting split up, too?" one of the guys asked.

Mr. Duncan answered. "We felt it might be more comfortable for you all to have a same sex team and manager. However, if you really wish to go with Mrs. Rose, or if you girls would like to join the boys on the other teams, that's fine. We just ask that you please wait until tomorrow. We've got specific things we need to go over today, and we can't have you hopping teams right now."

I pressed my lips together, eager to get started yet worried at the same time. Was I going to be able to handle a week of translation for Mrs. Rose? Also, I wouldn't be able to switch out teams after I'd promised to stick by her.

I waited as Mr. Buble counted off, almost random, among

the boys.

The girls naturally came together, except for one girl who stood alone, looking worried. She appeared younger, smaller, but had to be fourteen since she was here and not with the younger group. Something was different about her though I couldn't place it.

Mrs. Rose touched my arm to get my attention. She signed to me quickly. "Tell her to join us," she said and pointed to the girl.

I bit my lip. With Mrs. Rose unable to speak up, I would have to be her voice, and in a way, in charge.

I stepped closer to the girl and caught her attention. She looked at me with imploring eyes. Her sweater was pink with purple hearts, and she had short black hair around her face, cut at the jawline. She wore some makeup, too, lip gloss, eyeliner, and mascara, making her eyes stand out.

There was something else, too. A darkness above her lip. Like she shaved it. I knew some girls developed hair in places that weren't typical, but the closer I got, the more I realized her face resembled a boy's.

Was she a boy dressing as a girl?

It was easier to address a stranger when it was Mrs. Rose who told me what to do. "Pardon me," I said quietly, clasping my hands behind my back. "You're joining us, aren't you?"

She smirked. "I wasn't sure."

"I guess you can pick a team eventually," I said. "But for now, join us?" I glanced at the group of girls: there were six others. "There's plenty of room."

The girl nodded and slid over on the bench until she was sitting next to the other girls.

I returned to Mrs. Rose and looked over the group. While we might have been close in age, there was one in particular who seemed older, maybe seventeen. The girls studied one another carefully. Some were more tomboy, and a few wore makeup.

Mrs. Rose started signing quickly, and I struggled at first to catch up with what she was saying. "Mrs. Rose...wants to thank you all for coming," I said.

"Louder!" one of the girls called out.

I bit my lip, but Mrs. Rose continued. I watched her hands, focusing on her, and then talking as loud as I could. "Ah, she...wants to know if we'd like to go on a hike." I paused as Mrs. Rose continued but she got to one I didn't know, and I had to stop her to ask her to spell what she meant.

She did, but even then, I wasn't sure she was serious. "She says she's hoping we'll spot a bear today?" The question was more for her, but Mrs. Rose nodded enthusiastically and gave me a thumbs up. I had gotten it right.

"I don't have the right shoes," one of the girls said. "No one told me we were going camping. My friend just put me in the car and said it was a surprise."

The boys had almost done similar, except they'd given me Christmas presents to at least warn me I was camping. I assumed she had met someone like the boys, who brought her along as a surprise.

I thought of Kayli getting a lecture about secrecy. I wondered how many people were like me. If my parents knew, they wouldn't understand why I was here. Maybe they didn't have nice parents either.

Mrs. Rose signed. I translated. "Does anyone have shoes to share..." I paused and then continued on after Mrs. Rose had stopped, seeking out the girl who had spoken.

"What size?" I asked. She said and then I nodded. "That's my size," I said. "I've got sneakers. Almost brand new." I was sure Gabriel had packed more than enough. "You can even keep them if you'd like."

We were supposed to share, right?

Mrs. Rose had me check with everyone about clothing and shoes. We were directed to go back to our respective camps for now, and would meet at the latrine in a half hour to go on our hike. Mrs. Rose promised we'd be able to join the others after lunch in the normal camp activities, but she had to go over Academy basics and try to answer as many questions as possible.

When I was finished translating for the moment, I swallowed, my mouth dry. I was going to need lots of water if I was going to continue talking so much.

As girls began to drift away from the group, I checked in with Mrs. Rose. "Do you need me now?" I asked. "Otherwise, I'll go get those shoes."

She shook her head and waved me off, and then gave me another thumbs up with a smile that I knew meant I'd done a good job.

I breathed out a puff of air, relieved. She was nice but I sensed she'd be hard to keep up with all week.

I checked in with the girl who needed shoes; she was going to follow another girl to her tent for better clothes for hiking and would meet me at the latrine after.

I was finally on my way to check in with my team when I noticed the girl that seemed to be a boy standing alone by herself. She pressed her lips together, looking uncomfortable.

Mrs. Rose asking me for help made me feel like I was her assistant of sorts. I waved to the girl and motioned to her to follow me.

The girl smiled and moved up the slope until she stood beside me. "Sorry," she said in her husky voice. "I don't have a tent set up yet anywhere. I was sort of brought along at the last minute."

I wondered exactly how many of them were at least told they were camping. Did their friends, the teams that brought them, not bring anything for them?

"Do you need better hiking clothes?" I asked, looking at her dark jeans, the pink and purple sweater, and then the black boots. "Are you comfortable in that?"

"I guess," she said. When she blinked, it revealed very black eyeshadow covering most of her upper eyelid, making her seem dark and dangerous. "What's your name?"

"Sang."

She tilted her head and made a curious face. "Sang? Is that your real name?"

I nodded.

"I'm Lake," she said, brushing her hair back from her face. Her nails were manicured, painted black.

I blinked at her. I had strange name myself, and often got questioned on it, but I wanted to make sure to get it right. "Like...the water? Lake?"

She nodded.

I wanted to ask if that was her real name, too but didn't want to offend her. Did it matter? As long as that's what she wanted to be called. "Did a team bring you?"

"It was my psychologist," she said. "She said there was a school for people with gifted abilities, but without means to afford a private education. She asked if I wanted to come to this." She motioned to the area around us. "Crazy school enrollment, isn't it?"

She was told this was like a private school?

Didn't I think it was in the beginning?

I wondered if, by simply being around the guys, I knew more than most new recruits.

Not wanting to let on that I knew anything, and still not sure how much I even understood, I nodded and continued up the steps. "If you want to follow, I just need to go back to my tent."

She did follow, but I suddenly regretted bringing her when I looked up and found Gabriel, Kota and North standing at the top of the path, waiting for me. I couldn't see the others. I wondered if they'd left to do camp things.

I cringed, realizing I might not be able to say much now with her beside me, not knowing how much I *could* say.

When we got close, Kota smiled. The others were smiling, too, but Gabriel shifted on his feet, and North's smile was tight. Something was bothering them. Were they nervous?

Only Kota seemed at ease. He'd rolled up his sleeves, and was holding a stack of paper maps. "How'd it go?"

"Not bad, I guess," I said. While I wanted to tell Gabriel and North about Kayli and what she'd said, I knew it would have to wait. "I need to go back to the camp and grab shoes for one of the girls who didn't bring anything."

"Sounds good," Kota said. "You're staying with the girls today?"

He made it seem like my choice, but I hadn't been given the option to join my team. "They asked if I could help Mrs. Rose translate," I said, shifting, looking at North and Gabriel.

Their smiles faltered, just a fraction, but they recovered.

"Aw," Gabriel said. "Who's going to be my camping buddy now?"

"It's just..."

"Who's this?" Kota said before I could finish, looking at Lake.

I blushed as I looked at Lake, who was standing to the side, looking out of place. "Sorry," I said to her and then looked at Kota. "Kota, this is Lake."

"Hi," Lake said to Kota and then glanced at Gabriel. "Do we need camping buddies?"

"No," Kota said, rolling his eyes. "He's kidding. Congrats on getting here. I hope you like it."

Lake nodded but then said nothing more.

Kota handed me two maps and then gave Lake two as well. "Hang onto these."

"Rule of two?" I asked. "That's why we get two?"

"Just in case you lose one," he said. "Or someone loses both of theirs and needs to borrow one of yours. The rule of two is that if you have just one, you have none. So you have two, and you'll have enough."

I supposed that made sense. Lake shared a long look with me that I didn't understand but nodded.

"What are you all going to do?" I asked.

He motioned to Gabriel and then North. "Most of them will be making circles around the camp, joining activities. You'll see us later today. Except for me, Dr. Green, and Mr. Blackbourne. We've got training."

That was disappointing, but at least I could catch up with the other guys after this hike. "So I won't see you until tonight?"

"You're still sleeping in the tent, right?" Kota asked.

I nodded, hopeful that wouldn't change. Maybe Taylor and April were wrong. Why did it matter where I slept? Besides, most of my stuff would probably already be with Kota if he'd made up a tent already.

Would other campers believe we were a couple sleeping together in our tent?

"I guess we should go," I said. "I have to keep by Mrs. Rose and still have to get shoes from the tent."

"Good luck," Gabriel said. "Don't let her talk you into any caves."

There was so much I wanted to ask them about but knew I couldn't. I was doing exactly what Mr. Blackbourne had asked me to do. I was doing my best.

I tried to be brave, even if I missed them already.

$\mathcal{T}$HE $\mathcal{H}$IKE

$\mathcal{L}$ake followed me back to the campsite. She lingered, looking at the cars while I searched the big tent for clothes. When I didn't see any of mine, I tried going to the next campsite over where my pink tent had been.

There was a new tent set up, green and tan, but it was a slightly bigger size. An air mattress was inside beside a cot, but the cot was covered in bags. One was pink so I opened it, finding clothing and shoes. I pulled out a pair of mostly black shoes with some pink, hoping the girl didn't mind the colors.

Lake peered into the tent. "You've got two tents?" she asked. "Why'd you go in the other one?"

I searched for my phone but didn't see it. "I was going to be in the tent with the guys but then..." I stopped and then bit my lip, not sure how much I should tell her. "I...Kota and I were going to share this tent."

"Oh," Lake said. "I don't have a tent yet I don't think."

Was I supposed to be nice and invite her to stay in ours? "We should...talk with the others, I think," I said. "The other girls. It sounded like some of them might not have tents, either."

"I thought it was a private school, not a camp," she said. "You've got room?"

I couldn't invite her without asking Kota, even though I was sure it'd be okay. I also didn't know if the Academy had plans to put the girls without tents somewhere. "We'll figure it out later," I said, exiting the tent with the shoes, giving up on finding my phone. "I'm sure every tent has an extra bed or two. They're Academy." It was weird to say it out loud because I'd never been able to. Now was my chance to discuss everything about the Academy openly and learn as much as possible.

"What does that mean?" she asked. "Like Boy Scouts?"

I shrugged and started toward the road to the latrine. Lake followed. "Let's get back to Mrs. Rose," I said. "I don't want to miss anything."

We got there a little early. I excused myself to use the restroom and to give myself a breather in the stall alone.

I sat there longer than I needed to, needing a few moments to collect my thoughts.

By the time I returned, Mrs. Rose was there standing with Lake and four of the other girls.

"We're missing two," Mrs. Rose signed to me as I approached. She wore a backpack over her shoulders and held a walking stick fashioned out of a branch. She leaned it against her hip while she signed to me. "Do you remember their faces?"

I wasn't sure. I looked over the other four girls. Two had cinch bags on their backs, and another one had a water bottle in her hand. They were taking turns spraying each other down with bug spray.

I tried to pinpoint who was missing. "One was older," I signed to her. I don't know why I was using sign language when I was sure she could hear me. It was more a reflex like when I used sign language with Luke. "My age, I think."

"What's she saying?" Lake asked in the middle of my signing.

"We're missing two girls," I said after finishing what I was saying to Mrs. Rose.

"The car that they came in with was parked closer to the camper area," Lake said. "I overheard them talking. They had a long walk to get their gear."

Mrs. Rose nodded. "That's the direction we should head in for our hike—we can find them on the way. Let's go find a bear!"

I told the girls we were heading out and would meet the other two on the way. I avoided talk of the bear, not wanting to scare anyone.

Although *I* was scared. I tried to tell myself she couldn't be serious.

We didn't go far from the latrine before we caught up with the two girls. Mrs. Rose used the map and led the way. I started to fall behind but realized I needed to be in front to see what Mrs. Rose would say.

Mrs. Rose asked me to have everyone share names. They did, but there were a few of them and some spoke quietly and I didn't really catch them. After the gathering earlier and seeing everyone there, I wondered how many I would meet, and was sure I'd get some names mixed up.

At first, we trailed in a line, but Mrs. Rose asked me to tell the others we should walk more in a group. "Make sure they can hear you," she said.

Mrs. Rose showed the older girl and her friend the map and the direction we were taking. Once they understood, she signaled for them take the lead, putting them in charge of where we were going.

Lake and I were put in the middle, where Mrs. Rose walked. The four other girls fell behind us, close enough to where we could talk as we walked.

From what I could see of the map, we had a good distance to walk even before we hit any trail. Of the trails I had seen last night, those were dirt and gravel. Mrs. Rose touched my arm to get my attention and then signed, "Tell the girls to talk about what they already know about the Academy. I'll fill in the details."

"It's the Fernis Academy," someone said after I translated.

"The Grayson Academy is what they told my parents," said another girl.

The older girl in front with the map said, "They tell your parents fake names when they talk to them. But when you get your report cards, it'll say whatever name they said your school was."

We would get report cards? That was something I'd never

heard before.

"Is *this* considered a class?" someone asked. "I thought we were just enrolling."

Mrs. Rose got my attention and signed.

"She wants to start with the rules," I said once she was done. "Do you all know the rules of the Academy?"

"Family first!" a few of them replied.

"That's not the first one," the older one said. "The first one is: *trust* your family."

"Oh yeah," her friend said behind her. "And then it's...your family is a choice?"

"Family is a choice," said the older one. "The rules are, in order: Trust your family. Family is a choice. Family first, Academy second. When your family can't be there for you, the Academy always will be."

"What does all that even mean?" Lake asked. "Family first? My family sucks."

"It means your Academy family, or who you choose to let into your family," the older girl said. She looked back at Mrs. Rose.

Mrs. Rose nodded in confirmation but I was the one with the question now. "How long have you known about them...um...I'm sorry, I forgot your name already."

"Carla," the girl said. "I've been on their radar for two years, but this is the first time I've been invited down."

"But not everyone gets into the Academy," Lake said. "I was told that."

"That's true," Carla said. "You might not be a good fit. I mean, not you specifically but..."

"I know what you mean," Lake said, although in a grumble.

Mrs. Rose signed and I spoke. "She wants you to keep going explaining the rules, or what you know of them," I said. I wanted to know, too. I knew some but was happy to just interpret and learn from other people's questions for now.

"Okay," Carla said, handing the map off to her friend, who took the lead. "To talk about the first one, you need to know about the third one. Family first means when you've picked the family for you, you're to be loyal to them and focus your energy on making their lives safe. Not *easier*, not try to do things for them. Simply put them in a stable position so they can better themselves, or that could mean they stay where they are and live their lives.

"This could be your Academy family, or if you adopt someone, like your sibling or parent. Adoption means that you want to protect them and make sure they are happy and safe."

"How do you adopt your own mom?" someone asked amid a chorus of giggles.

I was wondering that, too. What about Marie? Or even my dad or my step mother? Did joining the Academy mean I adopted them?

"Once you're in the Academy," Carla continued, "you get to pick who you want to adopt. It just means they get put on a list, and the Academy will help you make sure they have a job, a house, and are healthy and safe. You might not be able to include everyone you want because they might not accept help. That's what the adoption process is for. To see if they're willing to accept help.

"Once they are taken care of, you get to work outside your family and help us help other people. If your family gets into trouble, though, you have to stop what you're doing and focus on family. That's why there's the rule about family is first. Once your family is safe, we move on. When your home life is stable, you're able to focus."

The girls behind us gathered closer as we walked. "What's the other ones?" one of them asked. "The rules?"

"Family is a choice," Carla continued. "It means you get to choose your teammates. No matter what, you can pick who you are with. You also choose who you adopt so it can be anyone. Simple enough."

I absently fiddled with the zipper on my jacket as I thought about her words. You could choose. It was a rule. Could it be that simple, though?

Before I could ask her to elaborate, she moved on. "But

the first one is trust your family."

One of the girls spoke, "I don't understand that one."

"It means, you have to be as honest as possible with your own Academy family, and tell them everything. Every tiny detail. There should be no surprises between you."

I swallowed. I wasn't a very good Academy person. I had secrets. The boys were holding out on Kota about a big one. I had taken their direction on it before but there was a conflict between trusting the others with doing the right thing, and trusting Kota to tell him.

"Why?" someone asked. "I was told the Academy was a secret, but they want our secrets? Why do we have to tell anyone?"

"Because..." Carla paused and then looked back at me.

"Uh..." I said and looked to Mrs. Rose.

Mrs. Rose smiled and then paused as she walked. Everyone else did, too, and made a circle to look at her.

She signed, and I translated. "I have a secret," she said. "When I was younger, I had a voice. I used to be able to sing."

I swallowed hard. I wasn't sure why, but I'd assumed she was born mute. Her eyes glittered when she spoke, but there was something dark hiding in there—I suspected it was pain.

She moved her hands to speak, but in some areas, I had to fill in some words as sign language was simple, and she was telling a story and I was doing my best to share. She continued. "I was a child of the state, and back then, they didn't have the regulations as we do now. I never knew my parents and was never adopted. I was in a foster home with other children who were forced to work. I worked every day with bleach to clean clothes and floors. Day after day, I smelled nothing but bleach. Because I breathed it in every day, my voice eventually faded, until I couldn't even whisper. It had eaten through my vocal cords."

Everyone was quiet. I couldn't believe her story, and had trouble remembering to translate what she was signing because I wanted to absorb the story.

"It was hurting my lungs, too," she continued. "One day,

when I poured the bleach into my bucket and breathed it in, I began to cough up blood. My foster parents tried to tell the hospital that I must have tuberculosis, but tests came back negative. Even then, doctors wanted to send me back to the foster home. The doctors gave me medicines, but I knew my foster parents would put me right back into scrubbing the floors.

"They said I must have gone off to smoke with some older boys. But I hadn't—I knew what was making me sick."

"I wanted to tell the doctors. They were the only adults that I thought could save me. Only I couldn't tell them what was really happening. I'd lost my ability to tell them."

"It was a young Dr. Roberts who saved me. Back then he was just an intern, but he knew. He won my trust by bringing me candy and would tell me funny stories, and never minded that I couldn't talk back. Then one day he handed me paper and pen and asked me to tell him everything that had happened to me back at the foster home."

I was so happy that someone would listen. I begged him to save the rest of the children in the foster home. Maybe it was too late for me, but I hoped he could at least save the others from this fate."

Her bright eyes darkened as she went on, her smile losing the glimmer she'd had before. "Forty-seven children in a three bedroom house, all forgotten by the state. But after I told my story to Dr. Roberts, the Academy took over. I eventually joined and with Dr. Robert's and my team's help, I made sure every single one of my foster siblings—all forty-seven of them—found a decent home. They are all—to this day— protected by Academy adoption.

"We tell our Academy family everything because they can *help* us with everything. If there are no surprises, there won't be anything they can't do for us. And once you're family, you'll want to know so you can help your family, too."

Once she finished, I realized my throat had closed up. Two of the girls standing with silent tears trailing down their cheeks. No one spoke. No one moved. We stood together, absorbing this story, with trees around us, the blue sky above, and the silence of mid-winter.

Mrs. Rose continued signing and I had no choice but to translate. "We need to talk about the third rule some more." She waved her hand, urging us to continue walking toward the trail. "Academy second."

We started walking again. "It means you work on your family first," Carla said, although her voice was softer than it had been before. "And..."

Mrs. Rose signed. "If there is a family emergency, while completing Academy work, family comes first. However, there's a second level to that same rule. If you do have an emergency, you rely on the strengths of your family first. Only turn to the Academy if you can't do it yourself."

"I thought the Academy helped others," one of the girls said.

"It's true," Mrs. Rose said. "But we don't offer training and assistance only to have you ask us every time something happens. Always, always come to us if you need us, but we encourage self-reliance. This is why there is a favor and banking system in place. It's to give you specific goals and train you while ensuring Academy resources don't get depleted."

I was relaying this information when something ahead caught my attention. There were figures in the woods on our left side, skirting around trees, but I could clearly see it. I panicked—thinking about Mrs. Rose and her talk of bears when I realized I could spot bright red through the branches of the low bushes.

It was hard to focus when I was trying to interpret but in the moments when Carla or one of the other girls spoke, I continued to look for it.

Was someone following us?

There was a break in the discussion as we got to the trail. This one was a red clay mixed with sand dirt path. It was bright and obvious, marked with a freshly painted "Hiking Trail" sign. I recognized Gabriel's handiwork. We didn't cover it last night, so he must have done it this morning.

"We don't know how far this trail stretches out," Carla said. She'd taken the map back from her friend and was looking at it. "The trails aren't marked, just the main roads."

"We didn't have time to hike all the trails and map them out," I said. "This camp is really big."

Mrs. Rose checked her gold watch on her wrist and then began signing instructions, which I relayed: "It's nine-thirty. Let's assume twelve-thirty is lunchtime, so we've got three hours."

"We could follow the trail for an hour and a half," Carla said. "And if it doesn't twist around and bring us back to camp by that time, we can just turn around and follow it back."

"That's a very smart answer, Miss Carla," Mrs. Rose replied. "Very Academy."

♥

FOLLOWING THE TRAIL

The girls chatted about the trail as we started out until Mrs. Rose brought us back to the Academy and what that meant.

"Your training—this week and beyond—will help you to help yourself and your family situation, both Academy-chosen family and your adoptions."

The way she said this, and with the way other girls nodded, it made me realized that what I'd suspected before might have been right. They were troubled teens. I didn't know their backgrounds, but I sensed they were eager, hopeful that the Academy was something much better.

"So it isn't a school?" someone asked.

"It's not a school like you're used to," she said. "But it's still an education. We train you according to your needs—both educational and so you may support yourself."

"You get us jobs," Carla said. "In fields we like."

"We create opportunities. The Academy has very smart, very connected people who can help you reach your potential. But it comes at a cost."

"I knew there was a catch," Lake said. "You're going to have us give you all our money once we get jobs."

"No," I said, even before Mrs. Rose could shake her head—I knew it wasn't like that though I wasn't exactly sure how it worked.

Mrs. Rose continued. "This is where the favor and banking system takes place. That's what I call it. I think their terms have changed over the years but I'm still thinking in old terms. Old bird that I am."

"Oh yeah, we're birds, aren't we?" one of the younger girls asked.

"But what about the dogs?" another girl asked. "The boys?"

As Carla tried to explain that birds mean girls and dogs mean boys and it was just Academy slang, I caught a glimpse of the red streaking through the bushes on one side of the trail.

Someone was following us.

I studied our surroundings. There were trees on either side, mostly uninteresting woods. There was no reason why I someone would follow us here other than to spy on us.

There was no telling who it was, either. I had some suspicious, though. There were times the boys followed me either in school or at other times, and it seemed similar. I wondered if it was practice...or if there was a reason.

Mrs. Rose went on as we continued our hike. "We don't take any money. You keep what you earn. However, internally, the Academy does have its own cash system. We use these funds collectively to start charities, to which we donate funds that go to our families in need. As our numbers grow and our needs increase, we occasionally hold additional fundraisers."

I thought about the fundraiser at Thanksgiving. I nodded and said, "So when we donate money to the fundraisers, that's when we're adding money to..."

She shook her head. "No," she signed to me as I spoke aloud for everyone else. "Let me explain." She paused, clearly trying to think of how to say what was next. "When you join the Academy, you'll be given an indirect 'fund.'" She did air quotes. "However, you do not have access to it. It's money you're provided with to help your situation and can only be dispensed with Academy approval. Consider it like a credit card. Do you all understand credit cards?"

"You charge money to an account," Carla said, "but you have to pay it back with interest."

"We don't charge interest," she said. "But we do need you pay it back. When you start out, you're given a debt in the beginning, usually ten grand."

Jaws dropped around me. "Ten thousand dollars?" one of

the younger girls asked. She lifted her hands up and shook her head. "I don't have a job yet. How am I supposed to..."

Mrs. Rose shook her head and lifted up a palm.

"Let her finish, please," I said. The girls looked to me, eager for an explanation. I realized they might be thinking I was some sort of leader because I was Mrs. Rose's voice.

Mrs. Rose continued. "Your Academy 'credit' total per individual right now is thirty thousand. Ten thousand is deducted the moment you get access. The money is used for your education and training. It's actually a real bargain." She smiled. "Colleges these days, that won't get you in the first year."

The girls chuckled, but there was still confusion on their faces.

"Anyway, you never pay any of this money back in cash," she said. "You must pay that debt back through the jobs you complete for the Academy. Jobs for your own family, helping your family, don't count. Helping your family, or your family helping you, that's always free.

"A job you do for the Academy might earn cash for the Academy. That cash is poured into your 'credit card'"

"When can we spend the money?" Carla asked.

"You can only spend it when your family needs it beyond what you can afford for yourself," she said. "Or if you wish to use it to better your family. As an example, say you lost your non-Academy job, and you're short on funds for bills. The money is used to pay until you're able to get another job."

"And then we pay it back?" she asked.

"Not in that sense. With Academy work. This is our way of boosting you up without having a constant debt owed to the Academy. It keeps our accounting simple, too, and under the radar."

"Because we're secret," someone said.

"Why are we secret?" someone else asked.

"While that's a long explanation, the simple answer is: people would try to exploit and take advantage of our system," Mrs. Rose said. "We are very selective of who we invite into the Academy and you should be very careful not to talk about it." She paused and shifted her bag on her shoulders as she looked around at the group. "Would anyone like some trail mix or water? I forgot to ask before we started. We should stay hydrated." She looked right at me.

I hadn't realized, but my stomach was growling. Two bites of burrito and a candy weren't going to last me through a three-hour hike.

Mrs. Rose opened her bag to pass out water to anyone who didn't have any. The girls who'd brought cinch bags offered their own bottles they'd brought along, too, along with bug spray and packets of crackers. Mrs. Rose had trail mix and she handed me a small bag.

When everyone had items in hand, we continued on the walk and Mrs. Rose signed to me that we'd take a break while I was eating.

As we walked, some of the girls talked but I concentrated on eating and the occasional streak of red zipping from tree to tree. I began to think there were two of them, the way my attention was drawn to different spots.

I glanced at the other girls, but they hadn't seemed to notice as they ate and chatted.

I remembered how Mr. Buble was adamant to the new teens about not being peeping toms, and I sincerely hoped it wasn't new boys who were spying on girls and would get kicked out. However, it didn't really make sense, either. Why us? We were just hiking and learning more about the Academy.

Then I remembered new people were probably in groups like this, so it shouldn't be them. So it had to be older Academy people who would know better, and that made me wonder why anyone would follow us at all.

Once I was finished eating, I let Mrs. Rose know I was ready to continue. She gave me a nod and began signing. "I also mentioned another half to our system. Favors."

"You earn favors from the Academy," Carla said. She was still in the lead, looking ahead at the trail, but spoke over her shoulder. "When you do jobs."

"But you also spend favors," Mrs. Rose signed. "And like the cash system, you begin with a debt."

"Don't tell me it's ten thousand," someone said.

"No," Mrs. Rose signed. "It's only ten favors out of a total of thirty."

"That's easy, then," someone said. "Thirty favors?"

"Not as easy as you think," she said. "This isn't asking someone a favor like babysitting for a night or mowing a lawn. Favors mean you're taking part in something big that could mean a life change for someone else, even if you might not see the result. Think of it like if you volunteer to build a house for the poor. It took effort and time and for that, you're rewarded a favor."

"How do we know it's a favor?" someone asked.

"When you're recruited to help," she said. "And you'll also know ahead of time when something costs you a favor as well."

"How do we spend favors?" another girl asked.

"It's the same principle as with the cash system. It never costs favors to work within your own team. I should also say that asking the Academy to help create a plan of action to help within your own family also never costs anything. We are always available for guidance."

Carla spoke, "It's when that plan of action requires more than your team can handle. That's when you spend favors."

"But you can also lose favors," Lake said. It had been a while since she spoke. She looked at her boots as she walked. "I heard someone lost favors."

Mrs. Rose signed, "Teams can choose to set rules within themselves. You can lose a favor by disobeying an important rule. You have to work to earn a favor back."

I paused in interpreting. Breaking rules. Like when the boys couldn't kiss me. Didn't one of them say they didn't have enough favors?

I had to concentrate to continue so I pushed the thought aside.

"Favors are earned back through our work in the community," Mrs. Rose signed. "Once your family life becomes stable, we don't simply stop. We reach out and use our skills and talents to help other people. Sometimes we're improving neighborhoods and making them safe. Sometimes we help lost children find parents. It could be anything. Usually, we try to focus on areas where we can do the most good but have been neglected by authorities. We may take preemptive measures to prevent harm."

"How do we find these jobs?" Lake asked.

"Your team will have an official Academy lead. He or she is our contact for your group. What jobs are offered might be dependent on your skills. This is why we keep a file, to highlight your talents and we try to create a match."

Kayli had known about her file. I wanted to know what was listed in mine.

She waved her hand. "Anyway, I'm not going to go into those details now. Do you all understand the cash and favor system?"

"So we spend it once we're a member?" someone asked. "The ten thousand and the ten favors?"

"You've got a credit limit of thirty thousand dollars and thirty favors, but as you go through classes and learn what you need to know, you'll eventually get to where you've paid off your credit and favor debts, and you gain a surplus."

"This is called graduation," she said. "Once you're able to support yourself and you have a surplus of favors and cash, you've officially graduated from member in training to full-fledged member."

"Does that mean we can graduate early?" Lake asked.

"The moment you're in the clear, you've graduated—there's no other prerequisite like a number of hours or making good grades." Mrs. Rose smiled at me. "Your doctor and his friend were the youngest pair to graduate, at age ten or twelve, I think. They were very young and did it all themselves."

I had said it aloud because I was in translate mode but then stopped to absorb what she said about Dr. Green and Mr.

Blackbourne. I'd heard it before but hadn't really understood it until now. Dr. Green and Mr. Blackbourne had been the youngest ever to graduate?

"How'd they do it?" Carla asked, her eyes wide. Everyone else looked at me, too.

I looked to Mrs. Rose, waiting for her answer.

"It doesn't matter," Mrs. Rose signed. "Focus on your own graduations. Before you get to that, though, you should think of getting into the Academy. Any questions about the basics?"

"So when do we pick our teams? And how do we pick them?" Lake asked.

"You can pick whoever you want," Mrs. Rose said. "As long as everyone agrees. We might make suggestions and ask you to try out other teams, based on what we know about you and learn this week, but it's always up to you."

She wasn't telling them about their desire to keep boys and girls on separate teams in certain cases. I wanted to ask about it, but I didn't know a way to bring it up and not reveal my own worries about joining a guy team too early.

The other girls started to talk to each other but then Mrs. Rose snapped her fingers to draw attention back to her. "I should tell you, though, that during your first few years, you will have trainers and a manager."

This was a surprise to me. "What's a manager?" I asked, looking at her.

Carla spoke instead. "All new teams need a manager," she said. "How else are we supposed to figure out what to do?"

Did our team have a manager? I wasn't sure. I had never seen one. Maybe we didn't because Dr. Green and Mr. Blackbourne were graduates, and the boys had been through a few years of training. I wondered who their manager had been.

"A manager will be picked for you," Mrs. Rose signed. "You might even live with your manager if you are young and in danger if you stay with your immediate family. It's all decided individually. This won't be a choice, however. Your manager won't be your family, but you should still trust him...or her." She paused, and then took a very deep breath before she continued. "This comes after you've gotten through application and become a member-in-training, though. I think it's time for a break for now. Let's enjoy this hike and give ourselves time to think. I don't want to bombard you with too much at once."

I was grateful for that. My voice was already scratchy, and it was hard to take sips of water when she was signing and needing me to talk. It also made me run out of breath more quickly as I tried to keep up with walking and interpreting at the same time.

"Why don't you take a break?" Mrs. Rose signed to me.

With a nod, I retreated, walking behind the others to give my voice a break and take sips of water. I listened as the girls talked about teams, wondering who would manage them, and how that worked. Who would be my manager? I suspected it would be one of the boys. Maybe North or Silas. I'd thought of Mr. Blackbourne, Dr. Green or Kota, but they were already very busy.

She had said though that we wouldn't get a choice in our manager. Was...was Dr. Roberts a manager? It would make sense since he shifted me in the line, and spoke for me within the group. I'd have to ask Kota.

♥

$\mathcal{O}$FF $\mathcal{P}$ATH

$\mathcal{A}$s we walked, I kept an eye out for whoever was following us. They weren't easy to keep tabs on, but occasionally I could hear the crack twigs or rustle of dry leaves from off the trail. No one seemed to notice except for me and I wondered if I should alert Mrs. Rose.

Whoever it was, they didn't seem to be doing any harm. They weren't spying on us naked in a latrine. I doubted from the distance that they could even hear what we were saying. For all I knew, it was part of some Academy training.

Until I smelled something familiar. Sugar and vanilla. It was faint, but the wind had shifted in our direction.

Luke?

Maybe he was practicing with someone on how to follow people, because whoever was with him was noisy and wearing red. We just happened to be easy to follow with the simple trail. That seemed like an Academy training course.

Eventually, our group came to where the main trail split of into paths.

One of the girls pointed into the distance. "What's that?"

There was a small dirt path that led through a group of trees to a clearing on the other side. We were uphill and could see the roof of a building.

I took out my map, wondering if we'd found some way around to where the rangers slept. Based on the map and the short distance we'd walked, I didn't think we were anywhere near it.

"It could be a hunting cabin," Lake said.

Mrs. Rose signed to me and I spoke. "If we're curious, we should investigate." I'd said the words, but I frowned. I didn't really agree with her. They'd said not to let Mrs. Rose do anything too crazy. What about bears?

"Maybe we shouldn't go too far from the trail," Carla said.

As she was talking, Mrs. Rose forged ahead. I shared a look with Carla and Lake as the other girls started along the smaller trail after her.

"She's a crazy old lady," Lake said.

"She's Academy, though," Carla said. "We should trust her."

We couldn't just stand and wait for them to return. We snaked our way down the path behind the others.

The closer we got, the more I realized it couldn't be a hunting cabin. The building would barely fit a cot inside, let alone much else. Was it an outhouse of some sort? A restroom along the trail?

Once we got to the clearing, the building came into full view, atop a small hill stuck against the rest of the slope. It had wood siding painted bright red, with a black roof, white trim, and little windows. There was a cranking noise coming from it.

The path wound around to the front of the building, meeting with a tiny, trickling stream.

The stream had formed a small trench, about waist-high and a couple feet wide, that wound north down the hill. I suspected it met up with the river eventually.

The little stream started from under the building, which had been built on top of the little gorge.

Underneath the building, the trench darkened as it deepened. A water wheel was on the far side of the building, turning as water flowed over it—this was what was making the grinding noise. The water flowed down, following a small ditch to a mini waterfall on one side.

"It's like a water house?" Carla asked and looked at Mrs. Rose. "It's pumping up water from a water source below?"

She nodded and signed. "Some sort of pumping station." Mrs. Rose started up the hill to peer into one of the windows. She started signing again as she turned back to me. "Possibly for the latrines. They just made it look like a pretty little cottage with a water wheel."

We all followed, taking turns looking inside. I stood at the end of the line, curious but also unsure. Was this what made this hiking trail interesting? This little water pump house? Maybe we should have taken the main trail further, and then tried another of the paths. Maybe it was part of the camp, but it didn't seem like we should be poking our noses inside.

When the girls had moved on to go look at the water wheel, I peered inside, finding pipes and the inside of the gear that turned the water wheel. The grinding noise was louder here and echoed from below. While there was a floor, there was a lot of open space around the pipes and darkness into the cave area. The pipe inside led down into the cave.

When I stepped back, Lake was nearby, ready to look in. "Don't let Mrs. Rose in the cave," I said, joking.

"Too late," Carla said behind me.

I turned, as did Lake. A trail of girls had dropped down into the trench. The stream wasn't the issue. You could easily step over it, and there was room on either side within the gorge to walk along its sandy bank.

But the girls were heading under the building, and into the cave, skirting the mini-waterfall as they went.

"Oh shit," Lake said. "The crazy old bat is going to get us killed."

"There could be bears," Carla said. "I read about it. This is Hunting Island. There's bears. And wolves."

"I'm more worried about snakes," Lake said. "Snakes like caves, right?"

I pressed my lips together. We couldn't just leave Mrs. Rose and the girls to wander around in caves that might lead on forever. "Do we follow them?"

Carla nodded. "One of us should." She pointed to Lake. "Can you circle the building? See if there's another side to this stream where they might come out." She pointed to me. "Go in after them. Try to encourage them to get out."

"What are you going to do?" Lake said.

C. L. Stone

"I'm going to stand at the entrance here and be here when they come out. If something happens, we don't want everyone stuck inside." She looked at me. "Whistle if they get stuck somewhere. I'll send Lake for help if you take too long. Make them use flashlights so they don't break an ankle in the dark. Don't trust the dark. Try to get in front of Mrs. Rose and encourage her out. Tell her there's a bear out here somewhere if you have to."

I couldn't whistle, but was hoping if I caught up to one of the girls, she would be able to. I didn't remember to bring mine and wished I had. I breathed in and out slowly and dropped myself down into the little canyon. I accidentally stepped in the stream on my way down, getting a bit of water on my boots. The little waterfall splashed into my face as I started in but I walked around it.

The air got colder the closer I got to the mouth of the cave and I could smell the musty dampness from within.

I stopped at the entrance, able to hear the echoes of the girls giggling inside, but it was all black from my perspective. I wasn't sure I would be able to see once I was inside.

I also didn't have a light.

"Hey!" someone above called to me and I looked up to find Carla holding a flashlight above my head. "Catch."

I did and then waved to her. "Don't you need it?"

"I've got my phone," she said. "Don't get lost."

Easier said...

I turned on the light. It was small and had a narrow beam, but it was enough to allow me to see inside.

The cave started out as a small circular area, the building above my head. When I looked up, I could see inside the building, the pump inside and a pipe going into the ground. Parts of the mechanisms were exposed down here. It was clear this part of the cave was used to get access to the pumping system, so at least this part was probably safe.

However, the cave continued and had two paths, leading deeper in.

This was exactly what everyone had warned me about.

Keep her out of caves.

The girls weren't in the main room but I heard voices coming from the paths stretching inward.

I sighed, shining a light toward one path and then the other. "Where are you?" I called. "Which way did you all go?"

"We split up and went both ways!" one of the girls said. "Talk so we can still hear you."

How could she have let them split up? I thought to go back to warn Carla, but I didn't want to lose them further, either. What if the paths split again?

I wasn't sure what to do, and I felt uncomfortable letting this continue. I thought the best solution was to get to them and encourage them out. We didn't know if this place was safe and everyone warned us to keep Mrs. Rose out of caves.

I picked the right side path, following it in. My plan was to get one side out, and then go back and follow the other path.

It wasn't long before I saw the beam of their flashlight, and I did my best to navigate in the dark, using the small light I had to make sure I didn't trip over any rocks. The cave floor was uneven and the walls closed in at several points, making trying to follow the girls harder than I thought.

I was so focused on the ground and where to step that I bumped into one of the girls before I actually saw her.

She stood in the middle of the path and turned toward me. "I can't go," she said in a shaking voice. "I can't go any further."

I shone my flashlight down the path in front of her, where the other girls had already wiggled their way further in.

"Why don't you go on out?" I said. "Carla's waiting at the pump house for us."

"I don't want to chicken out," she said. "And lose my chance at getting into the Academy."

I was pretty sure the Academy wouldn't kick her out because she was afraid to go into a cave. I tried to think of a good reason to encourage her to leave. "Carla could use your help. She's watching for bears just in case one gets curious about the cave while everyone is in here."

C. L. Stone

The girl nodded and then peered at me with wide eyes, barely visible in the darkness. "Walk back with me?"

I didn't want to risk losing whoever was in front of us. "I'll go with you until we can see the pump house again," I said.

We started back, adding my light to hers so she could find her way out. When we were at the pumping area, Carla was just inside the entryway, shining her phone light in.

"Hi," she said to the girl before turning to me. "Are they coming back?"

"They went both directions," I said. "And I wasn't able to get to them."

"I went around," Carla said, pointing above us. "There is a place further up the hill where the cave opens up again, like the creek, but it's steep. They won't be able to climb out, so they'll have to come back. And if there's two paths, then I'm not sure which one leads there. I had Lake go over there and stay to encourage them out."

I nodded. "I'll go back on the right, and get them to return."

"Do your best." She said and then looked at the new girl. "Can you stay here and shine your light into the cave on the left? I'm going to go in and see if I can get them to come out."

Were we being too cautious? Mrs. Rose was an adventurous spirit. I remembered following Nathan through paths in woods surrounding our neighborhood, and he was always eager to try new places we hadn't discovered yet.

This felt different to me, but perhaps because of the cave and darkness.

Or if there might be bears sleeping at the end.

Or snakes between the rocks.

I went alone down the right path, unable to hear the other girls ahead of me. I was alone.

Thinking of snakes made my knees tremble and I moved along the right path much slower now. If only the boys were here. It didn't seem so bad when someone else was here, and I had to be brave, but now it was just me with a tiny light facing

276

the darkness and silence and I was shaking all over, afraid of bugs, of bats, of bears who might jump out at me at any moment.

I tucked myself between rocks. The walls became narrow, and I had to duck and squeeze. At one point, I was on my hands and knees, suddenly disbelieving the group could have possibly wanted to go any further.

"Hello?" I called out.

A voice replied, but it echoed and I couldn't tell who it was, only that they were ahead of me.

Eventually, there was more light. I didn't know where it was coming from until I turned a bend, and saw it was coming from above where a small section had opened up.

This had to be the path that opened up, the one that Carla found. I hoped Lake was still out there.

I continued on, now able to use natural light to make my way through the cave, and eventually turned a bend to find the little stream and the small gorge it had formed, except the walls were taller here, well over my head.

The group of girls—three of them—stood together, where the trail ended. The stream trickled from a small crack where the walls met. The only way out was up the wall or back through the cave again. It was pretty, but it felt like we were stuck in a pit.

"We should climb out," one of the girls said as I got closer. "It'll be like rock climbing."

"I don't want to do that," another one said.

"I don't want to go through the cave again," the third said. She wrapped her arms around herself, shivering. "I don't like this."

"Girls," I called out, waving as I left the cave.

They turned to me, appearing relieved.

"Tell them to climb out," one of them said, pointing to the wall of the pit. "It'll be easier."

"I don't think I can," the other girl said. "Don't make me."

"We don't want to go through the cave again."

I sighed, looking up. "Lake?" I called.

It took a minute, but Lake appeared, looking down at us from the lip of the cave. "You found them?"

"I found three," I said. "Carla's going after the other group. Mrs. Rose must be with them. She's going to get them to turn back."

Lake nodded. "So go back. You can find your way, right?"

I looked at the girls, all folding their arms across their chests and regarding me with expectant eyes—they were waiting for me to make a decision.

I didn't like the idea of going back into the dank and dirty cave. "Maybe we should try climbing," I said.

We studied the walls, looking for the lowest and best spot to try.

Once we found what we agreed would be the best place to climb I stood at the bottom and assisted one of the girls up by clasping my hands together to give her a foothold, the way the guys had taught me before. I boosted and Lake put herself on her stomach to reach down from above to lift her up.

It took eons for the girl to find a foothold in the rock face that was sturdy enough for her to steady herself. Once she did, I boosted her, lifting with everything I had. The girl made it up, but barely, and I used up a lot of strength doing it.

Once she was up, I leaned against the wall and breathed heavily. Could I push up two more girls and still pull myself out?

Lake patted her hands against the dirt of the pit wall and reached down. "Come on," she said.

I bent over, ready to lift another girl. She was heavier than the first one, and while I tried to boost her, her balance was off and she wavered. We crashed backward, me on my butt, her on her side.

Lake groaned. "Come on," she said. "Or you'll just have to go back through the cave."

The third girl that was waiting shook and had tears in her eyes. "We're going to be stuck here forever," she said.

We needed someone stronger and taller. I thought of Silas or any of the guys. They could get themselves out.

Suddenly, I recalled the people in red who'd been following us. I'd had a suspicious feeling I knew who it could be as we walked. I suddenly hoped I was right.

"Lake," I said, swallowing against the dryness in my throat. "I need you to make a call."

"On my phone?" she asked. "It doesn't have a signal."

"I mean...make this noise." I made a squeal—the emergency signal I'd learned from kids in my neighborhood. I just hoped one of the guys were actually out there and remembered. "*Suu-weee*," I tried again. "Do that."

"Are you kidding?" Lake said, looking down at us with a frown. "Why?"

"Just do it," I said. "But do it loud."

She did, making the noise as loud as she could. The girl next to her joined in.

"Do it again!" I said.

They did, and then Lake stopped abruptly and turned, stepping away out of view.

My heart was beating hard in my chest as I stared up at the opening over our heads.

Please, please, please...

Nathan's face appeared, looking down at us, wearing a serious expression. Luke appeared beside him a minute later. Luke was wearing black pants and a camo long-sleeved T-shirt. Nathan wore the same, except for a red knit hat.

I was so happy to see them, I was going to ignore that they had been following us.

"How'd you know we were here?" Luke called down to us.

"Nathan's hat," I said. "I saw the red. And you were loud. I could hear you coming. And I could smell your vanilla scent."

I'd spent a lot of time walking in the woods as a kid, so identifying noises and what was human and just wood noises was easy for me.

Luke smacked Nathan in the stomach with a loose hand. "I told you that you were being too loud."

"Shut up," Nathan said and then peered down at us again. "Need a hand up?"

I nodded. "I'm not strong enough to boost them out."

Nathan squatted, and then crawled to the edge of the pit, lowering himself until he hung on with his hands, his feet dangling down. "Get out of the way," he said.

The two other girls and I backed up. He let go and landed with a thud at the bottom, dropping down to his hands to brace himself for the impact. Once he was settled, he stood, looking up. He whistled in a low tone. "That's a drop. That almost hurt." He turned to me and frowned. "What are you all doing in there? Did you fall? No one's hurt, are you?"

"Long story," I said. "Can you help the girls out?"

"Sure," he said. He motioned to them. "Come on. I'll boost you up. Luke will pull you out."

"We won't even ask a favor," Luke said from above us with a grin. "This one is on the house."

Luke lowered himself on the lip of the cavern like Lake had done, lying on the ground with his hands down, reaching.

Nathan picked up the first girl with ease, boosting her so she could reach up to Luke. Luke grabbed her hands, pulling her up. Lake continued to help, taking the girl's arm and pulling until she stood on solid ground. They worked again to lift the next girl out.

Nathan dusted his hands and then reached for me. "Your turn."

We were alone now, so I spoke quietly, hoping the other girls couldn't hear. "Are you guys going to keep following us?"

"Of course," he said. "Victor told us you made him promise to stay by you. We've got a schedule so we switch out, but we'll try not to get in the way. We need the practice apparently anyway. I volunteered today. I wanted to see how you were getting on. Probably a good thing, too. Mrs. Rose is a little...adventurous."

I smothered my proud and happy smile. Victor had kept

a promise I'd already forgotten about. It would make this job easier knowing the guys were going to be nearby the entire week. "Thank you," I said.

He winked and moved behind me to help me up, but gave my arms an extra encouraging squeeze. "You're doing amazing, Peanut. Keep it up."

I was glad it was him and Luke following, or any of my team. Anyone else might not have known to come help us.

Nathan lifted me up and Luke pulled when I reached for him.

"Except you," Luke said with a grunt as he pulled on my arms. He grinned through it, though, his brown eyes shining as a lock of blond hair fell into his face, escaping the clip he was wearing. "You owe me a favor after this."

"Just give him a cookie," Nathan said from below me, boosting me higher.

"I'll take a cookie," Luke said. "Or five. Homemade, though. Extra chocolate chips."

I was yanked up to the rim of the cavern, dirt smudging my sweater. When I got to the top and was standing by Luke, I brushed off my clothes. All the girls were covered in brown stains on the fronts of their clothes.

Luke dropped down to his stomach again and leaned further out. Nathan backed up, and then raced toward the wall of the pit, jumping up the side wall as he grabbed for Luke's hand. Luke caught and used Nathan's momentum to pull him up as the rest of us watched in awe.

Nathan and Luke stayed on their knees for a minute, breathing heavily and recovering.

"Whew," Nathan said, pressing a hand to his side. "No more falling into pits, girls. We might not always be around to call on."

"What was that?" Lake asked. Her eyes were narrow, suspicious. "The call. *Suu-wee*?"

Luke shrugged, brushing grass and dirt off his black pants. "It's an emergency call from our neighborhood. If you hear that, someone's in trouble." He looked at me to confirm.

"North made sure we all recognized it once we knew what it was."

"But that's not an Academy thing," Nathan said. "So don't expect other people to respond to it."

Lake nodded, shifting from foot to foot. Next to the guys, she did look more like a guy, just with feminine features, like a fine nose and the fact that she was small.

Luke waved at the girls to get their attention. "Now listen, you didn't see us here. I need you all to pinkie swear it." He held out his smallest finger toward the girls. While he was grinning, his brown eyes were steady; he was serious.

All the girls held out their fingers. He hooked his finger onto theirs and looked them dead in the eye in turn. When he was done, he smiled warmly and nodded. "That's what I'm talking about."

Lake pointed to me. "You didn't make her swear."

"She knows better," Luke said and winked at me.

"Thanks, guys," I said.

"For what?" Luke said with wide eyes as he backed away toward the woods. "We weren't here. We didn't do anything." He disappeared behind the trees. Nathan waved at us and followed him.

I was able to follow their movements for a little while, but they soon disappeared behind some trees.

With the guys gone, the girls all looked to me.

"What now?" Lake asked.

I looked around us. There hadn't been word from the other girls. "We should circle around."

"Are those guys going to follow us?" one of the girls asked.

"What guys?" I said, my eyes wide. I smiled like Luke had. "I didn't see anyone."

Since the guys didn't want anyone to know they were there, I assumed they weren't really supposed to be following us. Would it really be that bad if Mrs. Rose or someone in charge found out? They did help us.

Maybe because they were practicing following without

being noticed, so they wanted to continue that. If we told anyone else, we'd be looking for them.

The girl nodded and zipped her lips with pinched fingers and then started following Lake around the far side of the pit, back toward the red building. "I hope so," I heard her say as she walked on. "Just in case we find another cave."

I hoped so, too.

♥

ON WITH THE HIKE

The path Mrs. Rose had followed had ended and Carla convinced them to return. Once we were all outside. Mrs. Rose apologized when she returned, signing her explanation which I translated.

"The ranger said there was a nice little cave under a red building, which we were lucky enough to find. She said it was safe, just to watch out for critters that might have gone in through the night." She looked at me with an apologetic smile. "I told them this by writing it on my notepad before we went in beyond the water pipes. I'm sorry if I scared you."

I wouldn't have been surprised if she had specifically asked the rangers if there were any caves to explore.

We all said we were fine, but looking around at the group, I had a feeling we were all done with cave exploring.

Mrs. Rose suggested instead of following the trail back, that we follow the stream. She looked right at me. "This heads north to that river, right?"

She knew I could tell directions and she was giving me a chance to use it. I confirmed with them that the stream was heading north, and we'd be able to follow it to the beach and then back to camp. I gauged from the map that it wasn't very far. "Maybe a mile or two," I said.

It was enough to convince the others to enjoy a nice walk in the stream bed.

The gorge never got deeper than our waists from that point on, except soon it narrowed, so we had to walk single file. I wondered if we still needed to talk about Academy things, but no one asked questions at the moment.

A meadow spread out around us and it was a lovely walk following the stream along the sandy banks, with the sky overhead. I imagined during the spring and summer, there might have been flowers.

Sometime later, a girl ahead of me pulled her hand in sharply. "Ow," she said. "I think the plant bit me."

"Plants don't bite," a girl ahead of her said.

I was about to agree, although I suspected maybe she brushed up against poisoned oak. I'd had few experiences with it.

I was about to check her hand for the start of a rash, or a bee sting, when I noticed the overgrown plant she'd brushed up against. I'd been focusing on the stream we were following as we walked the sandy path and followed it north. I hadn't been looking around us for the last ten minutes.

The plants around us looked eerily familiar. As far as I could see the distant tree line, a hundred or so feet away, there were nettle plants. *Stinging* nettle.

Great.

"Girls!" I called out, my voice cracking after so much use earlier, plus my voice being broken since I couldn't talk so loud. I swallowed.

"Sore throat?" Lake asked. She'd been behind me, the last on the trail.

"Sort of," I said. I looked ahead and thought I saw the bigger river ahead of us as we continued down the gentle slope. The nettle didn't go as far as the river but was spilling over into the gorge, though. "Tell the girls to walk with their arms up and to not touch the plants. It's nettle."

"Is it like poison ivy?" Lake asked.

"No," I said. "It will make a little rash, but it'll go away in an afternoon if you don't scratch it. A little lotion can relieve the itch and I don't think it spreads like poison ivy does. It should be okay if their clothes brush against it."

Lake called over my head to the girls. "Keep your hands up!" she said. "Or cover your arms with a sweater and put your hands in your pockets! Don't touch the plants."

"Should we go back?" someone asked.

"We're almost to the river," Carla said. She covered her

brow with her hand, looking toward the river. "Can we get there?"

"There's no nettle up there," I said. "I think we're fine. Probably faster to go to the river than back."

Lake told the girls to continue forward. "Just keep your hands away from the plants, and you should be fine."

One of the girls said she didn't have a sweater with her, so another girl gave her a jacket.

Once we were out of the stream bed and away from the nettle, the girls collected on the beach.

"I'm not an outdoor girl," one of them said. "But this wasn't bad."

"A cool adventure," another one said. She held her hand up to give out high fives and then changed it up for a hug when Mrs. Rose opened her arms wide and almost tackled her.

"Group hug!" one of them called. "We made it!"

I gritted my teeth, looking at Lake. Lake shrugged, and moved toward the circle, joining in.

Hugging? My insides tightened as I held back.

"With Sang, too!" Carla cried out. She was somewhere in the middle. "She was great!"

Before I could get away, the group shifted and I was suddenly surrounded by hugging bodies.

Darkness washed over my eyes and my heart erupted into a thumping mess. I curled inward, making myself as small as possible, closing my eyes. I held my breath and tried not to move.

The feeling that washed over me was overwhelming. I didn't understand what I was feeling. I should have been happy, shouldn't I? They were being nice. This is what normal people did.

The longer they lingered, the more I wanted to sink down into the ground and escape. My skin crawled. My stomach clenched into a knot. My throat closed up. I couldn't even ask them to stop.

I was as still as I could by, my arms over my body, as I felt hands on my shoulder, my back, my arm. Someone's breasts pressed into my back as they hugged me from behind.

The girls broke it off and then they all giggled and started talking about the walk—the cave, the climb out, the nettles. It was nothing to them. It was a hug.

I rubbed at my face, pretending I had an itch and tried not to look at anyone as I wiped away the tears in my eyes. Overwhelmed and suddenly exhausted, I wanted to get away. I shivered and wanted to rake my crawling skin in a piping hot bath. What was wrong with me? I had been fine all morning until they all came close and touched me.

I was so awkward. So shy. So easily overwhelmed by simple, friendly touching. Would I have to get used to that kind of thing if I was brought into the Academy?

How come the guys could touch and hug me and this was so uncomfortable? Did I just need to get to know them?

"Follow the river!" one of them cried out, jolting me out of my dark thoughts but not enough that I wasn't still rattled by what had happened.

Mrs. Rose signed and I spoke for her, but in a low voice, not even registering the words.

It was Lake who heard me and became my voice. "Once we're in view of other teams, we're ready to split up for the rest of day. Go grab lunch. Join in activities. Tomorrow, meet me—Mrs. Rose—at the latrine at nine a.m. We'll review what we talked about today, go over some more Academy details, and open up for questions. If you need anything, come to me and I'll make sure you've got supplies, clothes and a place to sleep. I'll be at the cabins this afternoon."

It wasn't long before we came up to another Academy group.

A man sat at a table, with fishing gear and equipment around him. He had a beard and a wise old face. Beside him was a flagpole grounded in a bucket filled with cement to keep it in place. From the pole flew a flag with an emblem of a fish.

Along the shore of the river were several people, mostly guys, but a few girls of varying ages. Some had poles and some had nets and some sat on coolers behind those fishing, watching and chatting.

The man at the table smiled and waved at us to join him.

"Come on girls," he said. "Does anyone want to fish? Don't be shy. I should have enough poles or we can share."

Carla said something inaudible. The rest shrugged but seemed uninterested in fishing. I wasn't, either, but mostly because I was starving and wanted to find the guys and get lunch.

But then I spotted Silas, who had been facing the water and I didn't recognize him until he turned toward us. He had some string in his hand. The string was stretched out into the water, tugged taut by something on the other end. He held the string and was slowly dragging it in. Standing beside him was Ian, wearing the same Yankees cap from the night before. He watched Silas pull the string in.

"You got him?" Ian asked Silas.

Silas nodded but didn't say anything. Something tugged at the string and jerked it in another direction, but he held on, and slowly reeled it in. Just a bare string? Why didn't he have a pole? It took me a minute to figure out others around him had only strings, too. A few had poles, but they had split off to go further up the river. Silas's group all fished with their hands.

I peeled myself away from the girl group, grateful that we had permission to split up. I hoped Mrs. Rose would come to me if she still needed my help.

When I walked toward Silas, Lake followed, which I didn't mind. Then Carla followed her, seeming curious as well. Once she did, the other five girls followed her. I wondered if they had gotten used to following me and simply stuck close by. I imagined if they were dropped off and didn't see someone they recognized, they wanted to stick with someone familiar. I knew the feeling.

Mrs. Rose remained by the table, talking to the man in charge of the fishing station. He read her signing, nodding along, so I knew she didn't need me right now.

I walked up to Ian, who smiled at me. "I recognize you.

How'd it go?"

"We took a hike," I said. "Almost got stuck in a cave. Ran into some nettle. But we made it." I was on a roll with talking all of a sudden. Was it because they were Academy that I was able to talk more? Also, with Silas right there, I was feeling a little braver. I was relieved that I could join with him or any of the other guys. I was off duty for the day.

"You let Mrs. Rose in a cave?" Silas said over his shoulder. "Didn't anyone warn you?"

"Yeah," I said and stepped up beside him. "She had asked a ranger about the caves and led us right to it before we even realized." I paused as he was easing the string in. "What are you doing?"

Silas continued to pull the string, focusing on where it dipped into the water. "Hopefully, you'll see in a minute."

Lake, Carla and the other girls shifted around Silas, watching.

Something white appeared connected to the string. As it was still under the water, it was hard to tell, but it looked like a raw chicken leg, bone and all.

"You feed the fish with chicken?" I asked.

"It's not fish," Silas said. "Girls, step back. I don't want him to pinch."

The girls pulled back, as did I. Ian stepped up beside Silas, reaching a net out into the water.

When the net came up, it caught Silas's chicken, but attached to it was a blue crab. I hadn't even seen it in the water; it blended so well until it had nearly surfaced.

The crab dangled in the net, hanging on to the kitchen with legs wriggling.

"I'd rather eat the chicken," Lake said.

"Crabs aren't my favorite food, either," Ian said. He held the net carefully and swung it wide, bringing it over to a cooler that one of his team members had been sitting on. I couldn't remember his name. He opened the lid of the cooler quickly when he saw the crab coming his way. Ian dumped the crab inside. "But they're fun to catch."

"I'll eat one or two," Silas said. "They're good. Hard to find good blue crabs. This river is full of them today, though."

"Come here, girls," Ian said, waving us toward the cooler. "Come see this." His friend held it open so we could see.

We peered in, looking at a blue crab with its pinchers open and active. It had released the chicken and looked like it was feeling threatened and ready to strike. It backed up into the side of the cooler, its hard shell meeting up with the plastic wall.

"Aw, it's a girl," Ian said. "Pregnant, too."

I studied the crab, but couldn't tell how they knew it was a girl, or pregnant.

"Got to throw it back," Silas said.

"Why?" Lake asked. "Why not just eat it?"

"Because she'll have babies," Silas said. "She'll make more crabs for us to eat."

"We only want the big boys or the girls without babies," Ian said. He dropped the net and helped his friend bring the cooler back toward the river. They carefully tipped it until they dropped the crab into the water. The crab took its chicken and disappeared back into the depths.

"I don't want crab," one of the girls said. "Is this lunch?"

"I'm hungry," another one said. "We need real food."

"If you go down to the beach, there's a group making hamburgers and baked potatoes," Silas said. "Enough for everyone for lunch." He rubbed his stomach. "I had some, but I left room for a crab."

"Can we go?" one of the girls asked, looking to me, Lake and Carla.

The three of us looked at each other and shrugged.

"You don't need our permission," Lake said.

Still the girls waited. "Shouldn't we stay together?"

Carla and Lake again shared a look with me. Maybe they needed help finding their way around. I was hungry, too, though, so I didn't mind walking with them to lunch. "I could use a hamburger," I said.

"Might as well go," Lake said.

The guys waved goodbye to us.

We found the same grill the guys had used the night before, and it was surrounded by more tables dragged in from other camps. There was a pile of hamburgers already cooked, along with potatoes, all stacked in coolers with other supplies.

A woman was stationed there, in charge of directing us to eat and where to throw our trash. We sat together at one of the tables. I didn't see any of the other boys here and wondered if Luke and Nathan were still following and would they come out to eat, or if they had stopped following after we got back to the general camp area.

After eating, we explored different stations, one was first aid training, which was busy as Dr. Green and a couple other people taught people how to check vital signs is someone was unconscious. He was so busy directing the talks, he didn't see me. I didn't want to distract him, so I stayed in the background.

We were going to do a full circle of the entire camp until one of the girls said they were tired of walking. The others agreed with her.

"I've been up since four this morning," one of them said.

I shared a look with Carla, who shrugged. Lake nodded. "Me, too, actually," she said. "The people who brought me in had to give me the lecture on secrecy before we even got here. And I live over in Georgetown. It took a few hours to get here."

Carla checked her map. "Why don't we try the craft section?" she asked, glancing up at Lake and me. "That should give us a place to sit and still participate while giving us an opportunity to sort out who doesn't have a place to sleep tonight."

That made sense. Hopefully, they'd make friends with other Academy members, too, and they'd feel more comfortable going off together. I thought that was the point of the different booths: To get to know other people.

We stopped by the latrine for a break, but then followed the road that led to the designated arts and craft tables. Soon we came across another pole, this one flying a flag that had a paint brush on it.

The area was inside a pavilion, with a concrete floor and a wooden roof overhead set up on pillars, but was otherwise open. There was a stage made out of wood, where a few tables were set up.

On the concrete slab under the roof, there were dozens of tables set up in rows, and each row appeared to feature a different craft to work on.

A couple of older members stood and watched over the group, speaking to the people at the tables—giving guidance and advice, I assumed.

We didn't really look at the craft options, just for a spot where we could all sit. I scanned the tables for familiar faces, and I didn't see anyone. Carla pointed out a table with room for all of us.

We weaved our way through to get to it. It was covered in a bright yellow tablecloth and had several small buckets containing seed beads, fishing string, and some tools and clasps.

"Necklace or bracelet making?" one of the girls asked.

"Looks like," Carla said.

"It doesn't seem like Academy training," Lake said.

One of the gentlemen passing by to give assistance smiled at Lake's comment. "Some of the crafts do require more skill and perhaps a lesson. And some are just meant to be a break from lessons and just for fun. Take everything at your own pace." He motioned to the empty areas we had been walking toward. "Have fun."

I sat on the end of one bench. Lake sat next to me and Carla sat next to her. Another girl took up the spot next to Carla, and the other side filled in with the other girls.

I looked over our supplies. Besides the buckets, there were craft organizing kits filled with different sized and colored beads. Some were painted with designs and many with letters and charms, too.

One of the girls wiped her forehead. "Can we just stay here and make bracelets until it's time to go to sleep?"

I didn't have a problem with that. After all the hiking and

excitement, I couldn't wait until it was time to sleep.

It was Carla who taught us how to start off a bracelet. She didn't make one herself but spent her time checking knots in strings, going over the hundreds of charm options and finding colors for people.

I stood a little, with a knee in my seat, bending over the supplies, looking for different colors. I was thinking of making a bracelet one of the guys when I felt my hair clip loosen and get plucked away.

I whipped around, at first getting hair in my face, but already grinning. "Hey," I said.

Gabriel stood behind our seat in jeans and a neon orange sweater. He leaned forward to snap the clip at my face like teeth. "Worst camping buddy, ever," he said, pinching the clip so it would 'talk' along with his words. He was frowning but his crystal eyes were lit up.

"Meanie," I said. I tried to make a glare, but a smile spread across my lips at the sight of him. I missed him, too.

"Where have you been, Trouble?" He looked down at my clothes and then up to my face. "What the shit fuck...shoot...*fudge*..." He glanced over his shoulder and then at the girls. Then he leaned in to talk to me quietly. "God damn my mouth. But what happened to your clothes?"

"There was a cave," I said, looking him over. There were a few paint drops on his rolled-up sleeves, making me wonder where he'd been. He didn't have his hat on now, so the blond was hanging around his temples and the russet was brushed back.

Relief washed over me once again. The boys were here. I'd be fine.

"Aw fuck," he said. "We told you about her and caves."

I nodded. "You following me?"

"I've been here all morning," he said and pointed across the way to where there was a group of people sitting at easels set up outside the picnic area. An elderly woman was directing a painting class. "I had the morning shift. But I'm off duty now." He nudged me in the elbow. "Scoot your ass down. I'm tired of painting. I want to do something else."

I scooted, sitting closer to Lake than I was comfortable with, but Carla moved down, allowing Lake to make room.

"Prin—Sang," Victor's voice called, but I didn't see him until he was walking up behind the girls in front of us and waved to me. He had on a gray sweater and jeans, his hair a little messy. His fire eyes were curious, and his smile was small, fox-like. His cheeks flushed as if he'd been exerting himself. I had a feeling he had taken over for Luke and Nathan since we'd returned.

I was so happy to see him, too. I smiled and shared a look with him, wishing I could hug them both, but keeping my distance.

I quickly touched my finger to my lips, making sure he saw.

He quickly did the same and then dropped his hands. "Having fun?"

"Who are you?" one of the girls asked, turning to look up at him where he stood behind her.

One of the girls who had been in the pit with me leaned in to whisper to her but we all heard. "He's not here," she said. "Don't tell anyone."

I had a feeling despite saying not to tell the other girls, that all the girls knew about Nathan and Luke following us and how they had pulled us out of the pit.

Victor's eyebrows went up and the fire ignited as he shot me silent questions. I giggled, unsure how to explain.

"I don't think it matters right now," Lake said.

The girls looked to me for confirmation and I shrugged. "It's camp," I said. "We're supposed to meet new people and get to know others, right?"

"May I join you all?" Victor asked. He moved to the end close where I was sitting, across the table. The girls made room for him so he could sit across from Gabriel.

Once we were settled, Gabriel reached for a bucket of beads. "Aw yeah," he said. "Bracelet-making. This is great."

"You want an orange one?" I asked. "I'll make you one."

"I was going to make you one," Gabriel said. He scanned through beads. "Pink and...something. Some color..."

"I'll make her one," Victor said.

I realized then that if I made one for Gabriel, I'd probably have to make one for everyone. "Gabriel," I said. "We have to make nine."

"I was thinking the same thing," he said. He snapped his fingers and pointed to Victor. "I'll make yours and Sang's. You should make mine and Kota's. Sang, you make..."

"I want to make Sang's," Victor said. "And I can make one for me."

"Don't make your own. Defeats the purpose."

"There's a purpose?"

The girls giggled. Their eyes were wide, watching the boys. Lake squinted a look at the guys but then continued with her bracelet-making.

Carla waved to the girls to get their attention. "Come on," she said. "Make your bracelets. Ignore the boys."

I wasn't sure why she would say that. I knew the guys already, but it wasn't supposed to be 'us versus them.' Socializing was supposed to happen. They were supposed to get to know other team members and perhaps find their own team somewhere.

Gabriel waved a hand toward the girls over his head while he was focused on looking at a box of charms. "Yeah, yeah, pretend we're not here."

"Besides," Carla said. "We have to sort out where everyone's sleeping."

I remembered April and Taylor and Emma their tent. It was big like my group's tent, but they had plenty of room to spare since it was only the three of them. "Actually, I might have a solution. Gabriel, do you know where Taylor is? Or April or Emma?"

"Those girls? Uh..." His head shot up, and locks of blond hair fell in his face as he looked around. "I thought I saw one of them here earlier."

Victor stood up, scanning the area. "I think I see one.

Want me to grab her?"

"Yeah," I said. "Bring her over so we can ask if we can fill in some girls in their tent."

"Sure," he said and started off, winding his way around tables and disappearing among the group.

If nine could easily fit into the boys' tent, then there should be plenty of room for the other girls. That way, I could still spend the night with Kota in the spare tent.

"And then maybe we girls should make a bracelet together. Make ones for each other," Carla said. She looked at Gabriel. "If that's how it works?"

Gabriel shrugged, picking out beads from a bucket. "It's always better if you do things for other people."

"I'll make one for Sang!" one of the girls called out.

"I've got Lake's," another one said.

This started a chain until they had picked out who would make for who. I had Carla.

She spoke to Gabriel. "You boys can make your own for each other."

I bit my lip, glancing at Gabriel. Carla didn't seem to like Gabriel being there.

When Carla was busy directing the girls, Gabriel leaned into me. "Is she grumpy?"

I leaned into him to whisper. "No idea," I said. I thought someone needed to talk to her, but I wasn't sure I was the one to do it. Carla was older than me, probably eighteen from what I could guess, and had known of the Academy longer than I'd known about it.

But hadn't she said it took two years for her to get invited? Maybe she didn't know as much as she thought she did. I might be loyal to my team, but I wouldn't make anyone feel excluded.

I was thinking about this and picking out beads for Carla's bracelet, still intending to make nice ones for Gabriel and Victor, when Victor returned, trailed by Emma. She was wearing all black and with her dark hair, her blue eyes were very striking.

She was followed by Taylor.

"Hey, girl!" Taylor waved to me. Emma waved, too and to Gabriel as well. "Do I see a new girl group here? This is so cool. I almost wish it was my first year."

"First year was a lot of fun," Emma said. "But it's still fun."

Carla stood, wiping her hands on her sweater. "It's great, but some of us were brought in and weren't told it was camping. We don't have supplies but Sang said you might have room?"

Both of the girls nodded enthusiastically. "Sure! You can camp out with us," Taylor said. "We might need to ask around for more sleeping bags."

"We've got some," Victor said. "And extra air mattresses."

"I guess that'll be okay." Carla seemed to be unsure as she looked toward Taylor. "Do you have room for everyone?"

Taylor pointed as she counted the five girls and Carla. "Six, and..." She pointed to Lake. "Seven?"

Lake looked at me and frowned. "I think I'm staying with Sang," she said, her eyes wide.

I cringed, but also felt compelled to agree and let her stay with us. I could be wrong, but I suspected Lake wasn't really a girl. The other girls might be okay with hiking with her, but...if she had boy parts, would the girls feel comfortable with her in the tent? And what if the girls didn't know she was a boy, but then discovered it later?

I glanced questioningly at Victor and then at Gabriel. I wasn't sure they saw what I saw, but I hoped they understood that there was a reason we might need Lake to go with us.

The boys both nodded slightly. Fine by them. They didn't question me.

"No," Carla said. "We should all stick together. That way we'll be ready for Mrs. Rose in the morning."

I shared a look with Lake. Carla was taking this group thing a little far and was acting a little bossy.

"It'll be crowded with us," Lake said. "And Sang's got

her own tent already set up."

"I can give you all an extra heater," I said, trying to show my support. "And we're not far."

"We're supposed to be getting to know each other," Carla said. "I don't want two tents because it means one side will feel left out."

"I'm not going to feel left out," Lake said, saying what I was thinking.

"I want Sang and Lake in our tent," another one of the girls said. The others nodded their heads in agreement.

I was outnumbered. I pressed my lips together, not wanting to say anything but I didn't like Taylor's tent. It smelled. And what about Kota?

"It'll be okay," Taylor said with a smile, looking right at me. She was trying to tell me something, but unlike Gabriel and Victor, I couldn't read her face. "We should be able to fit. Can we bring your tent over and put our things in it?"

I glanced at Gabriel and Victor, who were sympathetic but were both serious now. They knew I wasn't happy with this decision.

What could I do? The girls wanted me with them, and they were new.

Reluctantly, I looked at Lake. She frowned but shrugged. "Whatever," she said. "It's just sleeping."

Taylor nodded and then pointed at me. "How about you and I go check it out and make sure everything's put together?"

"I'll walk with you," Victor said.

"Me too," Gabriel said, standing up. "I'll come back another time and make bracelets."

Lake stood, also. "Me, too. I'll help move things."

Carla was about to talk when Emma moved to where Victor had been sitting and smiled brightly at her. "You're Carla, aren't you?" she asked and then beamed at her and then the other girls. "So cool. What are we making here? I want to make something."

"We'll come back," I said to Carla, who was still looking at us. "We'll set everything up. Stay with the girls?"

Carla nodded and slowly sat back down.

Once we were away from them, I breathed out loudly.

"My God," Lake said. "She's clingy. And bossy."

"Happens," Taylor said. We walked in a line together, the girls in front, the boys trailing behind us. "Although she moves quick. Usually by midweek, the new girls try to stick together like that." She looked at us. "Something happen to you all on your hike?"

"A cave," I said, checking in with Lake. She shrugged so I continued. "And Nettle. Minor trouble but we got out of it."

"Crazy bonding?" Taylor asked.

I looked at Lake. Had we bonded?

Taylor waved her hand toward us to direct our attention back to her. "It's easy for new people to want to stick together, even if they aren't a good team, or don't even know anything about one another. It's good to get them to splinter out and get to know other people, but that 'we're new together' bond can stick fast if something happens. It can be hard to get them to split up until camp's over and they go home and reality sets in."

"We didn't do any of that," Gabriel said behind us. "Did we, Victor?"

"We already had a group going in," Victor said. "It's different when you come in solo. You're given a team—it makes sense you'd bond with them quickly."

"That's usually what happens," Taylor said. "Sometimes it works out and they stay together, or they get placed in temporary groups. My team was paired up to go on a mission. We started with five. Two split but the three of us stuck together."

"I don't think I want Carla in my group," Lake said.

"Give her a chance," Taylor said. "You don't know her story yet. You might not get along with her, but she's still Academy in training, and deserves a fair shot and our respect."

That was going to be difficult. Maybe because Carla was older than us, and considered herself responsible, she felt compelled to take charge, especially since she'd had something of a head start learning about the Academy.

We came up to Taylor's site first, stopping to look inside her tent.

The moment she opened her door flap, I froze, trying not to be obvious about my nose wrinkling at the very potent scent that hit me even outside the tent.

Gabriel had stopped when I did, his own nose wrinkling as he looked at me. "Wow," he said. "That's some strong...potpourri."

I elbowed him. I couldn't believe he'd said that out loud! Weren't we supposed to be nice?

"April spilled some perfume," Taylor said, looking back at us. Her eyebrows went up. "That bad?"

"What's wrong with fresh air?" Gabriel asked. "That's what we're here for."

"Our tent had a musty smell before," she said.

Gabriel shook his head. "Naw, you don't cover up must with perfume. You spray it down with some water mixed with baking soda. Actually, we've got some back at our camp in North's Jeep. We'll grab it when we get back. Leave your tent open."

"It's not that bad," Taylor said.

Victor went up to the open tent and poked his head in. "It's kinda bad," he said. "I don't think I could sleep in it. The other girls might not mind, but..."

"Shit," Taylor said. "Well, I guess I'll keep the flap open and let it air out."

"Hey, hey!" Gabriel said, pointing at Taylor. "You cursed."

"Uh, I'm an adult," Taylor said, standing taller with her shoulders back. "You're a kid. You've got to watch your language."

Gabriel grumbled about not being a kid, but Taylor ignored him, tying the door flap so it'd stay open while we walked over to the other camp. There were windows, too, and she unzipped the coverings.

It took us a good hour, but we managed to scrounge up

some air mattresses and extra cots.

Lake and I claimed cots; if we were going to be trapped in with a bunch of girls, we wanted to at least not have to share our sleeping spaces.

I hated every moment of moving their items inside the tent that belonged to me and moving the new tent Kota had set up over, putting his things back into the main boys' tent. Every piece I moved made it feel like I was pulling myself apart from the boys. I hated the thought of spending the entire week inside the tent with the girls.

When I got a moment alone with Victor, I tugged his hand, pulling him aside while the others continued setting up.

"I haven't seen Kota today," I said. "We need to tell him."

"He told us that you said you were staying with him in the small tent," Victor said. "Did something happen? He wouldn't explain it and I didn't want to press him."

I nodded, although it felt like centuries ago now. "I still need to spend time with him and explain things, but if I'm stuck with the girls..."

"I'll tell him you got roped in, but you wanted to stay with him. Maybe he'll be able to get away and come talk to you." He frowned. "It's only a week. We go home after. If you don't get a chance before the closing interview, then we'll just have to maybe say you're thinking about joining, but aren't sure of a team yet...or something."

I raised my eyebrows. "An exit interview? Is that like this morning?"

He nodded. "Maybe? It depends on how you do this week. Or if something crazy happens and they don't get to you. If they start asking you what you think of the Academy, and if you'd like to join, they might suggest to put you on a starter team, like what happened to Taylor."

"And I can't just say your team without Kota knowing...the plan? Because everyone has to be in agreement?"

He nodded. "You can try, but it'll be harder. Mr. Blackbourne said..."

"Hey!" Taylor called to us. She held onto a cooler and looked at us from the road. The others were carrying some extra food the guys had brought so the girls would have plenty to eat. "Don't get lost. Let's go."

"We're coming," Victor said, waving to her, and then slowly started toward the road that would lead us to their camp. He spoke to me quietly as he walked. "Look, I'll tell Kota to meet you tonight."

"Where?" I asked.

"At the latrine. Just pretend you're going to the bathroom around nine. He'll make sure to find you. Maybe go for a walk or something."

"Is that enough time before the ten p.m. curfew?"

"He might not be available before then," he said. We were catching up to Taylor and the others who had paused to wait for us. "Man," he said a little louder as we got closer to them. "Wow, that cave does sound kind of cool..."

I got that we couldn't let Taylor in on the plan. I didn't know why, though. She seemed trustworthy.

Once the camp was set up, we sat on the picnic table, looking over the site. The small tent that was now for storage had been placed beside the big one. Inside it were chairs holding the three brown suitcases, and now my things as well. If any of the girls had brought any clothes, they'd have a place to put bags.

"Good thing I brought... *you* brought extra clothes, Sang," Gabriel said.

"I already gave shoes to someone," I said.

"You're going to lose some clothes," Taylor said. "When the new recruits are brought in, they are being taught to ask for help when it's needed. At the same time, you're taught to give where you can." She glanced at me meaningfully with her brown eyes.

I understood. Everything we have, we can share with everyone else. That's just the way the Academy works.

"I brought extra clothes, too," Taylor said. "We'll have plenty. That's if you don't go on any more crazy hikes and get them all dirty like that."

"I don't want to go on another hike," Lake said. "I'm done with hikes."

We talked about going back to the art area but then kept getting distracted by talking about the different camp activities the others had discovered.

"I don't have to teach another class until Thursday," Gabriel said. "Which is good. I wanted to try crab fishing."

"I just want a nap," Taylor said and yawned, stretching her arms over her head. Her brown sweater was a little too short for her arms, and the ends slid down her forearms as she stretched.

"Me, too," Lake said, muffling a yawn by covering her mouth with her elbow. "Is that allowed?"

"Yup," Gabriel said. "You're allowed. It's camp."

I hated to say so, but I was feeling worn down, too, after moving all the supplies and the day I'd had. Gabriel had sprayed down the inside of the tent with his baking soda mix, and with the flap open, the inside was smelling better. The cot I'd set up with my pillow and sleeping bag looked really cozy. "We can just lay on top of the sleeping bags, Lake," I said. "And change later."

"Just lying on your back should be fine," Taylor said, standing up and trotting over to the tent. "Your back is clean."

Victor stood up. "If you all want to sleep, Gabriel and I will go tell the others you're here and where to find you."

"No way," Gabriel said. "I want to nap." He combed a lock of his blond hair away from his eyes and started toward the tent. "Let me borrow a bed."

"Buddy system, Gabriel," Victor said. "Come on. Let them sleep."

Gabriel grunted and shot me a look. "Don't let any bears in," he said and started following Victor toward the paved road. They soon disappeared on their way toward the craft station.

I was sorry to see them go, but at the same time, too tired to want to follow. I also wanted to calm my nerves with some sleep.

One week, I told myself. All I had to remember was this wasn't my group. The boys were. I just had to find the right moment to tell the others.

JUST TRYING TO GET AWAY

I slept deeply, and woke, not sure where I was when I heard voices. I opened my eyes and saw the material of the tent above me and remembered.

The other girls were inside, whispering and trying to be quiet, but Taylor woke up and took them to go outside to light a fire.

By the time I was able to get myself to sit up, I was still tired, but it was clear the sun had started to set. I needed to be awake, and aware of the time...

The time. I didn't have my phone. I'd looked for it while we were moving stuff but hadn't found it yet. I meant to ask Kota about it. How was I going to meet Kota if I couldn't keep track of the time? I glanced around, looking for anything that would have a clock on it, finding nothing.

Lake was still asleep in her cot, her arms over her face.

I'd have to ask someone around when I thought nine o'clock was and make my excuse to go then.

"Lake?" I said. I was trying to get myself to go out of the tent and join the others. I didn't want to, though. I didn't want to face Carla and the other girls.

"Yeah?" she said but didn't move.

"We should go..." It was a little better with Lake around. I wasn't sure why. I didn't know her as well. Maybe because she was a little calmer than Carla.

"Mmm."

"Are you hungry?" I asked. "Do you need water?"

Lake moved her arms from her face and sat up. Her short

dark hair was in all directions and revealed more of the shape of her jawline. With her fingers, she combed her hair around her face, locks falling in front of one eye as if to hide it. "I guess," she said. "I might not be able to sleep tonight. Let's get this over with."

I hoped she wasn't having a bad time. I knew it was tough fitting in when you felt alone.

The tent flap had been closed. When we got out, the other girls were sitting in folding chairs around the fire.

"Yay!" they cried when they noticed us. "They're awake! Now we can start!"

Taylor, April, and Emma were there. They pointed at the two remaining folding chairs nearby. "Come sit," Taylor said.

"Hungry?" April said and then pointed to a cooler. "There's burritos and coffee if you want."

"Or water," Taylor said. "And there's some Pop-Tarts and crackers in the cooler."

"Burritos?" Lake asked, and headed toward the cooler.

I waited until Taylor and April weren't paying attention anymore and I snagged Lake's elbow to whisper to her. "They're black bean and avocado burritos. Spicy."

"Ew," Lake said. "Black bean is okay, but I don't like avocado. I'll take a Pop-Tart."

We found strawberry Pop-Tarts and water and brought them back to the seats. Had Taylor and her team only brought spicy burritos? I wondered if I could exist on Pop-Tarts and water for the week. Luckily, I'd eaten a lot at lunch with the hamburgers and potatoes, and still felt fine. I hoped lunches like that were normal for camp. I wondered if we could team up with the guys around dinner time.

When Lake and I sat down, Carla gave us two minutes before she stood up. "Okay, now that we're settled, I wanted to go around the circle and have us all kind of talk about how we found out about the Academy and maybe go over what we learned today." She looked at Taylor and the other older girls. "Maybe you can fill in any holes we've got?"

"Sure," Taylor said. "We'll take turns, too."

"Well, I was hoping—" Carla said, glancing toward the younger girls, who were looking eagerly at her.

"Might be best for us to start," April said. "We're your hosts tonight. You should know who you get into tents with." She laughed, as did her teammates.

Carla sat down in her chair and nodded, seeming to lose her bossy nature.

Maybe Taylor had informed her team about Carla because April, Taylor, and Emma went through early chapters of their Academy careers, explaining how they tried different groups, and it took a while and some team changes for them to figure out what—and who—worked best for them.

"You never know with your group," April said. "One day, you run into people and you just click. You just know."

"But you had to work together on something and stick with each other for a while," Carla finally said after letting Taylor and her team speak for a long time.

Taylor shrugged. "Technically yes."

"So we should stick together," Carla said, smiling with some complacency.

"For now. However, you might also not be a best match within even your first team," Taylor said. "People switch all the time. You have to be open to change."

"They give up?" Carla asked.

"No," Taylor said. "Sometimes you just don't get along. Your manager might make suggestions to meet other people he feels might be a better match for you."

"Do we have a manager?" one of the girls asked. "Mrs. Rose?"

"Not yet," she said. "Not until you're officially invited to join the Academy. Your manager could be anyone, and he or she will basically be your team and family lead all in one for a while until a council feels you're ready to take over and assign your own lead. They teach you about the Academy, help you find a role to fill, give you jobs."

April snapped her fingers. "And that's another thing, did they tell you about women within the Academy? Our jobs?"

Everyone shook their heads, including Carla and me.

"Are we given different jobs than the guys?" one of the younger girls asked.

"No," April, Taylor, and Emma all said together and then laughed. April stood from her chair, her big sweater hanging big over her body. She folded her arms against her chest as she walked behind the circle of chairs, speaking as she did. "And technically yes. Us girls," she began, "we've got some of the most dangerous tasks within the Academy. And because there's so few of us, we're called on more within the Academy than the boys."

"We're recruiting more girls," Taylor said. She crossed her legs and leaned back shaking her head and smirking at April. "Every year, we find a few more."

"But it hasn't been enough," April said. She paced some more around the circle. The fire lit up her features, causing an orange glow the more the sun set beyond the trees. The trees blocked most of the sun and only looking straight up toward the sky could I tell it was still just sunset. I still needed to find a way to track time until my meeting with Kota...

"Why does this feel like a ghost story and you're trying to scare us?" Carla asked.

"It's the campfire," Lake said.

"Because you *should* be scared," April said, stopping short to put her hands on her hips and give the girls a look. "This is no joke." She pressed her hand to her chest, covering her heart. "I might be a little dramatic, but this is one of the most important lessons you'll ever be told about the Academy."

The girls silenced then, listening intently, watching April as she continued walking around the circle. Taylor and Emma sat back, occasionally whispering to each other but allowing April to take the stage.

"You see, while we can say boys and girls can do the same job, that's not always the case with real life. Especially when it comes to undercover work. In certain places, only a girl can blend in."

The group was dead silent. Taylor caught my eye, her expression serious as she gave me a slight nod.

I bowed my head, looking at my dirty jeans. Kota had warned me about jobs within the Academy, and that we might be asked to do them. Still, I had to know. "What...what kind of...?"

"Come on," Lake said over me. "Give us some examples here." She turned to me. "That's what you were trying to ask, right?"

"Yeah," I said.

"All jobs are different," April said. "However, women are often called on to be bait." She stepped around the circle, stopping behind another girl, eyes wide. "Or decoys. Or blending in and overhearing secret conversations if anyone underestimated us."

"Give us a real example," Carla said.

I watched April closely, wanting to know, too.

"For example," April said. She came through the circle and stood closer to the fire in front of Taylor, so her face was lit up with a flickering orange glow. "A few years ago, I was asked to join a state-sanctioned foster home. Most of them are okay, and the Academy will occasionally send kids in to make sure the homes are safe and clean. However, this one had a high report of girls running away."

"That's usually a sign of abuse," Taylor said. "The occasional foster kid running off is common, but if it's an unusually high number, it can be a sign that there's abuse of some sort."

April held up her palm toward Taylor. "I'm telling this story, hang on." She refocused on us. "Because it was the girls who were running, there was no point sending in a guy. The Academy had to ask one of us."

"They asked April," Emma said.

April nodded and moved on. "I suspected the father in the household, but I wasn't sure. My second week there, their biological son invited me out for ice cream, and seemed really cool, until he tried to force himself on me." She bent her head back and laughed. "He would never have gotten the chance if I hadn't been so caught off guard by blackberry swirl."

"So he got into trouble?" Carla asked.

"Of course!" April said. "He got a good kick in the crotch and blackberry swirl in the face. He told me he'd tell his parents I came on to him, and some other stupid nonsense. But I had collected evidence. Had my cell phone on record at the time. I was lucky I'd had it on. He didn't seem bad to me and I was thinking of saving the battery power."

Taylor finally stood up, smoothing down her brown skirt and standing next to April. She put an arm around April's shoulders. "The point is, you will all be asked to go into awkward situations, sometimes to fish out an abuser. It's one of the more common jobs."

I was holding my breath, in awe and a little bit of shock at learning about this part of the job. I didn't know what to think yet. Could I do this?

"It isn't the only type of job we get," April said. "But sadly, it's one of the worst."

"Why don't we report them to the police?" someone asked.

"We do," April said. "But getting evidence is the key. We would never ask an abused person to go back into such horrors to get evidence. We take it on ourselves. Sometimes, that isn't so easy." She pulled away from Taylor to focus on us again, the orange glow brighter as she appeared to get dangerously close to the flames. "I do what I do to protect other girls. I'm strong because of the Academy and the support group it provides and the training I've had. I know I will bounce back. When what I do helps others, it makes me stronger, and I'll endure anything..." she paused, looking each one of us in the eye. "Anything...Hell and back...to ensure the safety of girls who are unable to speak up for themselves."

"But you will never have to do it alone," Taylor said. "And that's not the only type of work we do. You may not be asked to do this at all. There's so much work we need to do that only girls can do and jobs will be assigned according to your strengths."

I stared at the fire while Carla and the other girls continued to ask questions. Kota hadn't wanted me to join the Academy because he was afraid of me getting picked to go into such dangerous situations.

For the first time, I wondered if he was right. Would I be able to handle going into a foster home to find out what was making girls run away? It would be an assignment the boys couldn't follow me into. However, if the Academy approached me and asked me, could I say no? If it meant preventing someone going through what I'd gone through, it was tempting to say I could. I stole secret looks at the other girls and thought of the younger ones from that morning, eager and ready to participate, and how I might be willing to help any of them.

However, images came to mind of Mr. McCoy, Jade...my own stepmother, who I'd thought to be my mother for so long.

It was horrible, and I'd had the boys help me so much. Could I willingly go back into such situations again? There were other jobs we could do. I helped once with Luke getting a camera. What if I focused on those jobs?

Was it different when you were aware and went into a situation knowing you were looking for evidence when it came to abuse? I wasn't sure.

April stood by and listened as the other girls spoke, but I suddenly had a different view of her altogether. If she had been through all of that and still went in to take on such challenging Academy jobs, then she was the bravest girl I'd ever really known.

Could I ever be half as brave?

As the girls continued talking about the Academy and then themselves and their backgrounds, I tried to gauge time using how long it had been since sunset.

Did Lake have a phone or watch on her? She was sitting back, eyes half open, staring into the fire. I wasn't sure if she was even listening to the other girls. Despite not knowing much about her, I'd felt her to be more of an ally. I wasn't sure if it was because she was a boy, or how she didn't seem fazed by Gabriel and the others when they were around.

"Lake?" Carla said, dragging our attention to her.

Lake sat up a little, blinking, making me think she'd been half-asleep. "Yeah?"

"Want to talk about yourself?"

Lake shook her head and sat back. "Uh, not really."

Carla frowned. "Just tell us where you're from."

"Not from here," she said.

"Is Lake your real name?"

"Is Carla *your* real name?" Lake asked with a raised eyebrow and a frown.

Taylor had been sitting by while the other girls talked, but now she stood and sliced her hand through the air. "Carla, we never force people to talk if they don't want to." She looked at Lake. "And Lake, I understand you might be tired and not want to participate, but we are always respectful to other Academy members. Always."

Lake tilted her head, looking toward the ground. "Sorry," she said. "I just don't feel like talking about myself."

Carla opened her mouth but Taylor cut her off. "Totally understandable." She looked at the group of girls. "I know some of you must be exhausted. You've had a long day. Why don't we make our way to the latrine and get some showers going? We'll get to bed early."

The younger girls jumped up, excited for a shower and bed. Carla, however, was still frowning as she moved along. We folded our chairs and April and Emma got to work putting out the fire.

Lake leaned into me to whisper as we put our chairs away. "That Carla's pushy. I don't like her."

I didn't want to say anything negative about her, even though I agreed with Lake. What I didn't understand was why Carla was so eager to keep us all together.

Maybe there was more to Carla's story than either of us

knew. She was here and there was a reason why she had been invited.

"What time is it?" I asked Lake.

She pulled out a cell phone and checked the time. "Eight thirty-ish," she said.

It was close. Could I stall for a half hour at the latrine?

I got my kit together and decided to join the girls to the latrine, planning to hang around and get ready to meet with Kota.

It wasn't like I was going to shower.

As a group, we headed to the latrine, Lake and I trailing behind.

At the entryway to the bathrooms, Lake hesitated. She had a few clothes she'd borrowed from me, sans underwear and a bra. She wasn't exactly my size, but a simple T-shirt and stretchy cotton pants should fit.

I paused and caught her elbow. "Something wrong?"

She stopped, looking at the latrine and then back down at the camp. "I don't know if I should go in." She looked at the ground, her hair falling over her face. "I don't think I should get in the shower."

If she was a boy, it would probably confuse the other girls. However, did she feel uncomfortable going over to the boy section? She could have gone in with the guys, but maybe she thought the other girls would notice and realize she was a boy. How confusing her life must be.

"There's stalls," I said. "We can just change and leave."

"There's another problem," she said. She looked up at me. "What if they're naked or something? Will they kick me out?"

It suddenly made me hesitate, too. With it being dark out, the lights inside seemed so much brighter, the fluorescents lighting up the entry.

Would they call her a pervert just for simply trying to wash up in the bathrooms? If she was in there, in the light, would they notice she was a boy? If she was caught and the girls protested to an Academy council, it could mean the end of her Academy career, even if she was just trying to change and use the bathroom.

I wished Mrs. Rose was there so we could ask her. I looked at Lake in the eye. "We could just tell them...they'll probably understand."

"I really just don't want to answer a thousand questions right now," Lake said. "I get enough of that at home."

I could understand she was tired and probably frustrated with what to do. I snapped my fingers. "Wasn't there another shower somewhere?"

"Where they park campers?" Lake asked. "It was on the map."

"It's a little further to walk," I said. "But if the others ask us later, we could tell them we were just splitting up so we wouldn't take up all the hot water."

Lake nodded slowly. "Okay," she said. "Should we go now?"

I nodded. "Sure. Why not? We're using the buddy system, right? There's two of us."

She nodded again and then turned. "Then let's go."

Did I have time to walk over there and get back for Kota? "Hang on," I said and started toward the boys' campsite. "I have to talk to someone."

"Someone from that boy group?" she asked. She kept pace beside me, holding the clothes and towel I'd given her. "Are they the ones who brought you in?"

"Yeah," I said. I'd debated for a second about telling her, but it seemed I should. She'd trusted me with her fears and I felt she might understand about my situation. "It's... my group."

She watched our feet as we walked. Our shoes scuffed along the grass until we met with the paved road. "Are you...like me?"

My heart raced. She thought I might be a boy? Did I look like one? "No," I said.

"I didn't really think so until those guys showed up. Then I thought maybe that's why you talked to me. I didn't know a girl could be on a guy team. So I just thought...maybe..." She shrugged.

"It's rare, from what I hear, to have a girl on a guy team, but it happens sometimes."

"So you're in?" Lake asked, looking up at me. "You're an official Academy member with your own team?"

"No. Not yet. I mean, I think I have my team, but I haven't told the Academy and...it's a little complicated."

"So why aren't you in training with them?"

Good question. I'd been wondering why Dr. Roberts had seemed to lead the discussion, giving give me such glorious recommendations where the result was I ended up on the girl team. "The...council this morning. When they asked our names and such, they asked me to help Mrs. Rose this week with translating for her."

But as I thought about it, I wondered if it had been lucky that I knew sign language or had the whole thing been orchestrated?

"Oh," Lake said. As she walked, she scuffed the back of her heels along the paved road. "I guess that makes sense."

We approached the guys' camp, and at first, I didn't see anyone, except there was a small fire still going. They wouldn't go far without putting out the fire, would they?

As if to answer my thought, the tent flap opened and North appeared. With his dark clothes and grumpy expression, he was a terrifying sight with the flickering light of the fire shining on his face.

Lake stopped instantly. "Whoa," she said, her eyes wide as she studied North. "Something wrong?"

North frowned at her and then looked my way. "What are you doing here? Aren't you supposed to be with the girls?"

There was an edge to his question. Was he mad? I tried to figure out if it was me sleeping in the other camp that had him upset, or if there was something else behind it. With North, it could be lots of things. "I..."

"Don't blame her," Lake said, stepping in front of me. "That crazy Carla wanted 'all us girls' together in one tent.

Otherwise, we would have been here."

I could handle North, but I was glad Lake seemed to understand and stepped in. It surprised me and made me feel like I really could trust her.

North's head jerked back and he turned the full force of his glare on her. "Who the hell are..." He broke off and the glare vanished as someone inside the tent pushed on him.

"Get out of the way," Luke said. "I haven't seen her all day."

While Luke and North argued over the tent flap, I leaned into Lake. "Don't mind North. He's always grumpy." That wasn't totally true, but I hoped she'd forgive him for being rude.

"I can handle guys," she said and turned her eyes on Luke, who dodged a punch in the gut from North and raced toward us.

"Sang!" he cried out and picked me up, spun me around once and then hugged me tight. "I haven't seen you all day!" he exclaimed, even though he'd seen me earlier—I knew he was saying it to cover up. He turned his eyes on Lake and then approached her as though he was going to give her the same greeting.

Lake raised her arms up, warding him off, but Luke ignored her, picked her up, whirled her once and put her back down. "And yay, you...whoever you are. You brought the Sang!"

"Aren't you *'not supposed to be here'*?" Lake asked with a smirk before she pushed him away.

Luke leaned in close. "That was earlier," he said quietly. "I can be here now."

North approached, looking past us, over our shoulders. "Where's the other girls?"

"At the latrine," I said. "We're heading to the other one, over by the trailers."

"That's a good walk," North said. "Why don't you just go with the girls to this one?"

I shared a look with Lake and then turned my full stare at

North. "To make sure there's enough hot water to go around," I said, hoping he'd catch my intent that this was a must and I didn't want to explain it and embarrass Lake.

He glared at me and then grunted. "Then hop into the Jeep," he said. "I'll take you over. It'll take too long to get back and forth."

"I was hoping to find Kota, too," I said. "I was supposed to meet him."

"I'll let him know where we're headed." He reached into his pocket, finding keys. He shot a look at Luke. "Stay with the fire. Don't let it burn down the forest."

"Aw, I have to stay?" Luke said and then walked over to the campfire, sinking down onto a log. "What about the buddy system?"

"And don't play with the fire, for fuck's sake. Last time I left you with it, you burned the tent. I have no idea how..."

Luke waved him off, although with a sheepish grin. "Go drive them to the bathroom." He waved at me. "Bye Sang!" He waved at Lake. "Bye, *Bringer of the Sang*!"

North grunted again and waved us toward the Jeep.

I hopped into the front while North held open the back door for Lake to get in. Once she had her seatbelt on, he shut the door and got in behind the wheel.

Within moments, we rolled slowly along the paved road, following the paper map toward the trailer site. He drove very slowly as we occasionally pulled up on people walking down the road in different directions. They parted to allow us through, some waving to us in the vehicle as we passed.

"I was there earlier," North said. He had a hand on the wheel, the other adjusting the temperature dials. "Are we hot or cold?"

"I'm fine," Lake said.

North took his hand from the dials and placed it on the wheel. "Anyway, there's a few trailers that have come in, but they're all Academy. No surprises. Nothing to worry about."

"Are these showers going to be busy?" I asked.

"Not likely. Not everyone's going to want to walk the

distance just for a shower. Everyone will figure out to try throughout the day to shower, or will skip days. It'll work out."

"And then we go home," Lake said.

North peered at her through the rearview mirror. "You got a ride home, kid?"

"I have no idea," Lake said. "I was told there was a school. Then I woke up this morning about a secret trip. I got in the car with the clothes on my back. I haven't seen the lady who brought me since this morning."

North huffed and dragged a palm down his cheek, the rasp of his stubble against his palm audible. "I know the feeling."

I wanted to ask him about it but wasn't sure he'd wanted to reveal so much with Lake around.

Soon we rolled into an area of the campground where there was a long field and small dirt roads leading in different directions. There were what I realized were RV sites—each with an electric pole and a small pad of concrete. I could only see three big campers, spread out from each other, but still close to the latrine.

The latrine was similar to the other one. Except this one was bigger, with brighter lights, outside and in. The doors were left wide open so we could see as we got closer.

When we got out of the car and approached, we could see the insides of these latrines had white tiles, smelled clean, and I didn't see any spider webs above our heads. Maybe it was technically an identical building, but it seemed better than the other restrooms.

"How are these so much nicer?" I asked. "How come they have bathroom tiles?"

"People in RVs expect nicer latrines," North said. "They pay more for their campsite because they use energy and plumbing. They bring in more money, so the campground spends a little more money on their latrine."

"Don't trailers have their own bathrooms?" Lake asked.

"Not all of them," North said. "And sometimes if you're here with family, you want a spare bathroom. Most of the time, people don't want to bother pumping out the waste if they don't have to."

Lake and I peered into the girls' bathroom. I could hear a shower running, but it sounded like it was coming from the guys' side.

Lake breathed out a sigh and shuffled over to a stall. "About time," she said, moving past me into the bathroom. I heard her close a stall door with a snap and set the lock. "I really had to pee."

North spoke, holding me outside of the bathroom. "You wanted to talk to Kota?"

"Yeah," I said, wondering why he was pulling me away from the bathroom. "He was going to meet me at..."

He pulled me behind the shadow of the door, out of view, and when I paused to figure out if there was a spider, he leaned in and pressed his lips to mine.

I froze, surprised. I'd been with other people all day, and I'd missed them, but still worried other people were watching.

But I assumed North wouldn't dare unless he was sure we were alone, so I tried to relax and kiss him back.

It was short but intense kiss, leaving me wanting more when he backed off. "May not get another chance this week."

I knew he was right. I wanted to talk about the night before when I'd bitten him, but I didn't want Lake to think I'd abandoned her and I was concerned that conversation may take way too long. "Okay," I said simply, and then wished I'd thought of something else to say, feeling stupid.

"I'll call Kota," he said. "And have him meet us here. I think he's still over by the cabins, so he isn't far."

"I'll go wash up," I said.

"Are you okay with him in there?" he asked.

I assumed he meant Lake. "Yeah," I said. "Sure."

"You know she's a guy, right?"

I wasn't surprised he'd picked up on it—they were all observant. "Yup."

"You're still okay with it?"

"Yeah," I said. "She's fine. She just wasn't sure

about...with the other girls..."

He stopped me with a finger pressed to my lips. "If they don't accept her for who she is, then they don't deserve to be here. But I understand that Lake doesn't want to cause any trouble. It doesn't matter to me. I just don't want you uncomfortable."

"I'm fine," I said, mumbling through my finger. I was pretty sure Lake was much more concerned about her Academy career than wanting to stare at naked girls. Otherwise she wouldn't have said anything. "There's stalls. We're not kindergarteners. We can keep our hands to ourselves."

He squinted down at me and then removed his finger from my mouth. He kissed me once more and then nudged me toward the door. "I'm right here," he said. "Maybe remind him of that."

I had to smile inwardly at his little warning, the mild jealousy he was hinting toward. "Her," I whispered, although I hadn't confirmed with Lake what pronoun she preferred. I'd just assumed by how she'd dressed and that she wanted to use the girls' bathroom.

I wasn't about to intimidate Lake by repeating North's warning.

I went in, relieved that other than us, the bathroom was empty. Lake stood at the sink, washing her hands, her clothes in a heap under her arm. "Did you want to shower first? There's several shower areas but they are completely open stalls. Thought I'd ask..."

I shook my head. "No," I said. "You go. I'll wash up out here."

"Huh?" she asked.

"I'm not that bad," I said, hoping she wouldn't think me gross for not showering after today. "I'm too tired to do a full shower. I just want to wash my face and brush my teeth and..."

"Tell me about it," she waved her hand over her head and then headed toward the shower. "I'm not even bothering shaving my legs this week." She paused and turned slowly back. "Uh...I don't suppose you have a razor."

I did have one in my kit and passed it over to her. "Keep it," I said as I deposited my things into a dry sink and headed toward a stall. "I may not shave this week, either."

I assumed she needed to shave her face if she was going to keep the girl appearance up.

I finished with the toilet and had changed into clean underwear, a long-sleeved T-shirt, and cotton pants when I heard the shower start up.

At first, I began to tremble, but as I forced myself to take deep breaths, I realized this shower was different. The echo of the tiles made the noise reverberate so much, that it didn't sound like a shower at all. It sounded more like kids were stomping around in puddles.

The odd noise made it easier to try to ignore and pretend it didn't even exist.

Would I be able to survive the week without fainting in a shower? Maybe with the chaos and us coming out to these showers, I had a better chance getting away with it?

I stood in the stall, waiting, wondering if Lake was comfortable with me being here while she showered or was it just that I was better than having all the other girls around.

Secretly, I was grateful she had been too scared to join the others. Changing for school gym was always slightly uncomfortable, and I'd always used the stall. I hadn't known what it would be like to be among other girls here at camp. Lake had thought maybe they walked around naked. Did girls do that? It made me uncomfortable thinking about it.

I forced away the questions and opened the stall door.

There was a shadow by the entryway, and I hesitated, thinking someone from the trailers was coming in.

I was relieved to see it was Kota leaning in, looking at me. He had dark circles under his eyes but was smiling. He had on his green jacket and wore jeans and sneakers. He was clean, so I wondered if he had been able to do any camp stuff at all or if he was in training all day. "Hey," he said softly. "I don't mean to barge in. Is it okay to come in?"

I shook my head, looking toward the shower area. "There's..." I wasn't sure how to explain. "Uh..."

"Who's that?" Lake called from the shower.

"It's Kota," I called back to her. "I needed to talk to him. Is it okay if he's in here?"

"I don't care," Lake said.

I turned to Kota, putting on a smile. "Hi," I said.

He smiled back, coming closer, keeping his hands in his jean pockets. "Hi," he said. "You okay?"

I nodded, but then spread out my arms, dropping my dirty clothes to the ground and then headed toward him. I needed this. Lake was in the shower; she wouldn't see.

Kota opened his arms wide and let me hug him, hugging me tightly back, letting me inhale his strong scent of sweet spice.

"You were all over the place today," he said. "I got twenty different messages about where you were."

"It's a long story," I said. I broke away, looking up at his face. I was looking past the black-rimmed glasses and dark circles, into his green eyes.

After all the problems I'd had that day, his bright eyes and inner calm somehow gave me a second wave of energy to keep going.

I just wish I could have more time with him. "And sorry for the change up last minute."

He waved his hand. "Don't worry about it. I get it. This is Academy. There's always something."

I moved away from him to pick up my kit so I could wash my face. He leaned against the sink next to mine, opening his mouth to talk, but then stopped, watching as I added foam soap to a washcloth and spread it over my face and neck.

I stopped, looking at him. "Something wrong?"

His cheeks turned red and he shook his head quickly. "No," he said. "Just feels like I haven't seen..." He paused as he tilted his head. "I don't think I've ever been in a bathroom with you while you do this."

I raised an eyebrow. "It's usually only Gabriel, I guess."

"Yeah," he said and continued to watch as I washed my face. "How'd it go with Mrs. Rose?"

"Fine," I said. "Although I think that Dr. Roberts might have tricked me into being her translator for the week so I was obligated and couldn't join the guys."

"They have ways of making it feel like you're doing them a favor, and the next thing you know, you're neck-deep in a job," he said with a small smile. "Whether it was intentional, we might not ever know, but I'm never surprised to learn something was part of a plan they've cooked up."

I glanced toward the shower, but the water was still running, so I didn't think Lake could hear us. "Does this mean I have to stay with their group?" I asked. "Are they going to ask me to join this girl team?"

"They might try to be clever to get you to join them or other teams they'd like you to be with. But you always choose your team." He frowned. "It's just...very hard to say no when they ask nicely or have good points why—they can make it sound like you're needed. And you're a nice person."

It *was* hard to say no. I remembered how the girls had gotten a little clingy after our hike, and while I'd wanted desperately to hang out with the guys, I was compelled to stay with them. "How can I say no?"

"Nicely," he said. "Although I recommend trying to get to know a wide variety of people. It might be easier if you mix up with different teams."

"The group I'm in is a little reluctant to do that," I said. I loaded a toothbrush with paste and started brushing, letting him go on.

"Carla's stupid," Lake said from the shower. The shower had turned off only a moment before, and I heard the sound of a towel being fluffed out echoing to us. "I don't like her."

I shared a look with Kota. Maybe our voices echoed in the bathroom. I tried to recall what we said, hoping Lake didn't think I wouldn't want to be on a team with her. She was nice, I just didn't know her. And I already had a team.

"You don't have to like her," Kota said louder, his deep

voice reverberating in the bathroom. "But you can't call her stupid. Do you even know her?"

Lake peeked her head out around the corner. Her hair was wet, slicked back against her head. Without her makeup, she resembled a boy even more. She scoped out Kota and then looked at me. "How many guys are in your group?"

"Nine," Kota said.

Lake disappeared again behind the wall. "Is that normal to have such a large group?"

"No," Kota said. I continued to brush my teeth, glad that Kota was so open with Lake. Maybe it was because this is where we were supposed to learn about the Academy. "There's varying sizes, but it's harder for larger groups to get along. Usually with so many different personalities, groups average between three and five people." He looked right at me now as he said the next part. "Unless...unless there's a couple team."

"What's a couple team?" Lake asked, her voice echoing oddly from the shower.

"If a couple is dating in the group, they can decide to splinter off and be just the two of them."

"You split from your old group?" Lake asked as she came around from the shower, hair still wet and wearing my T-shirt and pants. She'd tied the pants tightly at her waist and the T-shirt neck hung off one shoulder. She bent over, wrapping her hair up in a towel before standing up again. "I thought once you were in a group, you were in there for life."

"Not always," Kota said. He was looking at Lake, although there was no surprise in his eyes. North may have warned him. "You get older, and things change. Someone you got along with for years might change over time, and you lose your compatibility. That and if you're on a team where the others are getting boyfriends or girlfriends. Then you want to get married and have a family, maybe. So eventually, you might not even be able to join in on Academy jobs as much."

"Is that why there's so few old farts?" Lake asked.

I nearly choked on my toothbrush. I spat into the sink and

looked at her in the mirror. "Lake..."

"Sorry," Lake said and put a palm over her mouth, her eyes wide. "That's my dad talking."

Kota smiled and shook his head. "You're not wrong. At some point, you've made a family and you might not have time between a job and kids to go wander off in the night. So sometimes you...I don't want to say retire because sometimes you're still asked to join a council or step in on a quick task..."

"I get it," Lake said. "That's why there's so many young people." She came up to my arm and poked me. "Do you have a brush?"

I was scooping water into my mouth to rinse and spit again. I stood up, wiping my mouth with my towel and waved my toothbrush, eyebrows up in question.

"Uh...oh yeah, I don't have one of those, either," she said. "I meant a hair brush. You'd think after dragging us out here, they'd give us at least a basic bathroom kit."

"She's got an extra," Kota said. I looked at him, confused. He nodded toward my kit. "You should have two of everything."

I checked and he was right. There was a brand-new travel-sized toothbrush in the bag, along with a smaller brush, and a few other supplies. "Why?" I asked as I pulled the extras out, passing them to Lake.

"Rule of two," Kota said, winking at me.

I finished up, brushing my hair and clipping it up away from my face. Lake started brushing her teeth.

I really needed to talk to Kota alone. Was that even possible right now? I looked at him, unsure how to make it happen.

He looked right at me, nodded once and spoke. "Lake, do you mind if I take Sang with me? I wanted to show her the way to the cabins. North's waiting outside. He'll give you a ride back to the campsite."

"Can I hang out with them until she gets back?" Lake asked with a mouth full of paste. "I don't want to get cornered by Carla."

"Sure," Kota said, smiling. "They'll let you hang out. But if someone is bugging you, you really should tell her to try to work things out. When you keep your feelings inside, you stop yourself from getting to know the other side."

Lake nodded as she continued brushing his teeth.

Kota looked at me and nodded toward the door. "Ready?"

I slipped my feet back into my boots, collected my dirty clothes and bathroom kit into my towel like a bag, and draped it over my shoulder. "Ready."

I waved to Lake, who seemed fine being left on her own. I hoped North would be nice to her. I guess it said something that Lake would rather stay and face North than go back to Carla.

When we left the bathroom, North was leaning against his Jeep, talking to someone in the darkness. In the dim light coming from the bathroom, I could see he was talking to a middle-aged guy with graying, wet hair. I assumed he'd been the one in the men's side shower. He waved at the two of us before returning his attention to North and the story he was telling.

He seemed friendly, but North was quiet, simply nodding his head. I wondered if he'd gotten roped into chatting with a super-friendly Academy person.

Kota gently took my towel with my supplies and passed it quietly to North who took it but continued to nod toward the chatty camper.

Kota led the way down a path and I followed beside him, waiting to speak. He used his flashlight to guide our way.

♥
TAKING A WALK

The path wound toward a set of trees beside a small eating area with two picnic tables, a small fire pit, and a steel garbage can lit by a streetlight overhead. The grass was a little high around our ankles, but the space was clean.

Kota led me to the tables and sat on top of one, his feet on the seat. I climbed up beside him, scanning the area, noticing the ashes inside the fire pit, and the black trash bag that fluttered a little in the breeze.

For the first time all day, I let out a long breath. I was finally alone...with Kota, but away from all the new people.

I absently combed my fingers through a loose lock of hair, suddenly nervous. I'd wanted to talk to him all day, and I had so much to tell him, yet nothing wanted to come across my lips. My brain was tired. My body was a little sore.

I leaned into him, at first without thinking, and then pressed my cheek to his shoulder. "We leave tomorrow, right?"

He chuckled, put an arm around me and held tight, dipping his head to kiss the top of my forehead. "Do you not like camping?"

"It's fun," I said. "But...I don't like...I feel..." I struggled to explain. "I felt like I was sort of on stage all day today."

"You're in front of new people who are looking to you for help," Kota said. "I was wondering if this job was right for you. I'm glad you're helping out, but I know you're shy and how hard it is. From what I've heard, you seemed to do an amazing job, though."

I smoothed my cheek against his shoulder. "I hate to admit it, but I'm with Lake; I wish Carla hadn't insisted we have to stay in the girl tent."

"Might be better in the end," he said. "Give it a try." He kissed my forehead again and then shifted to rest his cheek against the top of my head. "You'll be able to say you gave it a royal effort. And who knows... maybe..."

"I'm not switching teams," I said. "I don't want to."

"It wouldn't have to be for forever," he said.

"Today felt like forever," I said. "It's not even over yet."

He pulled back to look down at me and I sat up a little. He kept his hand on my back, smoothing over my spine. "Was it really that bad?"

How could I tell him? They weren't bad, but they weren't for me. It was more than just missing the boys. Throughout the day, I had grown more uncomfortable being around the girls who seemed to be looking up to me. While I was sorry to disappoint them, I was also terrified of them. The hug that was supposed to be normal, had made me panic. Even thinking of being in the bathroom around them was making my insides tremble.

Lake had been the exception and the only explanation I really had was that she was really a boy. Why did that make a difference? Kota watching me wash up hadn't bugged me at all nor had being in there with Lake. Shouldn't it be the other way around? Weren't girls supposed to be more comfortable with girls?

Kota massaged my spine but remained quiet as I shifted through my thoughts. His lips dipped slightly into a frown. "Sweetheart, if we need to take you back...I mean I can go if you..."

"No," I said, sucking in a breath. I shook my head. I was going back home with them no matter what. That was what mattered. "It's nothing," I said. "It's a few days. I just wish I could spend more time with you all—with the guys. I know some of you are teaching classes and I'm helping out so we're busy. I guess I thought I'd see more of you."

"You'll see us more this week," he said. "Things start to relax after the first couple of days when new groups learn the ropes more and start to check out other teams. A few more days and we'll be packing up before you know it."

"I'll live," I said. "Been through worse." The words slipped out, and it wasn't until I'd said it out loud that I realized how terribly dark the joke was. I sensed how I was complaining about things and really shouldn't be. I should be grateful to be there at all.

His free hand reached around, touching my cheek, drawing me in. He hugged me, kissed my brow and held tight. "Try to have some fun," he said.

I held onto him. "I will."

He started to let me go, but when I still clung to him, he chuckled and wrapped his arms tighter around me. "I missed you, too."

I *had* missed him. I missed all the guys. Now that I was here, I didn't want to go back to camp, because it meant I'd have to let them go.

I tucked my head down against his shoulder. "Sorry," I said.

"Don't be," he said softly. He slid his hand up my back to hold the back of my head.

"I've been trying to go over what to say," I said. "When I'm asked what group I want to join. I want to make sure I say it right, politely."

"I wish I could tell you."

I backed up this time, realizing now that I did need to talk to him about the plan. If I said I wanted to be on their team, they had to be behind me, and it was only right if he knew the truth. "Kota, I want to stay with the team," I said, trying to sound confident. "All of us together."

He smiled weakly. "I thought that was the goal, but I know it's tough."

"I saw another team today," I said, "this morning at the interviews. A girl with four or five guys. She insisted right away that she wanted to stay with her team from the start. They let her."

His eyes went wide. "Is she a member?"

329

I paused and then slowly shook my head. "I don't...she was with the new people on the stage."

He frowned slightly. "Oh," he said, shoulders slumping. "Then they just brought her in."

"No," I said. "I don't...I think they are like us."

"That doesn't mean she'll stay with that team," he said. "It's kind of normal for new people to want to stay with the team that brought them in, even if it's not for the best."

"Is that like us?" I asked in a quieter voice.

He sighed, looking away from me and toward the fire pit. "I don't know. I don't think so. This feels different."

"They seemed different," I said. "Maybe they've got a strategy. Maybe we should compare notes." I wondered if they might have talked to Lily and Liam. They had told us that they got approached sometimes with a girl wanting to join a guy team.

I suddenly wondered where they were. It was the first day of camp so I could have missed them, but I hadn't seen any of them. Were they not at camp this week? Maybe they were busy.

"Maybe," he said, still staring at the fire pit. "I was kind of thinking..."

I pressed my lips together, waiting for him to finish. I was waiting to tell him about Lily, and to see what he'd say to learn about them.

"I don't know," he said, breaking his stare and looking at me. "I'm torn on the idea. Never mind."

"What?" I asked.

He shrugged. "If they give us a hard time, I was thinking about...about the couple teams..."

I stared at him, waiting for him to continue. "A...couple?"

"You and me," he said. "If we had to. If you...wanted..."

I was warmed by his train of thought—that he'd even consider it—but at the same time, fear crept in. "But the others...the guys..."

"I don't think it would change us at all," he said. "I could still work with them. They'd still be around." He sighed. "Only

I still haven't graduated and you're just starting, which would mean we'd need a manager." He paused. "They told you about managers, right?"

I nodded. "Couldn't Mr. Blackbourne do it?"

"No," he said. "They pick someone for you. We might not even get Dr. Roberts, who was Mr. Blackbourne's and Dr. Green's manager. The only reason our team doesn't have one is because they've already graduated and are guiding the rest of us. It wouldn't be too terrible to have a manager, I guess, but you never know who you get. I don't know...maybe I'm so used to Mr. Blackbourne that I'm biased..."

"I'm biased, too," I said. "And I don't want you to have to give up your team...*our* team." The secret plan we had was on the tip of my tongue. "Kota, we can't give up. We..."

"Yeah," he said with a smile. "I was just thinking...last resort..."

If they insisted for whatever reason that I needed to try out other teams, Kota was willing to give up his team for me.

My throat got tight as I thought about it. Deep down, I knew I could never make that decision. I couldn't pick him over the others, draw him away from his team. Could I ever be the reason they split apart? Would doing so cause some jealous war? I thought of North, who had told me he'd take me away somewhere if any of them tried to run off with me. The faces of the others swam in my brain. They struggled with the idea, but in the end, they wanted to try to carry out the plan, because they cared about each other like they cared about me.

However, if the Academy insisted we couldn't have one girl on an all guy team for whatever reason, maybe...if it was our only solution. "We'd still be near their team?"

"Yeah," he said. "I'm not sure how it would work. I might...I might have to talk to my mom about letting you stay with us. I would have to tell her more…then I've already told her."

I assumed he meant my family situation and how I didn't live at home anymore. "I couldn't stay with Nathan?"

"How would it look if we claimed to be a couple team

and a manager was coming around to check on us?" he asked. "We're still underage. We'd have to have my mom confirm it's okay and supervise us. Besides, I wasn't sure you'd want to."

This was so complicated, and it felt like I was betraying the guys just by thinking about it. It must have been what the other guys had gone through, considering their options: leaving the Academy, the thing they loved or splitting from the team they loved, just to keep me.

"Or," I said softly. "Or, I opt out of joining."

Kota's hand smoothed down to my lower back. "I've been trying to warn you."

I nodded, realizing how long he'd fought the idea of letting me inside the Academy. The Academy promised so much, a future, a place to belong, a feeling of being important as we helped our families and our communities. I'd thought it was the only way to really be a part of the team.

But Kota had been right all along. Bringing me in forced me to see that I was risking splitting their team, not to mention the dangerous situations I could be put into. Kota hadn't begged me to give up the idea of joining the Academy because he didn't think I could do it. He was doing it to keep me safe. He knew if I remained on the outside, we'd never have to defend our team to the Academy.

Was I willing to give up my chance at the Academy, at this thing that they all loved, a place I could belong? Would I be able to ignore it when the boys disappeared into the night, unable to ask what was going on? Could I live through years and years of them coming home with baffling scars and broken bones, without asking questions?

"I can't tell you what to do," Kota said. "All teams have mutual agreement that we're together and everyone wants to be in. However, the way they question us...they have ways to ensure we're making the right choice for us, forcing us to look at every nook and cranny, every little skeleton in the closet. They strip us bare to expose our doubts and fears about our team members."

I bit the tip of my tongue, wondering if that was what that exit interview was like. Maybe that was what they were worried about. They'd ask me questions from many different angles. If I wasn't sure that this was the best answer for us, then that doubt would come to the surface and the Academy might ask me to try something else.

He rubbed my spine slowly. "Sang, you're not the only one who has to be sure. I know Mr. Blackbourne has ideas about you joining, but I'm afraid he just sees all your potential and how good you could be for the Academy, but not how we would work this out."

He was wrong. Mr. Blackbourne did have a plan, but what was holding him—all of us—back was that it involved something the guys were still unsure about. If the Academy quizzed them, would they support me joining the team regardless of what the future held? It didn't help that we were all young and like they said, we could change our minds later.

"But if you want to be in the Academy," he said. "No matter what, we'll always be a team. As long as you want."

His words warmed me through. "I want to try, Kota," I said, still determined. "If it came down to it, I'd decline to join if I had to. Dr. Green might have been right saying it was too soon. I don't want to split the team. We're too...it's too..."

He nodded, but his face was unreadable as he kept his lips pressed tightly together. I hoped he didn't think I wasn't picking a couple team because I didn't want him. However, I knew the truth if the Academy questioned me about it, and how North and others had said they might not be able to take it if I split from the team. It still wouldn't work.

I reached for him, desperate make him understand. I touched his cheek, looking straight into his eyes. "I need you to promise me you'll do whatever you can to keep all of us together, though. All of us. You, me..."

In my head, I was gearing up to tell him why. I just needed him to make the promise first.

I was leaning into him, my hand on his face, so close.

His eyes dropped to my lips.

I lost everything in my brain the instant his eyes lowered. I was familiar with this look now. The guys did it just before they kissed me.

Only, Kota wouldn't move. Everything in him stilled, his lips slightly parted like he was ready, but it was like he didn't dare lean in.

The stupid rule. He was still holding to it. The others had jumped in, willing to break that rule.

Maybe he still assumed I didn't know about it. He'd been waiting for me.

I leaned in. My face was on fire. My nerves shook. It was a little strange to be the first to kiss, but I knew as soon as I did so, he could and I wanted to get to that point.

My lips brushed his very softly. How far did I have to move in before it counted?

Suddenly there were footsteps and voices.

We pulled apart, glancing at each other with wide eyes. He looked over my head, and then I pulled away a little more so I could lean back and see what was going on.

A small group of girls and guys were walking along the path, heading from where I assumed the cabins were toward the latrines.

They passed by, waved to us. We waved back, although my heart was still thundering a mile a minute. Had they seen who we were? What we'd been doing? I didn't recognize any of them but their faces were shadowed.

Soon they were gone and I breathed out a slow breath. I looked at him sheepishly. "I'm sorry," I said. "I don't know why. It feels like...school? Like we're not supposed to..."

"I know," he said and smiled. "I pulled away, too."

He had. "Were you worried it was Mr. Blackbourne?" I asked, assuming he was thinking about the rule and worried he'd get into trouble.

"What do you mean?" he asked.

I blushed, realizing I'd let slip what I knew. "Because...because you're not supposed to...there's a rule..." How had the others put it? I covered my mouth with my hand.

"Sorry," I said. "I found out about it. The others told me about how I was supposed to..." I stopped, realizing if I said more, it would come out that I had been kissing the other guys, not what I wanted to bring up right now.

Kota remained still for the longest moment. I couldn't speak and held my breath waiting for him to say something, anything. My heart raced and my entire face felt so hot. I was sure he could reach into my brain and would simply know the truth.

He frowned and reached out, drawing my hand my hand from my mouth. I was trying to come up with some quick explanation, but I never got the chance to say anything before he tugged me forward.

And his lips met mine.

I don't know what I was anticipating for a kiss, but in that moment, I was relieved. Memories flooded in my brain of all the times he'd gotten so close, how he'd looked at my lips, how he kissed my cheek.

All the times he'd tried to encourage me, being so patient, waiting for me to make that move.

It took me a moment to realize I wasn't moving my lips at all. He remained still. Slowly, he started to back away.

My hands fluttered up, finding his chest, and I clutched at his sweater. I responded, parting my lips, brushing them against his.

A long sigh escaped his mouth and his lips returned fully, kissing me in return. His warm hands slid up my neck, and he held my jaw with a steady hold. His glasses occasionally pressed against my cheek as he turned his head to kiss me.

His kiss was fresh air and relief. There was a strength behind it, the sort I felt when he was nearby and made me feel brave simply being around.

He stopped, leaned away from me and breathed out slowly, looking at me through slightly smudged glasses. "One," he said quietly.

I didn't understand and was about to ask when he leaned in again, giving me a short, gentle kiss, parting my lips, sucking a little on my lower one. I still had my eyes closed when I heard him whisper, "Two..."

He was counting our kisses from the very first.

We continued and he occasionally whispered numbers under his breath, making me smile. I held onto his shoulders, feeling the muscles, remembering how strong he really was. I breathed in the sweet spice over and over. My insides warmed. All I wanted was to stay there for as long as possible and kiss him.

At number seven, he finally pulled back a little. The smile on his face was wide, his cheeks red. "There were times I thought it would never happen," he said.

My cheeks burned and I was sure they were as red as his. "It took me a while to learn what the rule was. I thought it was like the Academy wouldn't allow you and then I found out it would cost you a favor."

"I would have given them all up," Kota said. "But I didn't have any left. I didn't want to ask Mr. Blackbourne for any more than I'd already borrowed."

I thought of some of the others. Had someone said they had some left? "Why? Why are you so low?"

"I didn't have many when I met you," he said. "And I spent them all, the last of my thirty allotted, on you." He smiled and then brushed his palm against my cheek. "Sweetheart, I couldn't get you out of that house without some outside help. You were complicated. All the background research..."

He spent everything on me? I bit my lower lip. "I'm sorry."

"Don't be," he said. "Totally worth it. But I've got zero now. I asked Mr. Blackbourne for more to help with you, which he didn't mind, but from my count, he's getting pretty close to thirty, too."

"The thirty original?" I asked. "The ones that are like credit?"

"Yeah," he said and then grinned. "You're learning fast. If you pay off your debt, any amount over thirty, that's when you graduate. Sort of. It's complicated."

I understood it. "How'd he get so low?"

"We've been working on getting more for everyone, but it's not always easy. There's been the situation with Nathan's dad, and occasionally Pam, and then Silas's brother, Theo. Family things like that can eat up a lot of favors. And then you, sometimes."

"I'm costing you favors," I said quietly.

"It's normal," he said quickly and hugged me around the shoulders. "But I didn't want to ask for any more. If I kept doing that, they would send a manager to our team to check out why we kept borrowing from each other. I didn't want to call attention to you."

I hunched down, putting my arms around my stomach and looking down at the fire pit. Now that I knew about the favor system, I wondered how much I had cost them all. Like the times I went to the hospital. "My stepmother? In the Academy hospital?"

"That's more cash than favors," he said quietly. "It's not a big deal. We've got plenty of that. We got another boost when we did the Thanksgiving Day donations."

Money and favors. Because of my stepmother, I must have been costing them a fortune, covering the hospital bills for so long. I was also risking Kota's Academy career, eating up his favors just to keep me around, to keep me safe. No wonder he hadn't dared to kiss me and break the rule.

The others had given in so quickly, maybe because they thought they had favors to spare. Or did they not realize how low their favors must be? Kota was family lead, right? Maybe he kept track of those things and knew the true numbers.

At this rate, if I got into the Academy, I might get a zero balance in each area right from the start.

Kota rubbed my spine. "Come on," he said. "We should walk back to camp."

"Is it ten already?" I asked.

"It's getting there," he said and stood. He reached for my hand. "Do you want me to come find you tomorrow night?"

I nodded enthusiastically. I wanted to talk to him about the plan, but I was suddenly lost in thought of favors and numbers. Perhaps because he worked with me and then spent so much time working as family lead that he never had a chance to earn a favor on other jobs. He spent, but maybe it was difficult to earn them back when he worked so hard to keep nine other people safe.

I held his hand as I walked beside him, lost in thought, my eyes trained on the road. I couldn't help but worry about my place in the team. If I joined, the Academy might not like me sticking with my team. We knew it would be difficult. We knew there would be problems; there were probably many issues we hadn't even thought through yet.

The Academy would force us to look at every single angle. With so many of us, and with me in the middle, I couldn't help but see them fighting over how things would work out with us. I'd already seen hints of jealousy and had to imagine there would be more.

Then there was the cost. I was expensive, because of my stepmother, and no doubt looking out for Marie would be expensive, too. I didn't think I could have the opportunity to be a member of the Academy without asking them to help me with my stepmother and Marie. Guilt would follow me through all my days if I simply abandoned them when I had the chance to at least make sure they were comfortable.

Maybe my father, too. Despite still being angry with him, and wanting to forget about him, what about the family he was with now? Did they deserve to be ignored? Or could they be at risk because of his past? I didn't even know them or anything about them, but something I did in the future might reflect back on him.

Maybe when the Academy did their digging, it might uncover if he really did rape my mother, or he'd get into trouble if anyone discovered she had been only sixteen.

And then there was me. I was in the middle of high school, already in trouble with Volto, Mr. McCoy and more. I might be too expensive to take care of at this point. There was no denying taking me on would be complicated.

Maybe all this talk of plans and how we'd work it out was moot. Maybe the Academy couldn't afford to keep me. Or worse, maybe they wouldn't even want me.

♥

A Rift Among Friends

I dwelled on dark thoughts the entire way back to the campsites, although I held Kota's hand. He quietly remained by my side, a small smile on his lips as he used the flashlight to guide our way back to camp.

Before I knew it, we were at the guys' tent and North was just putting out the campfire with a bucket of water. The others were putting away chairs and starting toward the tent.

Lake was with them, standing by. She was the first to see us coming. "Here she is," she said and pointed in my direction.

The others stopped what they were doing, looking at us.

It was instinct to pull my hand away from Kota, as I was feeling awkward but Kota held my hand firmly in his. I stopped fighting since he thought it was okay.

"It's been a long day," Kota said. He looked at Lake. "Think you can walk her back without running into bears, or another cave?" He said this with his smile firm, teasing.

Lake raised an eyebrow, looking from me to Kota. "Uh...yeah."

"Good," Kota said. He turned to me.

I looked up at him, thinking he meant to just say goodnight.

He leaned in quickly and kissed me square on the lips. It was quick, but that he'd done it meant so much. He pulled back and smiled. "Eight," he said. He squeezed my hand and walked toward the tent. "Okay guys, where are we at? Where can I help?"

I stood there frozen in place, stunned, surprised, shaken.

I glanced at North, Nathan, who had been at the tent holding the flap open, and Gabriel and Luke, who were dragging chairs around.

Nathan looked confused and backed himself into the tent.

North frowned, but said nothing, continuing to put out the fire.

Luke and Gabriel seemed curious, eyebrows raised, but then Gabriel spoke to Kota. "Not much," he said. "You want the coolers back in the car?"

They talked but no one had said anything about the kiss.

Lake approached me, distracting me by snapping her fingers near my face. "Hey," she said. "You sleepwalking? Let's go."

I nodded and turned away, unable to say anything. I hadn't been prepared for that goodnight kiss, especially in front of everyone. While I wanted to be happy about it, I was unsure about Nathan, who'd admitted to being jealous seeing that sort of thing, and North, who seemed to struggle with it, too.

"You took forever," Lake said as she walked beside me to the road. "Were you having sex or what?"

I gasped and my eyes widened as I stopped in the road. "No!" I said quickly.

Lake lifted her hands in a wait gesture. "Hey, I was just asking. I don't care."

"We were..." I said and then stumbled. "We...I..."

"I said I don't care," Lake said. She looked ahead and then started walking.

I kept up beside her. "There's complications with me joining the guy team. We were going over the problems."

"Find any solutions?" she asked.

I lowered my head, watching our feet as we walked. "No," I said. Not one I was satisfied with anyway.

The woods around us were very dark. Lake had a flashlight and carried her towel and supplies with her. I'd forgotten to get my own bathroom kit from North, but I suspected it was taken care of for now and I could get it tomorrow when I needed it.

Every so often, there was a pole with a streetlight, but they were so far apart, that you could be in the pitch dark in certain areas. We shuffled quietly along, eventually finding our way back to Taylor's tent.

Quiet, whispery noises drifted out from it.

"Let's scare them," Lake said.

I shook my head. "Not tonight," I said. I was thinking of the younger girls. They were probably exhausted.

Lake pouted. "You're no fun," she said and headed toward the tent to unzip it.

Despite my desire to not scare the girls, the moment Lake started unzipping the tent, the girls inside cried out in panic.

"It's a boy!" one of them said. "Coming to spy on us!"

"Or a bear!"

Lake chuckled and finished opening the zipper and then growled a little.

We went inside. Some of the girls were in bed, lying down but with blankets over their heads.

Emma was turned in her cot, asleep, as was April. Taylor was sitting up and grinned at us. "Ha," she said. "Good one, girls."

"Where have you been?" Carla asked. She had been sitting up and now dropped her pillow back into place at the head of her cot. "It's past ten."

"I don't have a watch," Lake said. I knew she had a phone so that wasn't really true.

I didn't want to get into where we'd been. I went to my cot, dropping down onto it and yanked off my boots. "We're here now."

Carla pointed a finger at us. "You could have been caught. You would have gotten into trouble."

"They're fine," Taylor said. "They weren't causing a ruckus. As long as you're quiet, no one cares if you're out of your tent after ten."

"They said it was a rule," Carla said.

"They say that every year," Taylor said. "But they aren't

prison guards. You don't get a demerit or get put into the clink."

Carla frowned, pursing her lips.

Lake paused, looking around after she zipped up the tent again. "Hey," she said. "Where..."

"You're over there with Sang," Carla said. "We rearranged some of the cots."

After I'd finished with my boots and had put them aside, I paused, checking out the cots, which had been moved around a little. An empty one was closer to mine than it had been before, and the others had made room for a big air mattress in the middle, where three girls were sleeping on it. The arrangement didn't make sense and wasn't the most efficient use of space. It seemed Carla had made sure Taylor, her team, Lake and me were shoved out toward the edges.

Lake rolled her eyes. "Whatever," she said and she dropped down into the cot next to mine.

"I didn't do it because of *you*," Carla said.

Lake frowned, lay down on her cot, and then turned toward me, putting her back to Carla not saying anything.

I didn't blame her. She'd been on the other side of the tent before and now it felt like she was being pushed away.

Maybe it wasn't what it looked like. Carla might have meant well; maybe the young girls had asked to sleep closer together and she'd complied. But I could see why it looked like they were trying to cast Lake out. Maybe Lake assumed it was because she was a boy.

It was obvious they weren't going to get along. They weren't going to be a team together. Lake was going to have to find another team sometime this week, or allow the Academy to put her in a team.

"Lights out," Taylor said.

♥

$\mathscr{C}$AMP $\mathscr{C}$ONTINUES

$\mathscr{F}$or the next two days, I saw very little of the boys, and Carla seemed determined to keep the girls together.

We met other people, but we were always together.

Mrs. Rose met with us every morning at nine. She went through explaining managers, more about the favors and money systems, and tried to answer questions. She also went over more details about the special jobs for girls, like April had done the night before.

I was her voice, and when my voice became weak and tired, I would relay to Lake, who had a louder voice and could go on for a long time.

Because Lake and I had turned into something like camp counselors for the younger girls, they followed wherever we went. Lake and I often tried to sneak away from camp activities in the afternoons when we split up, even going back to fish crabs with Silas. But we wouldn't be there long before we had five fourteen-year-old girls behind us, and Carla trailing behind them.

They did, however, participate in everything we did. They fished for crabs, took in a first aid training lecture, and painted. One day we volunteered to cook lunch and clean up after.

We never went on another hike, but Mrs. Rose occasionally joined us at these activities and continued to answer more of our questions. She talked about examples of inside jobs, too. Even though I'd been on a few, like that time when we helped a family of children from Mexico, and her examples were different from what I'd experienced, it just showed me how varied Academy jobs could be.

The burritos had a long cooler life, a fact Lake was surprised about, considering they had mashed avocado inside. However, not everyone wanted them, so Taylor made a vegan bean salad on the third morning.

Lake and I polished off a box of Pop-Tarts and started in on granola bars. Those held us until lunch when we could fill up. By the time dinner came around, Lake and I often were able to sneak over to the boys, but I was usually still full of lunch and ate a small bag of chips for dinner.

Every morning, a cooler loaded with a fresh collection of chilled mocha Frappuccinos appeared on the picnic table. I suspected Victor and one of the others made sure to stop by before we woke up. There was enough for everyone, including April, although she drank her regular coffee Frappuccinos, too.

Everything seemed fine, and Lake and I were sure we could probably survive the rest of the week simply existing on Pop-Tarts and putting up with a trail of fourteen-year-olds following us everywhere.

The one thing that became more of an issue every day was the fact that we had North drive us to the other latrine every night to wash up, and then tended to disappear for hours after that point.

Kota usually met up with us and listened to Lake and I talk about our day. There was always some complaining about Carla, and Kota encouraged us to talk to her. But the truth was that we both found it hard to talk to her.

After returning from the latrines, we spent our evenings with the guys around the fire. Lake and I often got too tired to even talk, but Gabriel and some of the others talked about the different teams, the classes going on, and what they might do the next day.

The boys were acting a little distant, I noticed. We were all friendly, but I wondered if something was going on because none of them pulled me aside or talked about the important issues: about me joining the Academy and the plan. No one brought up Kota kissing me, either.

The evening was the only time I really got to see them

all. I missed them so much that once Lake and I could join them after we'd been to the latrine, we lingered there until close to ten, leaving only then so Carla wouldn't make a fuss about us being out late.

On our third full official day, Lake and I, in an attempt to get the younger girls to leave us, spent all afternoon at the most seemingly uninteresting booths and activities. There was a geologist who pointed out rocks in the area and had us practice identifying them. There was a botanist who worked with us on identifying plants.

Unfortunately, those turned out to be really interesting. The lecturers made them fun. The most boring activity ended up being fishing because of all the standing around, waiting for a bite.

After twenty minutes at each station, we'd retreat, even if we liked the lectures going on, and try another booth, trying to shake the girls. But each time, they followed.

Carla was always last to trail behind them. Eventually, we ended up at the arts and crafts area, where there often wasn't room for all of us to sit together, so we were forced to spread out, finding seats where we could. It was as good as Lake and I could hope for.

"I don't understand it," Lake whispered to me, trying to weave the start of a sweetgrass basket as an instructor had shown us. "I would have ditched you by now..."

I smirked and shrugged.

"You know what I mean," Lake said. "How many times have we told them to mingle?"

"I don't know," I said, focusing on the grass. Weaving was harder than it had appeared and was already hurting my hands.

That night, we had a quick dinner of vegan hotdogs at Taylor's invitation, with Lake and I and a couple of girls opting for granola instead.

Every night, Carla tried her best to rally the girls into songs and skits and games. Lake and I often bowed out, not because we didn't want to. Carla, however, often didn't ask us to join in. Sometimes, she pretended we weren't even there.

Once Lake and I were done, we left to get to the showers early and then spent the evening with the guys. As we sat around the campfire making s'mores, the guys let us complain about the girls following us, sympathizing. At one point I looked up at Kota and could tell he still thought Lake and I should talk to her, but he didn't say anything and I looked away.

Part of me hoped the week would end without any sort of confrontation. I didn't want to fight. Why couldn't they understand we needed space?

When we returned from the guys' camp, Carla was waiting outside the tent.

"We have ten minutes," Lake said before she'd said a word. It'd been a really long day and I imagined she was as tired as I was and didn't want to get a lecture about being out past the scheduled time.

"I don't care about that," Carla said. She had her arms folded over her chest, standing close to the door, blocking our way. She leaned in, her eyes focusing hard on us. "I need to talk to you two."

"We'll be late," Lake said with a teasing grin.

"This is important," she said.

I cringed. Kota had been right. We probably did need to talk to Carla and get stuff out in the open. I'd kept my allegiance to the guys' team a secret, to not confuse the girls with my complicated situation, and because I simply didn't want to talk about it. Lake had never asked about it or let on what she assumed.

Maybe if Carla knew, she wouldn't lecture us about hanging out with the boys or wonder why we were out so late with them.

She kept her arms folded as she walked away from the tent, nodding her head for us to follow. I frowned, keeping my own arms around my stomach as we fell in step behind her. Maybe she wanted to kick us out for trying to escape all the time. Could she even ask that?

Maybe it would be better.

She walked until she was in the middle of the paved road, well away from the tent. She turned to us then, seeming to be thinking about what she was going to say

Lake and I waited. It was on the tip of my tongue to offer to get Lake and I a separate tent.

"The girls are worried you don't think they're good enough for the Academy," Carla said. "They've been asking to go home."

Lake's mouth dropped open. "What?" she said, shaking her head, obviously as surprised as I was. "Why? We don't have any control over that."

"I told them that," she said. "Probably because you two talk for Mrs. Rose. And you saved some of them from the pit. And Sang saved them from the nettle. You start out nice and helpful, but... I don't know..."

"Because we're supposed to split up," Lake said. "We've been trying to encourage them to spread out. We're supposed to get to know other campers."

"They're scared," Carla said. She dropped her folded arms from her chest to her stomach. Her lip trembled. "Everything seems like a test to them. They think this is part of getting accepted. I can't keep them confident and together when you two run off every night. Even Taylor can't convince them."

"Why are they scared?" I asked. "They aren't doing badly. We're not judging them. We're just trying to get them to try different things and talk to different people."

"They're worried," she said. "They think you two trying to ditch them means you don't like them or don't think they're good enough. And what happens at the end of the week with the exit interview and you two don't have nice things to say about them?" She breathed in deeply, letting out a soft whistle. "I understand you two are probably trying to explore and find your own teams, but right now, they're a split second away from demanding to go home because they feel like rejects."

Lake frowned and looked at me before she spoke. "We

didn't know," she said. "We were just..."

"I don't care," Carla said. "I know you're just doing camp activities. I know that's how it's supposed to work, but...they looking up to you two, not me."

"Maybe if you weren't so bossy," Lake said flatly.

Carla looked down, sniffing as she nodded. "I don't know what else to do," she said between deep breaths. "I thought if I took control a little, they'd want me to be their leader. But no matter what I did, they kept saying if Sang and Lake didn't think they were good enough, then they should just go home."

Lake rolled her head back, looking up toward the sky. "God, don't cry. How were we supposed to know? Why didn't you say something sooner?"

I trembled, tearful myself because Carla was crying, and also feeling sorry for the girls, who had directed their hopes into Lake and me. Carla wasn't trying to intentionally exclude us, she was trying to help the girls and give us our freedom. It just wasn't working.

And worse, Lake and I were letting the other girls down.

Carla breathed in deeply, looking up and wiping at her face. "I know you're probably trying to explore and look at other teams, but right now, I need your help to convince them they can't just quit the Academy. They don't believe they're good enough on their own. I just don't want it to be my fault if they decided they can't join if I could do something about it. They need us, all of us, to show them."

I sighed, looking at Lake. Were we responsible for this? Would the Academy ask us why we were making the others uncomfortable when we hadn't meant to? This had suddenly become more complicated than we'd realized.

"It can't be up to us," Lake said. "You heard April and Mrs. Rose and what they've been through. They can't need us backing them up. They need thicker skin..."

"They don't know as much as we do," Carla said. "We come from troubled families, don't we? Even if they don't join the Academy, they've been trusted with our secrets. What loyalty do they have to keep our secrets if we push them away?"

She was right. I stuffed my hands into my jacket pockets. I'd been so worried about getting onto my team, that I didn't stop to even ask them how they were doing.

"We have an issue," Lake said, looking at me. "Sang's already on a team or trying to get on that team. She's been trying to work it out with them. And I...I'm not..."

"Tell her," I said. She needed to trust other people, the Academy. It was time if Carla hadn't figured it out by now.

Lake groaned and then lowered her head. "I'm a boy."

Carla snapped her head up, looking at the two of us. "What?"

I cringed. Lake bowed her head lower, her hair falling in her face, covering her eyes. "I dress like a girl because I feel more comfortable like that. And I don't... I don't exactly like hanging out with guys."

I gasped and turned to her. "What?" I said, thinking back to the evenings sitting around the guys' campfire. "I thought you liked..."

"I don't mind *them*," she said with a frown, finally looking up. "And I don't mind talking and being around guys in general. I've just had bad experiences with guys and I'm not ready to join with a guy team. I was hoping there would be a girl or two somewhere that would understand. Finding a team for me is going to be impossible." She shot me a look. "I know you have your team already. Kind of wished you didn't though."

I frowned, suddenly torn and unsure. I didn't even know Lake that well and the guys needed me. But Lake was nice, and if she wouldn't feel comfortable with the guys in the long run, what did that mean for her?

She needed someone.

Carla spoke quietly then. "I didn't realize," she said. "I never would have thought..."

"Thanks," Lake said. "Kind of the point."

"And that's why you don't go to the showers with us?" she asked. "The girls were wondering. Like... I don't know.

Like you thought they were weird or annoying."

"We went to the other latrine near the RV area," I said. "So they wouldn't find out and feel awkward."

"I wish you would have told me sooner," Carla said. "We could have worked out a system."

That would have been helpful to us all. . We stood quietly together, the three of us, studying each other, our feet, the sky as we all seemed deep in thought.

I wondered what they were thinking about, but I now wondered about the boys, too. Here I was, in the middle of this girl group, suddenly feeling responsible to make sure no one bailed on the Academy. While at the same time, I was so lost trying to figure out *my* place in it.

"So," Lake said after a while. "What do we do now?"

Carla shrugged. "Help me help them," she said. "I can make up some excuse for the bathrooms if you can spend more time with them."

Lake pushed her palms to her face, pressing them into her eyes. "I don't understand. What do they want us to do? We've been spending all week with them."

"Maybe try not to run off like they're your annoying little sister you're trying to get away from," she said. "They need to feel like they belong here. They're not feeling that yet."

Feeling like they belong. I knew that feeling, or was more familiar with it now, thanks to Kota and his team.

Kota. *My* team.

I snapped my fingers, as wave after wave of memories flooded my brain, of all the things the boys and I did together that made me feel a part of their family team. It wasn't about our relationships, the complicated romance we wanted but had yet to work out.

It was the things we did together. It was the sleepovers. It was swimming in the pool and playing games. It was when we worked together to feed the hungry people of Charleston.

Carla was right, we couldn't run away anymore. "We can do this," I said. "But I need the guys. We need their help. And we need to find more people."

"Why?" Carla asked.

"Because they need a family," I said and started down the paved road, heading toward the guys' tent. I knew we had a curfew, but this was more important. The girls didn't have faith in the Academy, and that was the first step. "Trust your family, right? The girls need to believe the entire Academy is their family. That they can trust anyone here."

Carla didn't move at first, staring at Lake. Lake shrugged and then started following me.

I had a plan, but it would take an entire league of Academy teams to do it.

♥

WHAT THE ACADEMY CAN DO

When we got to the boys' tent, their lamps were off, and other than a few soft snores, they were silent inside the tent.

We slowed as we got closer.

"Let's not spook them," Carla whispered.

I paused and then thought carefully. It was risky, but it was too much to resist. I thought of Gabriel breaking my tent and the others giggling at me for not knowing my sleeping bag heated up. They could stand to be a little scared. "No, let's spook them," I whispered back.

Lake grinned, Carla shook her head. "They'll turn us in," Carla said. "They'll tell the others."

"They won't," I whispered and then motioned for them to get close. When they did, I let them in on the plan. "Let's sneak around the back. Carla, do you have your flashlight."

With it being a clear night, and the moon glowing above, we hadn't needed the flashlight. Carla had brought it, though. She pulled it out of her pocket and held it up.

"You stand back," I told her, figuring she'd want this job. "Shine the line toward the back of the tent. Lake, you and I stand close to the tent wall. When Carla shines the light, you pretend to be a bear and roar. And we'll make shadows."

"Sounds good to me," Lake said.

"Only we have to be quiet from here out," I whispered. "North can hear everything." I wasn't so sure he couldn't hear us out here now with his supersonic hearing. Maybe he was asleep...

The girls followed me as I tiptoed my way around wide toward the back of the tent. Carla positioned herself near the trees, so her light would cast a good glow. Lake and I stood halfway between.

Lake stood really close to me. "So we don't look like two people," she explained when I started to back away from her.

I realized she was right. Standing together, we'd make one big shadow.

We stood hip to hip and I counted down with hand signals to Carla.

Three. Two. One. Go!

Carla lit up the beam, creating a strong enough glow to spread across the back of the tent wall. She even angled from below so the beam went up, making our shadow taller.

Lake raised a curled hand like a claw and growled, doing a great bear impression.

I raised my own hand on the other side—another claw.

The tent erupted with the sounds of grunts, curses, and a few squeals.

"Kota!" Gabriel's voice erupted over the mix of noises. "Bear!"

"Bears don't have flashlights," Kota said.

"Shit," Gabriel said. "Fuck. Shit. Fuck."

"Enough," North said.

The three of us outside giggled and started making our way back around the tent, when I was tackled, and on the ground in a heap before I even realized what had happened.

The smell of leather and cedar wafted over me. I'd recognize the big bulk of muscle anywhere.

"It's just us!" I cried out in an eruption of giggling, struggling for breath with him on top of me.

"I knew it was you," Nathan said, leaning back while still sitting on my hips. "No one else at this campground would dare."

The others had been tackled, too. Silas was on top of Lake. Luke was on top of Carla.

"Get off," Lake said but she was laughing, pushing on

Silas, only Silas was bigger, and sat squarely on her hips.

"Silas," I called to him, remembering Lake had said she's had hard times with guys. In a stern voice, I said, "Get off of her, please."

Silas stood up instantly, offering a hand to Lake. "Sorry," he said. "I was just teasing."

"I know," Lake said and took Silas's hand, allowing him to help her up.

Luke picked up Carla, threw her over his shoulder in a sort of hug and twirl. "It's the second bringer of the Sang!"

I sighed. *Boys*.

"What are you doing back here?" Kota asked quietly.

Nathan backed off, helping me up. The other guys had come around the back of the tent, looking at us. They were all in warmer pajama pants, sweat shirts or long-sleeved T-shirts.

I brushed the grass and dirt off my butt and back. "I need your help," I said.

The guys looked at each other and then nodded.

"Anything," Nathan said. "Tell us what to do."

We moved inside their tent and sat on the cots as Carla, Lake, and I explained the situation.

Then I explained my idea. I didn't have to go far into it before the other guys were adding their own, even better ideas. They told us they'd take care of everything before they sent Carla, Lake and I back to our tent. We would have stayed to help, but we didn't want to be missed by the others and draw attention back to us.

Despite being sent back to our tent, as I lay on my cot, I was a jumble of excitement.

It would work. I was sure of it.

It had worked on me.

TRUST YOUR FAMILY

*D*espite not expecting to be able to sleep, I did manage to doze off sometime in the middle of the night, long after Lake had started snoring softly beside me.

I woke up with a hand over my mouth, stopping my breathing for a second. I startled, and tried to sit up, but a second hand kept me down against the cot. It was soothing, though, gentle.

I opened my eyes, finding Luke hovering over me. His brown eyes filled with delight at spooking me. He winked and held a finger up to his lips.

I should have known.

The dawn light was starting to come in. The other girls slept. I had no idea how he managed to get in so quietly. Only Luke could pull that off.

I sat up as Luke signed to me. "Breakfast is set up to be made outside. Do you want to wake them all now?"

I shook my head. I pointed at Carla and Lake. I wanted them to come help.

Luke nodded and shooed me toward Lake, as he went to wake Carla.

Lake seemed almost awake already when I poked her shoulder, sitting up almost instantly.

Carla took a minute and inhaled loudly. I think she would have cried out at finding Luke on top of her if he hadn't covered her mouth already. He pointed at Lake and me so she understood we were getting up, too.

We slipped out of the tent and took turns dressing in the spare tent with the luggage.

By the time we were done, Silas and North had come over

and set up the picnic tables together and had covered them with tablecloths, piles of paper plates, and plastic cutlery. Nathan and Victor were squeezing oranges, making juice.

Luke showed us the pancake batter. He held up a second box, pointing to me. "Vegan," he said quietly.

We got to work. North had hooked up camping griddle pans to some batteries in his Jeep that he and Silas had silently rolled onto the campsite.

Once some of the food was cooked, Lake and I took plates of bacon, opened the flap to the tent, and wafted the air toward the girls inside.

Two of the younger girls sat up sharply on cots almost instantly. They rubbed their eyes and peered out at us, blinking. Emma sat up, too, yawning.

One of them reached for another sleeping nearby, one on the air mattress. That one woke up, woke the others.

"Come on out, girls," Lake said in a happy tone.

"The world is spinning without you," I said, something Victor had told me once.

They all leaped out of bed, excited, following us out. April was up, too, and woke Taylor to join us, surprise on their faces as well.

Once they were outside the tent, the boys waved them over. Some of the girls grabbed jackets and boots to put on.

Nathan waved them closer, smiling. "Come on," he said. "Eat up. We've got a lot of work to do."

The girls looked to Lake and I, confused.

"We're going to make breakfast for some other teams today," I said. "We've invited them over—some of the other new ones—to help them feel welcome."

"Will you help us?" Lake asked. Kota had told us some things to say to make them feel like they were part of the helping team, which was a big deal.

Five heads nodded enthusiastically. They rushed over to the set-up table, where North stood by, teaching them how to make perfect pancakes. Luke stood nearby, asking if they wanted chocolate chips added.

357

April wrapped an arm around Taylor as they stood by watching the excitement. She tugged in Emma and the three of them stood together, watching the girls getting involved. "We've taught them well," April said.

I smiled. This just might work.

We were almost finished eating our own breakfast when the first other team wandered in. It was another team of young girls, led by Mrs. Rose—the ten-year-olds we'd seen before. They all had wide eyes and seemed eager to be included.

"We're here," Mrs. Rose signed.

I asked the new girls to come sit down and join us. Our team would take care of them. I invited Mrs. Rose to relax, even as she offered to help.

Luke taught the girls about serving like at the diner. "Ask them what to drink first," he said. "And make sure they have napkins and forks before they get pancakes."

Lake, Carla, and I monitored and helped, directing the girls, staying at their elbows.

We all took turns giving them thumbs ups and saying, "Good job."

While I'd never focused on the other girls before, right now, they were beaming with delight and I could tell they loved helping out and being useful.

They smiled. They talked to the little girls. They opened up a discussion about the Academy and what they hoped to do.

When the young group was almost done eating, a group of boys showed up. They were about the same age as their servers—around fourteen.

This time, the girls were nervous but the rest of us encouraged and helped where we were needed.

Soon there was a line, with people standing around with paper plates, making room for any younger kids at the table.

By the time we'd fed all the teams the boys had invited over, it was almost ten.

We offered to help clean up, but the boys shooed us away.

"Time for round two," Kota said.

I nodded and took the lead. I'd gotten permission from

Mrs. Rose, thanks to Kota talking to her and explaining the purpose.

I waved my arms and got the fourteen-year-old girls to pay attention.

"Are we ready for crafts?" I asked.

The girls looked at each other and then back to me.

"There's a trick," I said. "You can't make anything for yourself now. We're all going to make bracelets for someone else. You see, those younger girls and boys are new, and we want to let them know, they're welcome."

The girls nodded, smiling. "Yeah," one of them said. "We'll do that."

Lake gathered them together, getting them organized for a quick change of clothes, a latrine break until they were ready to go.

I paused by the Jeep, where North was cleaning off a griddle.

"Thank you," I said quietly.

"anytime, Baby," he said.

I waved and said thank you to the other guys, too, who were busy cleaning up and moving tables back. I hated to leave them to the mess but was grateful they had been so willing to participate.

Taylor, April, and Emma wandered off on their own. It was just Carla, Lake, and me now to guide the girls for the rest of the day.

Once we got to the arts and crafts area, Gabriel was there, waiting beside a cheery Dr. Green.

"Good morning, ladies," Dr. Green said. "Are we healthy and full of good food this morning?"

The girls nodded. A few of them giggled nervously, looking at the two of them with wide eyes.

Dr. Green wore khakis and a lime green polo shirt. Gabriel was dressed in a button up blue shirt and newer jeans.

Had they dressed a little more nicely just for the girls?

The five girls were seated, Dr. Green and Gabriel explained they would help pick through beads and assist with the clasps.

Working together with the five girls, and Lake, Carla and I participating, within an hour, we had over forty different bracelets, each with unique charms. Each one different.

When we were finished, we collected the bracelets in boxes.

"Are we going to give these to the others now?" one of them asked.

"Tonight we will," I said with a smile.

Lake elbowed me in the gut, gently. "Don't give away spoilers."

I winked at the younger girl.

She whispered to the others. "There's more. There's a secret."

I shared looks with Carla and Lake, unable to help grinning. It was fun to get them excited about the day.

Carla had gone over the girls' interests with us the night before. She'd told the boys, and they had spent all night setting up for the morning. All we had to do was walk them to the different stations at the right times.

The girls followed us to the beach after bracelet-making. First on our list was dancing. One of the girls wanted to be a ballet dancer but liked any sort of dancing.

Gabriel had followed us to where Luke and Nathan met us on the beach. There were other groups there, both younger girls, and another group of guys, including Ian and his team.

We took up a section of a flat area of the beach.

Gabriel led the class. I was nervous about the guys making the girls shy about dancing with them. Luke and Nathan were enthusiastic and joined in, which made it easier for the girls to get into it and not be embarrassed. It was the younger boys who hesitated but Ian's team participated and encouraged them, they all joined in.

Lake, Carla and I mixed in with all the kids, not just our

group, making sure everyone was part of the conversation.

Gabriel taught the steps to *Beat It*. I pretended I didn't know the steps and purposely fumbled a lot. I laughed at my own mistakes. The girls laughed with me and I shared secret winks with Gabriel when they did.

After going through the song many times, we were exhausted and sat down on the beach.

We'd spent the entire morning together and this was the time we'd been waiting for.

Lake, Carla and I had gone over what to say the night before. But now it was time, I was nervous. I felt like I was suddenly on stage, and with the other teams around, it was like revealing a piece of my soul to them all. I was rattling on the inside, not just with stage fright but because I'd be exposing part of myself.

Lake seemed to sense I was nervous and started for me. "Whew," she said. "This reminds me of the time when I was in on a team, and they took me to help out a bunch of Mexican kids."

Lake borrowed the story I'd told her. I didn't mind as it got the conversation going. She embellished a little, too. Luke laughed when she said he'd done crazy parkour back flips to get on top of the roof.

We wanted to show fun experiences with other teams, and open them up to the idea that you wouldn't be on the same team every time, but it was still fun. So we mixed up a few stories, mostly true, just to share with them between activities.

When she finished, I nodded and found the courage to join in. "That's nothing," I said. "There was this one time..."

"Speak up," one of the girls said. "We can't hear you."

My throat was dry from talking a lot over the last few days and my voice had never been very loud to begin with, so I was going to need help to be heard. I started looking toward Lake when I then focused on one of the fourteen-year-olds sitting close to me.

"Will you be my voice?" I asked her.

She nodded.

I spoke, and she repeated my words, shouting at first, but calming after a while. I told the story about Thanksgiving, the families we'd helped, about Academy neighborhoods, and what the one we had visited was like.

"I wish I lived there," the girl who had been my voice said to me after I'd finished.

I winced, wondering about her background. I suspected a lot of them had hard times at home.

The boys left after a while, leaving the girls to chat with each other, asking questions about their experiences at the camp so far.

Lake, Carla and I stood back, listening and smiling at each other. It seemed to be working. The girls were taking responsibility for the younger girls, becoming little leaders themselves.

Taylor appeared beside us as we were headed to the beach picnic area for lunch, watching as the girls continued excitedly talking among themselves.

"This was the best idea," she told us quietly.

"Getting them to talk to other girls?" Lake asked.

"Showing them others needed help, just like they needed you," she said. She winked at us. "When you stop thinking of yourself and focus on helping other people, suddenly your whole outlook changes. You're more positive and confident. You have to be when you're being looked at as a leader."

Taylor's team joined us and we all ate lunch together, listening to their stories about their history, their jobs, even how they'd picked their team.

After lunch, we headed out to a field where we met with Silas, who had brought his Wiffle ball set, as had a few others. We didn't play actual games, though; Silas pitched to whoever had the bat and other people tried to catch balls that got hit out into the field.

"This is almost better than softball," one of the girls from our camp said, smiling and obviously having fun. This opened her up, and she talked animatedly about her own softball team at home.

We were still playing around when Taylor's team showed up again and we were handed white T-shirts and were told to put them on over our clothes.

April handed out condiment squeeze bottles filled with different colors.

"Paint your friends," Taylor said.

"This is one of my favorites," April said as she stood back, shaking one of the bottles.

There was an eruption of giggles as the girls painted each other's T-shirts. At first, we signed names, but it was hard to do on shirts. So we stuck with initials and tried different variations of flowers and butterflies and smilies. Anything much harder and it became a mess.

It felt like I was initialing hundreds of shirts, and created little doodles on each: butterflies, moon and stars, swirls, smilie faces. All in pink. My hands were aching after all the squeezing.

Lake, Carla, and I spent the entire day with the girls, having fun and doing activities that Kota had called team building the night before, but since we were always mixed up with other teams, including the younger girls, it expanded the feeling of the team to more than the original group.

The teenaged boys joined us at dinner. We all still wore our painted shirts that had dried and while we ate, the boys tried to read all the signatures and identify all the doodles.

I noticed that as we mingled with the younger teams, our group seemed to repeat what we had been repeating to them all day long: Good job. You're doing great. Keep it up.

It was working.

We helped clean up from dinner and once it got dark, and we played games like Ghost in the Graveyard, which was sort of like hide and seek.

We made s'mores around campfires as we talked and told stories.

As it got later in the night, the girls kept asking if we needed to go back to the tents. We told them no and that we weren't done yet.

They were excited, but also eyeballed any grownup we passed as if they were going to tell us to go to bed.

We waited until about eleven before we had them follow us to the beach.

The beach was filled with other Academy members, old and young, all sitting in folding chairs.

There was a section just for our team.

It was New Year's Eve. I hadn't even realized until we'd talked about it the night before. This was one activity I didn't have to plan. It was happening and we simply sat and waited.

When the time came, we didn't even realize it until the first firework shot out over the ocean waves. Someone hooted, everyone cheered.

The fireworks lit up the sky.

Lake leaned into me from her chair beside me. "I think we did it," she said, and she nodded toward the other girls.

I peeked at them, and they were excited, looking up at the sky, and occasionally reaching out to hold hands with the younger ones. They were so engaged with them, they completely ignored us.

I smiled, admiring our handiwork when Victor caught my eye, sitting in front of me. He winked once, waited until Lake sitting next to me wasn't paying attention. He kissed his finger and quickly brought it to my lips.

I smiled. A quiet New Year's kiss. It was perfect.

♥

An

Uncomfortable Heart

When the fireworks ended, we helped put chairs into a truck that would take them away in the morning.

Someone mentioned it was our last night, and I was surprised. We were just in time and I hadn't realized it. For some reason, I assumed we'd stay through the weekend instead of going back on Friday. Maybe the adults would have to go back to work and needed to get home.

I'd gotten so familiar with the campgrounds, and while it had been stressful, it had also been fun. I was on a high, proud that I'd helped the younger girls see that there was more to the Academy than 'us versus them.'

I'd started to believe it, too. Everyone was so nice, so helpful and understanding. It was so different from school, where everyone kept to their own friends, never mingling with others. It was like a dream world, where everyone was amazing and supportive and I had become part of it.

As the girl team trailed back to our camp, I followed them, not meaning to separate myself. Just exhausted.

But when we got back, we had one more thing to do. We loaded everyone into cars with their bathroom kits and brought them all to the better latrine.

Lake and I did hobo baths, without taking off our clothes. "I'm not that dirty," she said to the others. "And I'm so tired." She kept her eyes down the whole time.

I, too, was focused on getting in and out quickly. Something about being in the bathrooms with the other girls sent a shiver up my spine. I blamed the showers, even with the strange echo they made. Once more than one shower was on, I became overwhelmed. I took in quick breaths as I brushed my teeth as fast as I could.

I told myself I'd be home soon. I wouldn't have to worry about showers anymore.

However, it wasn't just the showers. Like Lake, I kept my head down, focused on the sink. I couldn't help it. I couldn't look at the other girls, thinking at any moment one of them might undress around me.

Why did it bug me that much? It hadn't occurred to me until that moment. I understood Lake's reasons, but what were mine?

The other girls didn't seem to mind and were all chatting as they got ready for bed. They didn't ask Lake and I questions.

When we returned to the tent, everyone was still talking, buzzing about the day they'd had.

"This was the best," one of the girls said.

"We don't have to go home tomorrow, do we?" one of them asked.

"I still feel like I don't know much," another said. "I think I need to stay and learn more."

I didn't know what to expect tomorrow, either. There were more early activities, but when I checked the map, the paper said there was clean up scheduled in the late afternoon.

This was it. There might be an exit interview tomorrow. Was I ready? My heart was beating wildly as we got ready for bed. Now that the girls seemed happy, I had my own issues to worry about.

The girls continued to giggle and chatter. Carla and Lake, as well as Taylor's team, joined in. No one seemed to care how late it was.

"Okay everyone," Carla said. "This might be our last night. Let's group hug."

I'd been smiling absently while thinking and then froze. My eyes started to widen and my body stiffened. I glanced at the other girls, who didn't hesitate.

While the others had started to get up, I remained on my cot, holding tight.

I held my breath to prevent the feeling of panic sweeping over me.

I watched the girls who collected in the middle with Carla. Even Lake joined in. Arms wrapped around other girls, mostly around the neck, but some wrapped arms around waists. They closed in tight, pressing themselves against each other in a large circle.

In their rush to huddle together, no one noticed I was still sitting on my cot, hunching down, making myself small.

I hoped they wouldn't miss me, unsure I could hold myself together if they did.

Yet as I watched them together, I looked for signs that they were uncomfortable like I was. Why didn't anyone look as terrified as I felt?

"Sang?" Carla called, with her sweet, happy smile. "Come on. You, too."

I swallowed thickly, plastering a smile on my face and trying to smother a shiver. *Just stand and hold still*, I told myself. *Just don't move like last time.*

The others called my name and waved me in. I felt their expectations weighing around me. I smothered a grunt, got up and hoped to get it over with quickly.

I walked toward them with my arms tight against my sides.

"Girls, Sang can't get it," Carla giggled. The others laughed and opened their arms.

I swallowed a few times to keep back the trembling and the desire to run. I steeled my nerves, letting them pull me in. I closed my eyes.

Don't think of them. Think of the guys. Of anything else…

Arms encircled my waist, my shoulders. I felt hands on my wrists, trying to pat at me as if whoever it was couldn't reach me. My breasts met up with someone else's while someone's chest was at my back. I was surrounded, and I felt like I was drowning. My knees trembled, and all I wanted to do was sink down.

Why did it feel like the shower? Like I wanted to faint? My stomach twisted. Bile rose in my throat.

And then it happened. My vision blurred with tears, and suddenly, I wasn't seeing any of them.

I saw my stepmother.

She was yelling at me and held me in place while she poured vinegar and lemon down my throat.

I saw Muriel. Wrestling with me, trying to jab me with a needle.

I saw Jade. Touching me in places I didn't want her to.

My heart was in my throat and tears poured down my face. Panic and confusion whirled around in my brain.

The guys had hugged me before. I enjoyed their touches. Why was it now that I couldn't bear another moment of this? No matter how hard I bit my tongue, I couldn't stop the horrible feeling.

I cried. I couldn't hide it.

How stupid I was. I couldn't take a shower. I couldn't be hugged by girls.

I was a mess. And now I was humiliated

Carla laughed. "Aw," she said, tears welling in her eyes as she cried, too. "I'll miss you, too. But we can still stay in contact."

I swallowed, as hard as I could, and forced myself to smile and pretend that was what it was.

Some of the other girls cried and broke away. I covered my face now that I had the opportunity. Lake left her hand on my shoulder and I waved her off. She wasn't bad, but my skin still felt like it was crawling, and I wanted to rake at it with my fingernails. I felt dirty and disgusting, ashamed. "I'll be okay," I breathed through my tears, covering my face to hide my feelings. "Don't worry. I'm just sleepy."

"Let's get to bed," Carla said. "We've got all morning to exchange information."

"And don't worry about teams," Taylor said. "No matter what, if you've made it this far, you'll be put in a group somewhere."

I sucked in fresh air, dropping heavily on my cot and lying down. Lights went out.

My lungs burned with needing to cry more, but I held back, saving the others from my misery.

I turned toward the wall.

My mouth was open.

I was silent, but I was screaming on the inside, shaking and crying. I couldn't stop myself. The horrifying memories came flooding back to me. I knew. I couldn't help it but I knew.

I couldn't ever join a girl team.

♥

*S*ECRETS *R*EVEALED

I stared up at the ceiling of the tent, willing time to fly by. I wanted it to be morning already. I needed to find the boys.

How could I tell anyone about this?

I thought if I could stare at the tent fabric hard enough, my tears would eventually dry up. But the more tired I got, the harder it was to swallow them back.

I was going to fail Academy entry. I was fooling myself thinking I could make it work. If I tried to join the Academy, they might ask if I could work with other girls.

And I'd have to tell them why I couldn't. The real truth. It could never happen.

I couldn't. I was messed up. They wouldn't want someone like me. Someone who couldn't take a shower, and who couldn't get a hug from girls without crying.

Fear washed over me. I was sure Mrs. Rose would show up in the morning, and she would tell me if I wanted in, I had to stay with Carla and the younger girls. She'd smile at me and said I had done a good job.

And then she'd see how much of a mess I was.

There was no way I could do it. Maybe the guys saving me had been a bad thing. Not that I wanted to think so, but now I was so used to them, that imagining going through this with anyone else was unbearable. They had broken down walls with me no one else would be able to get through. They could hug me. They could be around me in the bathroom.

I wanted them. I wanted to feel their strong arms around me and their assurances. I wanted to go back weeks ago when Dr. Green said I wasn't ready, agree with him, and insist on not coming to the camp. I'd take it all back.

We'd been worried about nothing.

The Academy wouldn't want a broken girl. They needed strong ones who could stand up against bad people.

Time passed, and when sleep wouldn't come, I listened. Steady breathing from sleeping girls filled the air.

I rose, as silently as I could, with my heart pounding in my ears. I had no idea where I was going. All I knew was I needed out.

I thought about the guys, but I wasn't ready to talk to them yet. I needed to stop crying, or I'd scare them.

If I couldn't have the boys, I didn't want to be around anyone at all. I wanted to be the old Sang Sorenson. Being invisible and alone to get control of my emotions once again. I'd tell them I changed my mind. I didn't want to. I'd blame it on not wanting to break the team and was willing to be ignorant forever just to stay with them.

The floor of the tent crinkled, making it difficult to be quiet on, but I managed to slip into my boots and get to the door flap without waking anyone. Unzipping took forever, and when I was outside, I zipped it only halfway back.

The night was a little cool, but the heater was on and they all had warm sleeping bags. I didn't want anyone to follow me now. They wouldn't understand. They would think something was wrong with them. I didn't want the younger girls to see how much of a mess I was and lose their confidence.

I took a long route to walk away from the tent quickly, escaping to the road. From there, I walked quietly, hoping the exercise and brisk air would exhaust the seemingly unending waves of tears that flowed out of me. I didn't want to draw any attention to myself, so I avoided walking under the glow of any streetlights.

The chill cut through the soft long-sleeved T-shirt I wore, right through my skin, down into my bones.

I welcomed it. I wanted to be cold, to ease the feelings in my heart. I breathed in the cold air and scanned my surroundings, looking up at the sky, into the darkness.

Alone. For the first time all week, I didn't have anyone

371

around. I desired relief and expected it at first.

But the cold and being alone wasn't helping. An overwhelming sense of dread about my team came over me. I was costly. I was creating problems for my team.

I was also second-guessing my own spot inside their team. They couldn't afford me. Could any team afford me? Maybe even that was a problem.

Maybe Volto was right. Maybe going away was the better path. I didn't have the same reasons, but I couldn't help but think of Kota, and how he could possibly try to get back some favor points if he simply didn't have me to worry about. The others had risked favors, just to kiss me.

With me gone, they could get those favors back.

I was halfway to a crossroads when I heard the sound of footsteps, possibly heading toward the latrines. I paused, listening, wondering who might be awake now. I had no idea what time it was, but I didn't want to run into anyone.

With the help of the moonlight and a few of the streetlights, I found the footpath that weaved through the forest. I was pretty sure this was the one that led to the cabins, and eventually to the camper area, and then around to the boys' tent.

I dashed into the path, willing to take the risk of being caught by the Academy council for being out late. It was fine to head to a latrine, wasn't it? I could say I got turned around in the dark. Taylor had said as long as we were quiet, they didn't mind.

Still, when I heard footsteps still behind me, I hurried, keeping my head down. I didn't want to be caught out, just in case. Not like this. Not in the mess I was in.

When the main road was no longer visible, I paused, catching my breath. The shadows of evergreen trees had darkened my path, blocking the moonlight. I had to wait for my eyes to adjust a little, to even see the path ahead. I wondered if I wouldn't be able to see once I got further in. If it got pitch black along the way...

The dirt path wove around trees, and at times blocked out

the moonlight even more, making following it almost impossible. It came down to my feet, and moving slowly at times. I picked my way along the trail, thinking about tomorrow and what I was going to have to face.

Maybe I needed to simply go home, my old home, not Nathan's house. My stepmother wasn't there. Marie wouldn't be happy, but the Academy couldn't argue with me if I went back. I could transfer to a different school. The guys wouldn't have to spend any more favors or money on me. I could handle it.

I turned the bend and ran into what at first I thought was a tree until I caught the scent of spring soap.

I was stunned, sure I was wrong, even as the scent lingered deep in my lungs, and the warm body in front of me leaned in.

I spoke through trembling lips. "Mr. Bla..."

"Not here," he whispered. A hand closed around my wrist. I followed, letting him lead me away, through the trees and deeper into the woods.

The world was silent around us. I held his hand, my fingers nearly numb with cold but warmed quickly at his touch. I heard the swish of material, like a jacket, although I couldn't see very well at all.

How he could see so well was beyond me.

We went a good ways into the shelter of trees before he stopped, releasing my wrist. He turned toward me, and in the quiet of the night, I felt those gray eyes boring into me, silently commanding me to tell him why I was out so late at night, alone. He would never approve of this or my reasons.

I wanted to explain, but as I stood breathing in his scent, I realized that even here, with him right in front of me, he was still a million miles away.

He'd dragged me this far because we could possibly get into trouble, right? Here I was, putting him at risk again, maybe at the cost of a favor, or even being kicked out.

My voice cracked so much that I couldn't even say his name.

My head dipped and my hands lifted to cover my face. Hiding the tears that I couldn't stop, even for him. How could I ever explain?

"Miss Sorenson," he said quietly.

"I can't do it," I said, sobbing into my palms. "I can't do this."

"I've never known you to give up."

I wanted to answer him. I didn't have one to give. Instead, I let out all the tears I'd held back in the tent.

That's when I sensed his hands, hovering over my shoulders. I felt the warmth radiating from his palms. He rarely touched me, and now he was willing, but he was like Kota and the others who needed to be shown he could.

In the darkness, my hands found the material of his windbreaker jacket. I buried my face into his chest, gripping the material. The feel of his body, just being against him, had me crying all over again. I felt so stupid.

His hands lowered to my shoulders then. His thumbs smoothed over my collarbones. When my crying didn't ease, his palms ran down the outsides of my arms.

"What's wrong?" he asked. He knew this was more than just being homesick or being overtired from all the hard work. This was more than being singled out to join a group I was unfamiliar with. This was something much worse. But I was sobbing too hard to answer. "Miss Sorenson," he said, his voice commanding, impossible to ignore.

"I can't... I can't stand it when they touch me," I said, knowing I wasn't making sense, but my voice cracked and my muddled brain couldn't think of a better explanation.

"*Who* touched you?" the power in his voice grew stronger and his fingers clenched on my upper arms.

"The girls hug," I said. "They hold hands. They grab my arm. They group hug and they hug me. I know it's normal. I know I should be able..." Another sob broke through, but I took a deep breath and swallowed, wanting him to understand this part. "I'm trying. I thought I could..."

"What are you saying? They're touching you

inappropriately?"

"No," I said quickly. I lifted my head, wiping away my tears but no matter how many times I swiped at my face, they still fell. "I just can't do it. I don't know why, but I panic every time. It's so bad I want to pull away, even though I know I shouldn't."

His comforting hands on my arms disappeared instantly. "You mean anyone who touches you?"

"No," I said, and my hands sought out his jacket again, gathering the material into my fingers, silently telling him he wasn't who I was talking about.

My head dipped again into his chest, holding him close. I didn't want him to go anywhere else. I couldn't stop it from flowing out of my lips. "Not you. Not the guys. I want you to touch me. I always want it. Hugs. Kisses. Anything. It makes me happy. But with the girls... any girl, I think..."

"Any girl? Even Miss Newman?"

"Who?"

"Karen. Your friend at school. You didn't know her last name?"

"No. I talk to her in gym class. Sometimes I see her at lunch but she never touches me." I sighed. "I'm sorry. I wanted to try. I thought I could get used to it. I thought just for the week... If I have to join a girl group..." My voice cracked again and the sobbing took over.

I wanted to tell him more, about the shower, about how I felt about the guys and him. I wanted to confess everything, but my exhausted and wrung out body shook uncontrollably and my words were murmurs against his coat.

His hands found me again, and this time, he wrapped his arms around my shoulders. I felt a cheek press to the top of my head. "Miss Sorenson," he said, in a voice immensely softer than I'd ever heard from him before. "Are you telling me you're afraid of girls? What happens when one of them tries to touch you?"

The shock of him hugging me overwhelmed my senses. I froze, even as I welcomed his embrace. Afraid he'd pull back,

I kept still, pressing lightly back. I wasn't sure how to respond, but I somehow I found the words.

"I worry they'll hurt me. That they'll touch me like Jade did. I know they won't. I know...but I can't help it. It's every time they get close. I don't want to offend them and tell them. I don't want to..." I broke off because my thoughts went into twenty different directions at once.

Mr. Blackbourne's arms around me tightened. "So if they wanted to put you into another girl group..."

"The girls I'm with are nice and they're trying so hard, which just makes me feel worse. But I don't think I could be in a girl group."

Mr. Blackbourne's breathing was suddenly the only thing I could hear through my sobs and the blood rushing through my ears. The warmth of his jacket and body against my nearly frozen one had me seeking out his warmth, his arms around me. In the dark, I knew it was Mr. Blackbourne but it was still easy to forget it was him, too.

Just as I began to still against him, Mr. Blackbourne released me, to my utter disappointment. He quickly captured one of my hands, tugging. "Hurry," he said.

I followed close behind him, too distraught to question where we were going. He was going to let me go home. Maybe he'd drive me there himself. My life within the Academy was over.

It took me until we were at the door of a building before I realized we were at the cabins. My hand squeezed his, wanting to hold on to him. What was he doing?

Mr. Blackbourne twisted the handle, shoving the door open. He tugged me inside, but let go of my hand quickly, instead placing his palm on the small of my back.

The lighting was dim and close to the ground. When my eyes adjusted, I realized there were electric lights made to look like old oil lamps, placed strategically around the cabin to act like nightlights. There were eight sets of bunk beds inside against the outside walls, making it one long hallway with empty space in the middle.

There was a mix of older men and women inside, and they all sat up watching us.

Suddenly, everyone began moving at once: some got out of bed, others reached for robes and then joined them, approaching me.

If I could have melted through the floor, I would have. I stood with blurry eyes, embarrassed and I simply put all my faith in Mr. Blackbourne, that he knew what he was doing.

"What's wrong?" a man asked. "Is she hurt?"

"Ask her," Mr. Blackbourne said. His hand at the base of my back nudged me forward. "I found her sobbing alone in the woods." He said nothing more, seeming to expect me to explain.

I glanced back at him, questioning why he was making me do this. He nudged me again, this time, warmly, standing beside me and holding a palm to my lower back. "Trust me," he whispered in the softest tone I'd ever heard from him. "This is the last time you'll ever have to say it again, I promise. Tell them everything you told me."

I stiffened and found myself looking at the older women and men in the group, at the faces that were hard to recognize in the dark and with the tears still blurring my vision. My eyes lowered until I was looking at their feet, finding the floor easier to address than anyone else.

And I told them everything.

I was numb all over, simply repeating everything I'd told Mr. Blackbourne out in the woods. What did it matter now? I was a mess. He was having me tell them so he had a reason to take me home. I didn't care anymore. I was humiliated.

When I choked out the last of what I could explain, I began sobbing again, hiding my face once more in my palms.

Moments later, when I had quieted to hiccups and stuttering breathing, I felt hands on mine. At first, I thought it was Mr. Blackbourne, but a moment later, I smelled flowers, too heady to be him. I looked up quickly, and without thought, I jerked myself away from the touch.

It was Mrs. Rose. She had begun to lean in for a hug but

when I pulled back, she kept her arms down. Her eyes glistened and her face was full of empathy.

"I'm sorry," I said. She was the last person I wanted to offend. "I..."

She waved her hand in the air, cutting off my answer. She turned halfway away from me toward the group, using sign language to address everyone. Her hands were fast, but I made it out. "How could we have missed this?"

This was it. They now knew for sure I wasn't Academy material. My heart sank into my stomach.

"We know now," a familiar, very gentle male voice said. I turned, spotting Dr. Roberts wearing pajama pants and a dark blue robe. He held a tight, smile, sharing sympathetic looks with me. He spoke softly. "The question is, what do we do about it?"

"I don't know if now is a good time to make any decision," someone else said.

"I agree," someone else replied. "It's late. Please don't worry now. She can stay wherever she wants. If she needs to go, let her."

Mrs. Rose waved her hand at me and began to sign, "You're stronger than that. Please stay and talk to us tomorrow after some sleep. We can help. Remember what I told you?"

A warm hand found my arm, and I looked up to see Mr. Blackbourne give me a nod. The others continued to stand in the half-circle. I felt like I was being dismissed so the jury could make a decision.

I let Mr. Blackbourne guide me back to the cabin entrance. We left, closing the door behind us.

"They're going to kick me out," I whispered as Mr. Blackbourne led the way through the dark. "I'm sorry... With all the effort you..."

"You're not being thrown out," he said. His hand squeezed mine, drawing me down the path. "They're not that cruel. However, they will be considering this carefully." He paused. "You were very brave back there. I'm sorry for doing so right then, but they needed to see it for themselves, to hear it from you. I hope you understand."

He was probably right. Would I have so willingly told them so much if I'd slept? Or would I have hidden my feelings more? I needed to trust the Academy. "Thank you," I said. "But now what do I do?"

"They're right. Now isn't the time to decide. You need to sleep."

"I can't go back to my tent," I said.

He didn't reply but took my hand again and led me away from the cabin area. I followed, exhausted.

I looked up and was surprised to see not my own campground, or even the boys', but somewhere I hadn't been. I looked around, but couldn't place where we were.

We approached a small tent that glowed faintly—a lamp or flashlight had to be on inside—and Mr. Blackbourne yanked open the zipper before he stepped back. "Get in," he said.

My heart began to beat wildly again but for different reasons. This had to be his tent. Spring soap was stronger coming from inside, along with some ginger.

I angled myself inside, eager for warmth as well as to hide from anyone who might be nearby. Was he going to talk more in the privacy of the tent before sending me on to sleep with the boys?

The tent was dimly lit, but there was movement on the other side. Dr. Green's shadowed face appeared in the muted beam of the lamp. He let out a groggy grunt as he sat up on his cot, his hair mussed on one side. He lifted the lamp, adjusting it until the tent was illuminated.

He rubbed at his eyes and then squinted over at us. "What's going on?"

"Long story," Mr. Blackbourne said. He urged me toward the second cot, still neatly made. Had Mr. Blackbourne gone to bed at all?

A surge of crazy feelings emerged as I realized he wanted me to sleep in his spot. "What about you?" I asked, my voice barely a squeak.

"Just hop in," he said, pointing toward the sleeping bag.

I tried to look as calm as possible as I sat on the cot. I kicked off the boots and eased my body between the folds of the sleeping bag. The bag had been turned on to a low setting, but Mr. Blackbourne reached down, turning the knob up.

I glanced over at Dr. Green; his eyes were wide, as he looked from me to Mr. Blackbourne. "I thought we were..."

"Unforeseen circumstances," Mr. Blackbourne said. "Either come with me now to hear it, or you'll have to wait until the morning. Either way, she's not going back to the other group."

"Well, I have to hear about this." Dr. Green unzipped his bag. I caught the Led Zeppelin T-shirt, and the dark sleeping pants he wore before he pulled on a long fleece coat and stuffed his feet into boots.

They both moved toward the tent door, but Mr. Blackbourne paused, turning to me and his voice softening. "Will you be okay for a minute by yourself? You can sleep here, can't you?"

I nodded quickly. I'd sleep anywhere they told me. Just not with the girls. Not now, after...

His face tightened as if he understood. He ducked out of the tent and Dr. Green followed.

I settled in, calming myself and fighting tears. I didn't want to wet the pillow.

♥♥♥

I was almost asleep when I heard the zipper opening again. My eyes opened, my heart pounding as I remembered where I was.

I was expecting Dr. Green and Mr. Blackbourne to return. My body automatically shifted a little, expectant that Mr. Blackbourne would need a place to sleep, and I was willing to make room.

I spotted Dr. Green walking in, heading for his cot, but behind him was Gabriel.

My heart soared at seeing his beautiful rugged face, a couple of days' growth on his chin. His hair was mussed, the blond twisted into the brown. He shrugged off of his coat, wearing a bright orange tank shirt and black pajama bottoms.

But where was Mr. Blackbourne?

"Oy," he said, his voice gruff from sleep. "Trouble. Scoot over, will you?"

That I could do. I moved instantly, making myself as tiny as possible, feeling the sturdy bar of the cot at my back. He could have all the room he wanted.

Gabriel tucked his feet in first, sliding into the sleeping bag. He grunted, yanking it up and zipping it closed. "Get over here," he said. "It's fucking cold."

My face pressed into his chest as I clutched his shirt. I wanted to tell him I missed him. I wanted to say all the things I'd thought about since he'd been gone. I wanted to tell him what had happened, even though I suspected Mr. Blackbourne had told him already.

His lean arms went around me and his lips found the top of my head.

He kissed my hair and said, "You're the worst camping buddy ever, you know that?"

I smiled against his shirt. "Sorry."

"You're not sorry." He kissed my brow. "Are you going to stick by me this time?"

"Yes," I said, and I meant it. I collected his shirt into my fists, pressing my cheek against his body. I'd be his buddy. I'd stick with North. I wouldn't make anyone go near the ocean. I'd never question Kota when he tried to tell me something from the heart. I'd even squash all the spiders. I promised myself that for the rest of the trip, whether I was allowed in the Academy or not, I'd stay by Gabriel. I'd be the best camping buddy ever. I was so grateful. All I wanted to do was show them I cared so much.

"Lights out," Dr. Green said. "No funky stuff over there or Sang will have to join me over here."

I wouldn't have minded that, either.

♥

THE LAST DAY
OF CAMP

*A*s first light shimmered into the tent, I heard Dr. Green dress and leave. I couldn't force my eyes to open as he did; they burned and felt so swollen, it seemed I would be blind forever.

I almost wanted to be. I wouldn't have to face anyone then.

I held onto Gabriel the entire night. He snuggled into me, occasionally mumbling, humming some tune in his sleep.

As the morning wore on, I was sure the other campers would be awake, including the girls. I wonder what they would have been told about what happened to me.

I ducked my head against Gabriel's chest, embarrassed and knowing he probably knew everything. I pressed my cheek against him, listening to his breathing.

He reached up to rub at his nose, sniffing. "Fuck me," he said. "I don't want to get up, but I have to take a piss."

I moaned, not wanting to get up, either, but knowing I should. I wanted to stay in bed all day, for the rest of camp, until it was time to get in the car and leave.

Gabriel turned, pressed his lips against mine and then kissed my nose. "Trouble."

"No," I said quietly. I kept my eyes closed and hung on to him. "I don't want to get up yet."

Gabriel pressed his mouth to my cheek. He kissed the spot. "I can hold it for a minute, I guess."

I was so grateful, I trailed a line of kisses from his neck up to his jaw. I found his mouth with closed eyes. I had a fleeting thought about morning breath, but didn't care, and parted my lips, using my tongue as I kissed him again.

He turned in the bed toward me. He encircled me tighter in his arms, bringing me closer, and kissed back. He opened his mouth, accepting my tongue, tangling his with mine.

My heart sped up as the kiss deepened.

It amazed me how different it was compared to a simple hug the night before with the girls. I didn't feel sick. I didn't feel like I needed to recoil from his touch. I wanted it; it felt right. Like it did with all the boys. It gave me hope.

We had to make it work.

I heard a cough and then, "Ahem."

I gasped as Gabriel backed off. I blinked hard, forcing my eyes open, blinking at Gabriel's flushed face, too embarrassed to look toward the tent door.

I hadn't even heard the flap open. If it was Mr. Blackbourne, I'd be totally embarrassed, but at least he was aware and understood, even if it meant I was about to be told it wasn't appropriate.

As the silence loomed, I finally turned my head and found Kota, standing frozen just inside the tent, holding open the door. He was frowning, looking at Gabriel, and then he looked right at me.

Kota.

My heart stopped, for the hundredth time within the last twenty-four hours. My lungs froze. My face heated to a billion degrees.

There was no way he hadn't seen us. We were in plain view of the door.

I couldn't stop staring at his horribly distraught face.

"Kota," Gabriel said, backing away from me, trying to get the zipper down to let himself out of the sleeping bag. "Geez, man..."

Kota lowered his gaze to the ground. "Sang, they're waiting for you at the cabins. They want to talk to you. You should go there now." He paused, still looking at the floor, then he turned and walked away.

I remained in bed, frozen and afraid to move. Fresh tears filled my eyes, but they didn't fall. "Gabriel," I croaked out, my voice barely working.

Gabriel had stood up, but dropped to his knees, rocking back on his heels as he rubbing his face with his hands. "Fuck...Jesus...Anyone but him..."

I got up, pushing myself to the end of the cot, my head spinning at sitting up so quickly. "We have to go after him," I said.

"*I* have to go after him," Gabriel said. He reached for my hand, holding it. "I have to find him and tell him."

"I have to," I said. "It should be me."

"No," he said, shaking his head. "Liam said it was better if us guys told him ourselves. Now that he's seen you and me, he needs to know. But I have to get the others to go with me so we can tell him as a group. You have to go talk to a council at the cabins."

I shook my head, sure that I should go, too. "I could... I need to talk to him."

"No, it should be me," Gabriel said, shifting to kneel at my feet, looking up at me. He reached up, cupping my cheek while his other hand squeezed mine. "Sweetheart, this was my fault. We knew we should have told him as a team but no one wanted to do it. We were all uncomfortable and didn't want to tell him yet. But there's no way around it now. I have to go get the other guys and we have to force Kota to sit down and hear us out."

My throat tightened as more tears came. I couldn't get rid of the picture of Kota and those green eyes of his boring into me with questions and hurt feelings.

I was so close and had lost him. I should have told him before something like this happened. His finding out shouldn't have happened like this.

Gabriel cupped my cheeks, holding me steady so I had no choice but to look in his eyes. "Trust me, Sang," he pleaded. "Trust *us*. We'll make it right. We're too strong together to break up now."

I wanted to believe. I'd finally kissed Kota and he'd seemed so happy before. He must think I was the worst, after all this time and effort, and here I was kissing Gabriel when I'd been kissing Kota the night before.

How horrible I was.

"Sang," he said, his voice wavering, his eyes desperate. "You promised to stay with me. Remember? Remember when we were in your dad's closet together? You promised."

I nodded.

"Stay with me now," he said. "Only I need you to go face the council, and I need you to tell them that you have to stay with us. No matter what."

"They'll have to talk to all of you eventually," I said. "Won't they?"

Gabriel bit his lip. "Which means we have to tell Kota, and we have to tell him right now. But I can't do it if you're going after him. I need to get the guys." He pulled out his cell phone and looked at it.

"Okay," I said and then reached for his phone. "Can you set up a message?" I asked. "One that goes to all of them but Kota?"

He grunted, pushed buttons on his phone to make it happen, and then passed his phone to me.

I sent out a single message:

This is Sang. Please meet Gabriel at your tent. Bring Kota. You need to tell him everything.

I read the message, and then frowned, and added one more after that.

Please stay together. I need you.

I teared up and sent the message along. Mr. Blackbourne had said they would never fail if I asked them for something. I needed them now.

Gabriel shook his head and frowned. "Sang," he said,

reaching for me.

I handed the phone to him and then pushed him toward the door. "I'll be fine. Find Kota."

He nodded, stuffed his feet into boots and walked out in his pajamas, pausing only to zip up the tent door before he broke into a run.

I had to trust him that he knew what he was doing. That they all did.

♥♥♥

Sometime during the night, someone must have brought a set of clothes for me, because a fresh pair of pants and a pink sweater was set aside. I did a fast run to the bathroom and came back. I dressed quickly and used Dr. Green's hair brush. If I had to face an Academy council, I didn't want to look like a crazed lunatic.

Even though that's how I felt on the inside.

I breathed in slowly before opening the tent flap and felt a weird sort of calm. I realized I was suddenly devoid of emotion. I'd been through so much in the last twenty-four hours, that my emotions were drained completely.

I'd become the zombie.

As I emerged, it took me a minute to orient myself. They had placed their tent not far from the cabins. I wondered why they hadn't chosen to stay in the cabins with all the others. I wondered if it was so they could talk privately about me and the awkward position I'd put them in.

I walked, slowly, steadily, toward the cabin area. No matter how much I took my time, I was there all too soon. My thoughts were filled with Kota, worried about his feelings and what I'd done. If I said I wanted to join the Academy now, Kota might never approve.

Why would he want a girl who kissed someone else on his team? He must hate me.

The cabin area seemed so quiet like it had been during the night. The cabins had metal siding and shingled roofs, and were painted yellow with white trim. They sat on concrete slabs with concrete steps in front of each.

A group of people sat in chairs in front of one of the cabins. I didn't recognize most of the faces, but as I got closer, I spotted Marc, the guy from the team of older boys who'd been with the vocal girl from the first day—the one who wanted to join them. She wasn't sitting in the chairs; I wondered what had happened to her.

Marc was staring intently at the cabin they were closest to, lost in thought.

I wasn't sure why, but since the seat next to him was empty, and I didn't know the others sitting nearby, I sat next to him. "Is this where we're supposed to wait to talk to the Academy council?" I asked him.

He blinked repeatedly, his eyes coming into focus as he turned to me. His lips picked up in a small, tight smile. "Hi," he said. "If it isn't the little doctor, Sang."

I nodded, leaning back in the chair. I checked the others sitting beside us; a couple of older teenagers, some kids, a few adults. Some of them talked to each other, others waited quietly.

I wondered what I was doing here. Joining the Academy would be pointless without Kota.

"Are you in trouble, too?" I asked him, trying to distract myself and hopefully gain some answers as what was happening inside the cabin. "This sort of reminds me of waiting for the principal."

Marc laughed. A lock of long hair fell in front of his green eye. The blue one winked at me. "You don't seem like the type of girl who would be familiar with that."

"You'd be surprised," I said. I studied the cabin, wondering how long this would take. "Who's inside?"

"One of mine," he said. "New recruit. I'm waiting to go in and vouch for her."

I turned my attention back to him. "The girl?"

He nodded. "She wants to be on our team, or she's not interested. I told her she needed to actually...you know...get to know other people. Participate. Like you did." He snorted and shook his head. "She's so fucking stubborn, though. She won't listen to me. I don't think she'll make it."

"How...how are you going to convince them that she could go on your guy team?"

He shrugged. "I've heard rumors of other teams. We're good together. I thought they'd at least let us try it out." He looked at me and smiled. "They're letting you, right?"

I shrugged. "I don't know if I'll get in."

"Sure you will. You're a doctor." He winked playfully at me.

I understood he might have been joking but I wanted to be clear now. I wasn't in the mood for a game. "I'm not a doctor," I said. "I'm not even out of high school."

"Sorry. I was kidding. I knew before. Not that you couldn't be a young doctor in training, especially around the Academy," he said and paused. "Doesn't Dr. Green have a team?"

I nodded again. "Yeah."

He stared at me, shifting the hair away from his green eye now. He leaned in, talking quietly. "Another guy?"

I looked him in his eyes. "There's eight others besides Dr. Green."

His mouth opened. He coughed once. "Oh. So you and he are going to...like the couple teams?"

"No, I'm joining their whole team, if I can." I looked down and focused on my lap, sliding my hand down the jean material. "Or...or I might not join at all."

"You can't not join," he said. "Not if you're qualified. It's too good a thing to pass up."

"I don't want to pass it up," I said, and then lowered my voice to not be overheard by the others. "But I can't lose the team. And if I try to join without them, it means my team might split apart. It's too important to them. They are too important to each other. I can't do that to them." I ducked my head down. "Besides, I'm pretty expensive..."

"Huh?" he asked.

"I've caused them to use up a lot of favors," I said, looking up again. He was leaning close, his elbows on his knees as he leaned in toward me, focused. "And money apparently. They spent it trying to keep me with them and out of trouble."

He smirked. "So you're just going to walk away?"

I shrugged. "It would be less trouble."

His eyes sparked with amusement. "You're going to walk away after they spent all those favors and money?"

I was still now, looking at him, unsure. "It might cost so much more if I..."

"It's always a lot of favors when you take in a new recruit. If you walk away, though, it will all have been for nothing." He leaned in closer, and his voice lowered. "They've gotten you this far, haven't they?"

I nodded again.

"Well? If they've done this for you, then they must care a lot about you. Besides, you'll get favors when you join, right?"

"Right..."

"Think, dummy?" he said, reaching to poke me in the forehead with a long finger. "Wouldn't you spend the money and favors on them?"

I nodded, seeing his point.

He beamed and retracted his hand. "Same thing. You'd do it for them. Let them do it for you. Besides, if you're a girl, you've got a bargaining chip."

"What do you mean?"

"Girls are worth more," he said. "You can negotiate jobs pretty quickly, even before you're official." He blew a breath upward toward his hair that was falling in his eyes again. He brushed the strands further back with his hand and nodded toward the cabin. "I was hoping she'd go through with something like that, but I can't even get her to take camp seriously. They won't give her a job if they can't trust her. You might have a chance, though."

I considered what he'd said. "What can I say?" I said.

"How do I ask for a job?"

"You just say you're willing to do anything at all to ensure the cost of putting you on your team is covered by you alone, and not your team. Or something like that. My buddy Raven had to do that before they let him in. We were too low on cash to bring him over." Marc put a palm over his heart. "God, he was easy street compared to trying to get Kayli in."

"Maybe she doesn't want in," I said. "You're not pushing her, are you?"

He sat back now, shrugging. "I don't know. She says she wants in, but I don't think she's the team player type."

I looked at the cabin. It seemed so quiet—I couldn't imagine what was going on in there. "You'll go in to vouch for her? Is that normal?"

"Yeah," he said. "Family lead does that. They're supposed to go in after the council's had a chance to talk to them."

I gulped. It was why Kota had come for me. He knew he'd have to be here.

I sunk in my seat, sure that Kota wouldn't be able to say the words now. Not after what he saw. He probably didn't think I was Academy material now.

"Hey," Marc said. He reached back and pulled out his phone. "Can you...would you mind giving me your phone number?"

I blinked at him. "Why?"

He laughed lightly. "Not for what you're thinking. I just want to see how you're doing down the road. Maybe compare notes? Seems like we're in the same situation."

I wanted to tell him about Lily, although she might not want to be contacted. Maybe I could find a way to ask her if it was okay to give him her contact information so he could talk to her about her team. "If you'd like."

He nodded. "Sure." He paused and put his phone down in his lap. "Oh wait, maybe I should ask your doc. I don't want him thinking I'm flirting with his girlfriend."

I winced. In a few minutes, it might not even matter, in

which case I wouldn't have any insight for him, except not to kiss Kayli unless he's sure his other team members were on board.

Still, I told him my number. "You can still ask him, if you want. I don't have my phone on me right now, so I can't take your number."

"It's okay," he said and typed out a message. "I'm just going to send you a quick message so you know it's me."

That sounded reasonable.

He finished his message and sent it, but before I had a chance to say anything, the door to the cabin burst open, slamming against the side of the cabin with a bang.

Out walked Kayli, clenched fists at her thighs, stomping down the steps, glaring around until her narrowed eyes settled on Marc.

Marc whistled low. "This isn't good."

"Good luck," I said.

"I'll need it." He stood up and walked toward Kayli. He said a few things, pointed my way as I hunched down in my chair. Kayli glared at me and said something to him. He said something back, patted her on the shoulder, and headed toward the steps.

Kayli headed in my direction.

I tried not to cower. She was in properly-fitted jeans, a white T-shirt, black leather jacket and black boots. Her hair was straight, brown.

She was North as a girl: beautiful but angry, more terrifying.

I held tightly to the chair, swallowing. She stood over me, peering down. "He told me you have a guy team."

I looked down and nodded.

"You're with North, aren't you?"

This caused me to look up, blinking at her. "Yes?"

"I was talking to him yesterday," she said. She shifted and sat down where Marc had been. She bent forward, with elbows on her knees, like boys sit, and looked at my face. "Marc said he got your number?"

I nodded again, uncomfortable with the way she was staring at me. "I'm not...I'm not..." I was going to say something but I didn't want to say it wrong and make her angry.

"You're not interested in him," she said, an eyebrow going up. "Romantically? Is that what you're trying to say?"

I nodded, feeling like my head was going to bob off my neck. "My team...I have enough..." I paused, feeling weird and not wanting to go into those details.

She backed off and sighed. "I'm not interested in North," she said. "Believe me, I've got enough, too. And I don't date kids."

I pressed my lips together at her calling North a kid, but I didn't say anything.

"Marc said I should talk to you, but I'd rather talk to North," she said. "We kind of had a conversation last night and I'd like to continue. It's about...it's complicated. Do you mind? It's just talking."

"I don't mind," I said. This seemed like a fair compromise. I wasn't interested in Marc, but it would be nice to talk to someone going through the same struggles. Liam and Lily and their team were so far ahead, so much older. It was helpful, but knowing another team made it feel less...not normal. "I wouldn't mind talking to Marc." He was nice. "Just to...compare notes."

"On a girl joining a guy team," she said, her eyes going dark. "I told them I wouldn't even be interested in being on any other team. If it wasn't for them, I wouldn't even be here."

"You don't have to join," I said quietly, unsure if she wanted to hear it.

She stared at me. "They make such a big deal about it."

"But you knew about it before you came here? Maybe helped them a little?"

She stuffed her hands into her pockets and laughed, though I didn't know why. "Yeah, you could say that."

"Now that you can see a little of what the inside is like, could you live with going back to how it was? Knowing sometimes they won't be able to tell you things, or running off into the night without you?"

She pressed her lips together, not answering.

Those were the questions I was facing as well. I'd learned a lot about the Academy, but I was lacking a lot of the details, and if I quit now, I may not ever be invited back.

But I faced a much worse dilemma than Kayli, or at least I thought I did.

I stole a look at her, and then simply knew we'd come to a delicate truth. We were aware of each other and were possibly following the same path.

We'd eliminated the potential for any future surprises and jealousy right away. I trusted North, and she trusted Marc, and we knew that line would never be crossed by either of us.

We were Academy. Maybe we'd even have to work together someday.

The door opened and out walked Marc, his hands in his pockets, gazing at his feet as he stepped down the stairs and headed our way.

Dr. Roberts was at the door. "It's the only way," he told Marc as he left.

Marc frowned but ignored him as he continued walking from the cabin.

Kayli stood up in a shot, fists clenched at her sides. "What?" she asked. "I'm out, aren't I?"

"No," he said, still frowning, as he continued, toward the path. "But you're not going to like it."

"Miss Sorenson!"

I turned, forced to pull my attention away from Marc and Kayli, wondering what was in store for them.

I glanced at the others, wondering why I was called in ahead of them. I moved toward Dr. Roberts, who held the door open for me.

I should have been happy to get this over with.

THE COUNCIL

I wasn't sure if it was the same cabin as last night. They all looked the same to me. Inside, it was the same setup, with the eight bunk beds, all in a row, some stripped down to the bare mattresses, some neatly made. The air was a mix of musty mattress and perfumes, their colognes. The mix was a little much for my nose at first, and I smothered a sneeze quickly.

In the middle of the cabin were five folding chairs, all in a circle. All but two were occupied, and Dr. Roberts made his way to one of the empty ones, holding the back for me, looking at me expectantly.

"Would you like to sit, sweetheart?" he asked, his tone much gentler than the one he'd used with Marc.

In the other chairs sat Mr. Duncan, and Mrs. Rose, wearing casual clothes. Mr. Buble wore a suit today, all black, with a black tie and a white shirt. This seemed to be his regular outfit and reminded me so much of Mr. Blackbourne. Always dressed more formally than everyone else.

They all had pleasant but tense smiles as they waited for me to sit.

I went around the chair and sat, my back to the door. Dr. Roberts waited until I was settled before he lowered himself to the last empty seat, the one next to mine.

I crossed my legs, fighting the urge to fidget.

Mr. Duncan's large stomach protruded even more as he leaned forward. "Good morning," he said in a friendly voice.

I bowed my head toward him. "Good morning," I said softly. I couldn't help but remember what had happened the night before, causing my cheeks to feel like they were roasting. A light sweat started at my brow, even while the room was a little chilly. I was sure they all knew what I'd confessed to, even if they hadn't been there to witness it for themselves.

What a bumbling idiot I'd made of myself.

Mr. Duncan's eyes were very friendly, as were Mrs. Rose's, and Dr. Roberts's.

Only Mr. Buble looked dour. He had a polite-enough smile on his face, but otherwise, he was unreadable. He had his hands in his lap, legs crossed.

Mr. Duncan spoke after a long pause. "Normally, we'd start with talking about your week here and how you thought it went, but I understand your circumstances are...unique. I hope the girls you've been staying with haven't done you any harm."

I shook my head quickly, and without anyone there to talk for me, I needed to explain. "Please," I began. "Carla and Lake and the other girls are wonderful people. They did nothing wrong. No one did."

"We understand," Mr. Duncan said. "I just wanted to be clear and make sure."

"I want to assure you, this doesn't change things," Dr. Roberts said. He smiled softly. "We hope the experience hasn't scared you from us."

"No, I..." I paused suddenly, the air changing around me.

Sweet spice scent found me. It was faint, but it was there. Distracted, I turned my head, but the door was still closed. Was one of the others wearing a similar scent?

"What is it?" Mr. Duncan said. "Is something wrong?"

I shook my head, but couldn't say anything. My hope was suddenly dashed and my heart sunk, realizing I must have been delusional. "I thought...someone..."

"Don't worry," Dr. Roberts said. "No one will intrude if that's what you're worried about."

I sighed. "No," I said and looked at the ground. "I just thought Kota Lee was here."

"He's not hiding in here," Dr. Roberts said with a smile. "If that's what you're saying."

I was about to say of course he wasn't when the door

behind us opened. I turned again.

Kota stood in the doorway, holding the handle, leaning in. His eyes were dark, the shadows underneath them worse now.

I couldn't judge his mood, but he didn't look at me. My heart wanted to thunder in my chest and yet explode at the same time. I pressed palms to my lap to stop shaking. He was here.

Would he tell them what happened?

"I'm sorry to intrude," he said. "But...I wasn't sure if I was running late, and then I was about to knock when I heard my name."

Mr. Duncan's jaw dropped open, as did Dr. Roberts's. Mrs. Rose had her hand over her mouth.

Mr. Buble raised an eyebrow. "Don't tell me she's psychic now, too."

Kota's eyebrows shifted together and then he gave me a puzzled look before he looked back at them. "I don't understand."

"She knew you were here," Dr. Roberts said. He smiled at me, a bright twinkling in eyes. He slapped his palm against his knee. "Tell us how you did it."

"I..." I stammered out. My mind went blank.

"She can smell us," Kota said quietly, still holding the door open. I looked at him and this time, he was looking at me, a small smile lighting up his face. "You could put her in the dark and she could tell if one of us is around just by scent."

I swallowed, nodding, afraid to say anything, scared I'd burst into tears just because he was there.

I still didn't dare hope, but I was yearning to tell him everything inside my heart in that instant. He was stunning to me, with those green eyes, the way his hair was combed neatly. He was so strong, so smart. He had to know I cared about him and I would never hurt him on purpose.

Had the guys managed to find him? Did he know everything now?

The council stayed quiet and I'd almost forgotten about

them until Dr. Roberts started to laugh. "Oh my god," he said. "This girl...I'm telling you."

"She could smell you from the other side of the door," Mr. Duncan said. He waved Kota in. "Come on, you might as well join us."

Kota stepped inside, closing the door behind himself. He came around the circle and sat on one of the beds nearby, looking from me to the council. "Don't let me interrupt anymore."

"Well we can't pretend we're not interested in getting her involved in our Academy right away," Mr. Duncan said, his eyes on me. "You've shown so much potential this week."

Mrs. Rose signed. "You became a great leader to the girls, despite your feelings. You never let on to the others, either." She smiled. She pulled out a notepad and pen she had in her pocket. "I hope you understand, I did have to say something to the girls. Remember, we have to trust people with our feelings, right?"

I nodded. They knew.

I lowered my eyes. I'd hoped they'd never tell the other girls, and now I was afraid they thought I was weird or that I thought something was wrong with them. What else could she say?

"They told me they were worried something was wrong last night," Mrs. Rose signed. "Carla said something was wrong. I think they might have known. Please don't worry. They all have similar stories."

"Don't look so sad," Mr. Duncan said. "We had to tell them why you were missing, and the truth is normally the best way, especially among the Academy family."

"You did a great job bringing those younger girls back around," Dr. Roberts said. "They aren't members yet. They still have a lot to learn, but they're young and they've got time. And now they've got each other to talk to about the Academy when they go home."

"And the good news is," Mr. Duncan cut in, "Carla and Lake told us this morning that they've decided to become a team. They aren't sure if they'll stay together forever, but they asked if having a starter team was good enough." He chuckled. "And of course, it is. Those two have a fine future together. A little yin and yang never hurt anyone."

I was relieved that the others had gotten what they needed. I lifted my head up but still kept my eyes down.

"Anyway, on to you," Dr. Roberts said. He ducked, leaning forward to catch my gaze, and I picked up my eyes. He straightened when I was looking at him. "Don't be shy. This part is painless."

"The question is," Mr. Duncan said with a smile, "what do we do with you, knowing what we know now? Normally, we'd ask you to try out different teams. You can always pick your team, of course, but we like to put you with a group that would fit with your special talents. We would have asked you to join with Carla and Lake since you seemed to get on very well."

It was on my tongue to ask to stay on Kota's team, but with him right there, and not being aware of his feelings, or what, if anything, he'd been told, I thought it best to stay quiet for now.

At this point, my fate rested in him. He had the right to tell me I wasn't Academy-worthy, or that he didn't want me on their team and to suggest another one.

Kota coughed, shocking me out of my thoughts as to what I could say. I couldn't help but lift my eyes and look at him, but his focus was only on the other members.

"If you don't mind me speaking," he said quietly. "I don't want to speak for her, but I've got an option if she'd like to hear it."

"Of course," Dr. Roberts said, a small smile on his face. "We're here to discuss all options."

This was it. He was going to tell me to join Carla and Lake.

"The truth is, with all of her talents, we've been lucky she's been working with us on our current assignment," he said. "She's almost the center of our operation. We're also still working out her family situation, which is a little more complicated than we'd realized."

Hope started to rise through me. Was he really saying…

"I've been following this," Dr. Roberts said, addressing the rest of the council. "Miss Sorenson's much more valuable than she appears." He looked to Kota. "Do you mind if I tell them?"

Kota hesitated and then looked at me. "She doesn't even know all the details."

What was he saying? What else could there be to know? Was it my real mother? Did they find out details?

"Oh," Dr. Roberts said and then smiled. "Well then, this is sort of a shock. Brace yourself."

Dr. Roberts looked at me and smiled before he turned to the others. "Our Miss Sorenson here is rather an unusual case. The truth is, according to the government, she doesn't even exist."

I didn't know what he meant and maybe the others didn't, either, as there was a long silence.

"What are you saying?" Mr. Duncan asked.

"I'm saying, she has a false birth certificate on file: a copy made from her half-sister's. The only record of her is from her schools, and every time her file is cross-referenced in databases, it conveniently came up as an error, as her Social Security Number belongs to someone else."

"Which means the only record of her existence," Kota continued for him, "is in the direct school files, and we've deleted all but those at her current school." He turned his gaze to me. "She's never had a school photo. She's not in any school albums."

"She's a blank slate," Mr. Duncan said, sitting back in his chair.

"She's a ghost," Mr. Buble said, startling me as it was the first time he'd spoken.

I looked at him now. His eyes were steady on mine. His stare made me tremble on the inside, thinking of what he must be seeing: my dirty hair, my casual clothes. Every scar, every freckle, seemed under his scrutiny.

He leaned forward a little, his stare unwavering. "Do you know what that means, Sang Sorenson?"

I shook my head, afraid to say anything.

"It means, that if we're careful, you're one of our most valuable assets."

I still didn't know what that meant but it began to dawn on me that, I could be killed and no one would know to look for me because I didn't exist.

Did my father know this was the case? He had to have known about my birth certificate at least. Did he realize the full meaning? What about my stepmother? Would they have even cared to report me if I went missing or even had been killed?

I was nothing.

"She's not in yet," Mr. Duncan said with a small laugh. "Although we'd be idiots not to let bring in now."

"She's willing," Kota said. "And because of her situation, I don't think it'd be appropriate to take her out of school just yet. A wrong move there and the principal or someone who works for him might call the police on her. We've avoided that so far, but she's gotten close to needing the police."

"That sounds terrible," Mr. Duncan said. He sat back. "I know you've been having issues with your assignment at that school. Is it even safe for her?"

"It might be worse if we pull her out," Kota said. "I wish I could say it would be better, but we're doing our best to resolve the situation without causing more risk to her, despite her ghost status."

"You'll have to be more careful," Dr. Roberts said. "There've been instances where she's been photographed."

"Those might not matter," Kota said. "Since she has no official ID and nothing in any records, the best police could do with those pictures is ask individuals who she is. If we can get her out of school, and delete those records, if we handle this right, she'll be just a distant memory to them later. We'll have moved her out. Only her sister and the rest of her family could compromise this now."

"How do you propose to keep them from speaking out?" Dr. Roberts asked.

Kota smiled a little. "We're working on that, too," he said. He shifted his gaze to me. "But we need her help to do it, if it'll work at all."

Silence filled the room as the council members looked at each other.

Mrs. Rose was the first to move, tapping the floor with her foot to get our attention and then signing quickly. "It sounds like you're not finished with your adopted family yet," she said.

It took me a moment, but then I realized she meant Kota. It struck me as funny as I hadn't realized until just then that Kota and the others must have 'adopted' me into their family, according to Academy rules.

I nodded.

"I don't think we have a choice," Dr. Roberts said. "They need her. She needs them. With her past being so complicated, there's no resolution if she even tried another team at this point. They'd be at a severe disadvantage."

"Not to mention her preferences," Mr. Duncan said. "We'd have to find someone she was comfortable with, a boy perhaps. However, one couldn't do it alone, and we'd be back to a team of guys trying to sort her out. Is that even something we could do?" He looked right at me. "I'm sorry, we keep talking around you. Please understand. We're trying to offer you all the options."

I nodded, suddenly my heart soaring. I only saw one answer now. "I can stay with my team," I said softly. I looked at Kota, who nodded encouragingly. I continued. "I'm already familiar with them. I think they're comfortable with me."

"It doesn't have to be forever," Mr. Duncan said. "You know that, right?"

I nodded. Did he think they were a burden? "I understand."

"They could be her starter team," Dr. Roberts said. "I can

keep an eye on them, though, if you'd like."

"We'll have to sort some details," Mr. Duncan said.

"We will want updates," Mr. Buble said. His intense gaze hadn't lessened a bit. "However, given the circumstances, if we want her in the Academy with her ghost status preserved, she might be stuck with that team for some time."

"She could get out of such a situation much sooner if it's very bad," Mr. Duncan said. "If she doesn't have a birth certificate, and we're forced to, we could make one up for her and change the birth date. We could make her eighteen right now. There's no proof other than her parents' word."

"There might be other relatives out there," Kota said. "She might have extended family. We won't know until we do more research and if they exist, we'll need to locate them and talk to them to find out what they know."

Dr. Roberts sighed and then stood. "Then it seems like we're the ones that need to ask her."

My eyebrows lifted. The others in the council stood, and I did, following their example.

They all looked at me, but Mr. Duncan was the one who spoke. "We would like for you to join us," he said with a tight smile. "However, the path you've got in front of you is filled with a lot of work, possibly more than any other recruit."

"We can't let you in," Mr. Buble said, "without asking *your* permission to continue with the team that found you. Also, we'll need your consent to allow them to probe into what will probably be upsetting information, and to stay with them for as long as it takes to get their current job done."

"You may never be safe until it's resolved," Dr. Roberts said, making hand gestures as he spoke. "Even then, to keep your ghost status, you may never have a typical life, a normal one. By agreeing to this, you'll be granting us favors."

"Many favors," Mrs. Rose signed. "We'll be in your debt for your putting up with this, even before you're initiated."

Marc had said I could ask them for work before I was in. "I...I only want any cost for joining the Academy to be put on me, and not my team," I said. I looked toward Kota, unsure if it was fair to even ask but it was important to me. "I don't want them to take on any more debt because of me."

Kota smiled, and nodded, just once.

"Spoken like a true Academy member," Mr. Duncan said, now beaming. He reached out with a hand and offered it to me. "I think we've got a deal."

I shook his hand, Mr. Buble's and then Dr. Roberts's as well.

When I looked at Mrs. Rose, she had her hand out, but then began to pull it back.

I reached for her. I could handle a handshake.

She beamed as she shook mine. Then she signed, "You go, girl."

I smothered a giggle.

"Mr. Blackbourne and our Mr. Lee here will continue with your Academy training," Mr. Buble said. "You're not official yet, but you'll start try-outs."

"That's the step after you've passed the initial application, which is what you did this week," Dr. Roberts said. He waved me toward the door. "I hope you realize, we'll probably need to ask you to talk to a specialist, given your circumstances. We want to make sure you're happy and healthy. It's important."

A specialist? A psychologist? Who?

"Don't worry about that right now. Your family lead and team lead will explain it all if you have questions. If you don't mind, though, we've got many more people to see."

I was in. I smothered a bright smile by pressing my lips together as hard as I could, turning away and heading toward the door.

Kota followed me.

"Mr. Lee," Dr. Roberts called out. Kota and I both turned around before Dr. Roberts said, "Keep that one safe."

"I will," Kota said.

♥

ℛETURN

here were people still waiting outside, in fact, a there were a few more than before, some even standing as there weren't enough chairs.

We walked away from the cabin and I didn't even look at where we were going. Just toward the trees, eagerly seeking out a place of refuge from others' eyes.

While I was happy that Kota had found the answer we'd been looking for to keep the team together, I still wasn't sure how he felt, especially after what had happened that morning. He'd used our circumstances as an excuse to keep me around, my safety being his biggest concern.

Given my outburst the night before, they had no alternative. No girl team could step in on my behalf, working so closely, without me being uncomfortable. A single guy joining me couldn't do it alone. I needed more guys, and their group was the one that brought me in. They were technically stuck with me.

The council had called it a starter team, but it gave us time to work things out before we would be called on again to talk about my future within the Academy.

I walked beside Kota in silence, afraid to speak. I stared at our feet, wondering why he'd chosen to say the things he had. He'd been so adamant before. He didn't want me in the team any longer because of my situation, and now suddenly he'd used it to keep me in.

It wasn't until Kota started to slow, and wind away from the path that I lifted up my head and looked around. We were at a picnic area, and it took me a minute to recognize it to be the same one we'd sat in a few nights before.

The night where we'd kissed for the first time.

My heart dropped as he headed toward the bench. I didn't want to ruin this place, the memory I had, if he was going to tell me off here.

I climbed up, sitting beside him and wrapped my arms around my stomach, waiting for the worst. I'd seen breakups at school. Usually, they involved yelling, accusations, and at the end, the couple parting and walking away, angry and sometimes even swearing. Sometimes, it was done quietly with text messages, one person complaining to friends about the news.

Kota rubbed his hands together and then stuck them into his jacket pockets, looking at the ground. "I guess you made it in," he said, his voice light in tone. "Congratulations."

I wanted to tell him thank you, but I couldn't get my lips to move, and my voice was gone. I was terrified of saying the wrong thing. I had already done the wrong thing and didn't want to make it worse.

"Sang," he said, his voice soft now.

Tears filled my eyes, tears I was sure I'd used up the night before, but now they came back, fresh and ready to spill over.

"Sang, don't look like that," he said even softer.

I bit my lip, trying to hold it in, not turn into a mess. I sniffed hard, trying my best, but once the first tear rolled down my cheek, the guilt overwhelmed me and I was done. My win with the council and getting into the Academy didn't matter if Kota didn't like me anymore.

A gentle hand rested on my spine. "Sang," he whispered.

I stilled. I wanted him to forgive me, but I couldn't get the words out.

The hand on my spine shifted to my shoulder and tugged me toward him.

"Come here," he said.

That was it. I broke down completely, sobbing loudly against his shoulder. I bawled, unable to speak, unable to explain or defend myself at all.

I should have told him. I was a terrible Academy member. I kept secrets from the people I cared about most.

I wrapped my arms tightly around his neck, afraid that it would be the last time.

He held me quietly, his palms rubbing my back lightly.

I cried until I couldn't breathe and had to stop to catch my breath. I sucked in every bit of that scent of sweet spice I could.

When I'd finally quieted, Kota spoke softly into my ear. "I wish you would have told me," he said.

"I tried," I croaked out. "The guys...they said *they* wanted to tell you. I was going to tell you this week when I said we should..."

"How...how long have you been talking about this with them?"

I sniffed, backing away from him so I could wipe my eyes and stop soaking his nice shirt with my tears. I used the sleeve of my sweater. "Since around Gabriel's birthday. We went to go see Lily."

His head tilted, an eyebrow going up over the rim of his glasses. "Who's Lily?"

Had they not told him about her? "She...she's another bird with all guys on her team. North and Mr. Blackbourne went to see them before, to ask them how they did it. Only...only Gabriel, Luke and I didn't know and went to see them ourselves. She talked to me about it. She told me about how they did it."

He slowly reached back into his pocket. He pulled out an iPhone.

It had a pink case. The glass was cracked on the surface.

The crack must have happened the night Gabriel broke my tent. Kota had my phone the whole time?

"I got your message," he said. "And...I didn't mean to look, but I couldn't help it."

"Message?"

"The one you sent from Gabriel's phone," he said. He swiped at the screen but didn't turn it on. "The one where you asked them to tell me something."

What happened to Gabriel looking for him? "Did...did

they not find you?"

"I didn't want to be found," he said, frowning. "And I had to prepare for your interview, but I needed some time to go calm down." He smirked a little. "Had to count to nearly a thousand."

They'd never reached him! He'd returning on his own; that had to mean something.

"You came back, though," I said. "You vouched for me with the Academy."

He looked up at me. "Sweetheart, I knew you were dating the others," he said.

My lips parted. "What? I..."

"I know Dr. Green kissed you," he said. "It was you in the pictures. I know the others do, too. They talk about it sometimes when they don't think I'm in the room, but I've overheard them. I know you've been on a few dates." He shrugged a little. "I guess, at first, I just thought...that was normal. Dating, right? Sometimes, you have to date other people to find the one you want."

I pressed my tongue to the roof of my mouth, afraid to speak.

He looked down at his jeans, picking off some dirt that had collected in a fold. "You've never committed to any of them, from what I understood. It was just dating because I know they wouldn't want to step on each other's toes over a girl. We've never had a problem with that before. And for a while, I guess I put the idea of dating you out of my head. I wanted to give you distance to not overwhelm you. But then you kissed me and it changed everything. I assumed there was something of a commitment in it. It was wrong of me to assume."

"It wasn't wrong," I said in a quick rush, wanting to explain everything to him quickly before he learned it from anyone else. "I just never told you the whole story. Or the plan."

"I know you've been working on trying to keep us together," he said. "Like researching other teams. I saw that

Marc sent you a message."

I nodded. "Yes, and then there's Lily."

"Yeah," he said. "How come they didn't tell me about this Lily? Was it a dead end? Did it not work out for their group?"

I shook my head. "No," I said, and then lowered my voice. "No, not a dead end. It was an answer. Maybe. For us."

His eyebrows lifted together. "How?"

I sucked in a breath, letting it out in a rush. The other guys might have wanted to tell him, but maybe it didn't matter who he learned it from. He needed to know.

Before I could speak, a voice shouted from the path. "Found him!"

We looked up. It was Gabriel and Luke. They came running. Gabriel was in the same clothes as before, without even a jacket, though Luke had thrown one on over his pajamas.

"Oy! Don't be mad at her," Gabriel said and then looked at me, which made me instantly tear up.

"No, no, no..." Gabriel said as he pointed a finger at Kota, at the same time grabbing my arm and tugging me toward him. "Don't you dare make her fucking cry. So help me, I'll kick your ass. This was *our* fault. You can't blame her."

"I didn't," Kota said, stepping off the table. "Hang on a second."

Gabriel came over to me, picked me up on his shoulder, pulling me away. "Nope," he said. "She's cried enough. Don't say anything to her you're going to regret. We need to talk to you first."

"Put her down," Kota said in his commanding voice. "We were talking."

I hung upside down on Gabriel's shoulder, unable to find my voice as it was hard enough to breathe. I tried smacking at his butt, but it didn't seem to affect him.

"Kota," Luke said, although I couldn't see where he was. "We all want to date her. And..."

"I know," Kota said, a little louder, sounding

exasperated. "I know that part. I was just telling her that. Gabe, put her down, please."

"What?" Gabriel said loudly. "How in the world did you know?"

"You all aren't that sneaky," he said. "I'm family lead for a reason."

"Oh," Gabriel said and then finally put me down on my feet. He held onto my shoulders, keeping me steady as the blood rushed through my head. "So why did you walk out earlier and why is she crying now?"

"Because I knew about it, but I hadn't ever...witnessed it. It was surprising and it was hard to see you and her..." He paused, frowning. He sighed and looked at me. "I didn't mean to stress you out."

"He doesn't know about the plan, yet," I said. "We should tell him."

"What plan?" Kota asked.

There were more voices over ours as more people walked toward the camper area, perhaps to the latrines. They waved at us.

We forced polite smiles, waving back.

"Maybe not here," Luke said. "But first—is she in the Academy?"

"Yeah," Kota said. "At least for now. We're her starter team."

"Kota bought us more time," I said.

"I imagine it's for while she's still in school, and while we're on this job," Kota continued. "So we've got until June, at least, before they might want to reevaluate."

"Then maybe we should go home," Gabriel said, looking over his shoulder. "I don't want to get into the plan here. I don't want word to get out what we're up to, and then be questioned to death by a council."

"What plan?" Kota asked. "Just tell me."

"We will," Luke said. "Somewhere private."

"But if you're cool with us dating her, then it might not be as bad as what you're probably thinking," Gabriel said.

"Just trust us."

Kota slowly nodded. "Okay. Let me take Sang to get her cleaned up. Have someone bring us a towel and some new clothes? I'll find some empty showers somewhere. The rest of you, pack up everything. I want to leave right away."

"Yes!" Luke said, raising a fist. His eyes lit up and he grinned. "No campground clean-up duty!"

"They've got enough volunteers," Kota said. "And we were here early to set up. It should be fine as long as we're picking up after ourselves." He reached for my hand. "Shall we go?"

I nodded, relieved, enthusiastic and hopeful. "Yeah," I said. We had a chance.

Maybe it would work out after all.

♥

ALL LAID BARE

s we approached the camper latrine, we could tell by all the voices that it was full of people. The secret was out that these showers were nicer.

I didn't want to go in anyway. I was afraid Carla and Lake or any of the others were in there, and I couldn't face them now.

I told Kota this and he agreed to walk with me to the other latrine. He promised to scope it out and ensure I got a space to myself. We'd wait if we had to.

It took us some time to get there. Once we did, the only noise was from the girls' side.

Kota peeked in the boys' area and then looked back out at me. "No one's in there," he said. "You can clean up in here."

He reached for my hand and led me in. Compared to the camper latrine, this one looked so much more dingy, with the paint peeling from the concrete block walls, the rusty sinks, and the spider webs up in the corners.

I could deal with that for now.

I used the toilet first and washed my hands. As I did, I looked at Kota, leaning on the sink next to mine, doing something with his phone. The door was closed. "Did you lock it?"

"It'll be fine," he said. "If anyone comes up, I'll tell them...something." He finished with his phone and slipped it into his pocket. "Someone's bringing soap and other stuff. Do you want to...uh..." His cheeks turned red. "Hop...hop in the shower?"

I bit my lip, shaking my head. "I'll...just wash in the sink..." I reached for the water, intending to wipe my face. I could feel the streaks of tears across my cheeks and I imagined I looked like a mess.

"Sang," he said, with a tight smile. "Don't take this the wrong way, but you've got sand all over, and you're filthy. I don't care personally, but I wouldn't want to get sand all over North's Jeep. He'll complain for months if it gets everywhere and he can't vacuum it all out. He still swears there's sand in his bike after you all went to the beach."

Now that he said so, I could feel the sand in creases, the dirt in my hair.

"Turn around?" I croaked as the panic rose in my throat. "Maybe you should stay by the door?" My goal was to shoo him out, wash very well in the sinks, and fake it until we got home.

"Don't worry about someone coming in," he said. "I locked it. That should be good enough. I'll answer it when someone comes with soap and clothes." His cheeks reddened again. "Oh, do you mean...I'm not going to look. I swear."

I had to agree. It wasn't about him possibly seeing me naked.

He faced the door and waited. "Maybe...should I stay outside? But the showers are around the corner. I can hand you soap and a towel without looking."

He still assumed I was taking a shower. "I can wait for soap," I said. I turned, and he appeared to be heading for the door. I kicked off the boots and stepped out of my jeans first, then pulled the sweater over my head. I left the clothes in a heap on the floor, hoping spiders didn't crawl into them. I was still in a modest bra and underwear, more material than some bikinis.

I squirmed as I padded my way to the sink. Touching the cold concrete floor with my feet, compared to the clean white tiles of the other bathroom, made me feel even more dirty. Like bugs could crawl up my legs at any moment. I imagined the showers were horrible, too.

I turned on the faucet; I had to at least rinse off most of the packed-on dirt until I could get proper soap. Once I was undressed, I realized just how dirty I was, parts of me caked with sand even some bits of grass in places. I glanced in the mirror at my hair, which looked stringy and dull. I really needed a full bath.

Kota turned slightly the moment the water started running, keeping his eyes on the wall, but clearly able to see what I was doing in his peripheral vision. "Sorry, I thought..." He paused and then looked up again in surprise. "That's not going to work," he said. "Go get in the shower."

"This will be fine," I said, although I squeaked it out.

"The showers aren't that bad," he said and then started to look my way but stopped himself, his body going rigid. "Can I turn around?"

"I guess," I said. He'd seen me in a bathing suit, skimpier underwear than what I was wearing now, and a towel.

He turned, looking once at me before he walked past me, toward the shower area. "Yeah, you need this," he said. He disappeared beyond the wall. "I'll warm it up for you. Come back here."

I froze at the sink. "I don't need to," I squeaked out. He's going to make me take a shower! I had to tell him. My heart was in my throat. "Kota..."

He came back around, and headed toward me, gesturing me toward him. "Trust me," he said with a smile. "There's no spiders, either. I can stay nearby and squish any if you're worried about it."

Spiders were not the problem right now. The sound of the shower running full blast now made me freeze. I shook where I stood, terrified. My throat closed up, I couldn't speak. I could barely focus on breathing.

The water seemed to get louder until it was all I could hear, besides the blood rushing through my ears.

I didn't even hear Kota until he was right next to me.

"Don't be such a scaredy cat," he said. "I said there's no spiders. And it's not that bad. Come see."

Before I could move, he scooped me up, carrying me toward the showers.

C. L. Stone

Panic washed over me, and I clung to him. "No!" I squeaked out, but it was so light. I tried to hold tight to him, but my body wasn't working. I couldn't grip. I tried to squeak out more words, but they caught in my throat as the shower got even louder the closer we got.

"Sang, calm down. North would have a fit if you got into his Jeep so dirty. I'll go in with you if you're so afraid a spider will get in there. Nothing to be afraid of. I'm here."

I tried to get him to drop me to stand, but he was strong. I couldn't get the words out past my throat, my breathless whispers falling on deaf ears.

Once Kota passed the wall into the actual shower area, my eyes darted everywhere. The rusty shower heads. Several poking out of the wall.

Like the showers at school.

The paint was peeling from the walls here, too. The concrete slab floor had a simple drain in two spots where water was already running into it.

Kota put me down on my feet but my legs were boneless and I sunk down, crouching with my face on my knees. I wrapped my arms around my body, making myself into a ball.

I couldn't move. I could barely breathe. The echo of the shower was deafening. I didn't even hear Kota getting undressed. I didn't notice anything until he picked me up again, in his arms.

"Come on," he said. "No spiders, I swear. There's no one else here. We'll go in together. I know it's a lot of rust and looks dirty. Two minutes and we're done. I promise. I know after I've had a stressful day, a shower always perks me up. Don't let the rust scare you."

He was using such a soothing voice. He thought I was just tired and overwrought. He didn't understand.

I couldn't speak, but inside, I was screaming.

I can't go. Please, don't make me.

I gripped his shoulder and pressed my face into his shoulder. I was too weak to hold stronger, and my throat closed up.

414

"No spiders," he said, his voice rising. "Sang, stop panicking. What's wrong with you? It's just a shower."

There was something terribly wrong with me.

Water splashed down onto my face as Kota held me.

Blackness swallowed me up.

"Princess," Victor's voice sounded far away.

It felt like he'd woken me from a deep sleep and I struggled to remember why I'd been so tired.

Hands were on my shoulders, but I was lying on something cold and hard. I was wet, and confused, wondering why I was so cold.

The hands gently shook my shoulders. "Sang," Victor called again, sounding closer this time. "Wake up."

I couldn't for some reason. Maybe I was dreaming. My return from sleep took so much effort, and I was using that effort to breathe, and I couldn't breathe enough for my lungs to feel full, and to give me the energy to wake further.

"I don't understand," Kota's voice echoed, but it was strange. High pitched. "I thought she was overtired and worried about maybe being alone after today and didn't like the dirty shower, or was worried about spiders."

"Spiders? Sang?" Victor scoffed, his voice getting louder. "Didn't she tell you no?"

"Yeah," Kota said, the power gone from his voice. "But I thought if I went in with her, she'd see it was okay."

"When does she ever tell you no?" Victor asked, his voice firm. "Ever? You should have listened to her." My body was shaken again. "Sang. Come on. Wake up."

I moaned, too cold to move. My lip trembled. I was awake, but my body was stiff. I couldn't lift my own arms.

A towel was wrapped around my body. Victor pulled me to sit up. I could smell the moss and berries.

"We should get a doctor," Kota said. "Maybe it's her blood pressure. The hot water..."

"It's not the temperature," Victor bit out. I'd never heard him so angry, so loud. "She can't take showers."

"What are you talking about?"

Victor held me, held my cheek, warming me a little with the towel wrapped around me. "Don't cry," he said softly. "I'll take you home."

I didn't realize I was crying until then. I sniffed and tried to whisper. "I was trying to wash up," I said. "North...so North's Jeep wouldn't get dirty."

If they'd give me a minute, I could wash. I'd do anything they wanted. Just not the shower.

Victor kissed my forehead. "No, Princess. You can ride home with me. We'll go to my house." He picked me up, holding me close. "I've got that big tub, remember? You can stay in there all day. I don't care if my car gets dirty."

"Wait," Kota said, and I sensed him moving closer, blocking Victor. "I don't understand. What happened to her? Why can't she take a shower? What's this about?"

"How would you feel if your mother tied you up in the shower, with the water running over your face for hours and hours and left you there, not caring if you died?" Victor said, his voice firm, but not as loud as before. "How do you think you'd feel about showers then?"

"But...she...never said..."

"She was embarrassed," Victor said. "But she told me. At the time, we were dealing with Volto, and she said she didn't want to bother anyone with it."

"Then *you* should have told us."

"It wasn't life and death at the time, and she wanted to tell you herself," Victor explained and I was so grateful that he could speak for me. "She can take baths, and it wasn't interfering with her health, so I let her take her time with it. She's had enough to deal with. What she *doesn't* need is you not listening to her when she says no to something. Now get out of my way."

There was no resistance from Kota and Victor walked toward the door.

Silas was there, holding the door open, looking in.

I was wrapped well in a towel, and then another one, so I was covered, but knowing Silas was nearby, and probably the others, too, I buried my head into Victor's shoulder, ashamed to look at any of them. Afraid to see even more strangers' faces who would wonder why Victor had to carry me in a towel.

He walked endlessly, and I kept my eyes firmly closed and just held on, breathing in his calming scent.

When he slowed, I opened my eyes to find Silas had run ahead of us, and now was holding Victor's front passenger door open.

Victor placed me inside, tightening the towel around my body.

"Princess," he said, and he put a warm hand on my forehead, focusing on my face. The fire of his eyes had risen to an inferno. "You'll be okay. I'm taking you to my house. Are you okay with that?"

I nodded.

He looked over his shoulder, to somewhere I couldn't see, and then back at me. "The others are going to follow us. They are going to stay nearby. Are you fine with that?"

I nodded again. They all had to know now that I was messed up. More than they could have imagined.

He leaned in, kissed my lips softly and then strapped me in with the seatbelt. "Hang in there," he said. "We're leaving."

I settled back into the seat, my eyes closing. I didn't want to see any more.

It took a while before Victor returned. Kota and Gabriel got into the back seat. Victor started the car and backed up out of the camp site.

I was the worst camper ever.

The drive was quiet the whole way. I stared ahead at the road, the towel wrapped around my body like a blanket. The wetness of the bra and underwear was chilly, but I eventually warmed. It was a little uncomfortable, but I was unable to move to get them off. Victor held the wheel tightly, his knuckles nearly white, as he sped along. I could only guess how many miles an hour he was over the speed limit, but it felt like a lot.

I couldn't look at Kota and Gabriel. Staring ahead was all I could do.

It felt like eons before we were finally rolling through downtown Charleston streets. I covered myself more, thinking strangers could look in and see that I was basically naked.

When we were finally at Victor's large yellow house, the entrance gates opened for us. Victor parked the car as close to the house as he could, one of the front wheels in the yard. He threw the car into park and jumped out immediately, leaving his door open. The car dinged to remind him the keys were still in the ignition.

Before Kota or Gabriel could even move, Victor had yanked open my door, had my seatbelt off and was already pulling me out of the car.

"I'll take her," Gabriel said in a small voice.

"Go run ahead of us," Victor commanded, a tone as strong as the one Kota usually used. "Go fill the tub. I'll bring her up." He lifted me carefully out, so he could scoop me up, an arm under my knees and another at my back.

Gabriel ran off, disappearing into the house.

"I can help," Kota said, somewhere out of view. "Let me carry her."

"You've done enough," Victor spat back at him. "Hasn't she been through enough this week? Then you had to go and force her into the shower."

"I didn't know," Kota said, sounding helpless. "She should have trusted me enough to tell me she was afraid..."

Victor stopped on his path toward the door to face Kota full on. "*You* should have listened," he barked. He held me tighter to his body. "She told you no. She has never, ever, told you no, even when she's not sure of what she wants. This girl would rather suffer in silence, would rather go through hell than disappoint you. We told her to go with the girls, and she did, even though it killed her to do it. We ask her to go into danger with Mr. Hendricks all the time, and she does. Now the one time she's telling you not to make her do something, you don't listen to her? How is she supposed to trust you when you do something like that?"

I loved Victor for defending me. I did. I loved Kota, too. I wanted to tell him so. He'd made a mistake. I wasn't as upset as Victor was. It also wasn't totally his fault, as I put myself in such a position.

Kota said nothing. He bowed his head, looking at the ground.

Victor readjusted me in his arms. He was strong, but he couldn't hold on to me forever. "I can't even talk to you right now. I've got to get her upstairs."

Kota didn't protest, instead running ahead, getting doors for Victor.

Victor carried me all the way up the stairs to his bathroom.

"It's ready," Gabriel said. "It just warmed up. It'll fill in a few minutes."

Victor put me down delicately on the edge of the tub, remaining close. I glanced over and saw Kota, standing in the doorway, looking in. His eyes were wide, his lips pressed together like he wanted to say something, but he didn't.

Victor was breathing a little heavily as he cupped my cheek. "Is this okay?"

I nodded.

"Do you want Gabriel to stay in here with you?"

I nodded again.

"Okay," he said and he smiled tightly. "He's going to stay here with you. I'll get some breakfast for us. Do you want pancakes? Chocolate chip, right?"

I nodded, realizing how hungry I was, and yet still sorry for what had happened with Kota. Victor had yelled at him. I didn't want them to hate each other now.

I thought after I was clean, and we had some breakfast, I

419

would talk to them about it.

Victor turned halfway around, the full fire in his eyes an explosion as he faced Kota again. "Out," he said. "Now."

"I don't..." Kota mumbled then glanced at me pleadingly before looking back at Victor. "I wanted to..."

"I don't care what you want right now," Victor said. He snapped his fingers, clapped once and then made a shooing motion toward him. "Get out."

"I need to talk to her."

"She's had enough of you right now," Victor said. "Trust me. Trust Gabriel. We've got her. Just step back and let her get herself together. Give her some time."

Kota bowed his head and walked back out into the bedroom.

I let out a slow breath, still trembling, still feeling the cold of the concrete from the latrine at my back, despite having been in the car for so long. It was the first time I'd seen them have an out and out fight, and it was about me.

A minute later, Victor left, too, but before he closed the door, he looked at me and then at Gabriel. "No one comes in here until she's ready."

"Hell fucking right," Gabriel said.

Victor twisted the lock on the door until it was set and closed it. The lock clicked into place as the door closed.

Gabriel reached for me. He was still wearing the pajamas. "Come on," he said, in a much gentler voice. "The tub has enough water in it."

Gabriel got me to release the towel, and I eased back slowly into the tub. I was still in my underwear, and I left them on. They were now dingy, dark pink material, possibly ruined, not that it mattered now.

The moment the water enveloped me, I felt all the dirt and sand again, the grossness of my hair, the stain of tears across my cheeks. I must have looked like a monster.

Victor's tub was so big and round, that when I sat back where the seat bench was, Gabriel was too far away to reach.

He frowned. "Hey," he said. "If I leave my boxers on, can

I get in?"

I nodded and waved him in.

He stripped down, although his cheeks and ears turned bright red. His lean body wasn't as dirty as mine, but he still had some splotches of dirt around his feet and some along his arms. His hair was wild, the brown sticking up at the back, the blond mixed in.

He left in his earrings, the pink crystal studs, the three black rings, and the one pink ring.

He lowered himself in, and then eased his way over until he was sitting beside me. "Okay," he said with a sigh as he put a hand on my knee. "Now, sit back. Let's just chill out for a minute."

We found rolled-up towels nearby and used them as pillows. Once they were under our heads, we could relax in the tub and almost nap.

I didn't want to nap, but it helped to calm my nerves. The water was still. Gabriel remained still.

Slowly, it started to sink in that we were back. Despite Kota and Victor being upset and how I needed to try to smooth things over with them, we were back home.

We had survived the week. And we had won.

"Gabriel," I whispered.

"Hmmm," he said, his eyes closed.

"I'm here for another six months," I said. "At least until the school job is done."

"I know," he said and opened his eyes, lifting up his head. His crystal eyes glowed and his grin came back. "That's plenty of time."

"Is it?" I asked.

"Sure," he said. "We'll work on our family dynamic here. Kota knows now, well, we still need to tell him the details, but he seems willing. I mean, he doesn't really understand, of course, but I bet once they're done fighting, and we've all calmed down, we can work it out."

I smiled, reaching for his hand. I squeezed it. "And then we can talk to council and make it official?"

"That'll probably happen," he said. "But next time, we'll be ready for it."

"You think they'll let me in on the team?"

"Trouble, now that they know you're a ghost, and how talented you are, I bet they're out there right now thinking of what they could bribe you with to get you to stay."

"I told them I just wanted...I wanted for me to be able to pay my own way in with favors and cash."

He laughed. "You know what's funny?"

I shook my head.

"They offered us to pay off all of our debts just to encourage you to join Carla and Lake. At least, up until you freaked out and came to them crying. We couldn't do it. We said no." He lifted an eyebrow. "Did you even know we said that?"

I shook my head, surprised. "You didn't?"

"We were letting you make your own decision. We said we wouldn't encourage you one way or the other."

My heart pounded. They had given up favors and cash? "You..."

"We would have graduated, all of us in one day," he said with a smile. "It was tempting. I couldn't go through with it, though. My heart wasn't in it. Neither were the others'."

I sighed. "Maybe I should have asked them to graduate you all, too."

"We're fine," he said. "Actually, with your coming into the Academy now, we're still in the same place, just we don't have to worry about any more costs on your part." He lifted an eyebrow. "You know what? I don't know what that means now. Does that mean everything until you're an official member, or just your cost of membership, what they usually take in favors from us to bring in another team member?"

I wasn't sure. "We'll have to ask Kota. He was there. He could tell us."

Gabriel was about to say something else when raised voices came through the closed door.

I groaned and braced to get up from the water.

Gabriel reached for me, taking my hand and tugging me back down. "Hang on," he said. "Don't worry. They won't come in. They said not to let anyone in..."

"I just don't want Victor yelling at Kota anymore," I said. I pulled away from him. "Not about the shower."

"They might not be yelling about that," he said, getting up, the water flowing off him, the boxers clinging to his body.

"I'll listen," I said, standing up beside him. "If it's about something else, I'll come back." I threw the towel I'd brought in to the floor and stepped on it so I wouldn't drip all over the place.

Gabriel followed. He wasn't going to give me an inch of space, and I didn't mind.

No matter what, we'd get through it. It'd be fine.

I put my ear to the door and listened.

Gabriel did as well.

And we heard it all.

*K*ota Lee stood by the piano. He counted the keys, white, and then black, all of them together, and then white again. Victor had retreated, for now, having gone downstairs to ask for a maid to bring up pancakes.

Kota paced the floor, counting, waiting, listening, although he heard nothing from the bathroom.

Oh god, her face. Her pale face when she was passed out. He'd screamed. He'd called her name.

He'd never been so scared.

He was still scared for her.

Other images flashed through his brain. Things he couldn't erase.

Why couldn't he stop thinking about Gabriel kissing her in there? He'd seen it before and he had been able to calm himself, but now, he couldn't. She was half-naked, and trembling and weak.

And it had been his fault.

They should have taken her to the hospital. She needed to be checked out. Fainting wasn't nothing that they shouldn't worry about. He should go in there right now and demand to take her to a doctor.

But did he really believe that? Or was he jealous that he was out here and Gabriel was in there? Was he looking for excuses to go in there, check on her, to see with his own eyes that she was okay?

Kota trembled with fear and anger. He was angry with himself for not listening to her. She'd struggled, and she'd said no. Victor was right, he should have listened.

He had been so sure she was just being oversensitive because of all the stress. He'd heard from Silas how she wouldn't even step foot inside the girls' latrine without Silas going into inspect for spiders.

He had assumed that's what the fear was about. He hadn't meant to scare her so badly. He was just going to show her there weren't any. Face your fears. That's what they always said at the Academy.

Even though he'd undressed to his boxers to join her, to stand with her and ward off spiders, she'd still fainted from terror. Victor had come in with her bathroom kit, only to find Kota standing over her in a panic, trying to bring her back.

He'd been screaming for help, and too afraid for her to leave her side to do anything more than cry out. He checked her vitals, and he made sure she was still breathing.

He didn't think he'd ever been so afraid in his life.

Victor had said it had happened before, but seeing it for himself, it scared Kota senseless. What if someone else, not him, had brought her to a shower, and she'd fainted, hitting her head on the concrete? What if one of the girls—already an area where she clearly had some issues—had forced her in and...

He breathed in deeply, and pressed his hands against his face, the coarse stubble scratching his palms. One...two...

Despite his eyes being closed, it was her face he saw.

And Gabriel's.

And they were kissing.

He opened his eyes again. He counted piano keys again. Somehow focusing on something real, like the keys, kept his imagination at bay. It was the only thing keeping him sane.

The sound of the front gate opening outside was enough to draw him out of counting to check on who was coming through. He sincerely hoped it wasn't George.

It was his home, and he had every right to be there, but with Sang in the tub, Kota worried what would happen if George tried to come up and see what was going on. He crossed the room, pulling back a curtain to look out.

It was North's Jeep rolling in. Kota frowned, doubting his team would have been able to get all their things and pack them in the Jeep that quickly. They were one car short and it wouldn't have fit so easily.

He could understand they were upset with him, but that didn't mean they could leave a mess for others to pick up. They still had responsibilities.

Maybe he'd send them back to pick it all up. He was still thinking about this when Victor returned.

He stood by the door opening, looking over toward the windows. "Who's here?" he asked.

Kota watched as some of his team got out of the car and came toward the house. He turned, walking away from the window back toward the center of the room, near the piano. "The others," he said. "All but Mr. Blackbourne and Dr. Green."

Victor grunted, heading toward his piano, dropping heavily on the bench, his back to the keys. He leaned forward, putting his face in his hands. "I don't think I've been so stressed out in my entire life."

"I'm sorry," Kota said, something he'd said to Victor before they had left the campground, and again before Victor had finally gone down to get pancakes. "I didn't know."

"It's not just this," Victor said, suddenly sitting up straight.

There were times when his eyes were insanely intense, just like his mother's on the rare occasions she fought with her husband. Kota had only seen them like that when Victor was upset about one of them.

His eyes now were a fury, ten times worse.

Victor got up and paced the floor behind the bench, his voice rising as he glared at his surroundings. "She said she wanted to be with us, and we sent her to be with the girls. We weren't listening."

"She didn't say no girl team, she just said she wanted to stay with us," Kota said quietly. "She never said anything before like she was afraid. She never even hinted."

"But we weren't listening, either," Victor said, still pacing. The sleeves of his white shirt were rolled up past his elbows still. There were stains on his black pants. The dirt from the shoes he wore dirtied the white carpet. He didn't seem to care. "I knew it. I knew bringing her to the camp was a bad idea."

"She *wanted* to join," Kota said. "She wanted to go. We told her..."

"We didn't tell her enough," Victor snapped back. He stopped mid-step, turning the full fury of his eyes on Kota. "We should have told her more."

"She had to see for herself," Kota said. "She had to learn it on her own. That's how it's done."

"She wouldn't have said anything if we'd told her ahead of time," Victor said, waving his arms toward the bathroom door. "She wouldn't have let on she knew anything about it."

"It's too easy to read her face, and she can't lie," Kota said. "She's lousy at it. Besides, why are you yelling about it now? She's in. It's done. And she's still here with us."

"I don't know!" Victor turned and kicked his piano bench. The leg snapped and the bench leaned, supported now only by three legs. "Because it shouldn't have happened this way! Because she didn't deserve to have her first true Academy experience completely ruined because we didn't take the time to find out."

Kota stepped toward him, his own anger burning in him now. He'd been sympathetic to Sang and had truly blamed himself for her fainting in the shower. He'd taken Victor's abuse, but now, he couldn't stand it anymore. His hands curled into fists at his sides, as he focused on Victor's angry eyes.

"Enough," he barked. "There was no way we could have known."

"We should have known," Victor cried out. He pointed a fist at his own chest. "We should have taken the time, instead of fighting with each other about who gets her for the night, or whose sleeping bag she stays in."

"What does that have to do with anything?" Kota asked.

"We've been so focused on ourselves and this stupid plan that we haven't even spent the time with her to get her to tell us when things like this happen." Victor covered his face with his palms. "I'm so stupid. I knew something was wrong."

"Hey!" North's booming voice cut through, startling Kota. North stood in the doorway. Five days without shaving had left him with a dark beard, and his eyes were wide, dark circles under them. His clothes were dirty and rumpled. He looked dangerous.

Behind him were the others, all pushing at North to let them by.

North came in, letting the others in behind him, as he focused on Victor. "You're not stupid. And stop yelling." He pointed at Luke, who was the last to come through. "Close the door."

Luke shut and locked the door and then looked at Kota. "Where is she?"

Kota nodded toward the bathroom. "In there with Gabriel taking a bath." He frowned, unable to stop another vision of those two kissing.

Luke started in that direction but North snapped at him. "No," he said. "Stay out here. We're finishing this now."

Nathan and Silas started toward the bathroom door. "We didn't come all this way back to fight," Nathan said. "We're going in to see her. I want to see her with my own eyes and make sure she's okay."

"The fuck you are," North said and then forced his way between the boys and the door so they couldn't enter. "Leave her alone. If anyone's going in there, I am."

"No one goes in there!" Victor shouted. At the sound, everyone froze. Victor rarely ever yelled, but in that moment, he sounded like his father.

Victor pointed, his finger sweeping from North, and Luke, to Nathan and Silas, and then to Kota. "All of you," he said. "I promised her she could have the bathroom as long as she needed to calm down. Gabriel's in there with her, so we know she's fine. She's not going anywhere right now. North is right. We need to get this out now before we're reduced into fist fights. The last thing we need is to end up facing an Academy council to explain why I've killed you all. But if you try going in there again before she's ready to come out—so help me god—I won't hesitate."

The boys fell silent, their breathing the only sound in the room as anger dissipated.

Kota looked at his shoes, caked with mud from the week, trying to calm his heart, his anger, before he said something he'd regret forever. Victor was right. Sang could come out at any minute. No doubt she could hear the yelling. They'd scare her away for good. She'd refuse to join if she saw them fighting like this, especially over her. She'd hate that.

Nathan shared a look with Silas. They moved quietly toward Victor's bed, sitting on it. Luke dropped to the floor, on his knees, sitting on his heels, frowning.

North moved away from the bathroom door, leaning against the other one that led to the hall. He pressed his back against it, folding his arms over his chest. He looked at Kota. "How much do you know about our plan?"

"I don't know anything," Kota said quietly, not wanting Victor's parents or any servants to overhear. "What plan? Sang said you all had a plan of some sort. Something about us..." He shook his head. "Just assume I don't know anything."

North frowned, looking down at the floor to where his brother was sitting. "This is complicated."

Luke fell back until he was lying on the floor, his hair spilling out from the clip he'd been wearing. He stared up at the ceiling. "Tell me about it."

"Look," Kota said, stepping forward, waving his hand through the air. "Just tell me, okay? It's been a bad day. You can't make it much worse."

Silas grunted. "I didn't think it'd be this bad, either," he said.

"It's not just Gabriel," Nathan said. He was looking at the floor, kicking at the carpet with a dirty sneaker. He stopped and then leaned forward, elbows on his knees, covering his face. "We're all dating her."

"I know," Kota said quickly, and then paused to think about it. He'd known about Dr. Green already. Then Victor had made it clear he was interested, and there had been the kiss when she was in his sleeping bag. He had only kissed her forehead, but Kota had suspected if he'd let it go on, there would have been more.

It would have kept him—and maybe the others—up all up all night, hearing it, knowing what was going on. It's why he'd told him to get out for the evening and cool off.

"Well, I didn't know about..." He looked at the rest of them. He'd suspected Nathan, but not so much the others. He strained his brain to fully realize the truth. "Wait...All of you?"

But now, as he looked at the guys, their similar guilty expressions and the way they wouldn't meet his eyes, he knew. They were all interested in her.

Kota bowed his head in defeat. This was it. It was what he had been worried about from day one. The minute she'd first met the others, he could tell they liked her. "It's over," he said quietly, feeling his heart breaking because he was about to lose her. "Isn't it? You're going to ask her to pick one of us? One of us leaves and joins her on a couple team in six months?"

"No-o-o," Luke said, sitting up quickly. His hair spilled around his shoulders as he frowned. "God. You'd think we'd do that?"

"You think *she* could do that?" Victor grumbled. "Do you think she could pick one of us, and then split us up like that?"

Kota slowed his breathing, shaking his head. "I don't... I don't really understand. What other option is there?"

The guys shared looks with each other and then returned their eyes to Kota.

Nathan was the first to speak. "We share her," he said. He frowned and then leaned forward again, covering his face. "Shit. That's hard to admit out loud. I'm sure that's not really the right way to say it."

Kota struggled to understand. Share her? He had to have heard that wrong. "What are you talking about?"

"We stay with her," North said, his voice strained. He cleared his throat and continued. "All of us. We care enough about her, and each other, to stick together. And...we share her."

Kota made a face, shaking his head. "You can't mean... that's not..."

"It can work," Victor said. "And it happens. Not every relationship is one plus one equals two."

"Yeah, I know," Kota said. He'd heard about love triangles before and more complicated relationships, but he'd never really given it much thought. "But..."

"It's not going to be easy," North said. "I didn't like the idea at first. But I'd rather give it a try than assume we have to split up." He pointed at Kota. "Because trust me, I will follow her. I don't care if she picks you after it's all said and done. I'm behind her and I'm not leaving. And like hell if I'll let her go on Academy jobs without watching her back."

"Me either," Victor said.

"You all can't really believe it would work," Kota said, looking around the room at them. He couldn't picture it. Did they really know what they were getting themselves into?

He looked at Nathan, his oldest friend, and usually the most sensible in their group, second only to Mr. Blackbourne. He stared at him and waited. He couldn't formulate all the questions he wanted to ask at one time.

Nathan groaned, sighing. "I don't know if it will work," he said. He faced Kota straight on, his serious blue eyes focused. His shoulders straightened like they did when he was confident. "None of us do. But what's the alternative? She leaves because she feels guilty about splitting us apart? Or she chooses one of us and the rest of us are all angry at that person? And what happens when she does need to go on an Academy job and one of the others are there? Are we going to fight the whole time?"

Kota swayed on his feet. They all looked at him, determination in their eyes like he'd never seen before. He'd seen it in Gabriel, too, when he'd come at Kota, ready for a fight over Sang. Now he knew there had been more to it than just him being angry over Sang crying.

Unable to stand anymore, Kota sunk to his knees on the carpet. He sat back on his heels, counting as he tried to make sense of everything.

But the counting couldn't take away the thoughts floating through his brain, the visions of Sang kissing Gabriel. Victor kissing her in his sleeping bag, in plain view. Dr. Green in the photo.

They thought they'd hidden the pictures, but he'd found them, and even though only her head and back were visible, he'd known it was her.

"I don't think I can do this," Kota said.

"We can't do it without you," Luke said moving toward him. "You can't say no. One of us not going for it breaks everything."

"I can't," Kota said, closing his eyes. "I can't... stop thinking about her with someone else. I can't watch that. I can't..."

"I know," Nathan said. "I see the same thing...when...after you kissed her at the campsite."

Kota slowly opened his eyes, looking at Nathan.

Nathan was glaring at him, the hurt and pain in his eyes. "I get angry just thinking about it, even though I know you're not being stealing her away. I can't help it."

"I feel it, too," North said. "I force myself to just get over it."

"Well one of these days, we're not going to *just get over it*," Nathan said, looking over Kota to North. "Not unless we work this out. We're not ready. Not until I don't feel like punching your teeth out anytime you get close to her."

North opened his mouth, lips pulled back, teeth bared, ready to snarl, when Victor stepped in, hands wide.

"Wait," Victor said. "I've been reading about this in psychology studies and through examples people talk about in articles. First, we need to establish we're okay with this, including Sang if we're ready. Then we need to set up boundaries."

"I'm not going back to not kissing her," Luke said. "That

took too long last time. We already know she wants to."

"That's not what I'm talking about," Victor said, looking at them each, in turn, his eyes intense. He peered at each of them and waited for their attention. Kota recognized it as something he did on stage before he spoke. When he did speak again, his voice was calmer, quieter than before, so they all had to strain to hear. "Clearly we have issues with kissing her or doing other things in front of each other. So now if we're in on this and she's okay with it, we need to set up rules. If someone else is around, you don't get to kiss her."

Luke raised his hand. "I don't mind seeing it. It doesn't bug me."

"This is the way it is for now," Victor said, turning to Luke. "We can't risk anyone getting angry. We need Gabriel to agree to this, too." He looked around, waiting for someone else to say something. "The other part is, we need to divide our time with her better."

"She's already dividing her time," Nathan said.

"Not enough," Victor said. "And not evenly. She's there with you every evening."

"Well, I can't help that, can I?" Nathan asked as he leaned back on the bed.

"She can sleep at my place," Silas said in his deep voice, surprising everyone. "Charlie doesn't mind."

"It's more than just sleeping," Victor said. "It's dates and how we spend our time with her."

"That's not going to work," North said. "We've got school. And there's seven days in a week and nine of us."

"Nine?" Kota burst out. "Who...Mr. Blackbourne...he...?"

The others nodded.

"It was his idea in the first place," North said.

"His plan," Nathan said.

Kota tilted his head back, groaning. He couldn't believe it. He'd thought Mr. Blackbourne was the most sensible, and here he was suggesting this very strange plan. Kota wasn't even sure why they were talking about it. "North's right," he said. "Nine of us, and seven days. How are we supposed to wait so long between to see her?"

"You'll see her nearly every day since we're working together," Victor said. "If we're still a team, we're going to have to still work together. And for the time being, we're still in school together."

Kota looked at his knees on the floor against the white carpet, shaking his head in disbelief. He wasn't convinced. "I don't know. Does she want this?"

"She was willing to try," North said quietly. "Her main concern was us fighting about it."

"All of these things won't work anyway without us all in agreement," Victor said. "You don't even have to choose right now."

Kota lifted his head up to meet Victor's eyes. "You said we had to figure this out."

"Yes," he said, "but this only works if you're ready for it. We can't do it without you. I can't do this without *all* of you." He looked again to the others. "This only works if we're willing to work together. It'll be hard enough going into it, learning our boundaries."

"Are you sure she wants to?" Kota asked. "This has to be a lot for her."

Victor continued. "She'll bail if she thinks we'll fight over her. She'll find another team or leave altogether." He paused, his shoulders dropping. "She'd do anything to stop us from killing each other over her, even if it means her joining another team. We all have to give this serious consideration, and then come to her when we're ready. We'll have our work cut out for us just to convince her we're serious. And hopefully, we haven't driven her insane enough that she'll want to."

The room silenced once more. Kota breathed in, counted, breathed out, counted some more. Never, ever, would he have guessed this would be a solution.

"I don't know," he said. He needed to think, to go over whatever Victor was reading and see it for himself. Hadn't

Sang said something about Lily? Or was it Marc? Something about their team?

Before he finished the thought, there was a pinch of electricity zapping his butt. Emergency call shocked his body. His heart skipped as he reached for his phone.

"Tell whoever it is to fuck off," North said. "This is more important."

It was Mr. Blackbourne calling through, so while he wanted to follow North's suggestion, he couldn't ignore the call and answered the phone.

"She's fine," he said. He suspected Mr. Blackbourne had heard about what had happened with Sang. He'd forgotten to text him as well as Dr. Green on the ride in and cringed, afraid Mr. Blackbourne was probably pissed. "If you want a doctor to..."

"Stop talking," Mr. Blackbourne said, his voice loud enough that Kota was sure the others could hear. Still, he put him on speaker. "Where is she?"

"In the bath," Kota said. "Why? What's wrong?"

"It's her father."

Kota stood up, still holding the phone. His heart began racing even as he told himself it could be anything. "Did something happen to him?" He shared a look with the rest of the guys. From Mr. Blackbourne's tone, he knew something was terribly wrong.

"He's at the Sunnyvale house now," Mr. Blackbourne said. "And he's demanding his daughter back."

Thank you!

Thank you for purchasing this book!
For new release and exclusive Academy and
C. L. Stone information sign up here: http://eepurl.com/zuIDj

Connect with C. L. Stone online
Twitter: https://twitter.com/CLStoneX
Facebook: https://www.facebook.com/clstonex

If you enjoyed reading *First Kiss*, let me know. Review it at
your favorite retailer and/or Goodreads

BOOKS BY C. L. STONE

The Academy Ghost Bird Series:
Introductions
First Days
Friends vs. Family
Forgiveness and Permission
Drop of Doubt
Push and Shove
House of Korba
The Other Side of Envy
The Healing Power of Sugar
First Kiss
Black and Green (Late 2016) – Turn the page for a sneak peek!

The Academy Scarab Beetle Series
Thief
Liar
Fake
Accessory
Hoax (2016)

Other C. L. Stone Books:
Spice God
Smoking Gun

READ AN EXCERPT FROM THE NEXT BOOK IN
THE ACADEMY GHOST BIRD SERIES

The Academy

The Ghost Bird Series

BLACK
AND
GREEN

Book Eleven

Written by C. L. Stone

Published by

Arcato Publishing

♥

$\mathcal{T}$HE $\mathcal{R}$ETURN

$\mathcal{W}$e'd just returned from camp. I'd listened as the others discussed the plan of keeping the team together when a phone call interrupted everything.

I'd thought I couldn't panic any more than I already had after simply listening to them.

Until Kota called for me in alarm. I'd never forget the desperate tone in his voice.

I dressed quickly and rushed out of Victor's home in downtown Charleston. Kota drove North's Jeep, with Nathan in the passenger seat, and Victor, Gabriel and I crammed into the rear seat together. The others would follow after gathering laptops and other supplies.

My father was back and from the way Mr. Blackbourne had described it, he had called the school, asking for Mr. Hendricks or someone who could bring me back from school camp; what we had told my sister about where we'd be for the week.

"We need to make sure he doesn't do anything desperate," Kota said. "If he came home to check in and found you gone, he might be worried. Remember, he's just as desperate to keep your background a secret. Now that your stepmother hasn't been around to keep you at home, he's probably worried about exposure."

What we couldn't have was Mr. Hendricks finding out, either.

My heart was in knots, still in turmoil over the argument I'd overheard when in Victor's bathroom. Gabriel had held my hand as we listened, and the more they argued, the closer he got. By the end, we were clinging to each other. We'd stared into each other's eyes, knowing what the other was thinking.

It can't end. We have to stick together. The more they fought, they more it was obvious to us. We had to find a way to convince Kota. Mr. Blackbourne had been right. Kota was the core of the team. Without him believing in it, the others would doubt. We would fail. We would break.

But right now, we had more immediate problems. We hurried as quickly as we could on Mr. Blackbourne's orders. He and Dr. Green were on the way, although we would still get back to Summerville first.

Most of them were still dirty from the camp we'd been at hours before. I was the only one relatively clean. In my rush, I'd dressed quickly inside Victor's closet, not daring to waste time. I'd put on fresh underwear, no bra and a bulky sweatshirt I suddenly realized might have been Luke's because it was baby blue and too big for me. I'd also pulled on cotton shorts that were the first things I'd seen inside Victor's closet that were about my size. I didn't recognize them, and for all I knew, they weren't shorts at all, but one of the boys' boxers and I was too panicked to notice the difference.

Hope filled my heart on the way to Sunnyvale Court. Maybe my father was just worried about me. Maybe he was upset that I'd left Marie alone for a week. Had something happened to her? An accident?

"What about my mother?" I asked Kota as he drove and then regretted looking to him for an answer. His hands were locked at ten and two, and he edged over the speed limit, despite normally being such a stickler for road rules. He hadn't even gotten on my case about my seatbelt, which at first I'd forgotten about, but had slowly, quietly put on. I turned and focused on Victor beside me. "Is it because of her? Is she back?"

"She can't be," Victor said quietly. They'd all been so quiet in the car, so intent on the road, and consumed by their thoughts. Victor held my hand, my fingers almost numb at the strong way he held on to me, although I returned the squeeze. "They wouldn't dare, although she's been demanding a transfer to a different hospital."

"We're working on pretending to get her a transfer, and then just drive her around the city in an ambulance and bring her back inside the hospital from a different entrance. We'll give her a new room and a new doctor," Nathan said. He spoke to the windshield at first, and then bent over the middle console to look back at me. "She wants medications she overdosed on and a different doctor that will listen to her demands. She thinks a different doctor will release her from the hospital."

"We won't be able to keep her forever," Kota said. "But she's still there. We would have been notified if things had changed."

I settled into the seat, bringing up my legs and pulling the sweatshirt over my knees to cocoon myself inside. I lay my head on my knees. "He's probably just checking up on me," I said. "He came back, but...he'll go again."

Victor's palm found my back and he rubbed warmly, leaning in. "It'll be fine. We'll be there to listen."

"We should have done something before now," Nathan mumbled under his breath. "This shouldn't be a problem."

"We don't know what's going on," Kota said. "And he wasn't the one tying her up and leaving her to die. Despite whatever we might assume about his past, he's never laid a finger on her." His head lifted, the first time since getting in the driver's seat. He peered back at me in the mirror. "Right?"

I nodded. I couldn't remember the last time my father touched me at all. A hug? A handshake? Funnily enough, now that Kota mentioned it, I couldn't recall it ever happening.

"Hopefully, he's back just to check on the house, and panicked when she wasn't there," he continued. "It's why we left her room the way it was. So he'd think she was still around, and she could slip in if he came back. Remember?"

I did remember. Some clothes, books, and other things had been left behind. The bed had been made. My old trunk was still there.

In the secret attic space, I'd left the old wardrobe, too, despite wanting to bring it out. It was still soundproof, and had pictures inside, along with lights and a beanbag chair. We'd thought he'd come back at least every couple of weeks, maybe to refill the fridge and pantry with food, and to pay the bills. Instead, he paid the bills from wherever he'd been, leaving Marie and me to figure out how to get food and take care of the house. He sent Marie cash to pay for it, although she didn't tell me until I'd moved out.

I wished the car ride could last forever, or at least until my father gave up and left. I probably shouldn't feel the way I did about my own father, but it was simpler when he was gone.

Despite my wish, we got to Summerville quickly and soon turned onto Sunnyvale Court. We turned into the road next to Bob's Diner, the parking lot empty since it was New Year's Day. It was odd to see it like that, though I imagined most of the staff was at camp this week.

Kota pulled the Jeep into the parking lot and then turned off the engine. He twisted, turning to face me. "Remember," he said. "You've been at a camp for school, a girls' retreat. It's why Mr. Blackbourne got the forwarded call. Your father was trying to call the school."

Despite his calm demeanor, his eyes were wide and his knuckles were still white from having gripped the steering wheel so tightly.

Victor pulled out his phone and passed it to me. "You'll need to hang onto this so we can listen and track you," he said. "I turned the sound off. It's probably best if you hide it."

I didn't have a bra on, so I tucked it into my underwear at my back. With the tight shorts, it should stay at my waist if I didn't bounce around too much. "Is that good enough?"

"It should pick up enough sound," Victor said. "And we'll have the cameras running."

"No matter what," Nathan said as he opened his door, "you feel threatened, walk out the door. I'm not going to be far."

The others exited the car. Nathan opened my door.

There was no time to tell them what I'd heard and I didn't dare bring it up now anyway.

My heart was pounding so loud. This was worse than the week leading to the camp. I was returning home for the first time in what felt like eons to face my father, not having any idea why he'd come back.

I breathed in the cold January air. I wasn't sure of the time, it had to be past noon by now.

How different my world had been since this morning, or even yesterday. Camp had changed me. It had shown me how nice people could be. Despite my issues with being around girls, and the disaster I'd become around the shower, the Academy had shown me a world of kindness.

Coming back had been a trip through a wardrobe. Academy had been Narnia, and now I was back, blinking, wondering if it was all a dream because the real world wasn't nearly as nice.

I stared at the path through the woods that led back to my house. I would go and tell him I'd been dropped off at the diner.

"If you need someone to vouch for you, we can always call Carla back at camp," Kota said. "She'd even do it without a favor."

I didn't want to bother Carla. She was nice, even if we'd started out at odds when we'd first met. As much as she and the other girls were very nice, I'd left them under poor circumstances in the middle of the night, and never wanted to see them again. I was too embarrassed.

I walked with the boys. I was going to tell them they could wait at the diner. I knew at least one of them had a key. Or they could go to Kota's house, or Nathan's.

I could have told them that, but then I didn't think they would listen. They would be at the doorstep if they could get that close. They'd sneak in, and even sit inside the attic space, waiting and listening.

I swallowed a thousand times on that walk, trying to get my heart to settle. My nerves had been made worse through my week of anxiety. I didn't think I'd ever feel calm again. Especially not now.

When the path twisted and I found the bridge that would take me to my house, I paused, looking at the two-story gray building that used to be my home. The boys stood with me, Victor to my left, Kota to my right. They each held onto my hand.

Nathan was behind me and his hands found my shoulders, holding me strongly.

The house didn't seem any different to me, but we saw the back. The shed blocked the view of the drive. The back porch, the screened in area, those were all still and quiet. The trampoline the neighborhood boys often came to use with Derrick when he was over visiting Marie, was still there. The grass was a little tall, but patches of it were brown. Despite the break in clouds and blue sky above, the day still felt gray and gloomy.

"I'll get this over with," I said, suddenly determined. My father wouldn't stay on. He didn't dare. His job called him out on business trips for long periods of time. "He's just here to pay a bill and to check up on us. He'll leave again."

"Let's hope so," Kota said. He continued to hold my hand and found his phone with the other. He turned it on, checking the cameras. "I see him," he said. "He's in his bedroom, making the bed."

"Okay," I said and turned to look at them. "I'm going. He's probably just here for the weekend. He'll be gone on Monday. I can probably even sneak out during the day for walks like before. So I only need to show up sometime in the afternoon and sleep there."

"We'll send someone in," Kota said, ignoring his phone now and looking back toward the house. "We'll keep an eye on it and find a good time to head up. Someone will be in the attic at all times."

"We shouldn't need to go that far," Victor said. "You said he wouldn't hurt her."

"It's not about him," Kota said and returned his eyes to me. "Do you want us to?"

I swallowed, of course, I did, although that was a risk.

"Don't if it's not safe," I said. "Don't let anyone get caught."

He nodded sharply.

That was it. Decision made. Despite heading back, I wouldn't be alone.

I was never alone.

I left them, and crossed the bridge, still feeling their warm touches in my palms and on my shoulders. I tried to keep that memory with me. I ducked my head and kept going.

When I was halfway across the yard, I heard a short whistle. I panicked, worried someone inside would hear, and I stopped, turning back.

Kota had stepped out, waving to me.

I started to turn back. Was something wrong? I stood in the yard, puzzled, trying to figure out if he was telling me to hurry up, or to go back. With the vague way he was waving at me, I couldn't figure out his meaning.

"Sang!" Marie's voice came at me like a punch in the back. I spun around again, hoping Kota would retreat.

Marie sprinted halfway to me. She was barefoot, wearing jeans and a sweater and was urging me toward her. "Come quick."

Was that what Kota had been warning me about?

It was too late to turn back now. I hurried to her. I was back.

ABOUT C. L. STONE

Certification

- Marvelour of Wonder

- Active Participant of Scary Situations

- Official Member of F.A.M.E.

Experience

Spent an extraordinary number of years with absolutely no control over the capping of imagination, fun, and curiosity. Willingly takes part in impossible problems only to come up with the most ludicrous solution. Due to unfortunate circumstances, will no longer experience feeling on a small spot on my left calf.

Skills

Secret Keeper | Occasion Riser | Barefoot Walker Strange Acceptance | Magic Maker | Restless Reckless | Gravity Defiant | Fairy Tale Reader | Story Maker-Upper | Amusingly Baffled | Comprehensive Curiousness | Usually Unbelievable